AW YEAH
COMICS!™
MAKE WAY...FOR AWESOME!

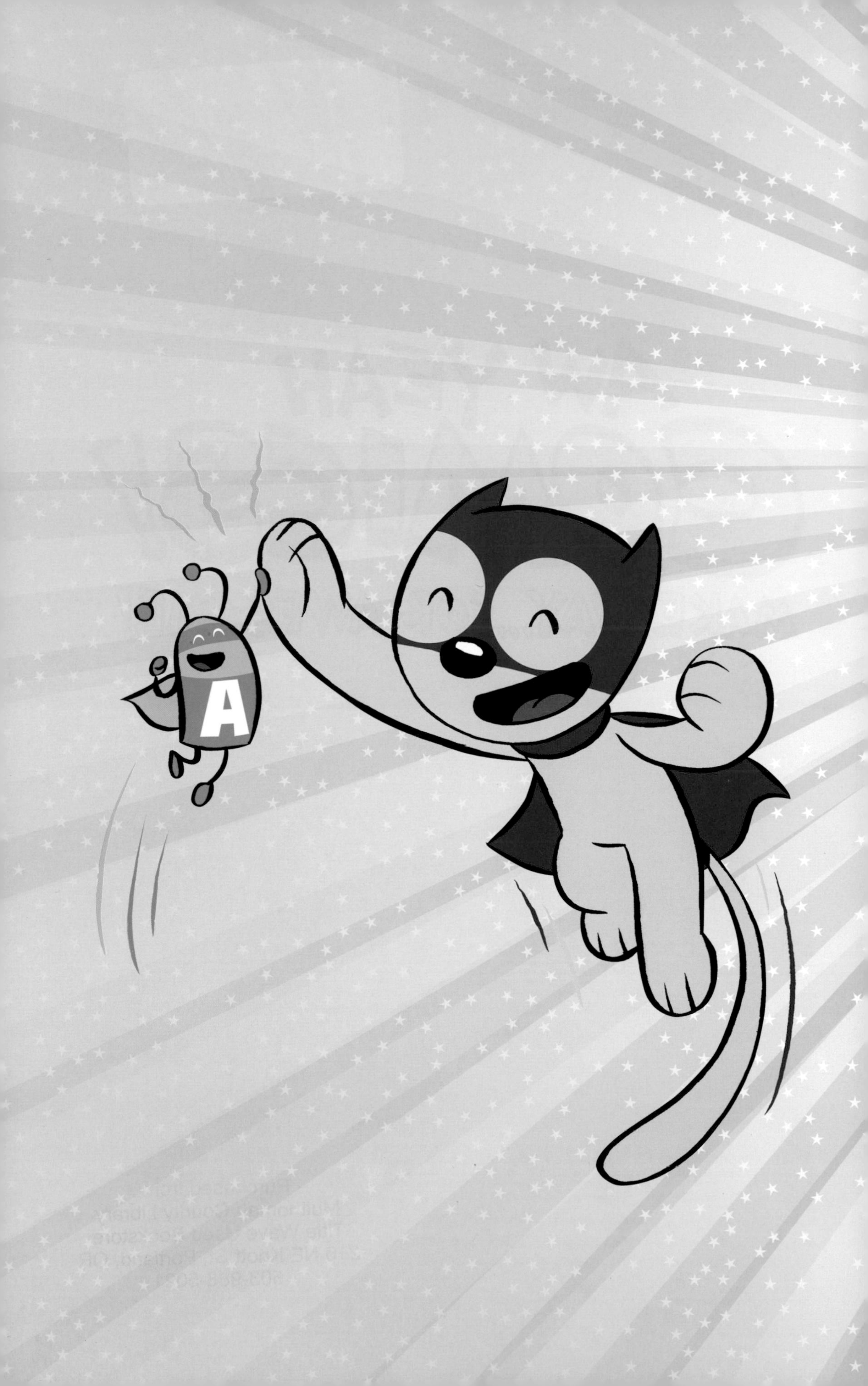

AW YEAH COMICS!™
MAKE WAY...FOR AWESOME!

STORY AND ARTWORK BY **ART BALTAZAR** AND **FRANCO**

Chapter break artwork by Art Baltazar

FEATURING
Scoot McMahon, Denver Brubaker, Marc Hammond,
Kurt Wood, Dave Scheidt, and Vince Dorse

Dark Horse Books

President and Publisher MIKE RICHARDSON
Editor SHANTEL LaROCQUE
Assistant Editor KATII O'BRIEN
Designer SARAH TERRY
Digital Art Technician CHRISTINA McKENZIE

Published by
Dark Horse Books
A division of Dark Horse Comics, Inc.
10956 SE Main Street
Milwaukie, OR 97222

DarkHorse.com ★ AwYeahComics.com

First edition: JUNE 2016
ISBN 978-1-50670-045-8

1 3 5 7 9 10 8 6 4 2
Printed in China

This volume collects *Aw Yeah Comics!* #9–#12, originally published by
Aw Yeah Comics! Publishing, as well as new material created for this volume.

AW YEAH COMICS! MAKE WAY . . . FOR AWESOME!

Executive Vice President NEIL HANKERSON ★ Chief Financial Officer TOM WEDDLE ★ Vice President
of Publishing RANDY STRADLEY ★ Vice President of Book Trade Sales MICHAEL MARTENS ★ Vice
President of Marketing MATT PARKINSON ★ Vice President of Product Development DAVID SCROGGY
★ Vice President of Information Technology DALE LAFOUNTAIN ★ Vice President of Production and
Scheduling CARA NIECE ★ Vice President of Media Licensing NICK McWHORTER ★ General Counsel
KEN LIZZI ★ Editor in Chief DAVE MARSHALL ★ Editorial Director DAVEY ESTRADA ★ Executive Senior
Editor SCOTT ALLIE ★ Senior Books Editor CHRIS WARNER ★ Director of Print and Development
CARY GRAZZINI ★ Art Director LIA RIBACCHI ★ Director of Digital Publishing MARK BERNARDI
Director of International Publishing and Licensing MICHAEL GOMBOS

Library of Congress Cataloging-in-Publication Data
Names: Baltazar, Art, author, illustrator. | Aureliani, Franco, author,
    illustrator. | McMahon, Scoot, illustrator. | Brubaker, Denver,
    illustrator. | Wood, Kurt, illustrator. | Scheidt, Dave, illustrator. |
    Dorse, Vince, illustrator.
Title: Aw Yeah comics! Volume 3, Make way... for awesome! / story and artwork
    by Art Baltazar and Franco ; chapter break artwork by Art Baltazar ;
    featuring Scoot McMahon, Denver Brubaker, Marc Hammond, Kurt Wood, Dave
    Scheidt, and Vince Dorse.
Other titles: Make way... for awesome!
Description: First edition. | Milwaukie, OR : Dark Horse Books, 2016. |
    Summary: "Your favorite superheroes return, led by Action Cat! But what
    evil will threaten our heroes this time? No doubt Evil Cat will pounce
    again! And Parallel-O-Ham menaces beautiful downtown Skokie! Follow the
    continuing adventures of Art Baltazar and Franco's superhero
    creations!"--Provided by publisher.
Identifiers: LCCN 2015050937 | ISBN 9781506700458 (paperback)
Subjects: LCSH: Graphic novels. | CYAC: Graphic novels. |
    Superheroes--Fiction. | BISAC: JUVENILE FICTION / Comics & Graphic Novels
    / General.
Classification: LCC PZ7.7.B33 Awe 2016 | DDC 741.5/973--dc23
LC record available at http://lccn.loc.gov/2015050937

★ CHAPTER ONE ★

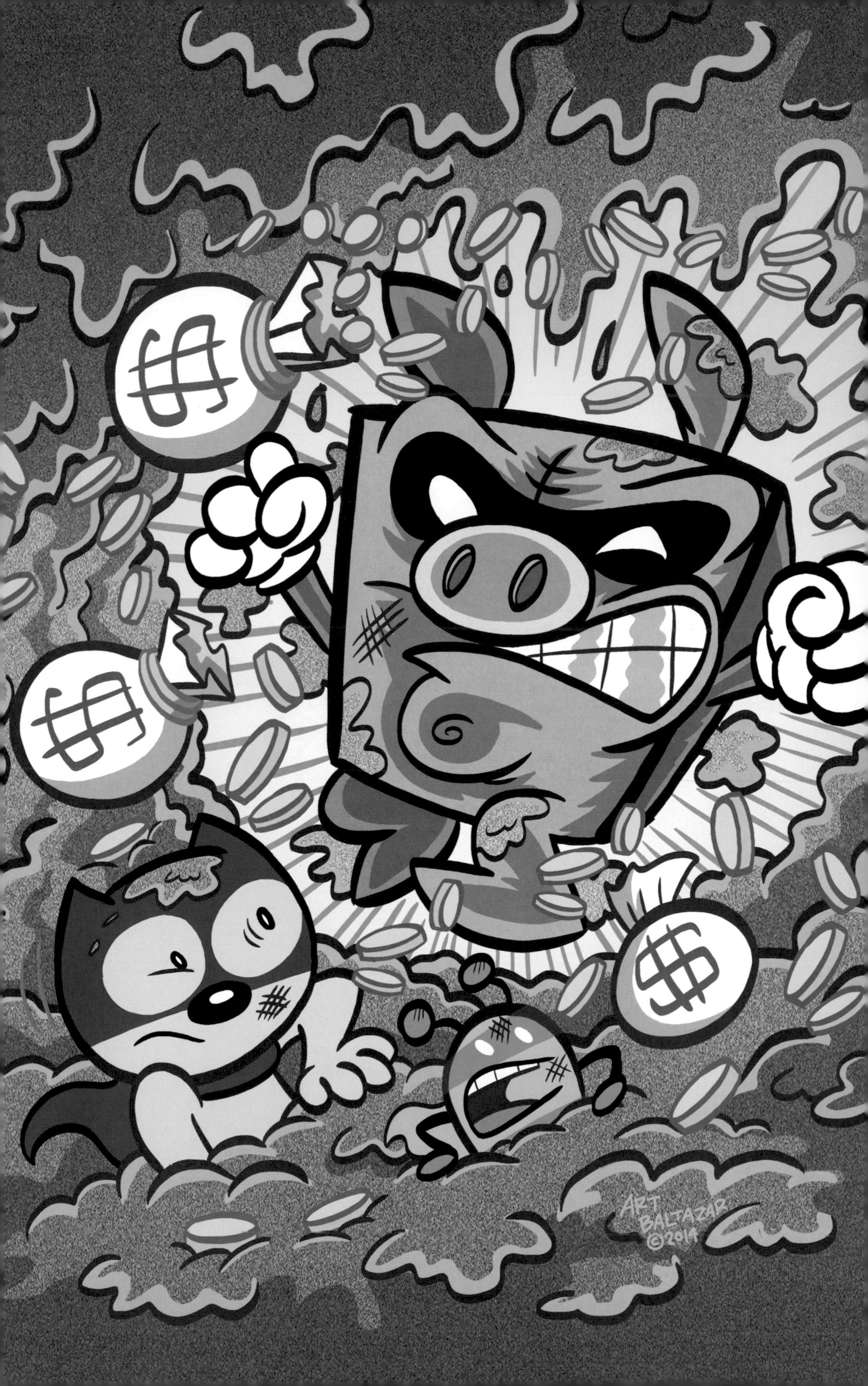
ART BALTAZAR ©2014

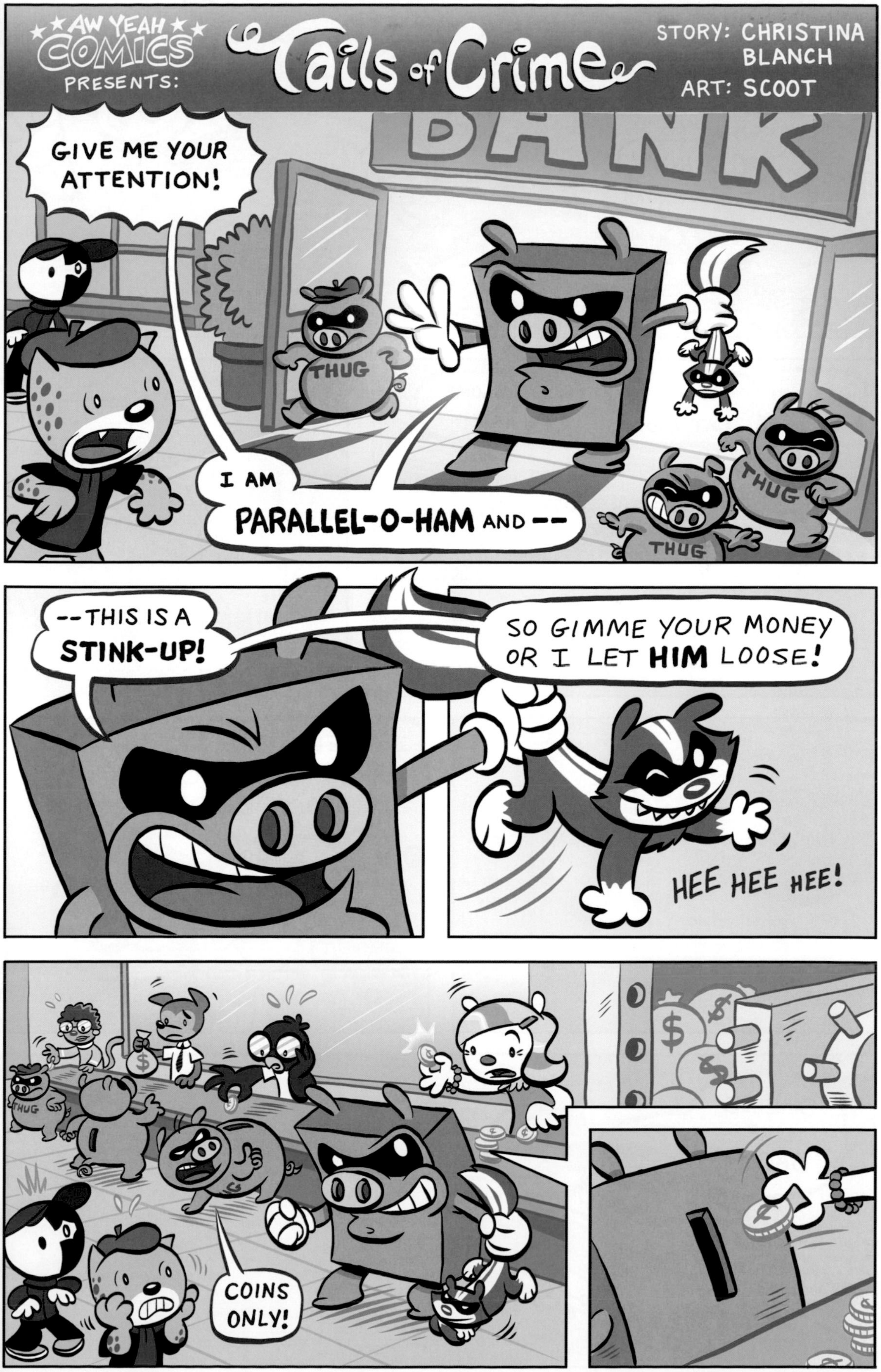
AW YEAH COMICS PRESENTS:
Tails of Crime
STORY: CHRISTINA BLANCH
ART: SCOOT
BANK
GIVE ME YOUR ATTENTION!
I AM
PARALLEL-O-HAM AND --
THUG
THUG
THUG
--THIS IS A STINK-UP!
SO GIMME YOUR MONEY OR I LET HIM LOOSE!
HEE HEE HEE!
THUG
COINS ONLY!

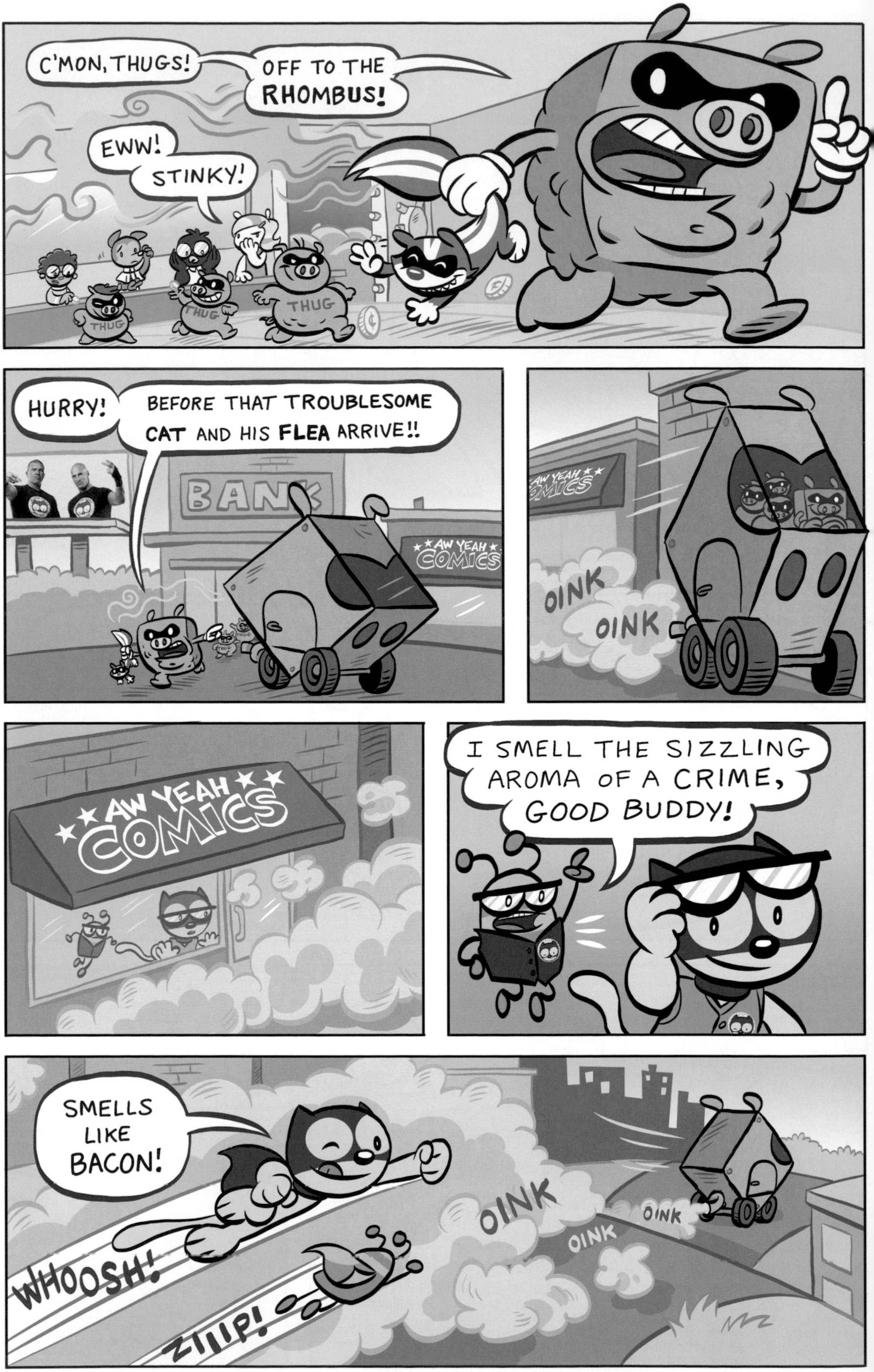
C'MON, THUGS!
OFF TO THE RHOMBUS!
EWW!
STINKY!
THUG
THUG
THUG
HURRY!
BEFORE THAT TROUBLESOME CAT AND HIS FLEA ARRIVE!!
BANK
AW YEAH COMICS
AW YEAH COMICS
OINK
OINK
AW YEAH COMICS
I SMELL THE SIZZLING AROMA OF A CRIME, GOOD BUDDY!
SMELLS LIKE BACON!
OINK
OINK
OINK
WHOOSH!
ZIIIP!

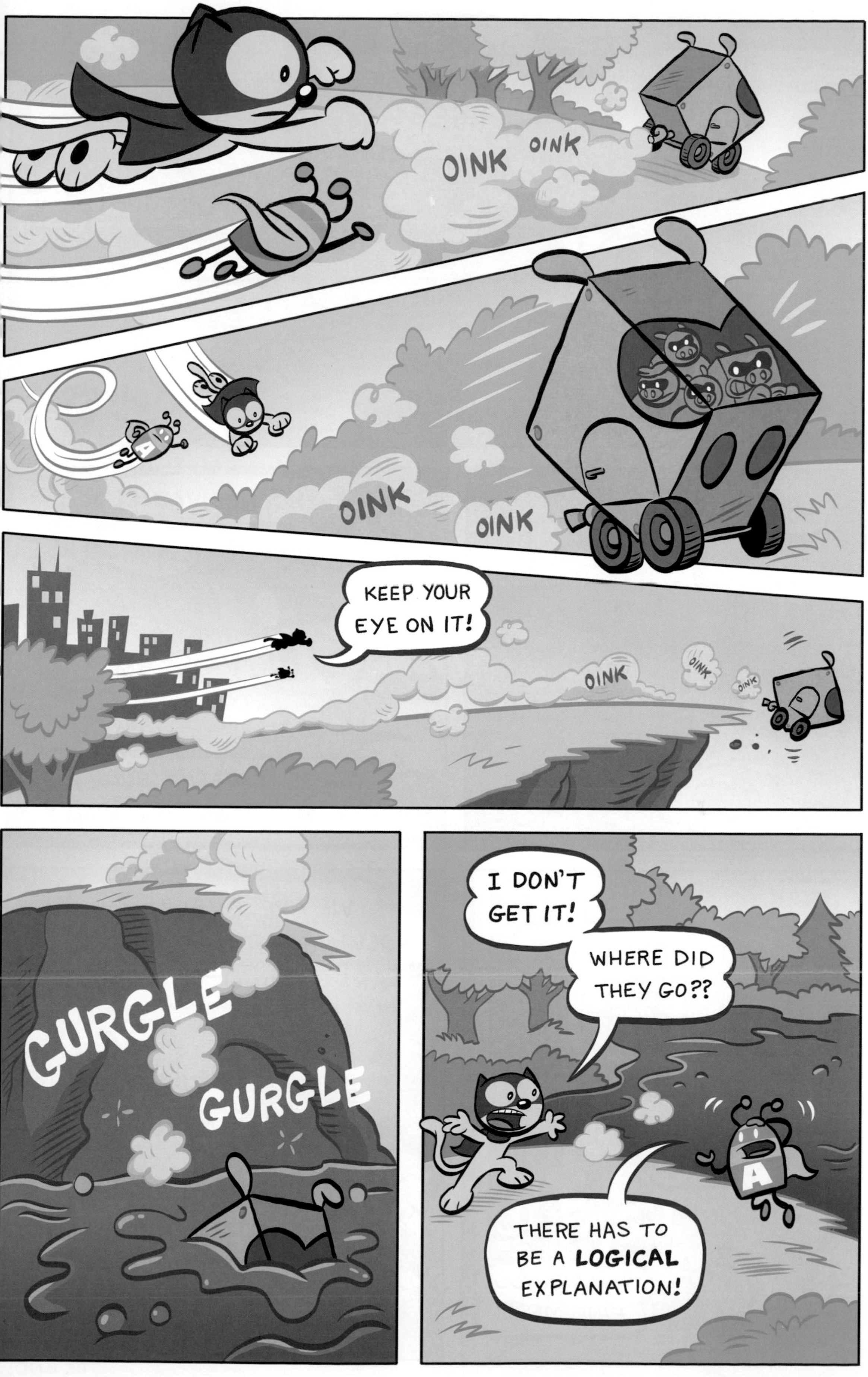
OINK
OINK
OINK
OINK
KEEP YOUR EYE ON IT!
OINK
OINK
OINK
GURGLE
GURGLE
I DON'T GET IT!
WHERE DID THEY GO??
THERE HAS TO BE A **LOGICAL** EXPLANATION!

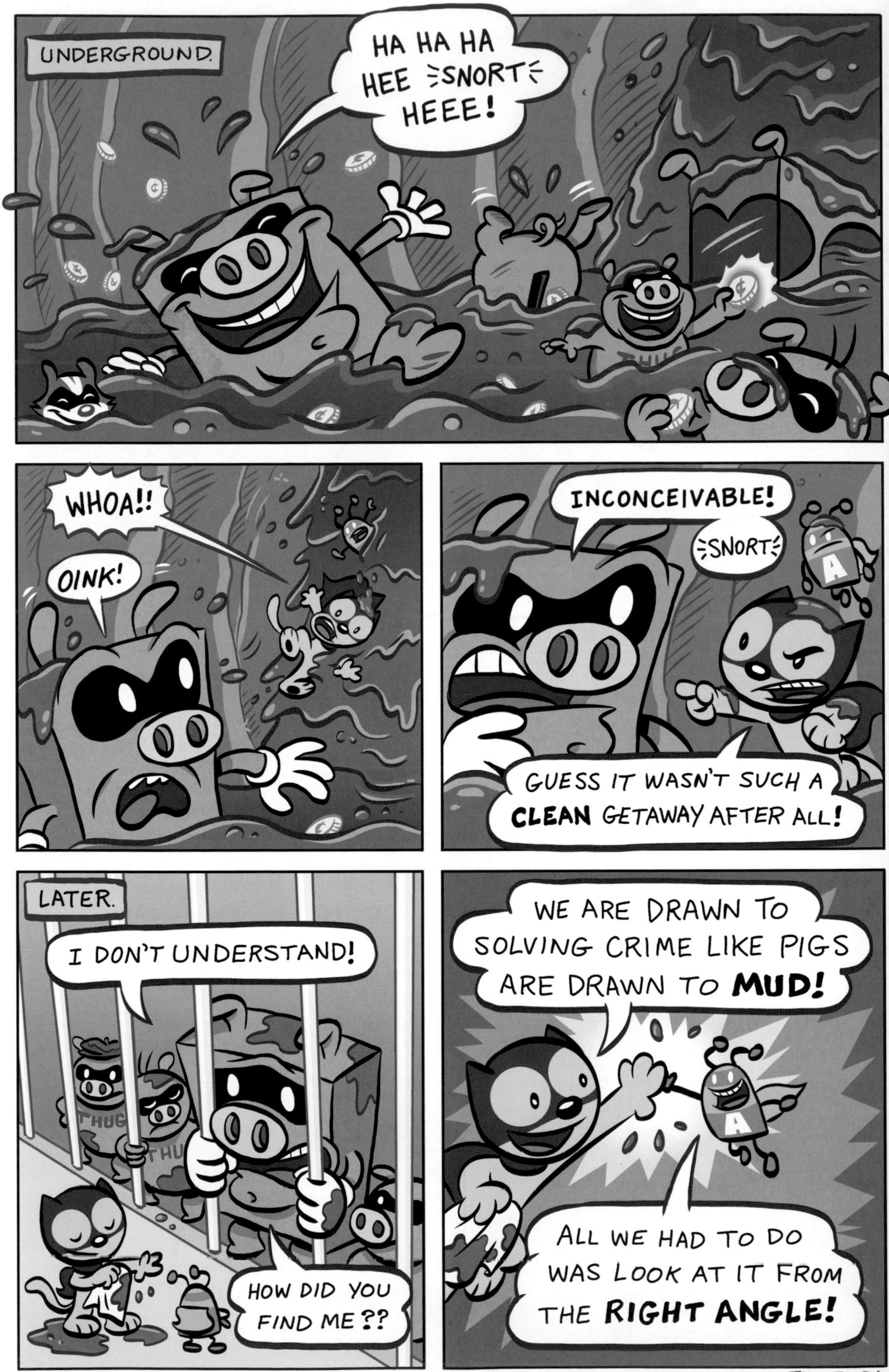
UNDERGROUND.
HA HA HA HEE SNORT HEEE!
WHOA!!
OINK!
INCONCEIVABLE!
SNORT
GUESS IT WASN'T SUCH A CLEAN GETAWAY AFTER ALL!
LATER.
I DON'T UNDERSTAND!
HOW DID YOU FIND ME??
WE ARE DRAWN TO SOLVING CRIME LIKE PIGS ARE DRAWN TO MUD!
ALL WE HAD TO DO WAS LOOK AT IT FROM THE RIGHT ANGLE!

THE END!

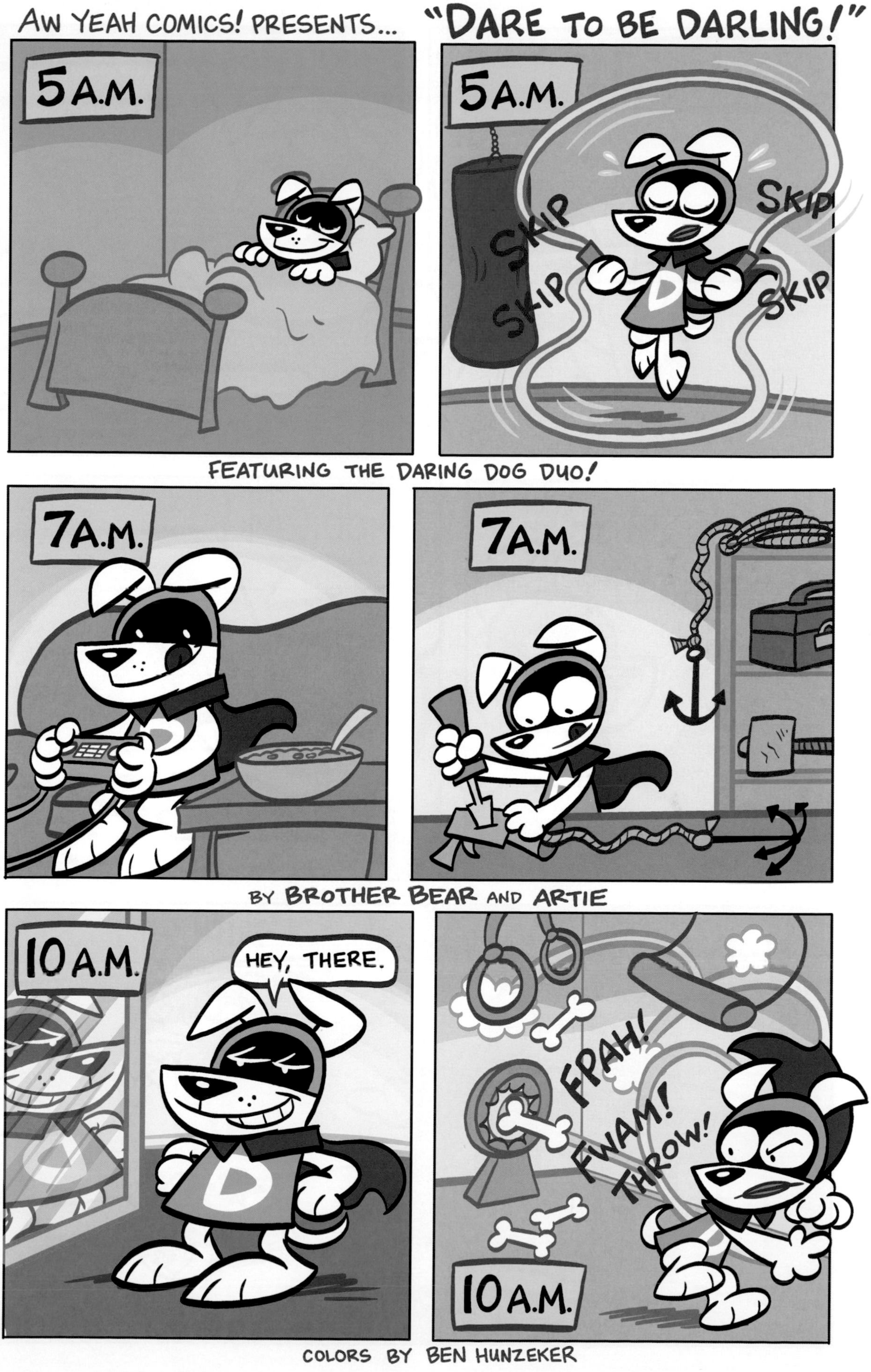
AW YEAH COMICS! PRESENTS...
"DARE TO BE DARLING!"
5 A.M.
5 A.M.
SKIP
SKIP
SKIP
SKIP
FEATURING THE DARING DOG DUO!
7 A.M.
7 A.M.
BY BROTHER BEAR AND ARTIE
10 A.M.
HEY, THERE.
FPAH!
FWAM!
THROW!
10 A.M.
COLORS BY BEN HUNZEKER

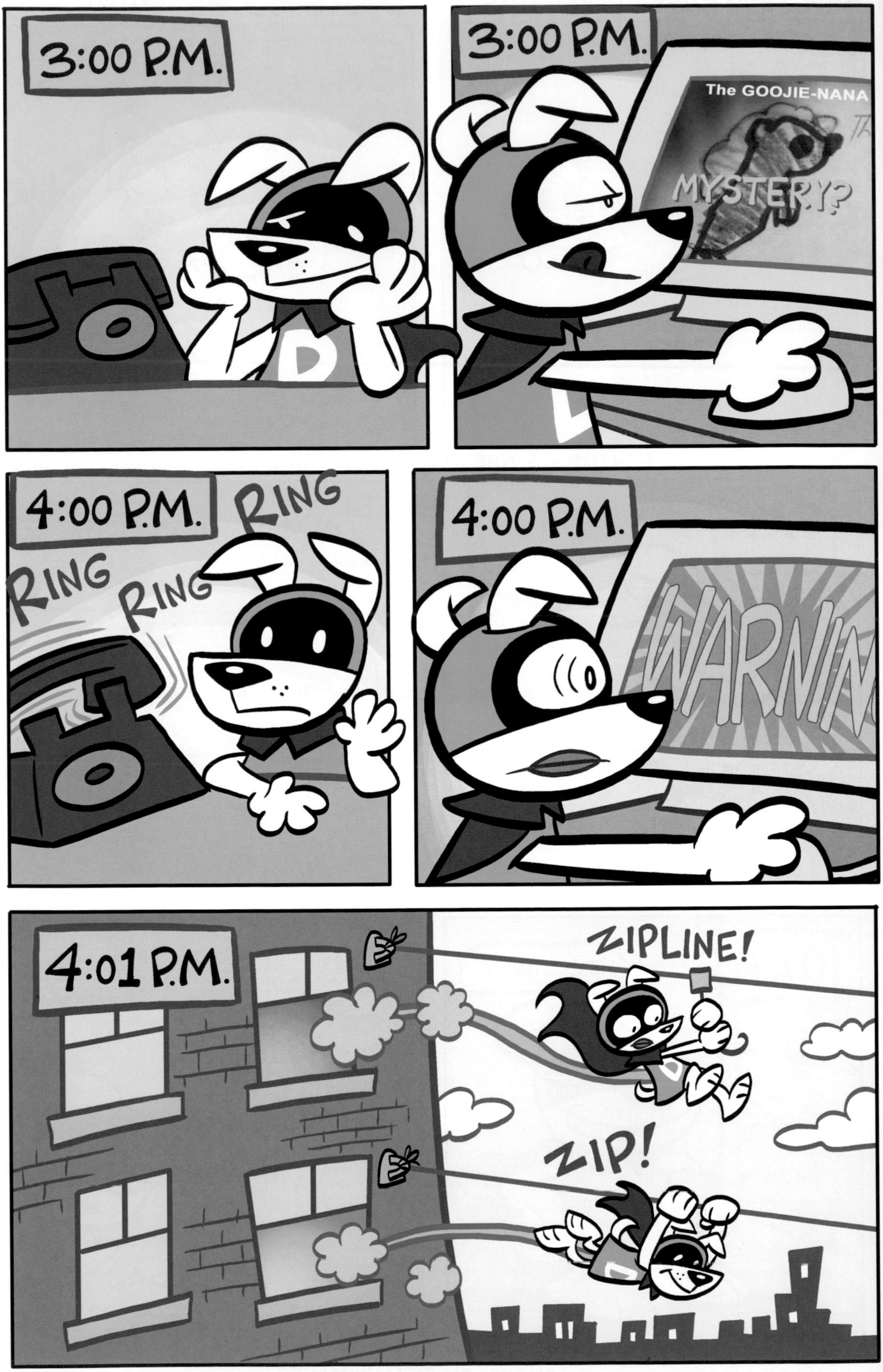
3:00 P.M.
3:00 P.M.
The GOOJIE-NANA
MYSTERY?
4:00 P.M.
RING
RING
RING
4:00 P.M.
WARNIN
4:01 P.M.
ZIPLINE!
ZIP!

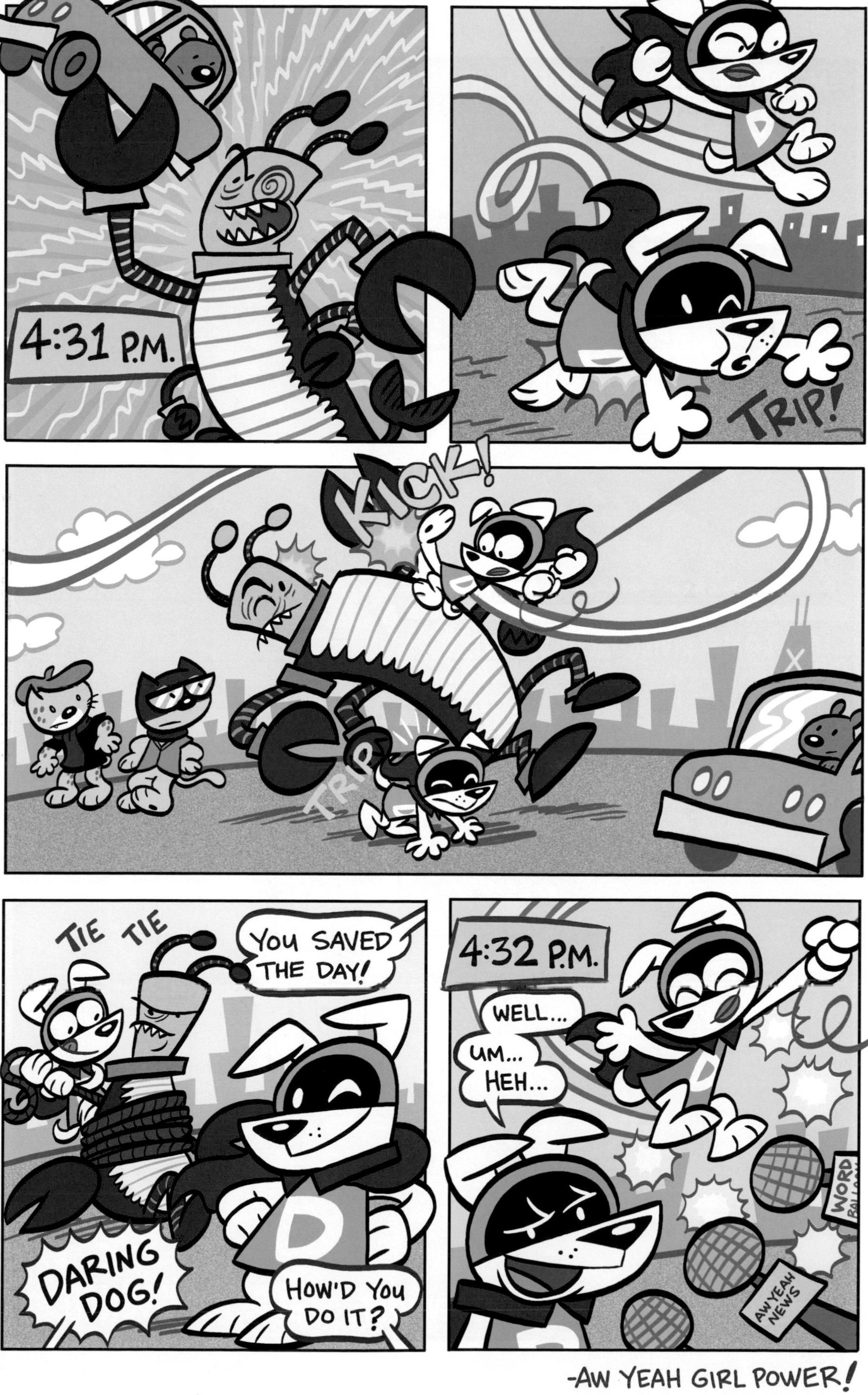
4:31 P.M.
TRIP!
KICK!
TRIP
TIE TIE
YOU SAVED THE DAY!
DARING DOG!
HOW'D YOU DO IT?
4:32 P.M.
WELL...
UM... HEH...
WORD
AW YEAH NEWS

-AW YEAH GIRL POWER!

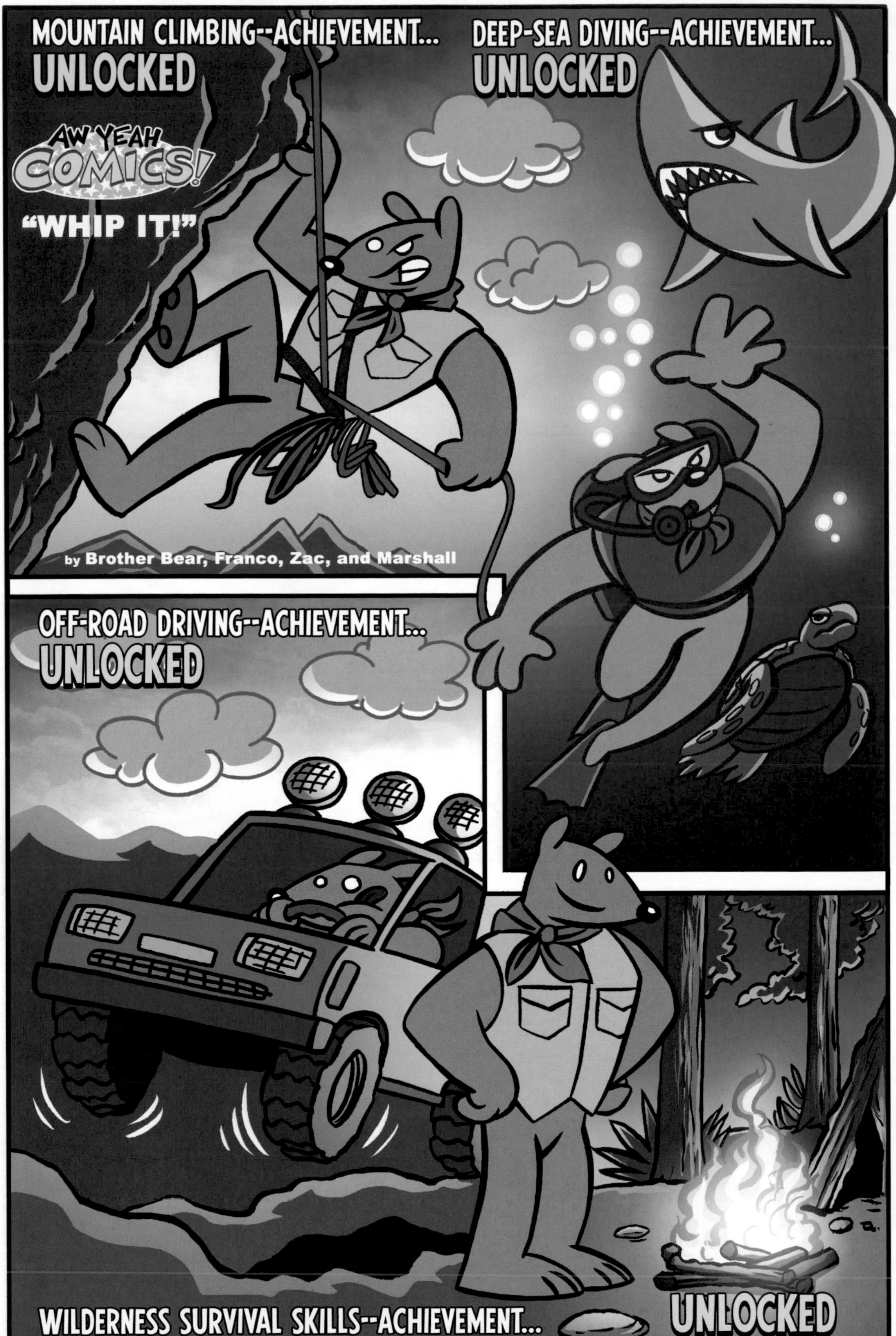
MOUNTAIN CLIMBING--ACHIEVEMENT...
UNLOCKED
AW YEAH COMICS!
"WHIP IT!"
by Brother Bear, Franco, Zac, and Marshall
DEEP-SEA DIVING--ACHIEVEMENT...
UNLOCKED
OFF-ROAD DRIVING--ACHIEVEMENT...
UNLOCKED
WILDERNESS SURVIVAL SKILLS--ACHIEVEMENT...
UNLOCKED

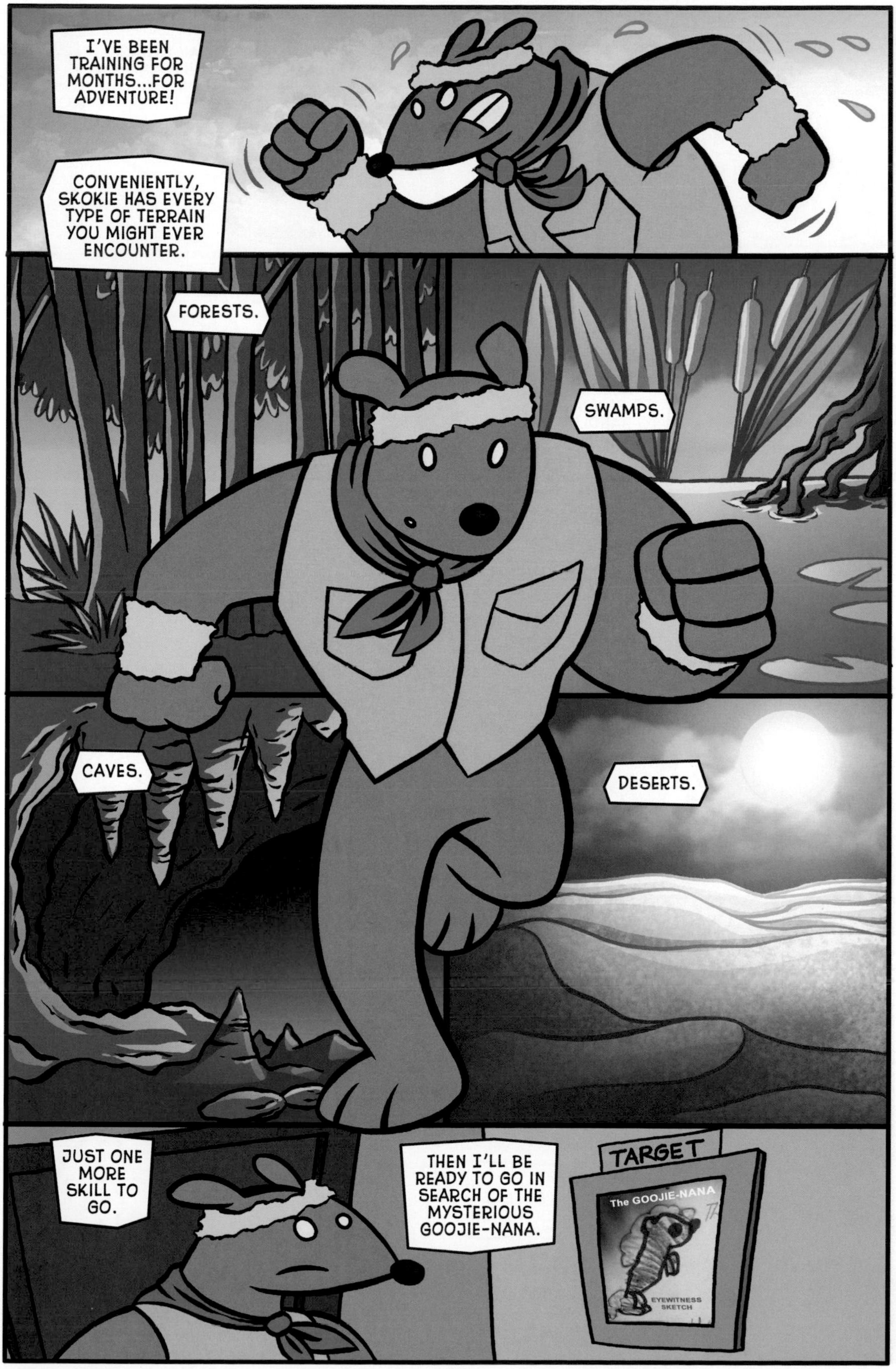
I'VE BEEN TRAINING FOR MONTHS...FOR ADVENTURE!
CONVENIENTLY, SKOKIE HAS EVERY TYPE OF TERRAIN YOU MIGHT EVER ENCOUNTER.
FORESTS.
SWAMPS.
CAVES.
DESERTS.
JUST ONE MORE SKILL TO GO.
THEN I'LL BE READY TO GO IN SEARCH OF THE MYSTERIOUS GOOJIE-NANA.
TARGET
The GOOJIE-NANA
EYEWITNESS SKETCH

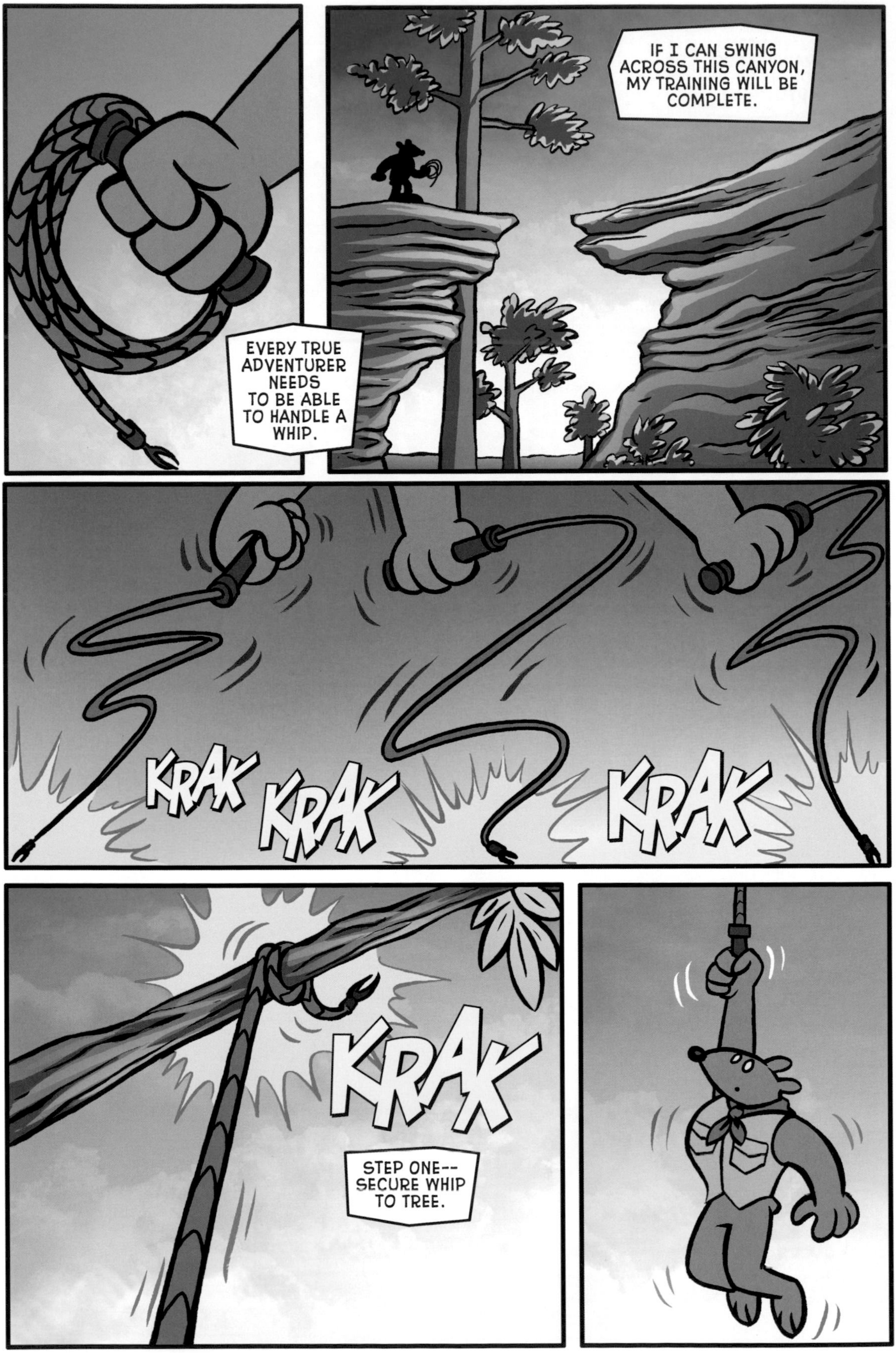
EVERY TRUE ADVENTURER NEEDS TO BE ABLE TO HANDLE A WHIP.
IF I CAN SWING ACROSS THIS CANYON, MY TRAINING WILL BE COMPLETE.
KRAK
KRAK
KRAK
KRAK
STEP ONE-- SECURE WHIP TO TREE.

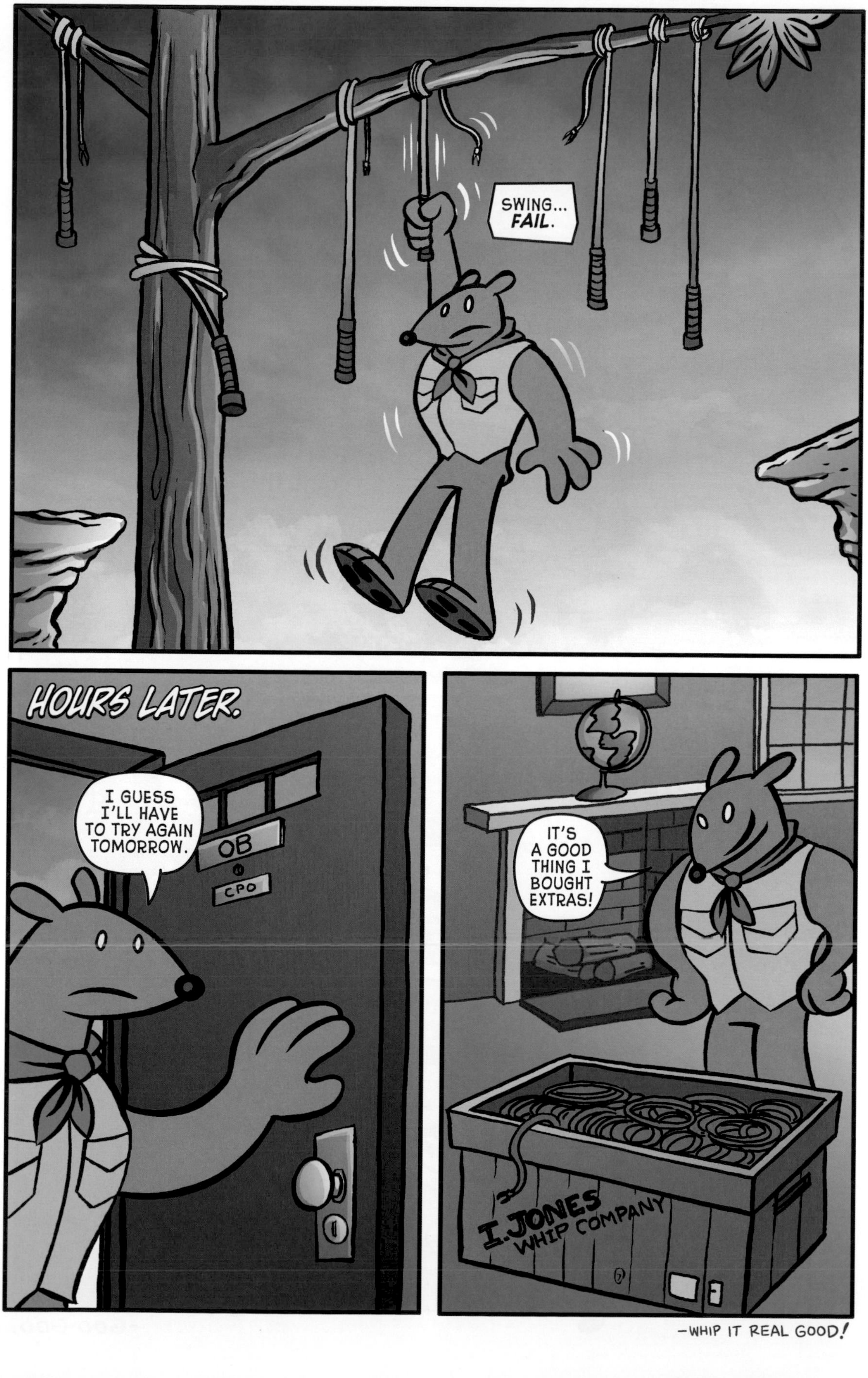
SWING... **FAIL**.
HOURS LATER.
I GUESS I'LL HAVE TO TRY AGAIN TOMORROW.
OB
CPO
IT'S A GOOD THING I BOUGHT EXTRAS!
I. JONES WHIP COMPANY

—WHIP IT REAL GOOD!

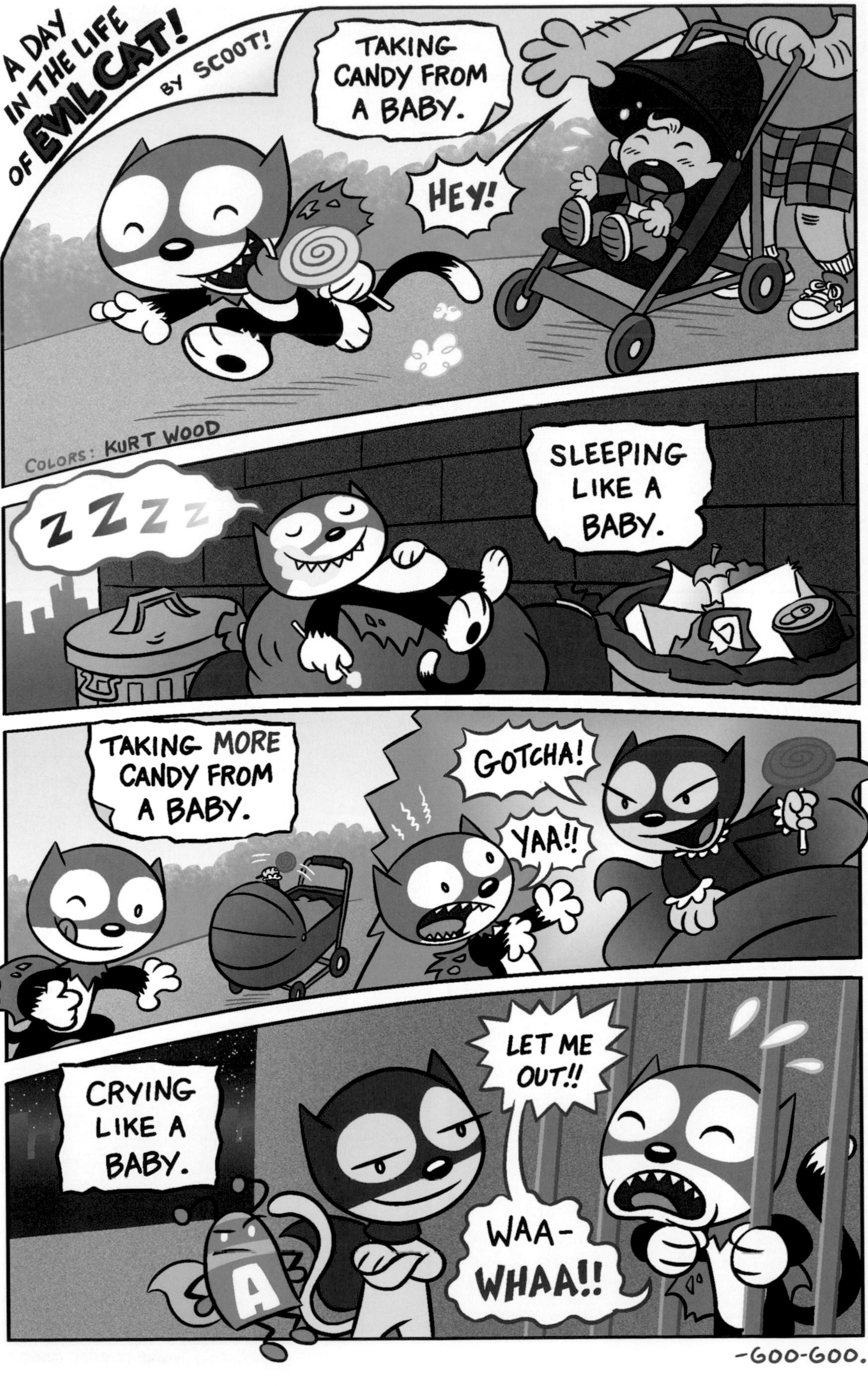
A DAY IN THE LIFE OF EVIL CAT!
BY SCOOT!
TAKING CANDY FROM A BABY.
HEY!
COLORS: KURT WOOD
SLEEPING LIKE A BABY.
Z Z Z Z Z
TAKING MORE CANDY FROM A BABY.
GOTCHA!
YAA!!
CRYING LIKE A BABY.
LET ME OUT!!
WAA-WHAA!!
-GOO-GOO.

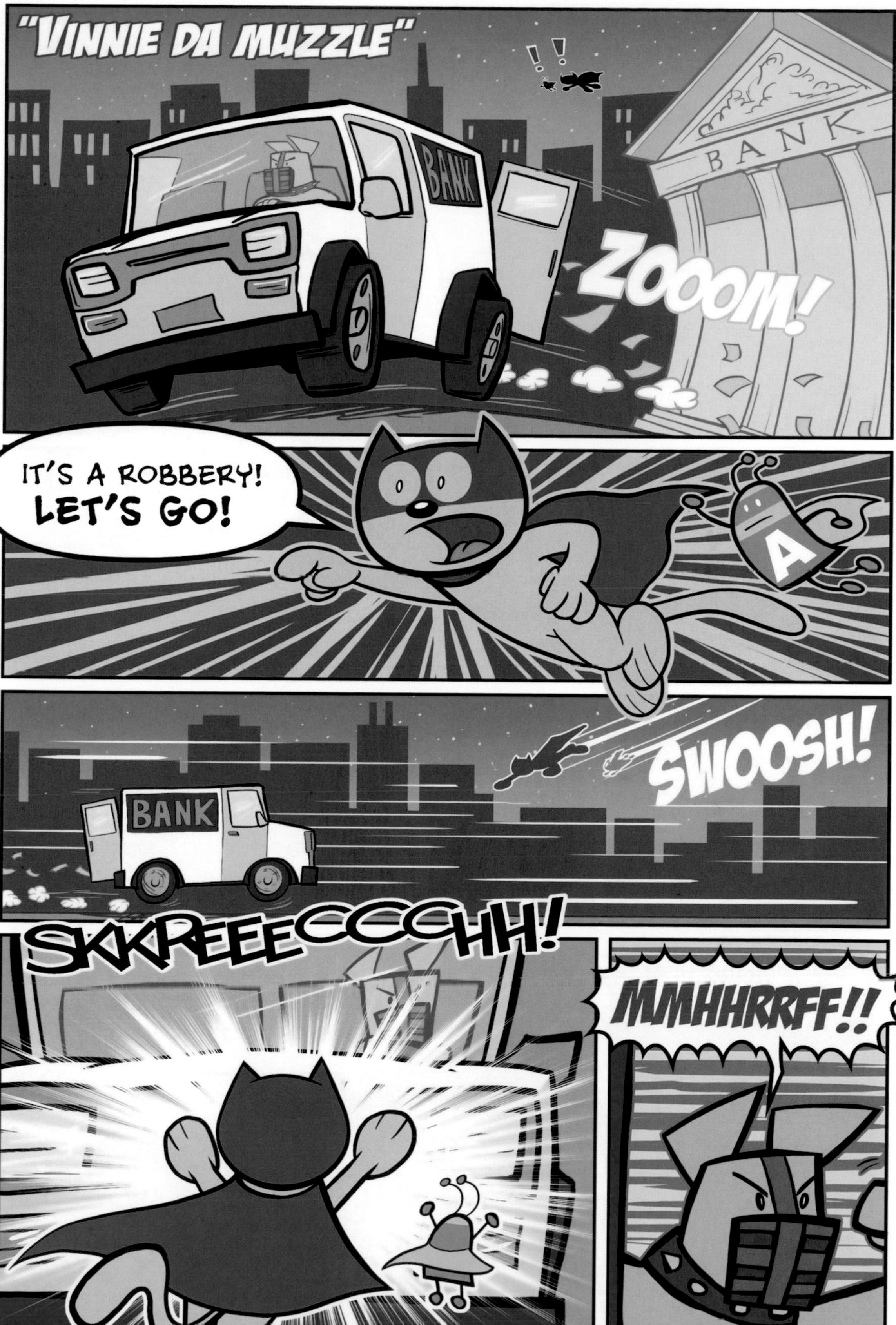
"VINNIE DA MUZZLE"
! !
BANK
BANK
ZOOOM!
IT'S A ROBBERY! LET'S GO!
A
SWOOSH!
BANK
SKKREEEECCCCHH!
MMHHRRFF!!

ART BY PATRICK SCULLIN STORY BY PATRICK & HUNTER SCULLIN

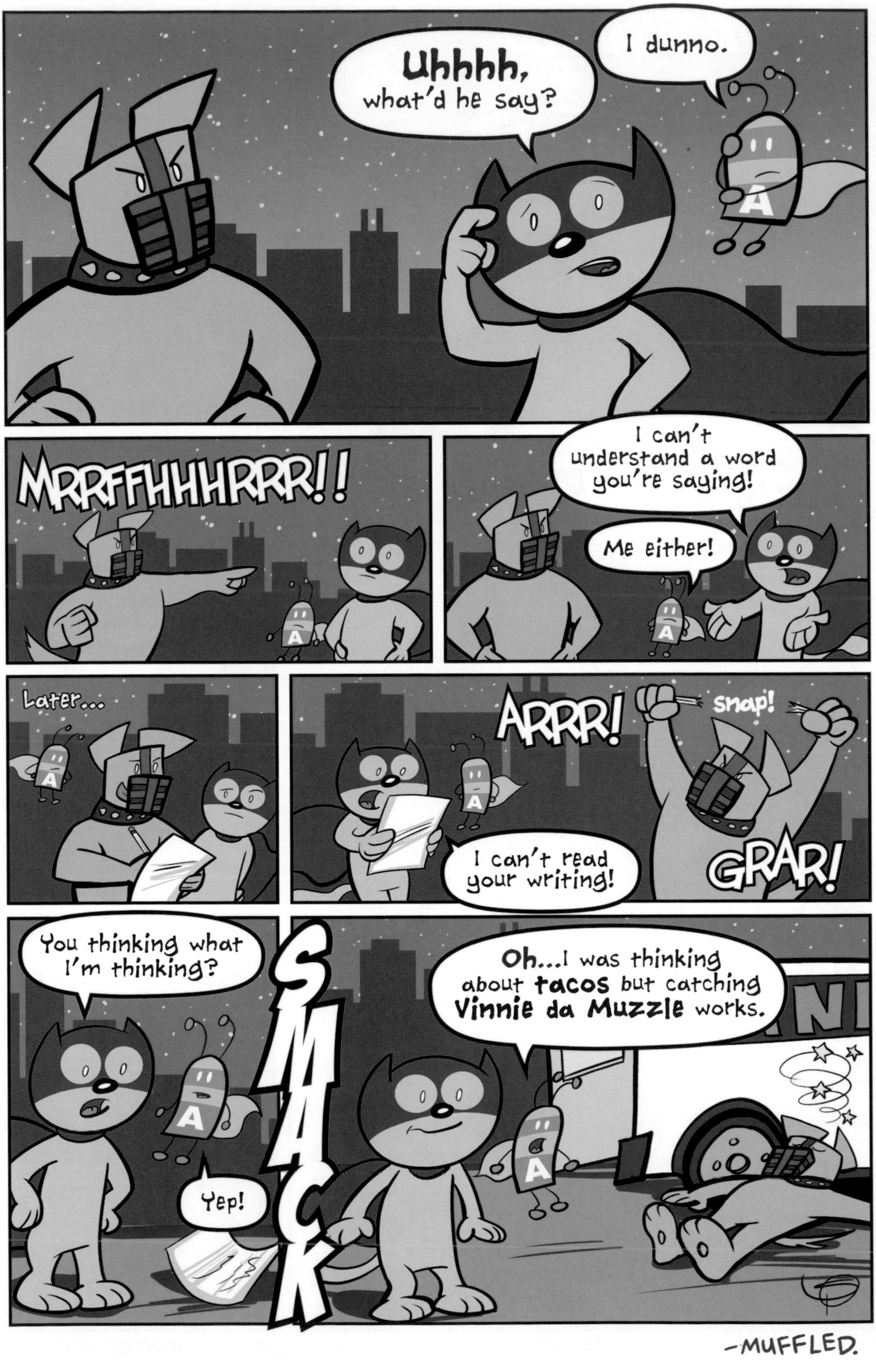
Uhhhh, what'd he say?
I dunno.
MRRFFHHHRRR!!
I can't understand a word you're saying!
Me either!
Later...
ARRR!
Snap!
GRAR!
I can't read your writing!
You thinking what I'm thinking?
Yep!
SMACK
Oh...I was thinking about tacos but catching Vinnie da Muzzle works.

-MUFFLED.

ZOMBIE LUNCH!

by SCOOT

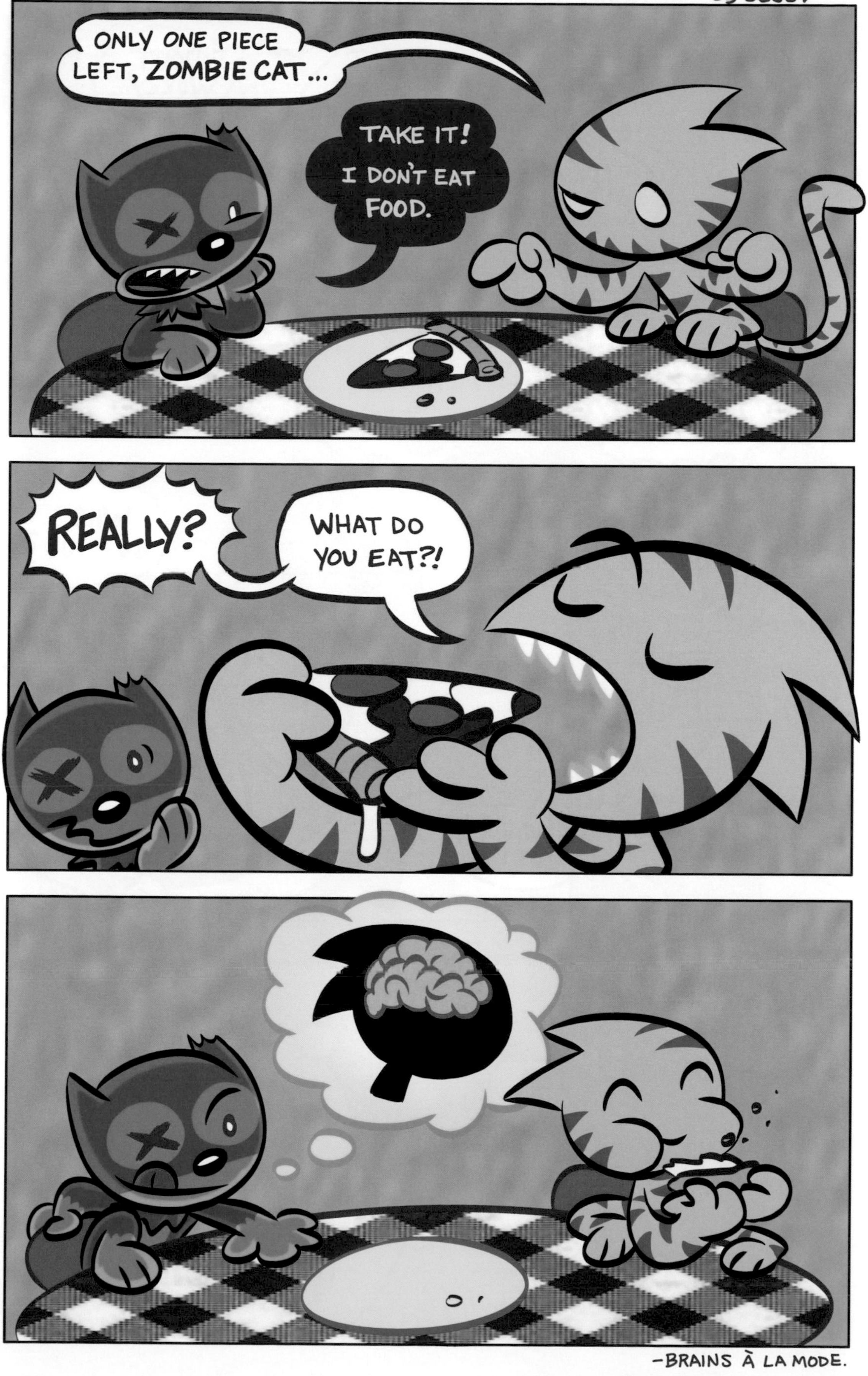

ONLY ONE PIECE LEFT, ZOMBIE CAT...
TAKE IT! I DON'T EAT FOOD.
REALLY?
WHAT DO YOU EAT?!

-BRAINS À LA MODE.

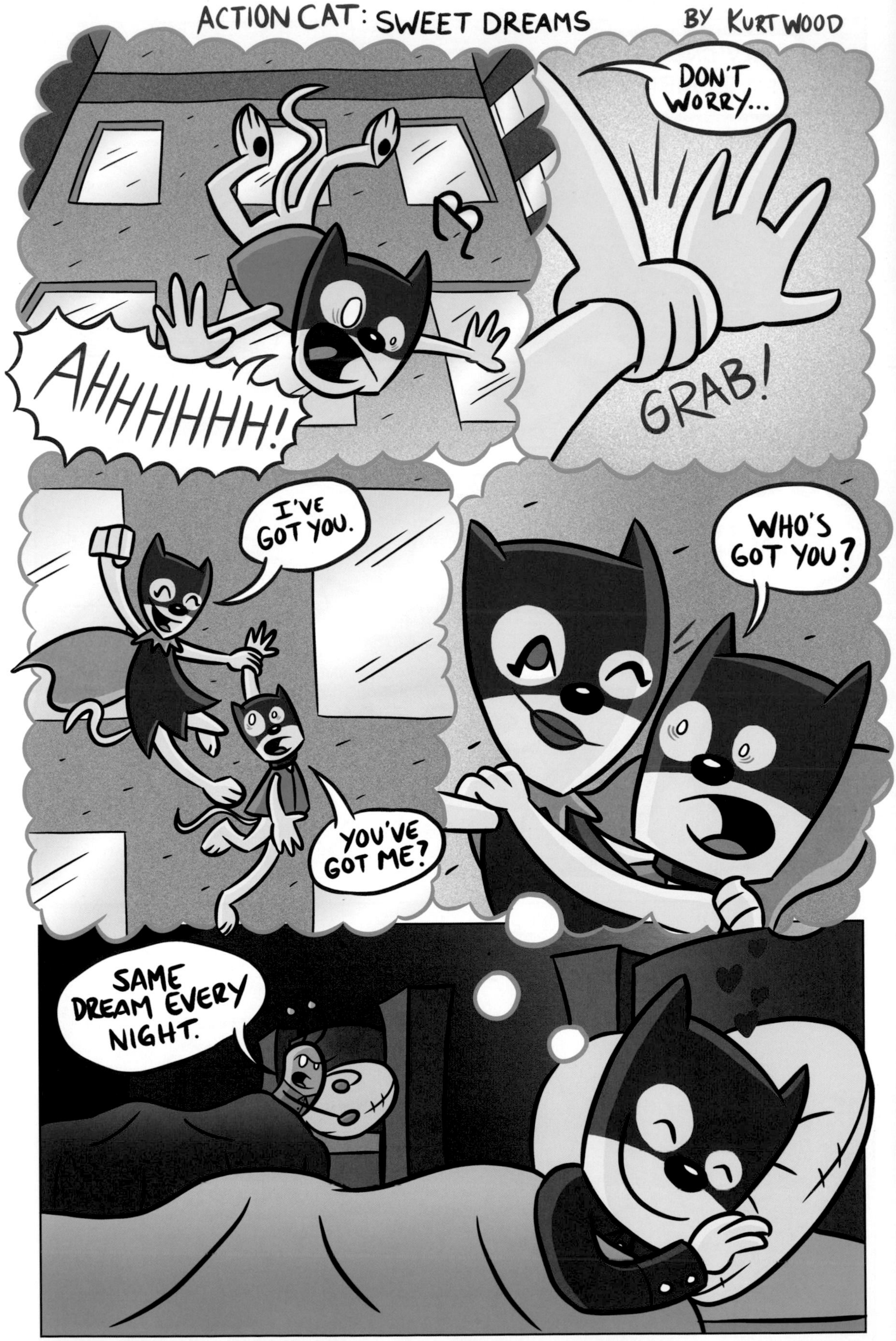
ACTION CAT: SWEET DREAMS
BY KURTWOOD
AHHHHHHH!
DON'T WORRY...
GRAB!
I'VE GOT YOU.
YOU'VE GOT ME?
WHO'S GOT YOU?
SAME DREAM EVERY NIGHT.

CORNELIUS and ALOWICIOUS in: DIGITAL FIRST by: SCOOT

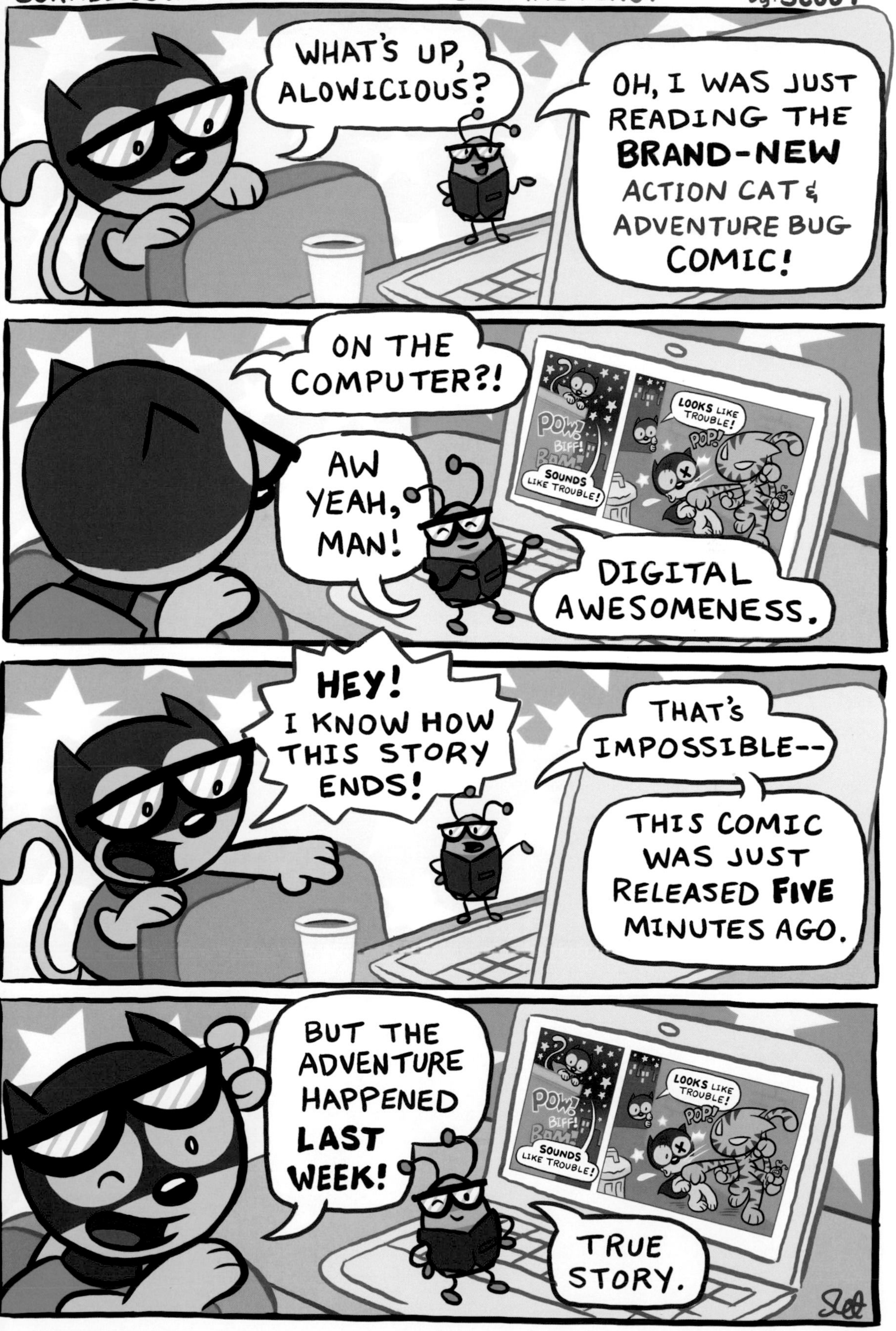
WHAT'S UP, ALOWICIOUS?
OH, I WAS JUST READING THE BRAND-NEW ACTION CAT & ADVENTURE BUG COMIC!
ON THE COMPUTER?!
AW YEAH, MAN!
DIGITAL AWESOMENESS.
POW! BIFF! BAM!
SOUNDS LIKE TROUBLE!
LOOKS LIKE TROUBLE!
POP!
HEY! I KNOW HOW THIS STORY ENDS!
THAT'S IMPOSSIBLE--
THIS COMIC WAS JUST RELEASED FIVE MINUTES AGO.
BUT THE ADVENTURE HAPPENED LAST WEEK!
TRUE STORY.

★ CHAPTER TWO ★

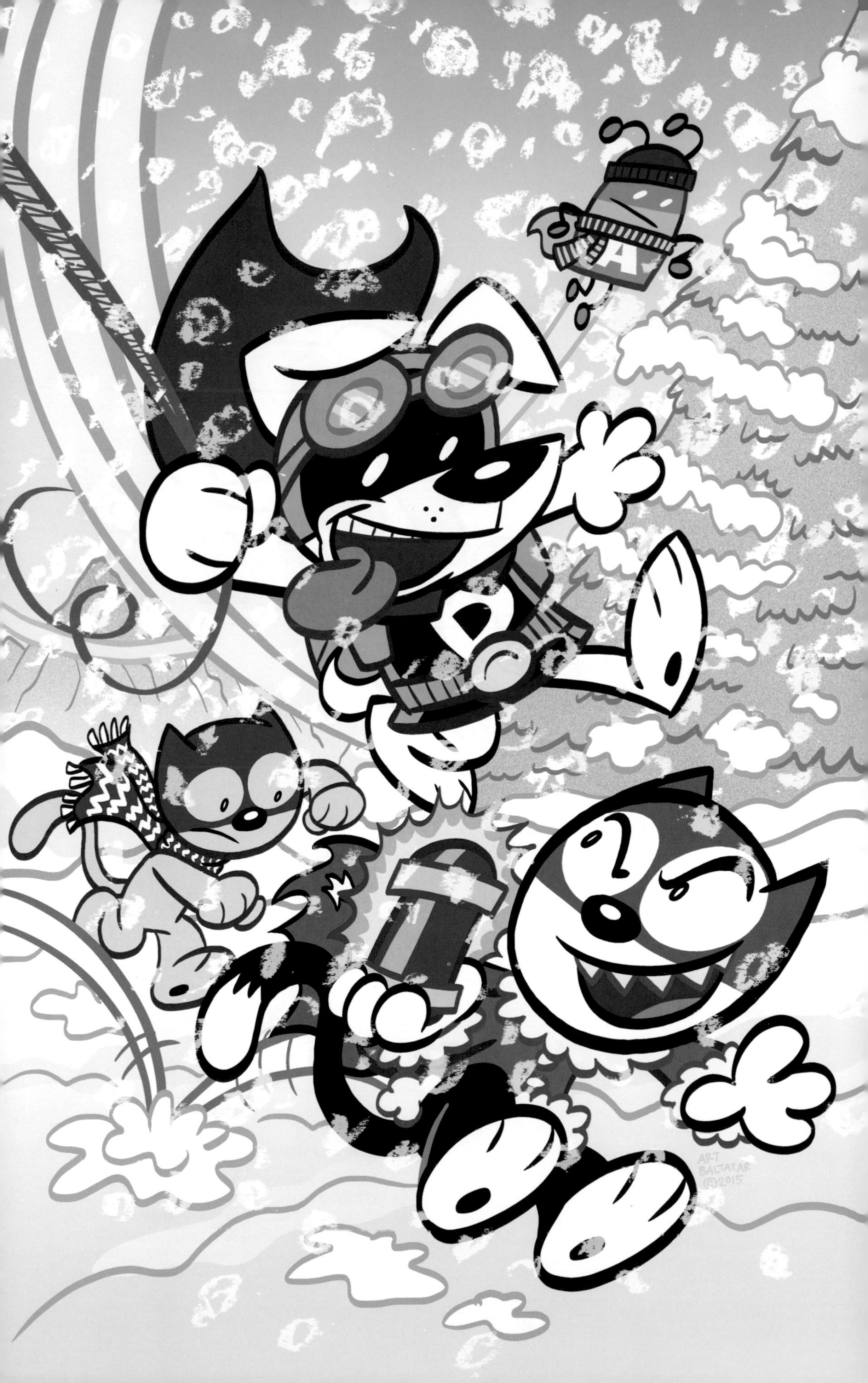
ART
BALTAZAR
©2015

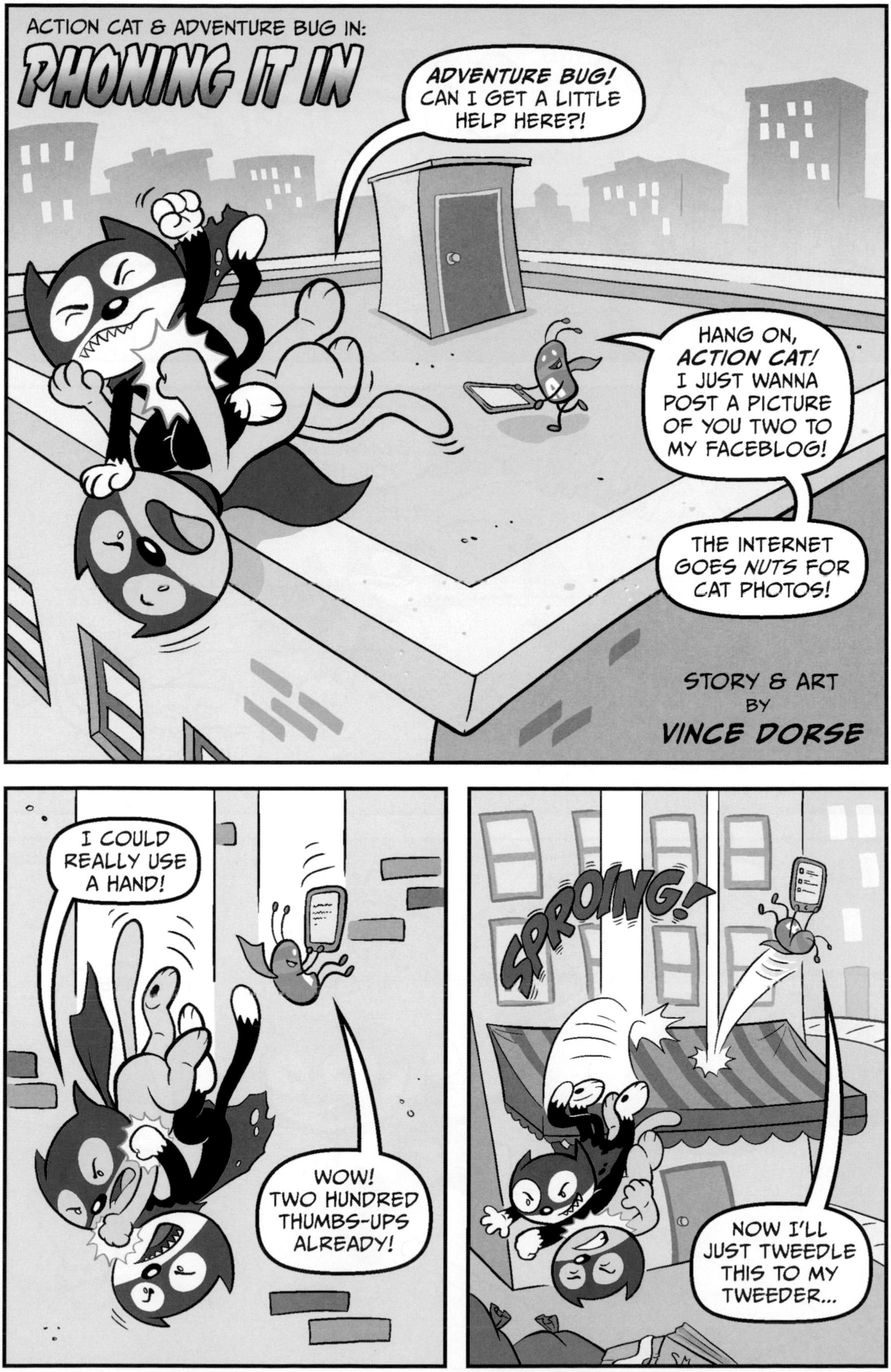
ACTION CAT & ADVENTURE BUG IN:
PHONING IT IN
ADVENTURE BUG! CAN I GET A LITTLE HELP HERE?!
HANG ON, ACTION CAT! I JUST WANNA POST A PICTURE OF YOU TWO TO MY FACEBLOG!
THE INTERNET GOES NUTS FOR CAT PHOTOS!
STORY & ART BY
VINCE DORSE
I COULD REALLY USE A HAND!
WOW! TWO HUNDRED THUMBS-UPS ALREADY!
SPROING!
NOW I'LL JUST TWEEDLE THIS TO MY TWEEDER...

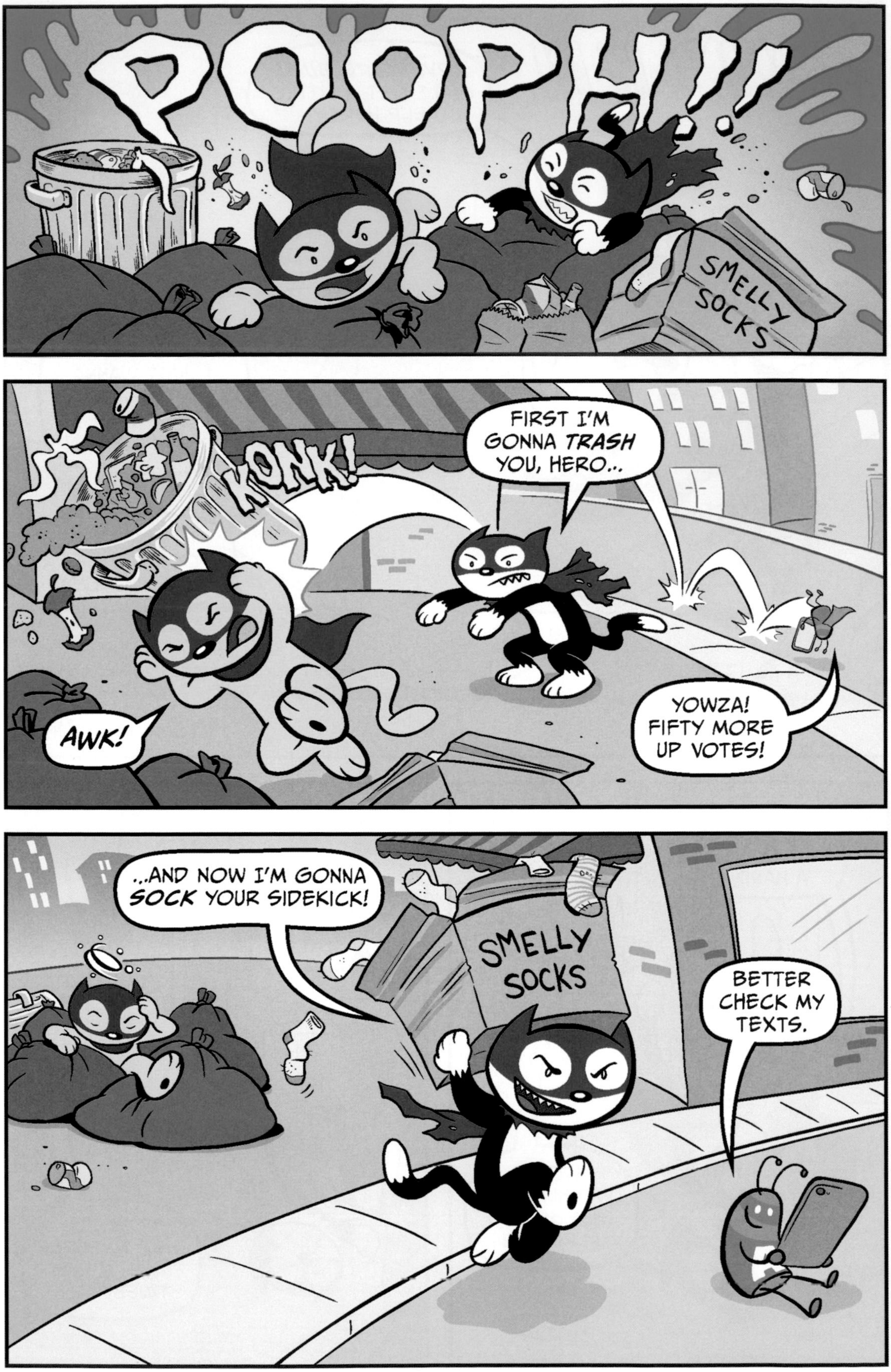
POOPH!!
SMELLY SOCKS
KONK!
FIRST I'M GONNA TRASH YOU, HERO...
AWK!
YOWZA! FIFTY MORE UP VOTES!
...AND NOW I'M GONNA SOCK YOUR SIDEKICK!
SMELLY SOCKS
BETTER CHECK MY TEXTS.

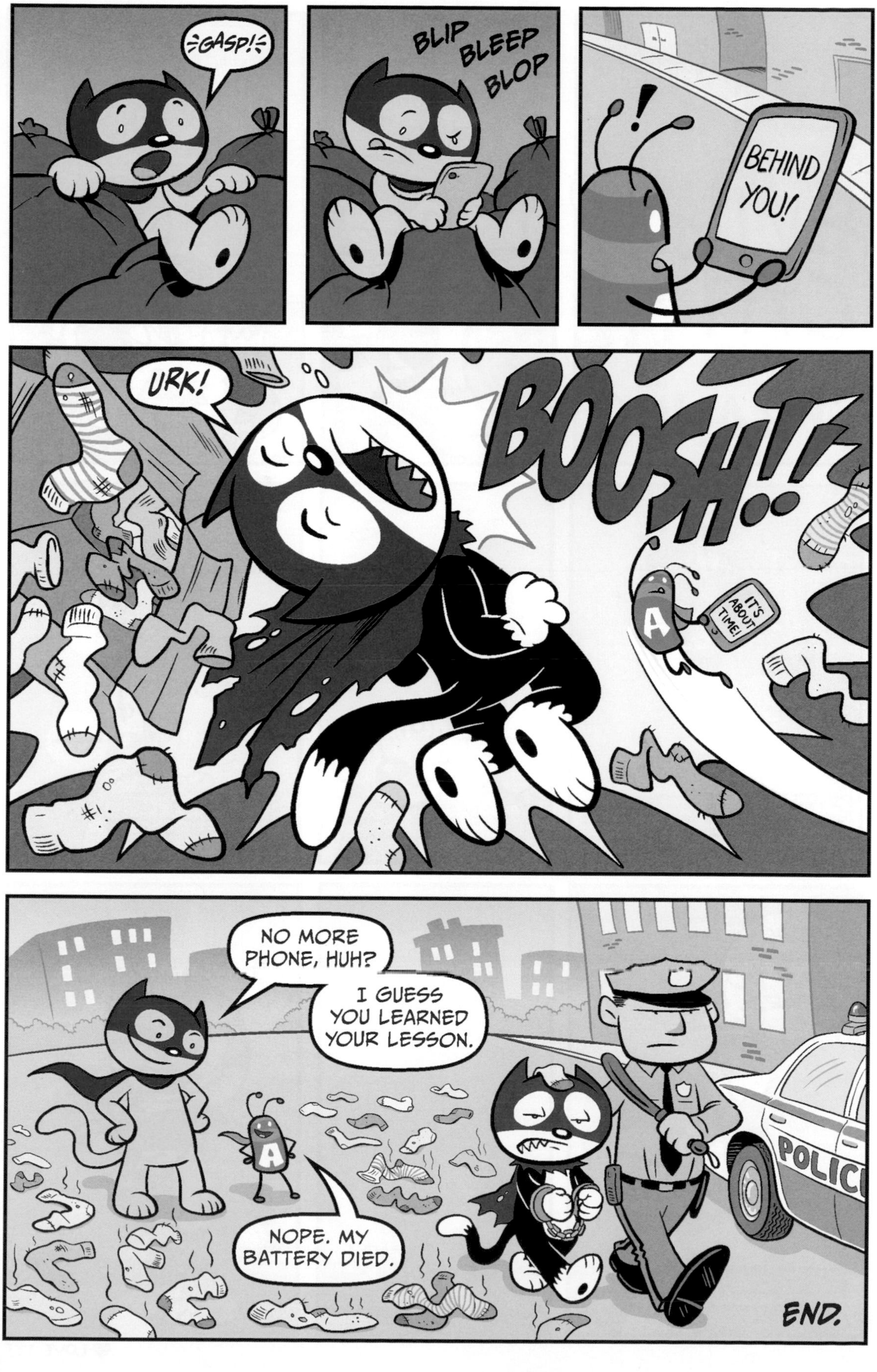
GASP!
BLIP BLEEP BLOP
!
BEHIND YOU!
URK!
BOOSH!!
IT'S ABOUT TIME!
A
NO MORE PHONE, HUH?
I GUESS YOU LEARNED YOUR LESSON.
NOPE. MY BATTERY DIED.
POLIC
END.

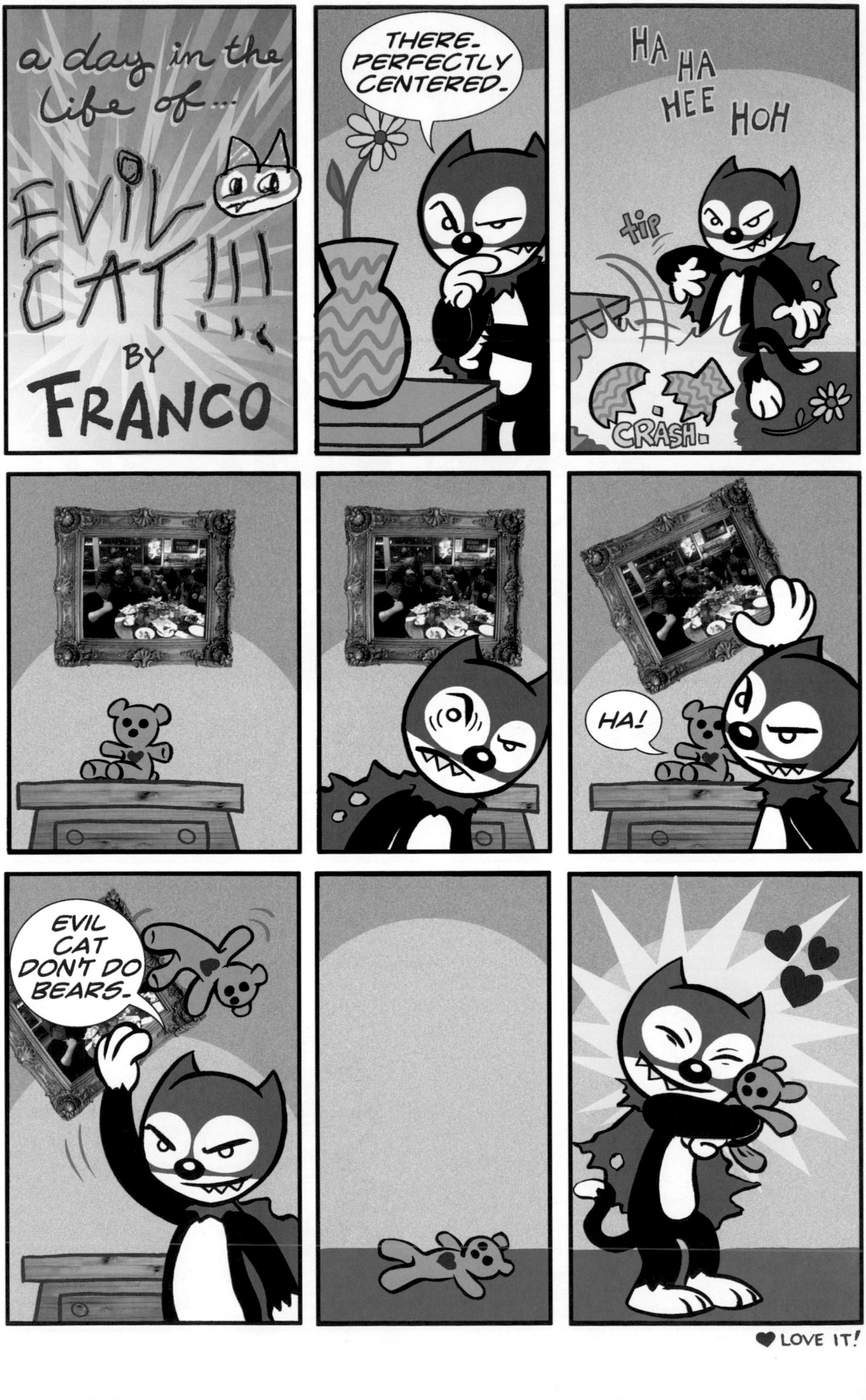
a day in the life of...
EVIL CAT!!!
BY FRANCO
THERE. PERFECTLY CENTERED.
HA HA HEE HOH
tip
CRASH.
HA!
EVIL CAT DON'T DO BEARS.
LOVE IT!

ACTION CAT and ADVENTURE BUG: LAUNDRY LESSON

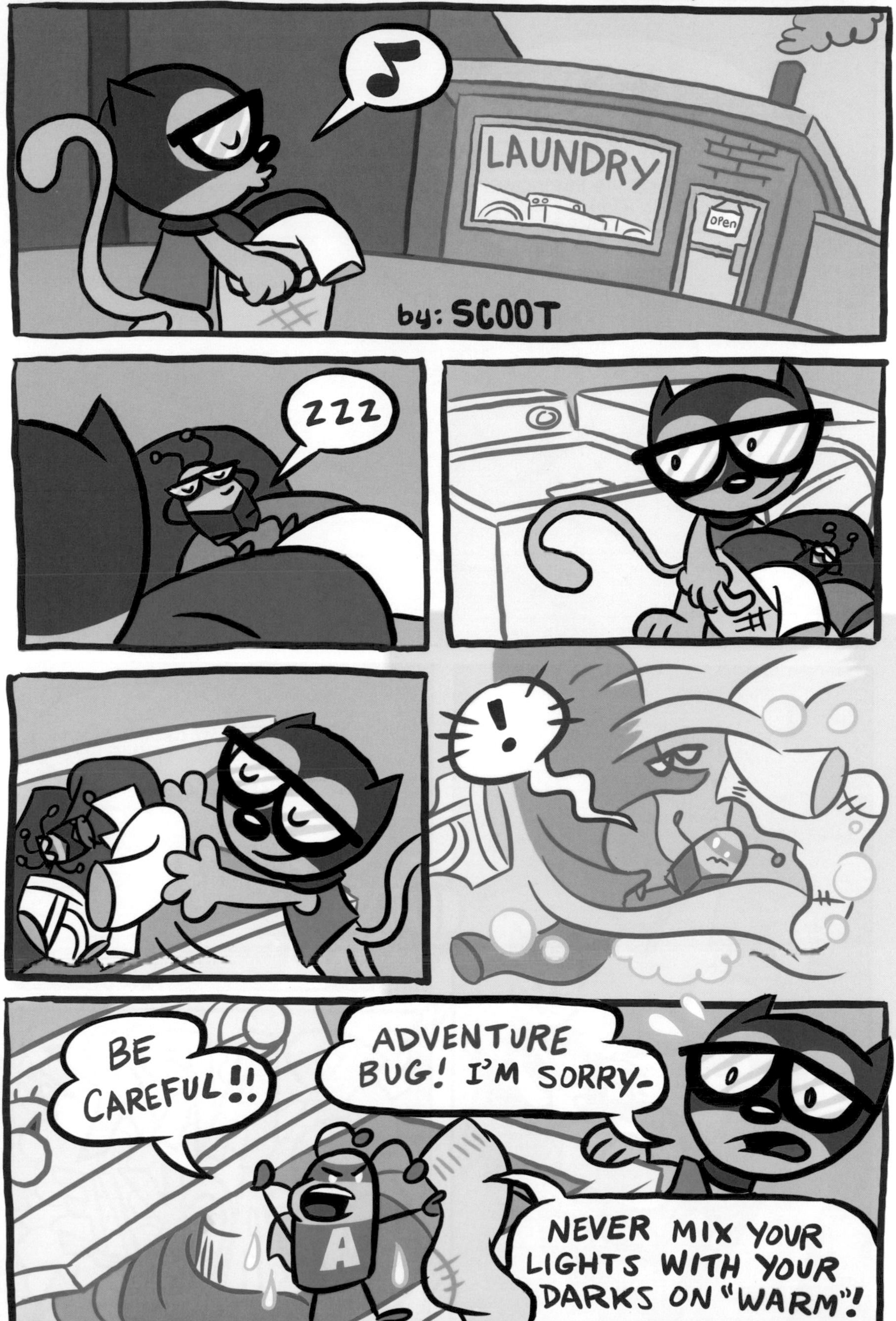

LAUNDRY
OPEN
by: SCOOT
ZZZ
!
BE CAREFUL!!
ADVENTURE BUG! I'M SORRY-
NEVER MIX YOUR LIGHTS WITH YOUR DARKS ON "WARM"!
A

EVIL CAT AND GHOST BUG IN: MONSTER CAT

BY KURT WOOD

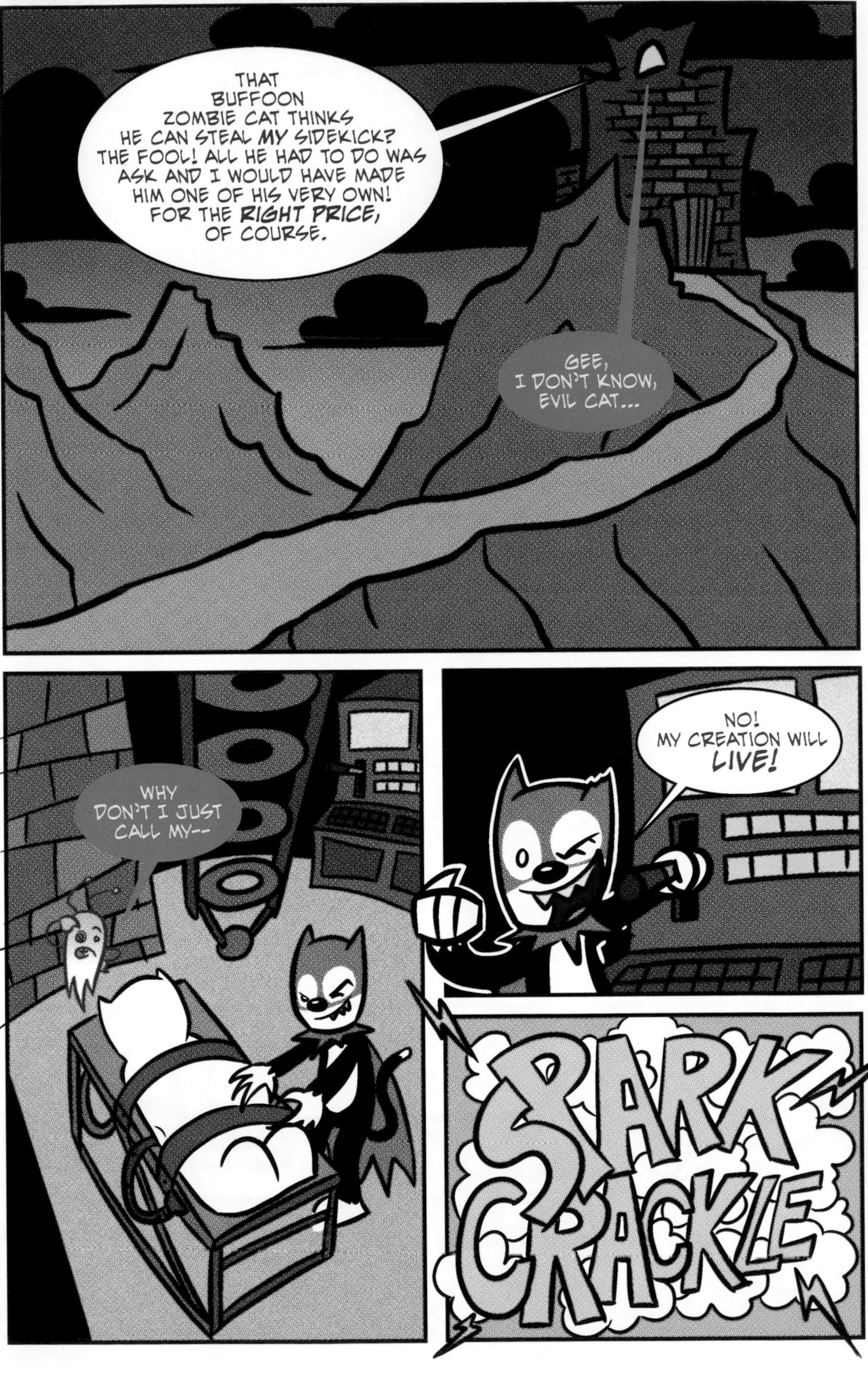

THAT BUFFOON ZOMBIE CAT THINKS HE CAN STEAL MY SIDEKICK? THE FOOL! ALL HE HAD TO DO WAS ASK AND I WOULD HAVE MADE HIM ONE OF HIS VERY OWN! FOR THE RIGHT PRICE, OF COURSE.
GEE, I DON'T KNOW, EVIL CAT...
WHY DON'T I JUST CALL MY--
NO! MY CREATION WILL LIVE!
SPARK
CRACKLE

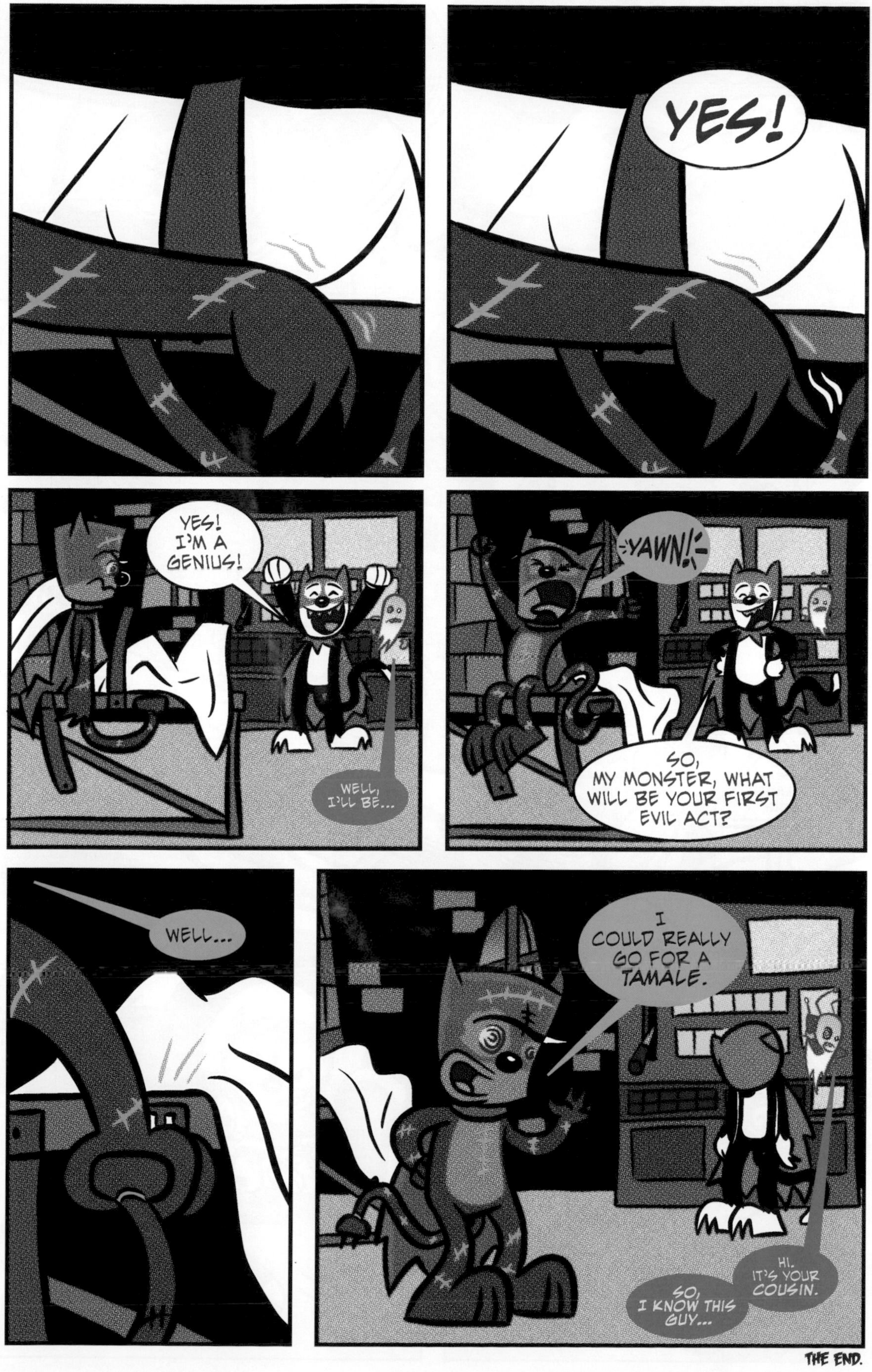
YES!
YES! I'M A GENIUS!
WELL, I'LL BE...
YAWN!
SO, MY MONSTER, WHAT WILL BE YOUR FIRST EVIL ACT?
WELL...
I COULD REALLY GO FOR A TAMALE.
HI. IT'S YOUR COUSIN.
SO, I KNOW THIS GUY...

THE END.

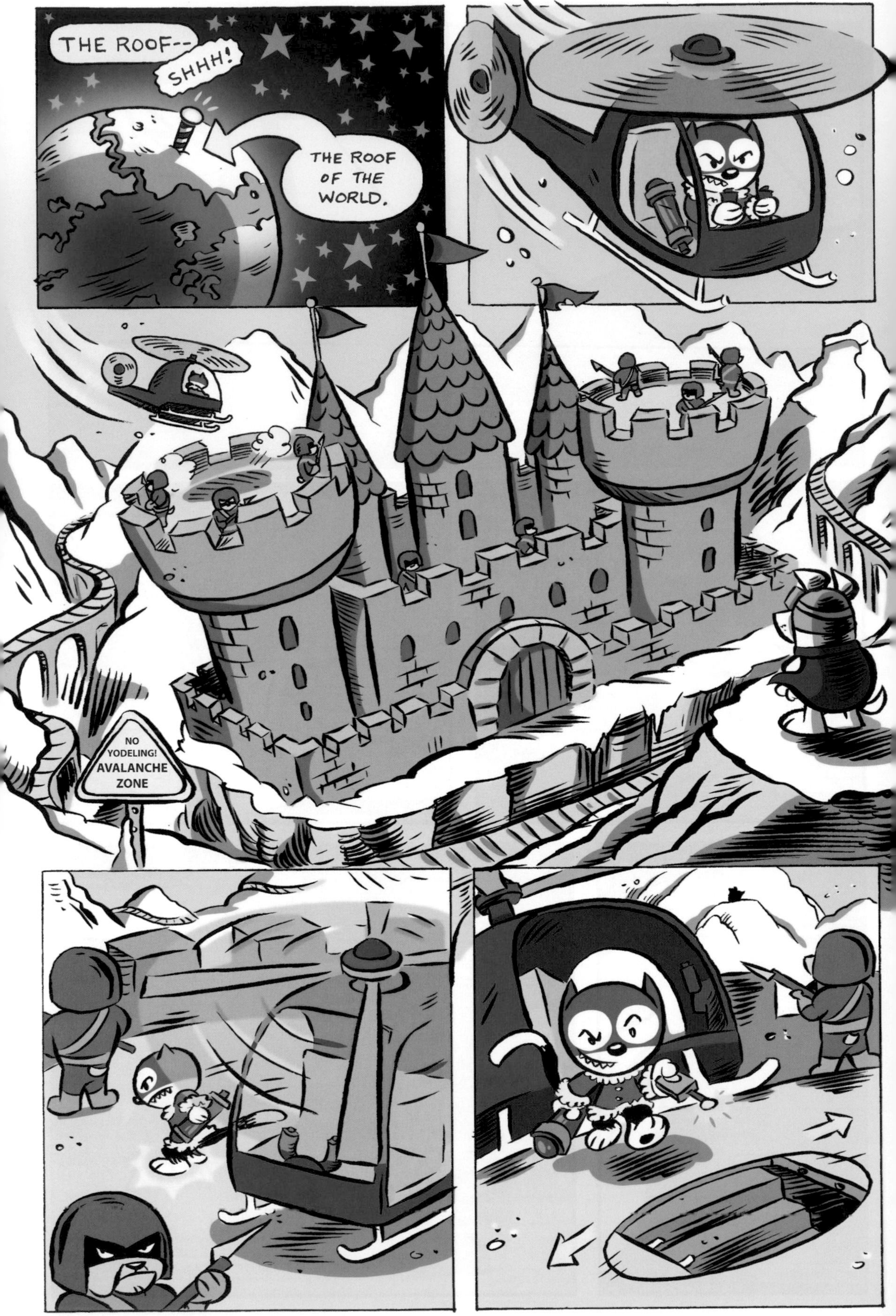
THE ROOF--
SHHH!
THE ROOF OF THE WORLD.
NO YODELING! AVALANCHE ZONE

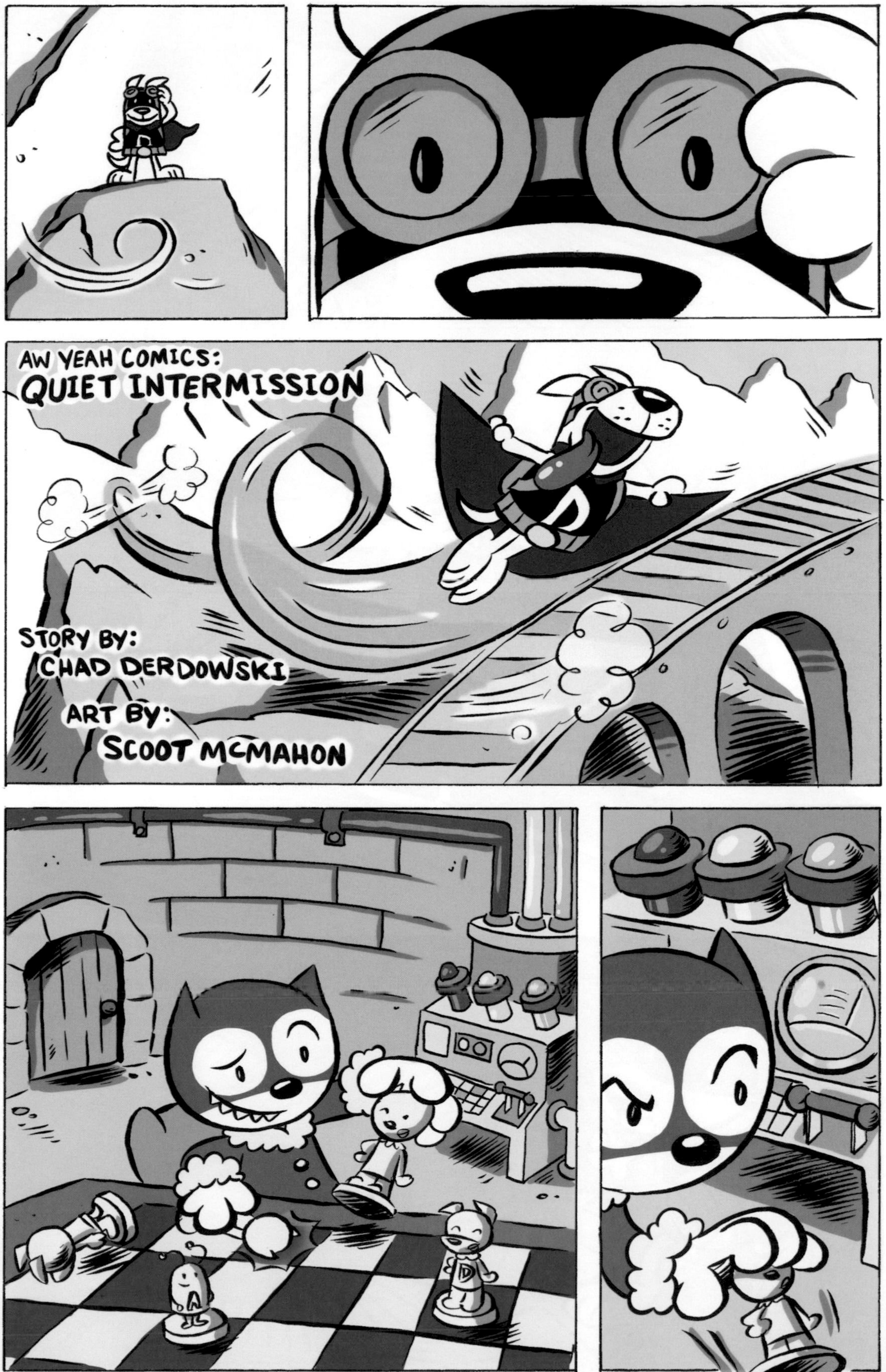
AW YEAH COMICS:
QUIET INTERMISSION
STORY BY:
CHAD DERDOWSKI
ART BY:
SCOOT MCMAHON

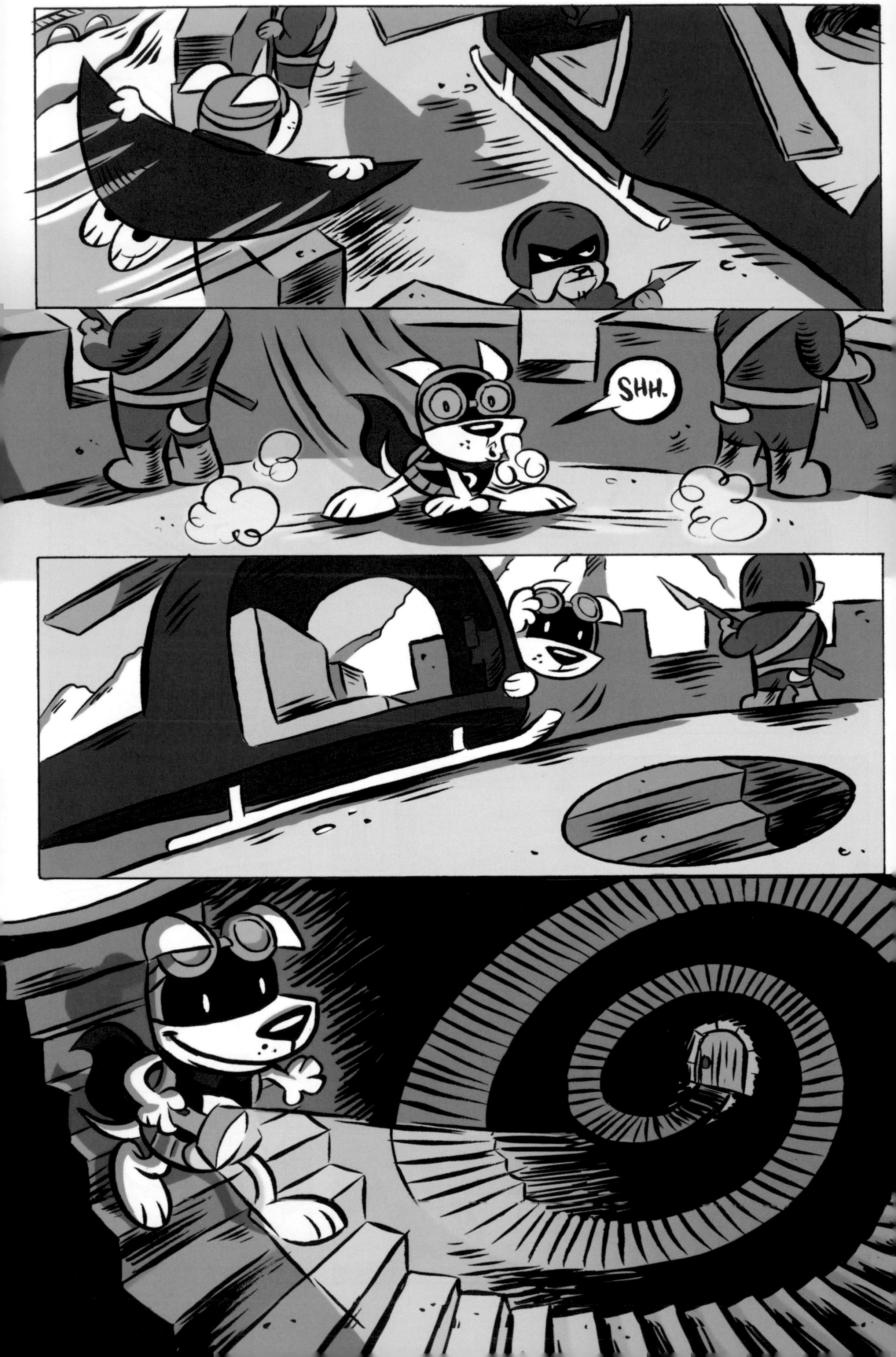
SHH.

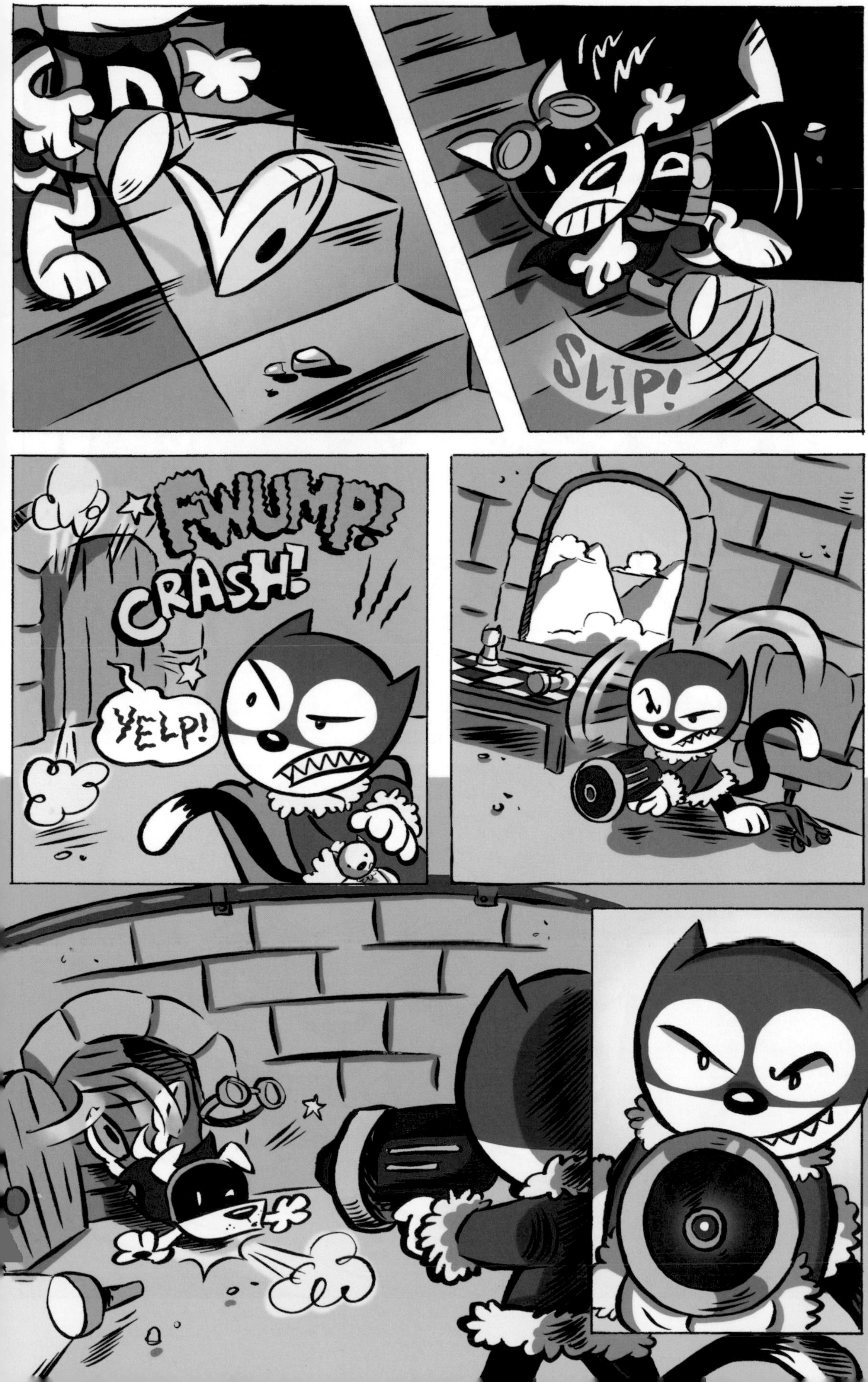

SLIP!
FWUMP!
CRASH!
YELP!

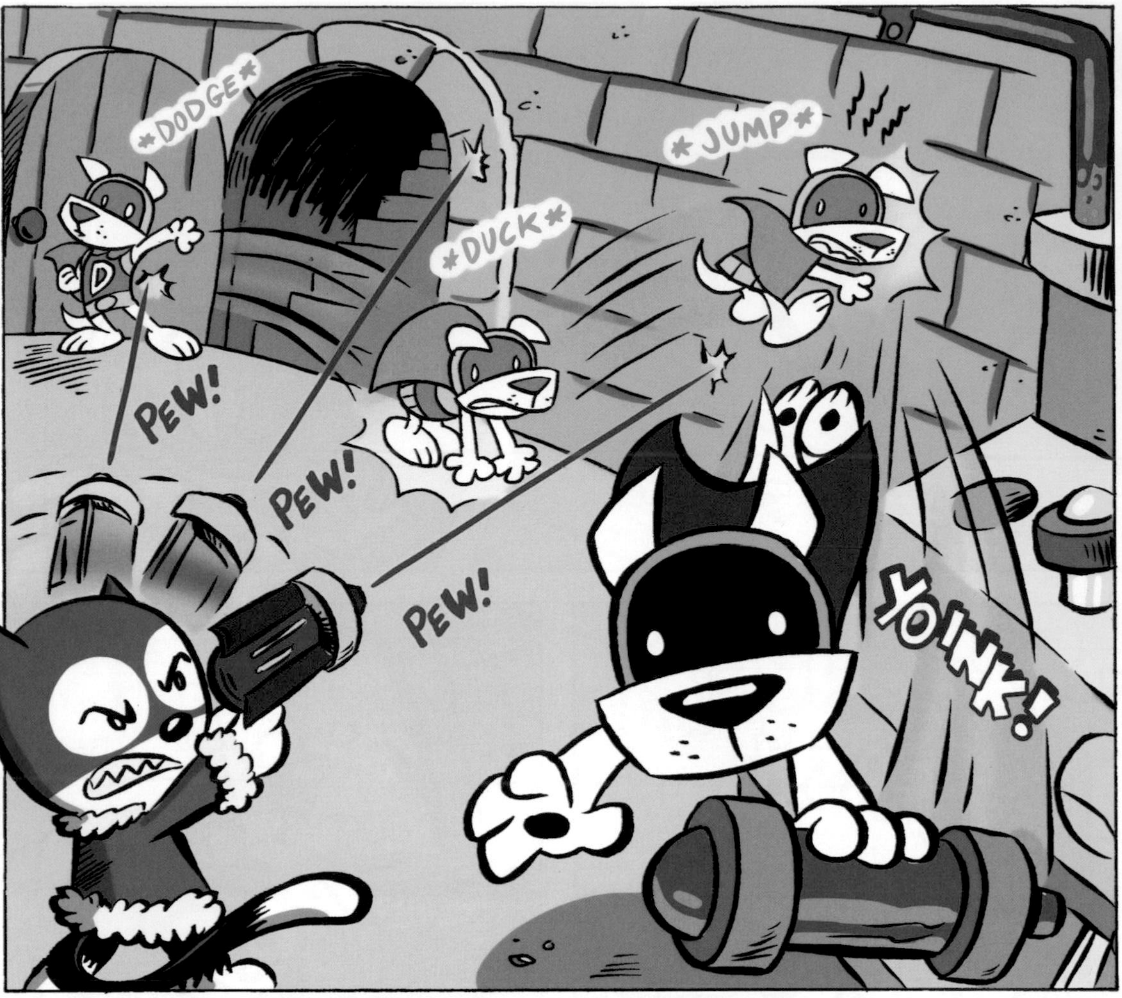
DODGE
DUCK
JUMP
PEW!
PEW!
PEW!
YOINK!

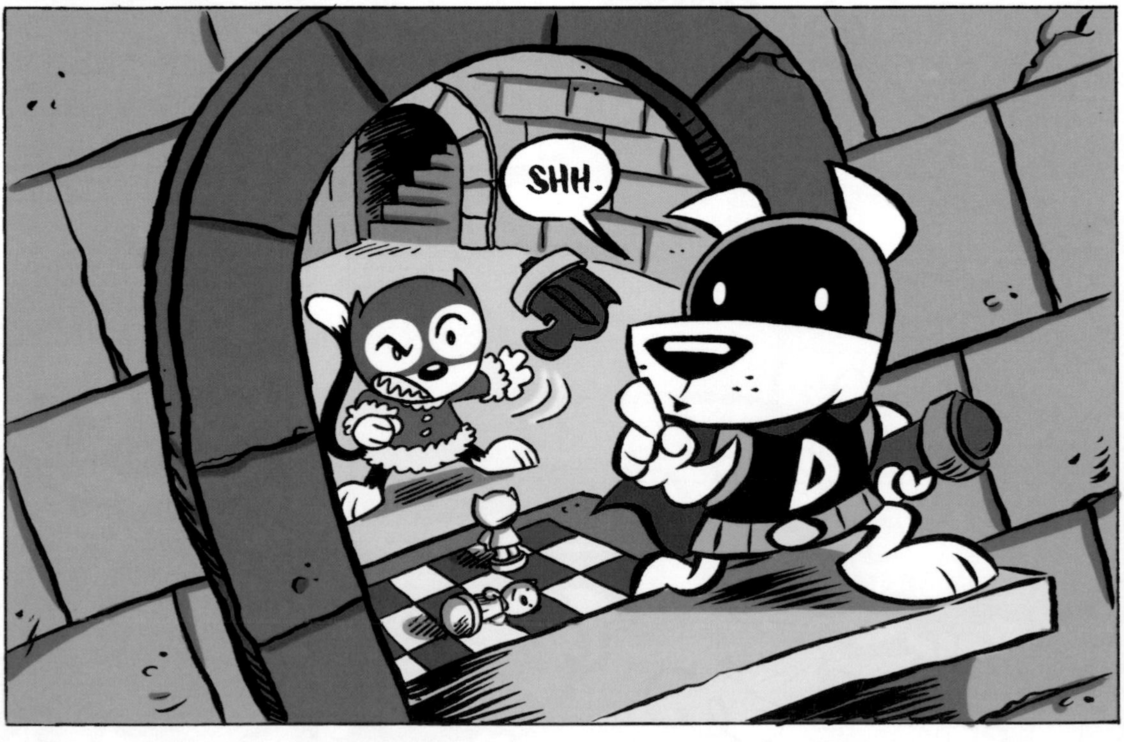
SHH.

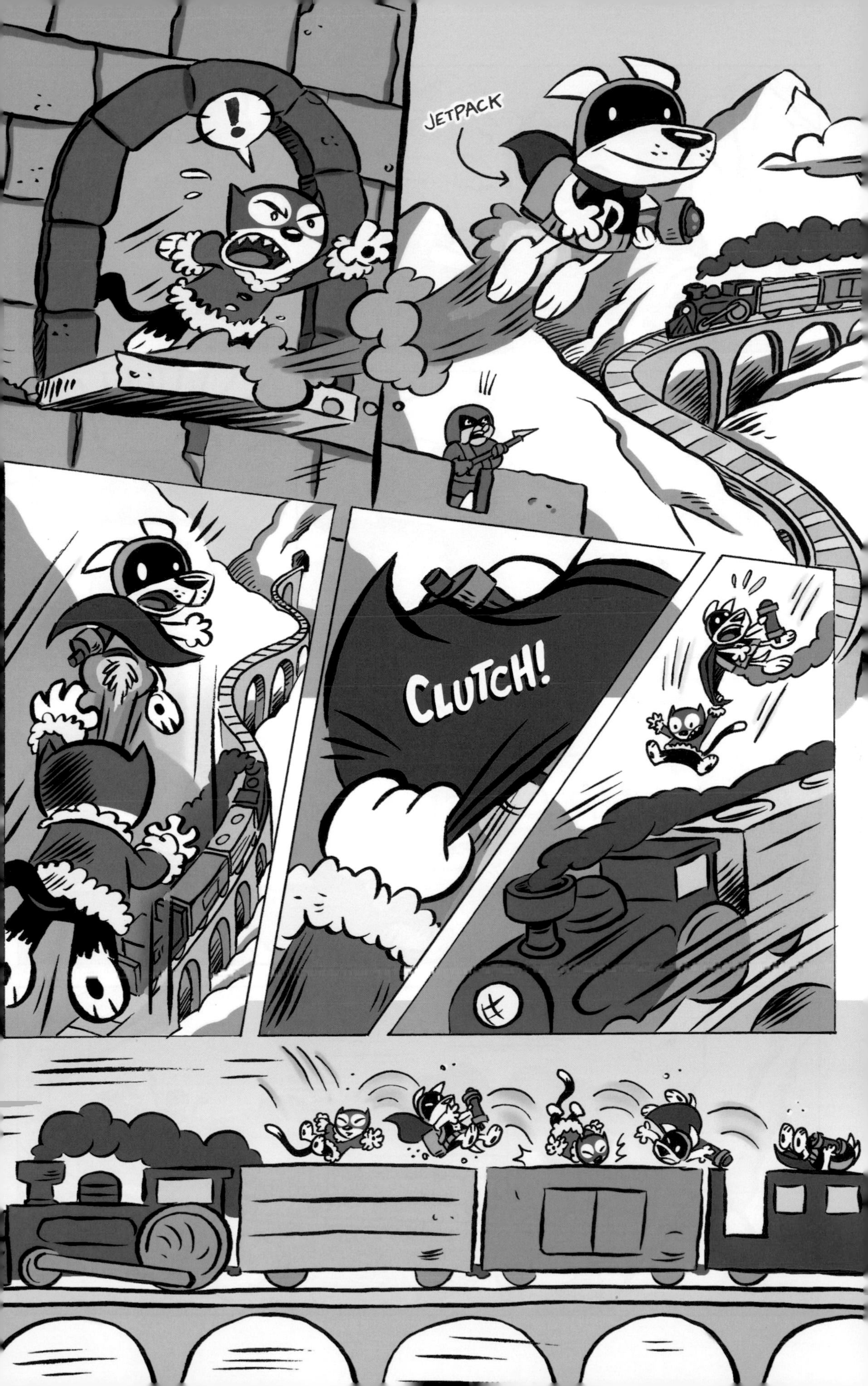
!
JETPACK
CLUTCH!

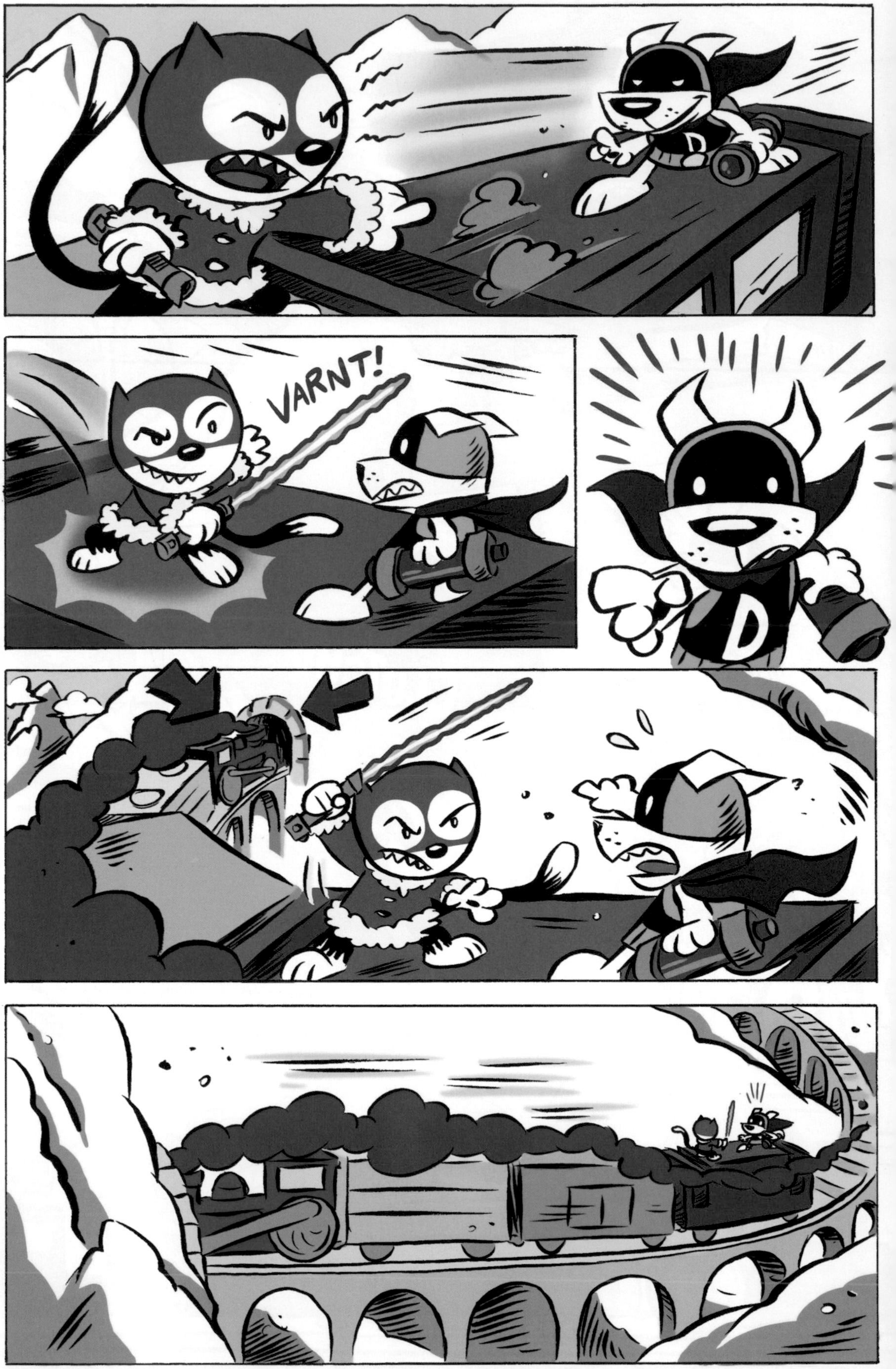
VARNT!

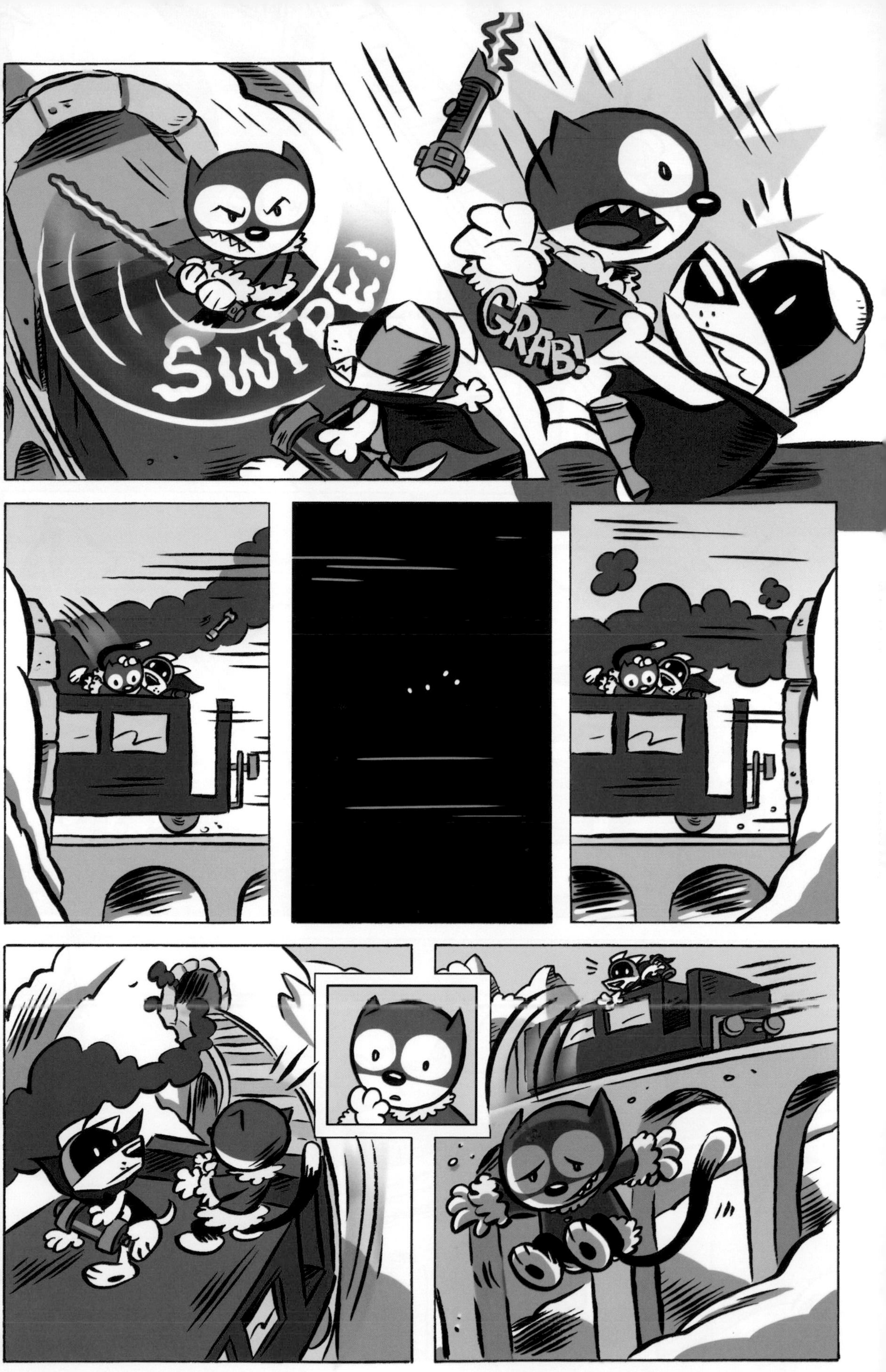
SWIPE!
GRAB!

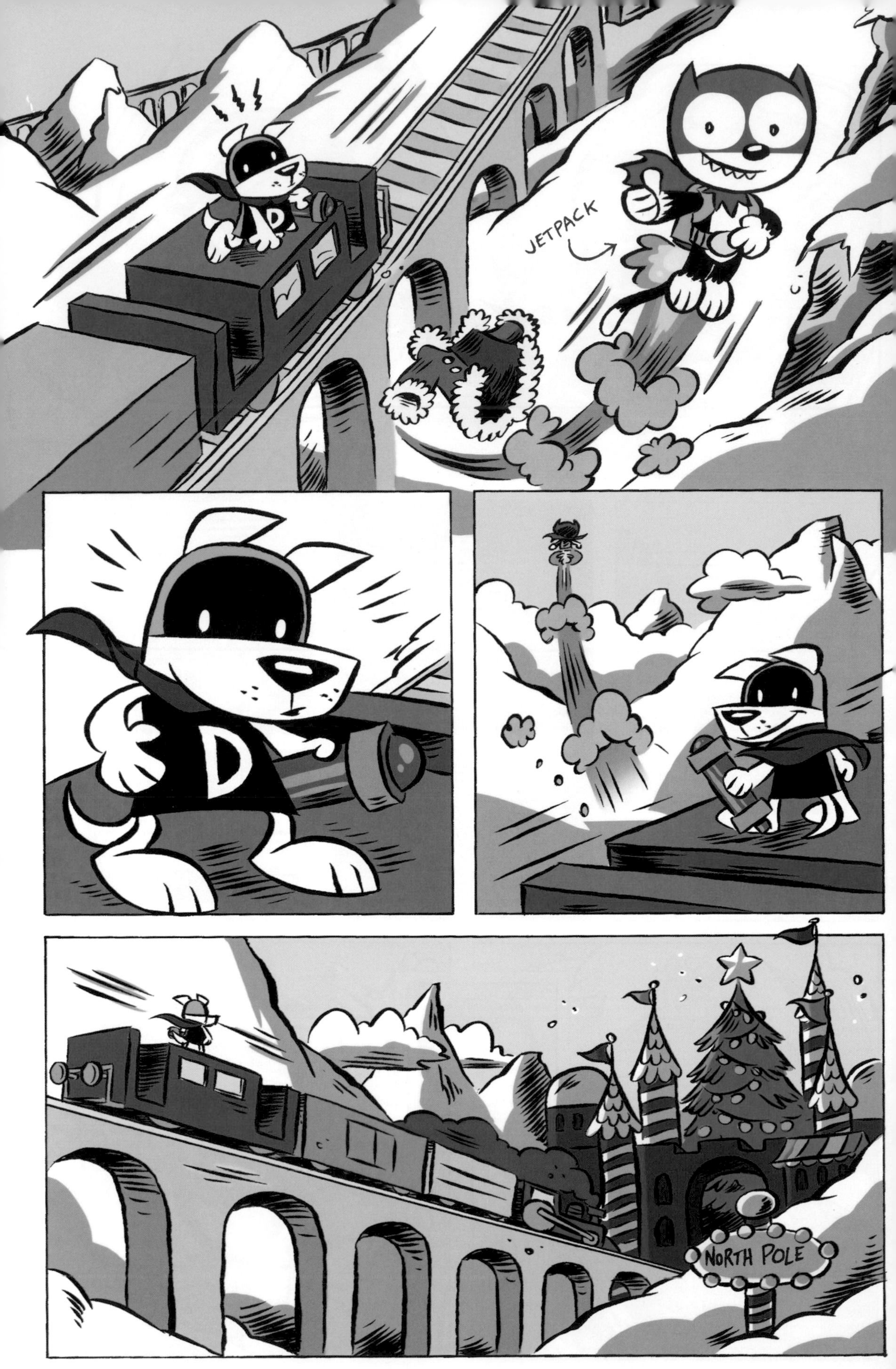
JETPACK
NORTH POLE

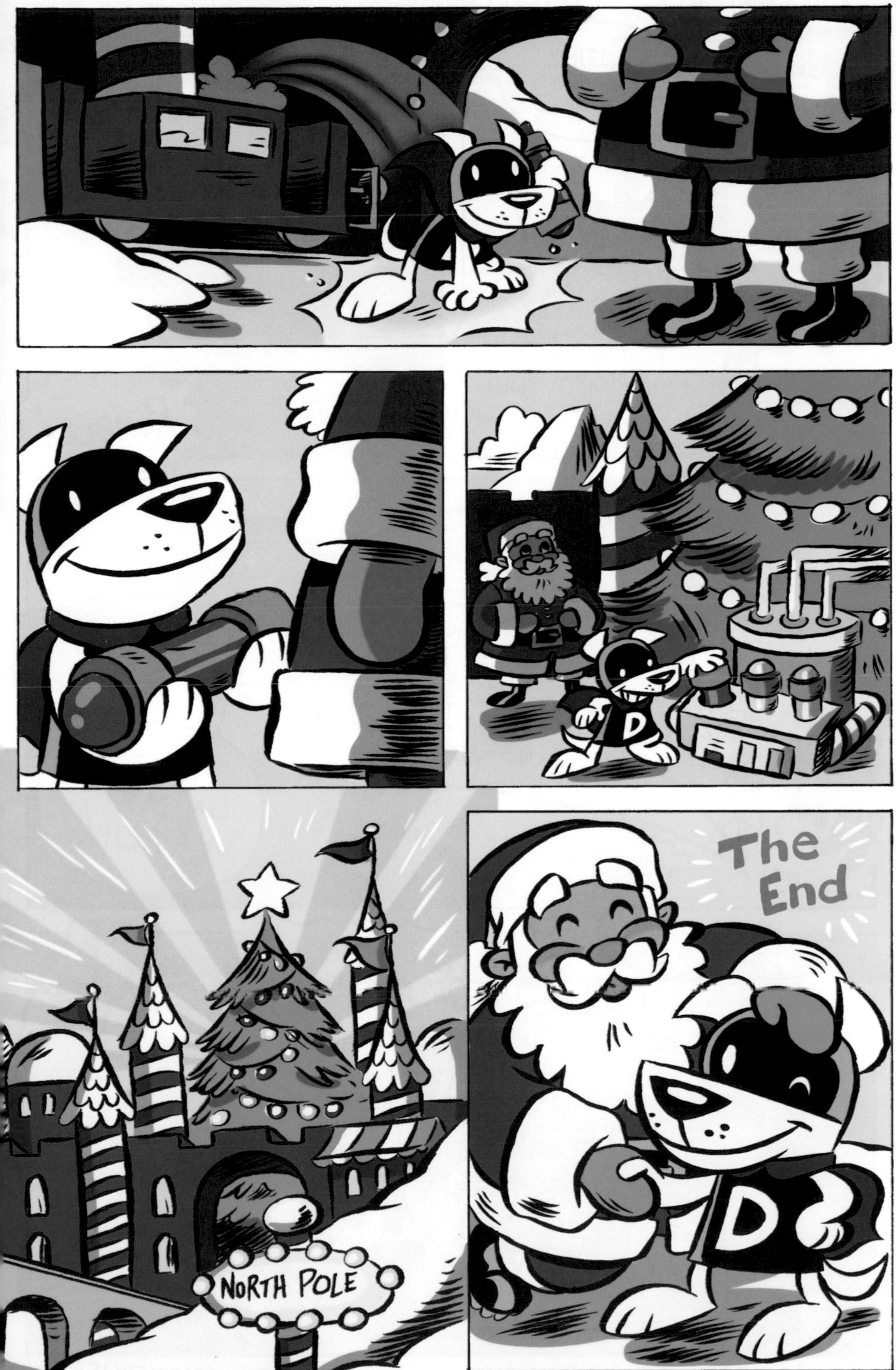

The End
NORTH POLE

AWESOME BEAR: LISTEN CAREFULLY

BY KURT WOOD

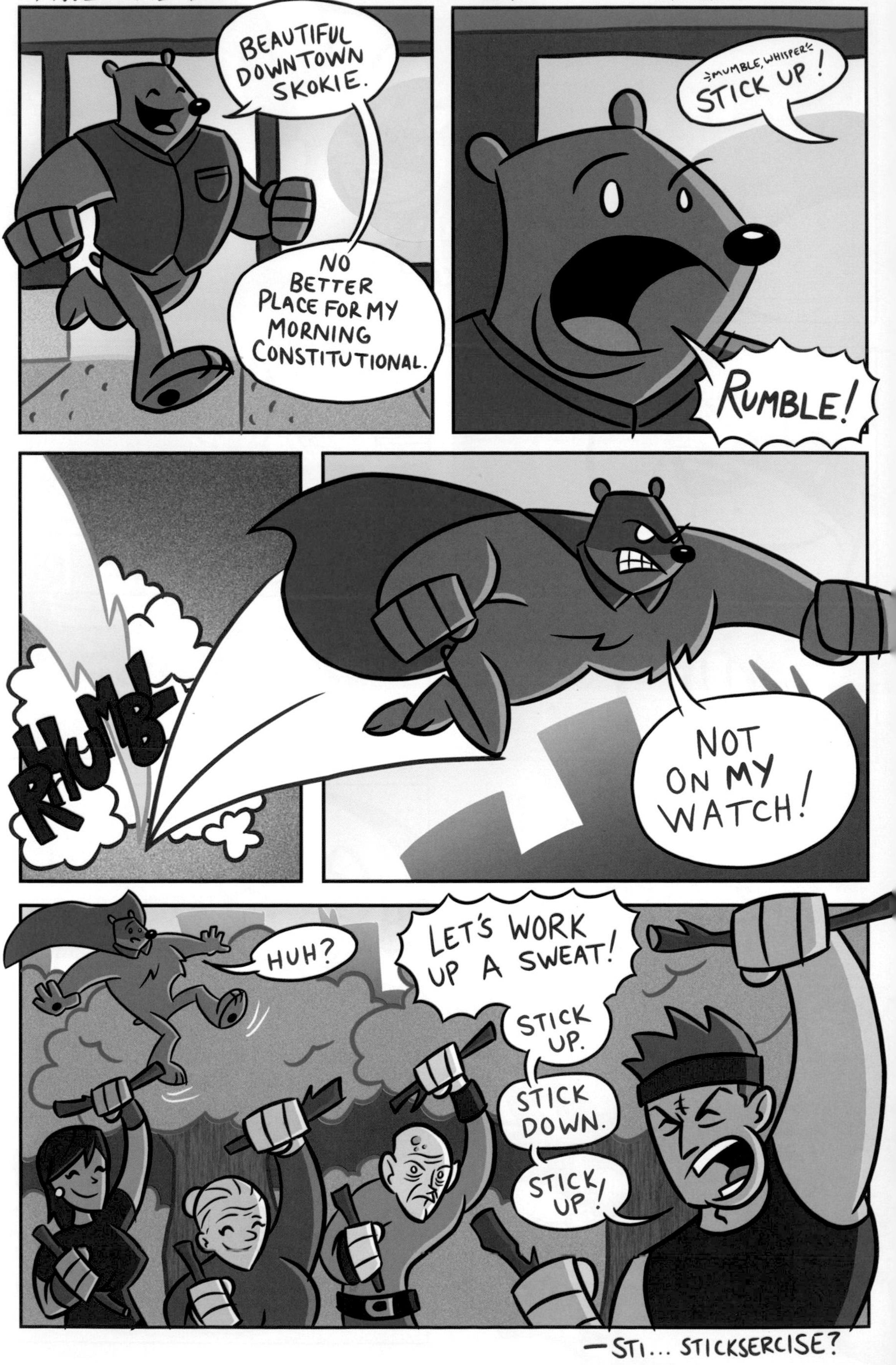

BEAUTIFUL DOWNTOWN SKOKIE.
NO BETTER PLACE FOR MY MORNING CONSTITUTIONAL.
MUMBLE, WHISPER
STICK UP!
RUMBLE!
RHUMB!
NOT ON MY WATCH!
HUH?
LET'S WORK UP A SWEAT!
STICK UP.
STICK DOWN.
STICK UP!

—STI... STICKSERCISE?

aw yeah comics! presents:
ice-cream MARAUDERS

STORY BY ALEJANDRO ROSADO

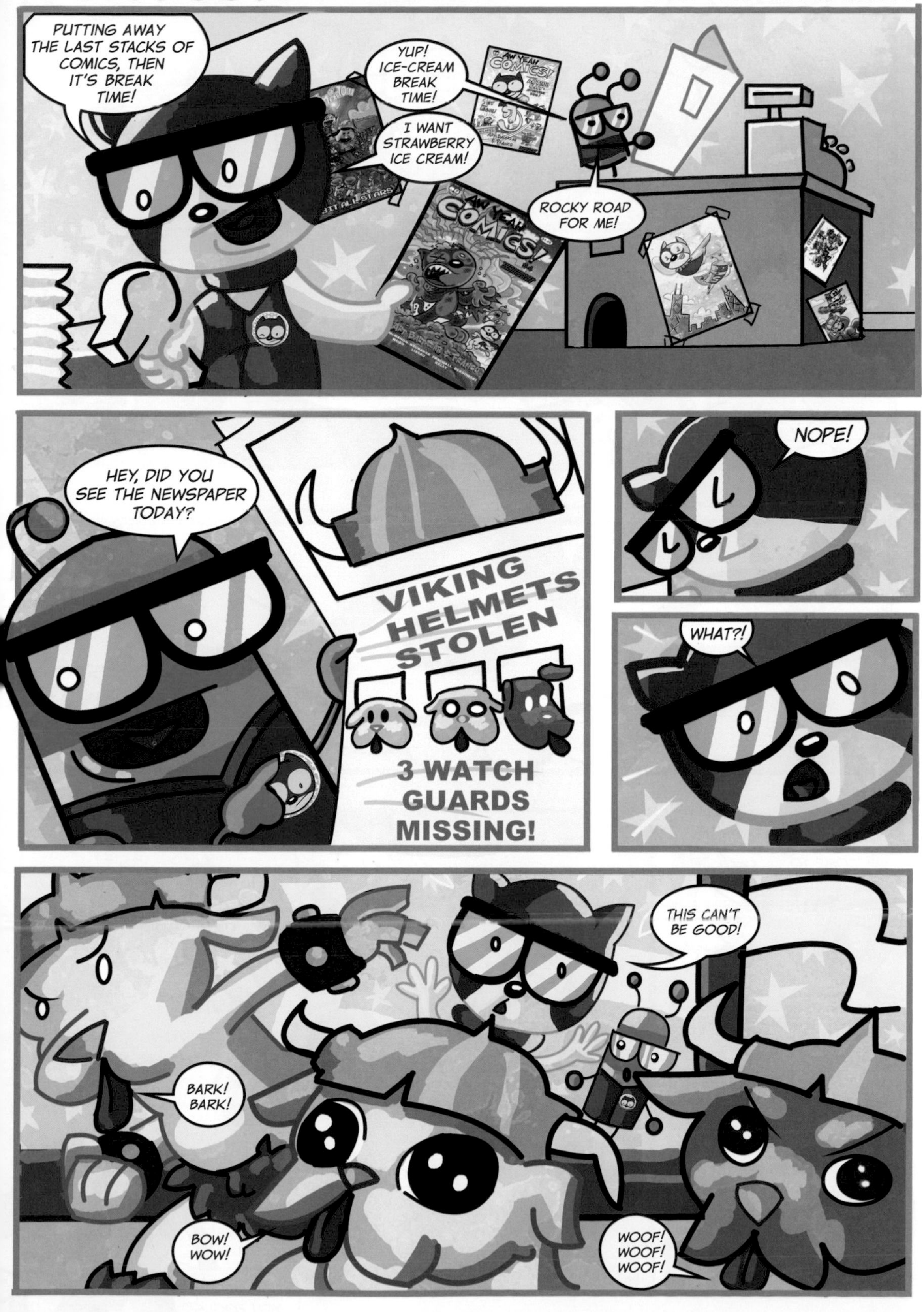
PUTTING AWAY THE LAST STACKS OF COMICS, THEN IT'S BREAK TIME!
YUP! ICE-CREAM BREAK TIME!
I WANT STRAWBERRY ICE CREAM!
ROCKY ROAD FOR ME!
HEY, DID YOU SEE THE NEWSPAPER TODAY?
VIKING HELMETS STOLEN
3 WATCH GUARDS MISSING!
NOPE!
WHAT?!
THIS CAN'T BE GOOD!
BARK! BARK!
BOW! WOW!
WOOF! WOOF! WOOF!

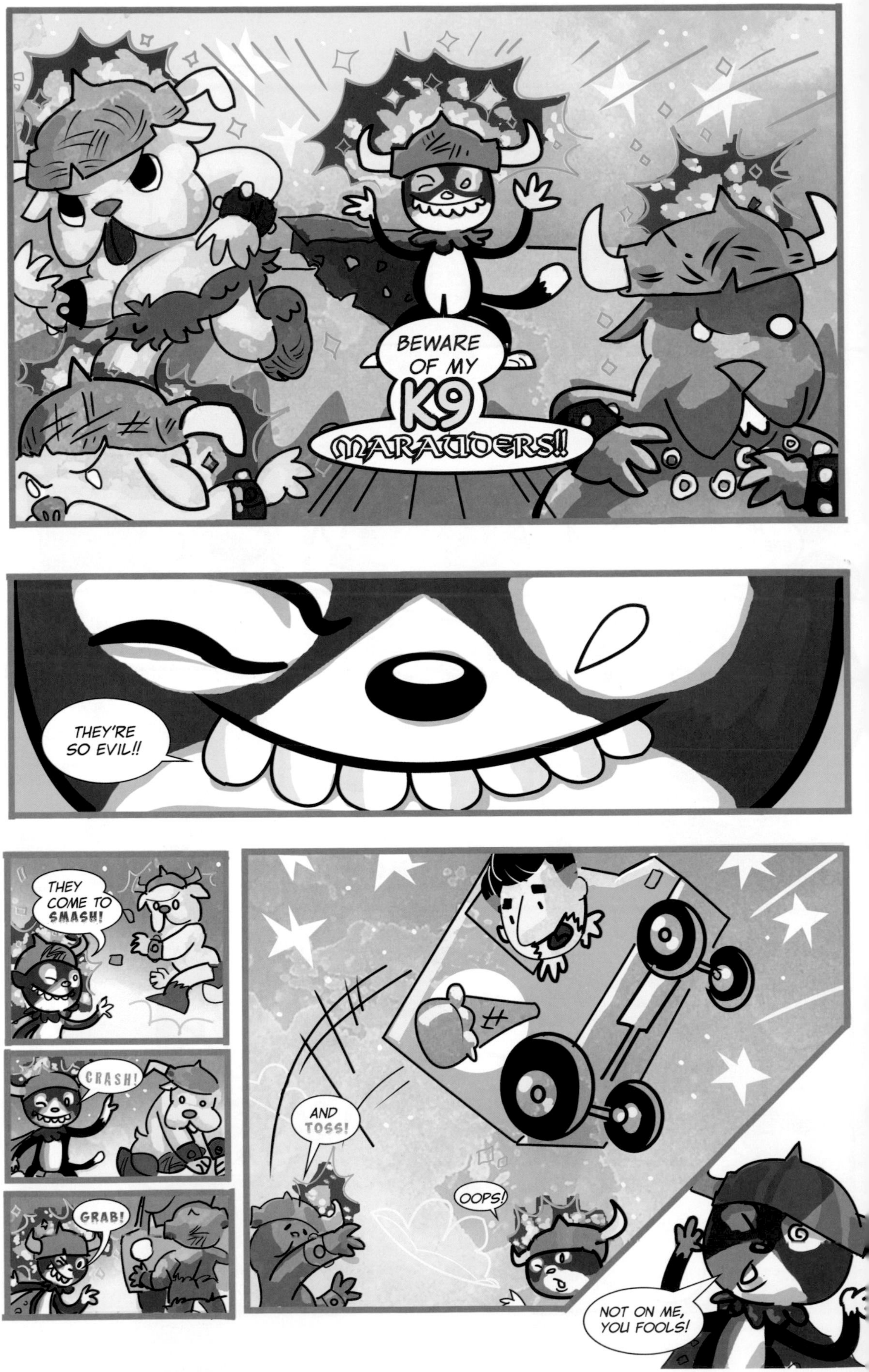
BEWARE OF MY K9 MARAUDERS!!
THEY'RE SO EVIL!!
THEY COME TO SMASH!
CRASH!
GRAB!
AND TOSS!
OOPS!
NOT ON ME, YOU FOOLS!

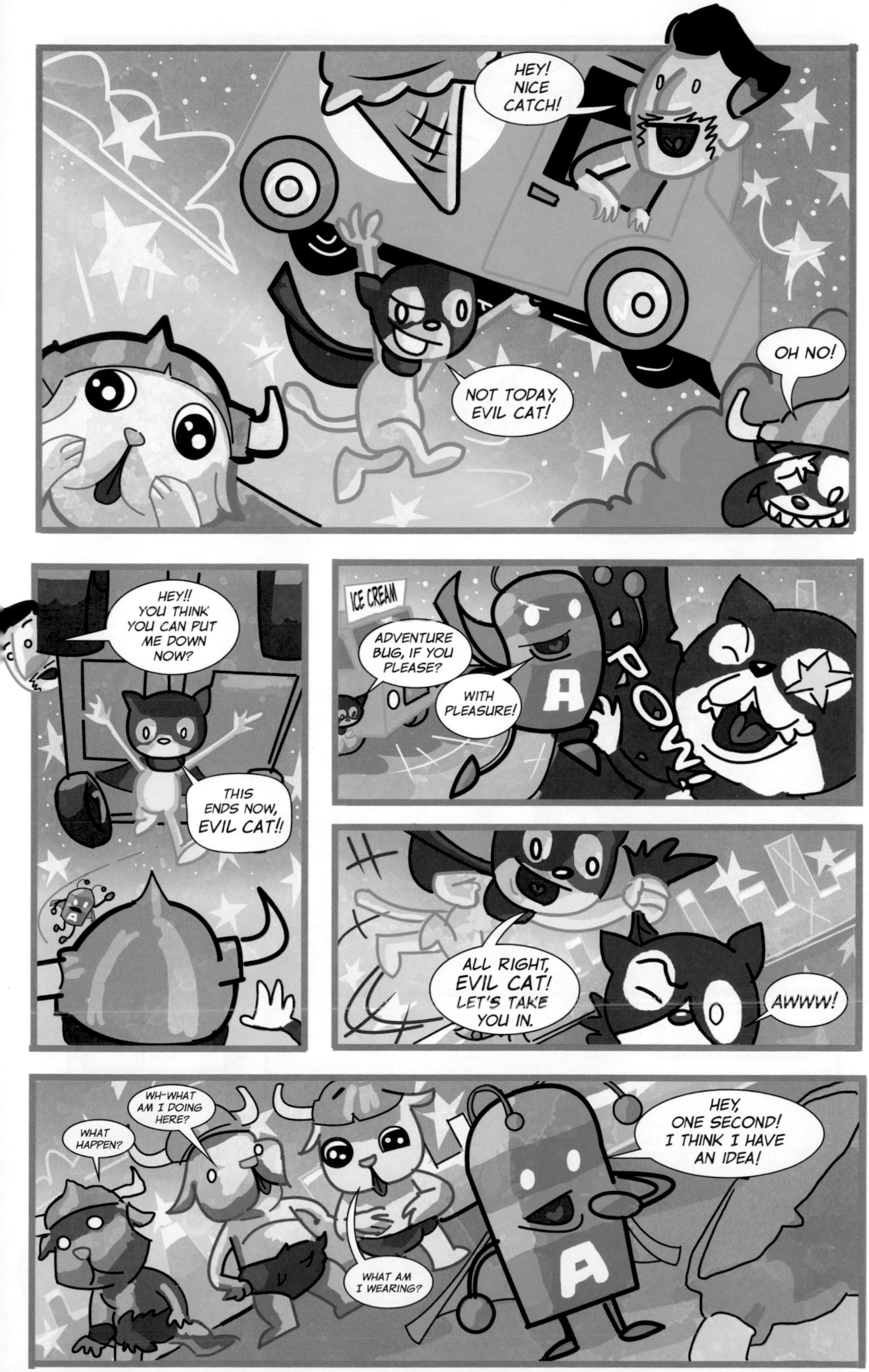
HEY! NICE CATCH!
NOT TODAY, EVIL CAT!
OH NO!
HEY!! YOU THINK YOU CAN PUT ME DOWN NOW?
THIS ENDS NOW, EVIL CAT!!
ICE CREAM
ADVENTURE BUG, IF YOU PLEASE?
WITH PLEASURE!
POW!
ALL RIGHT, EVIL CAT! LET'S TAKE YOU IN.
AWWW!
WHAT HAPPEN?
WH-WHAT AM I DOING HERE?
WHAT AM I WEARING?
HEY, ONE SECOND! I THINK I HAVE AN IDEA!

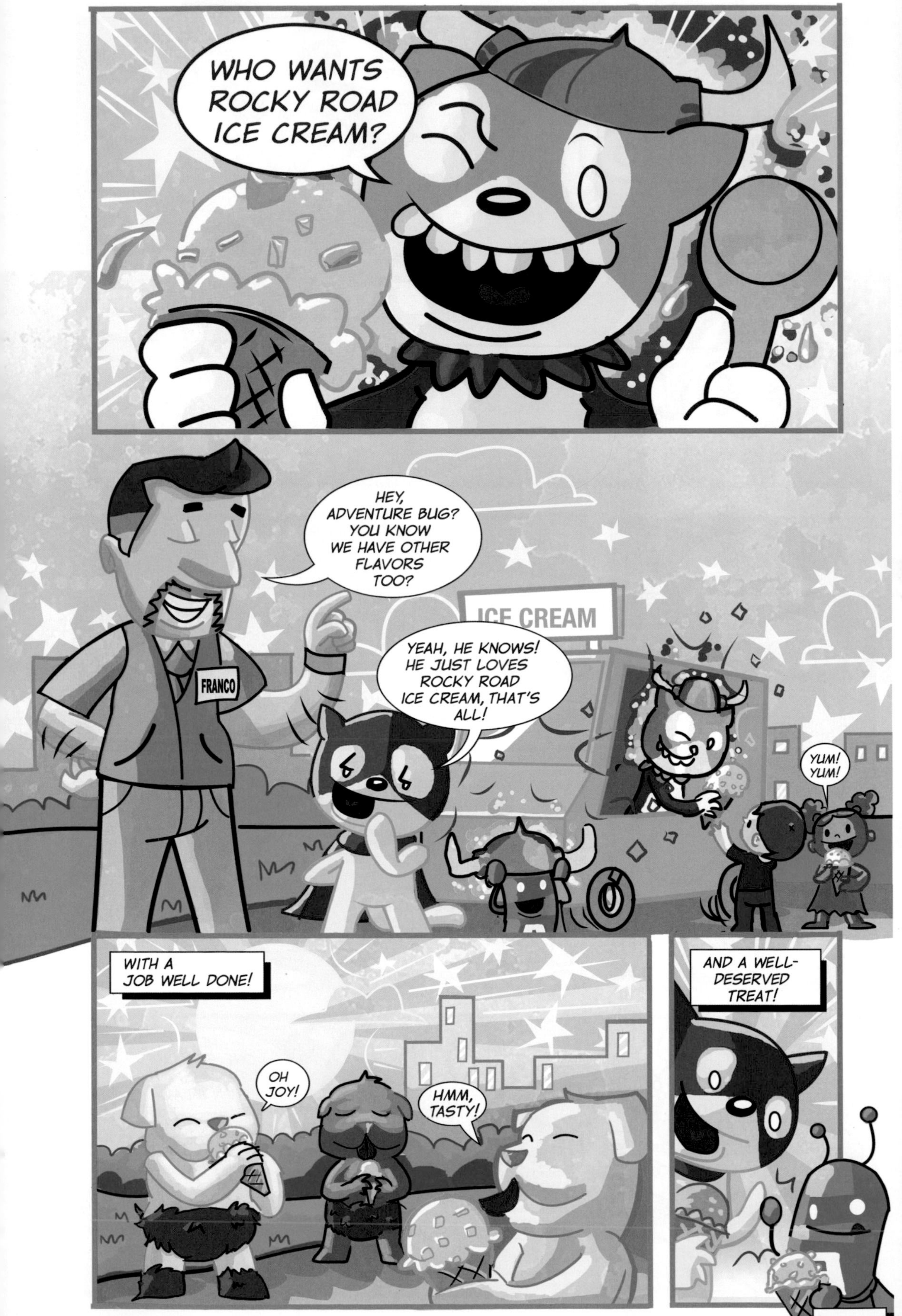
WHO WANTS ROCKY ROAD ICE CREAM?
HEY, ADVENTURE BUG? YOU KNOW WE HAVE OTHER FLAVORS TOO?
FRANCO
ICE CREAM
YEAH, HE KNOWS! HE JUST LOVES ROCKY ROAD ICE CREAM, THAT'S ALL!
YUM! YUM!
WITH A JOB WELL DONE!
OH JOY!
HMM, TASTY!
AND A WELL-DESERVED TREAT!
THE END!

ZOMBIE CAT: NO FREE LUNCH

BY KURT WOOD

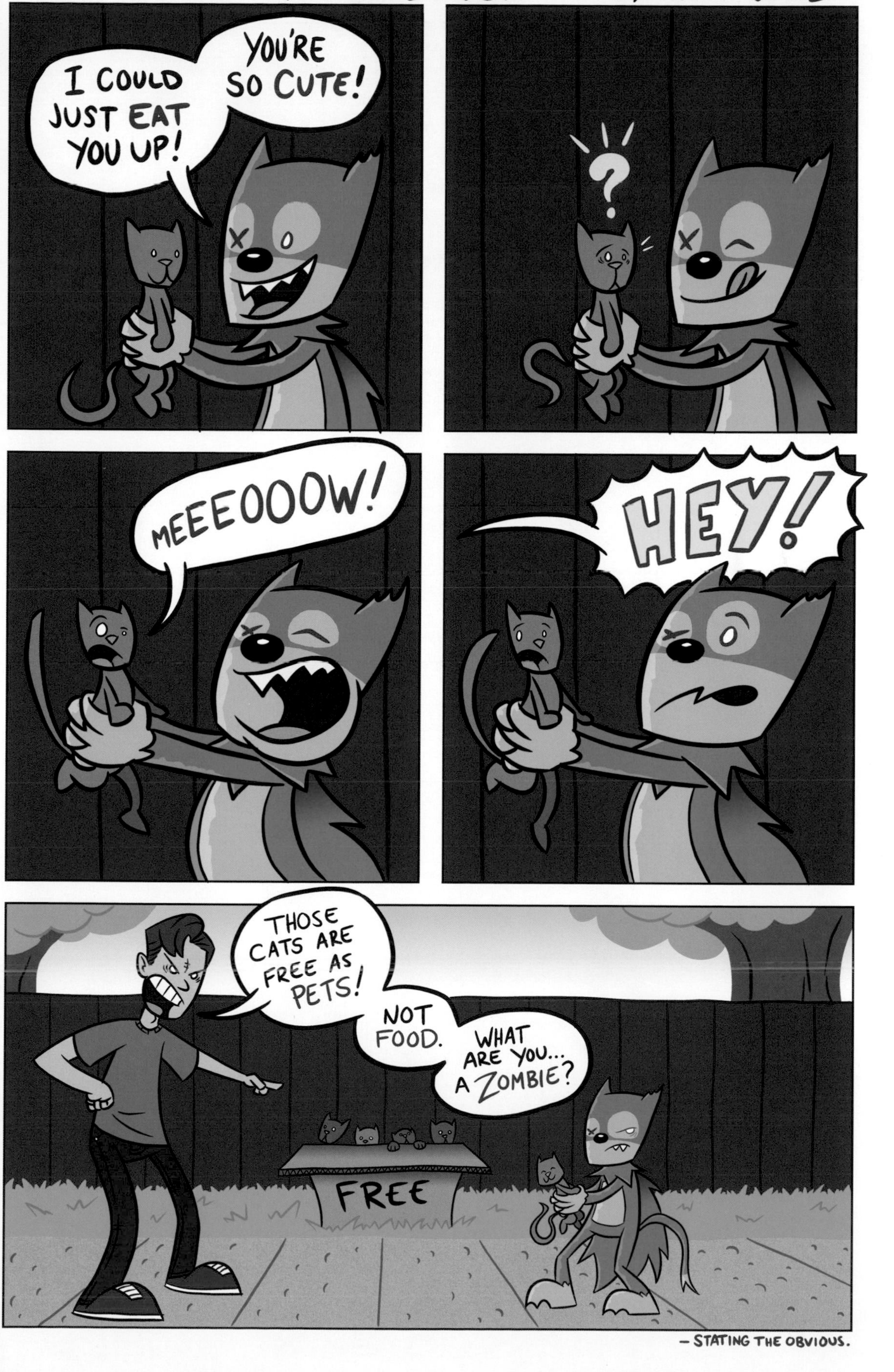
YOU'RE SO CUTE!
I COULD JUST EAT YOU UP!
?
MEEEOOOW!
HEY!
THOSE CATS ARE FREE AS PETS!
NOT FOOD.
WHAT ARE YOU... A ZOMBIE?
FREE

– STATING THE OBVIOUS.

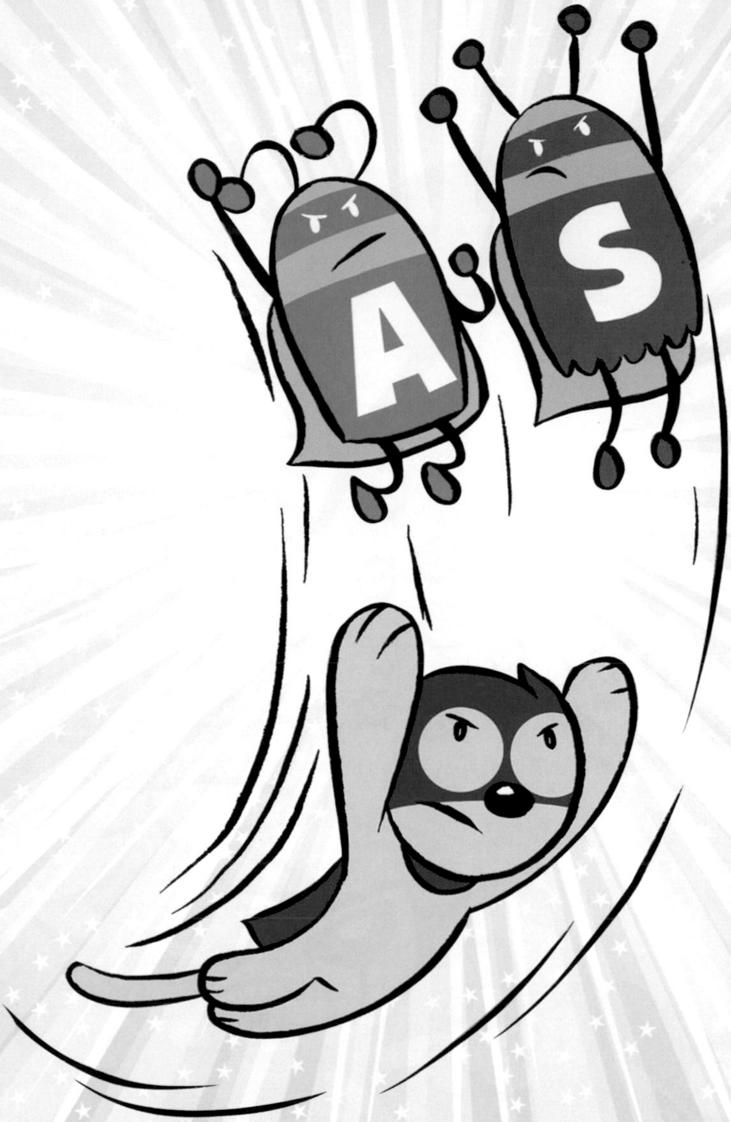
A
S

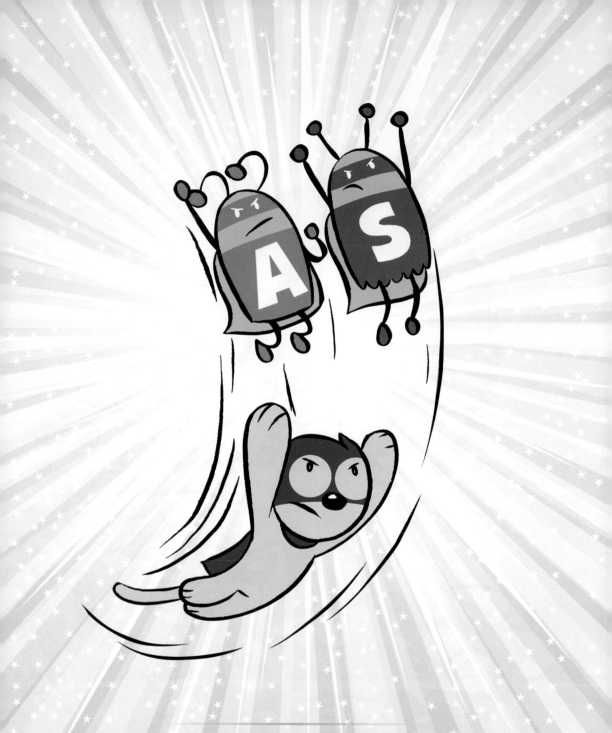

CHAPTER THREE

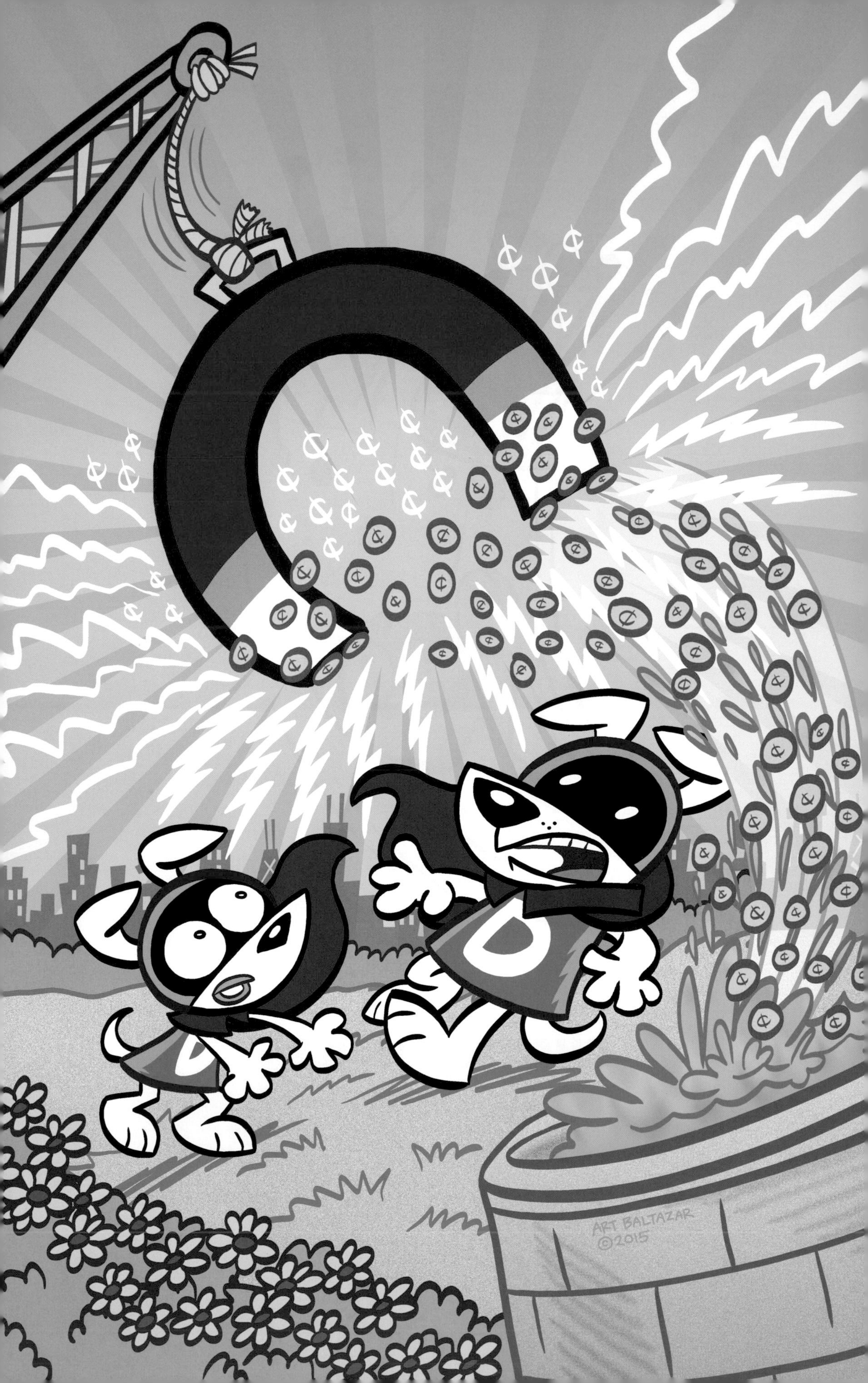
ART BALTAZAR
©2015

AW YEAH COMICS! PRESENTS...

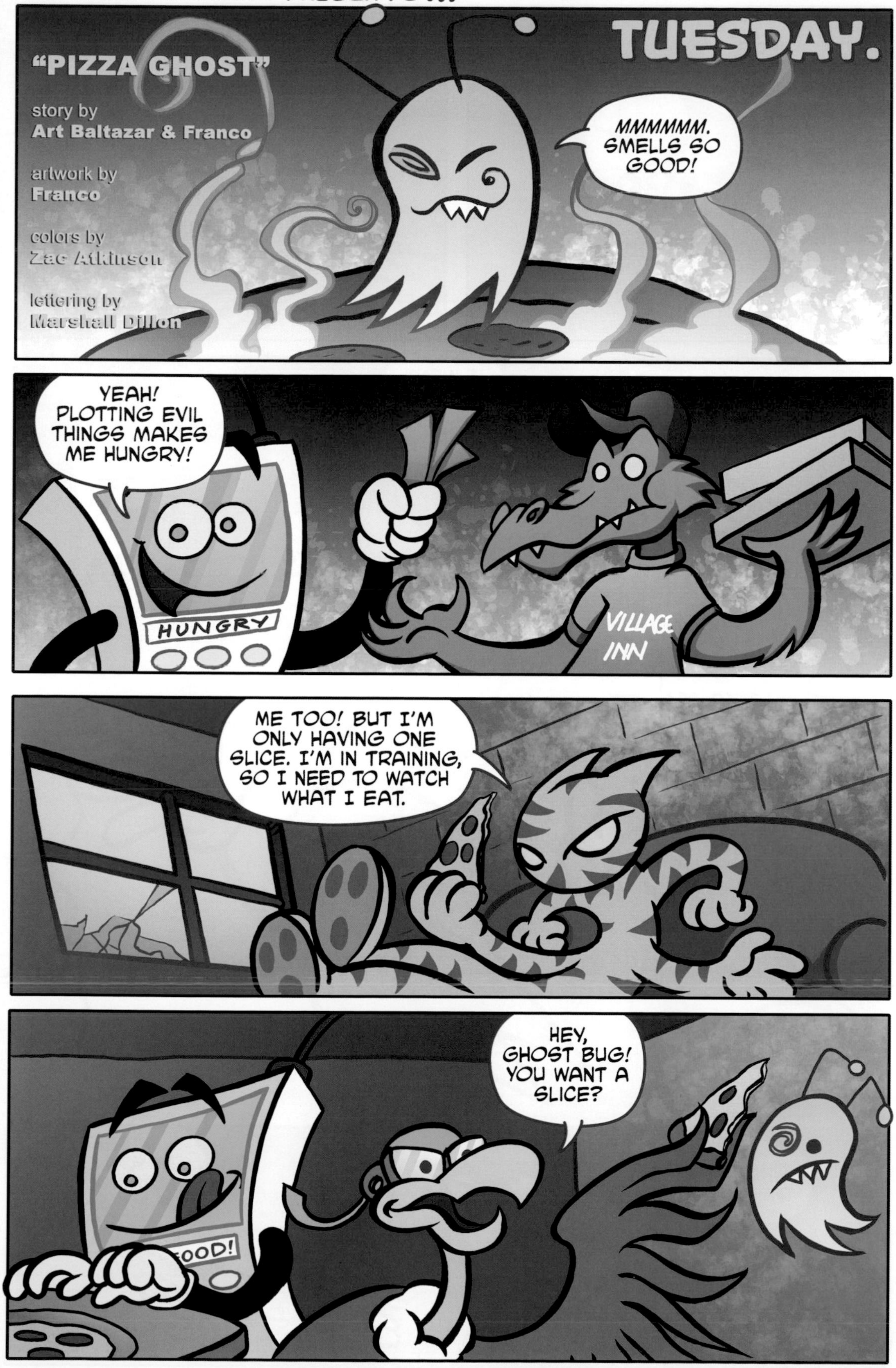

TUESDAY.
"PIZZA GHOST"
story by
Art Baltazar & Franco
artwork by
Franco
colors by
Zac Atkinson
lettering by
Marshall Dillon
MMMMMM. SMELLS SO GOOD!
YEAH! PLOTTING EVIL THINGS MAKES ME HUNGRY!
HUNGRY
VILLAGE INN
ME TOO! BUT I'M ONLY HAVING ONE SLICE. I'M IN TRAINING, SO I NEED TO WATCH WHAT I EAT.
HEY, GHOST BUG! YOU WANT A SLICE?
FOOD!

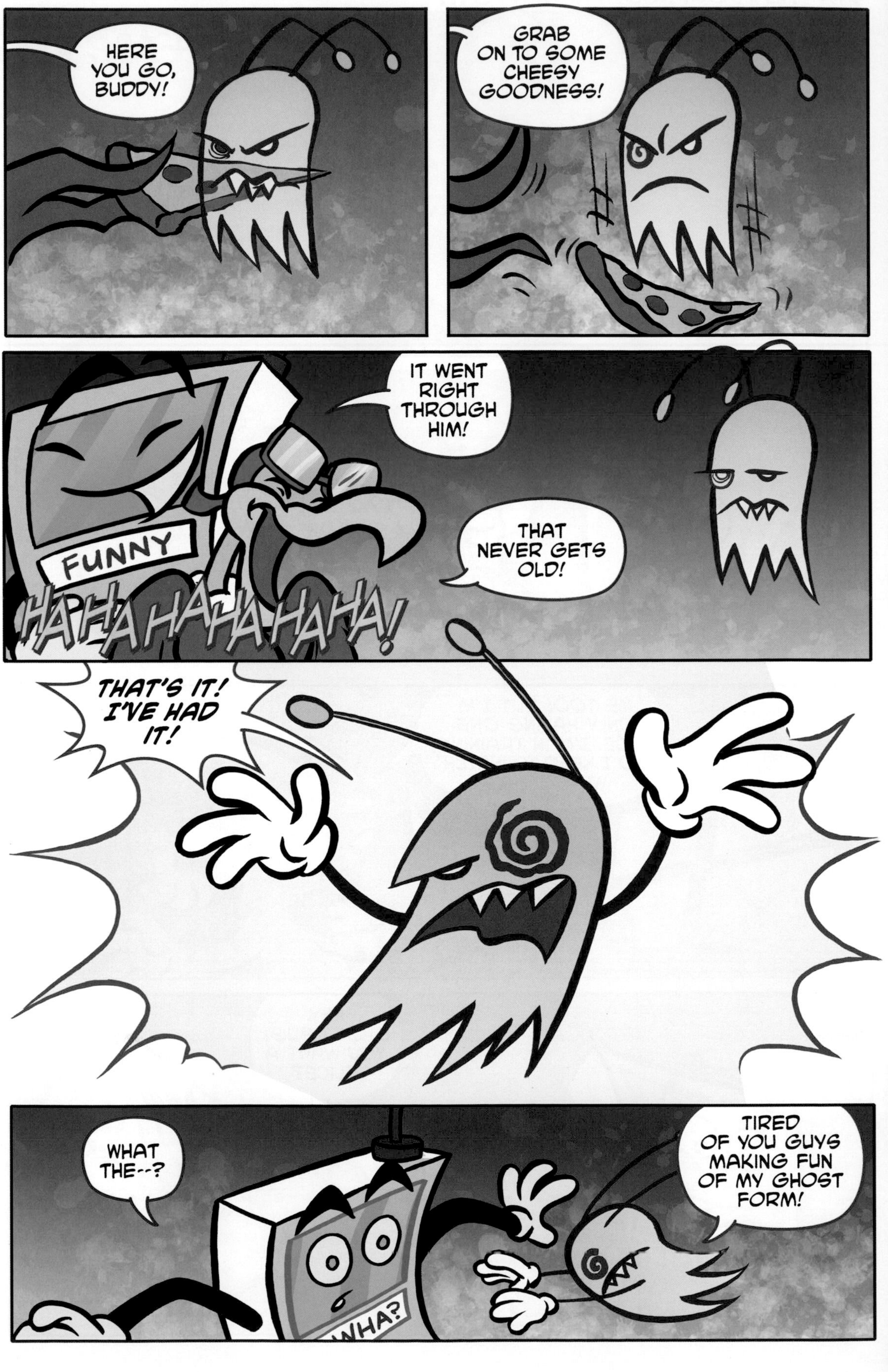
HERE YOU GO, BUDDY!
GRAB ON TO SOME CHEESY GOODNESS!
IT WENT RIGHT THROUGH HIM!
FUNNY
HAHAHAHAHAHAHA!
THAT NEVER GETS OLD!
THAT'S IT! I'VE HAD IT!
WHAT THE--?
WHA?
TIRED OF YOU GUYS MAKING FUN OF MY GHOST FORM!

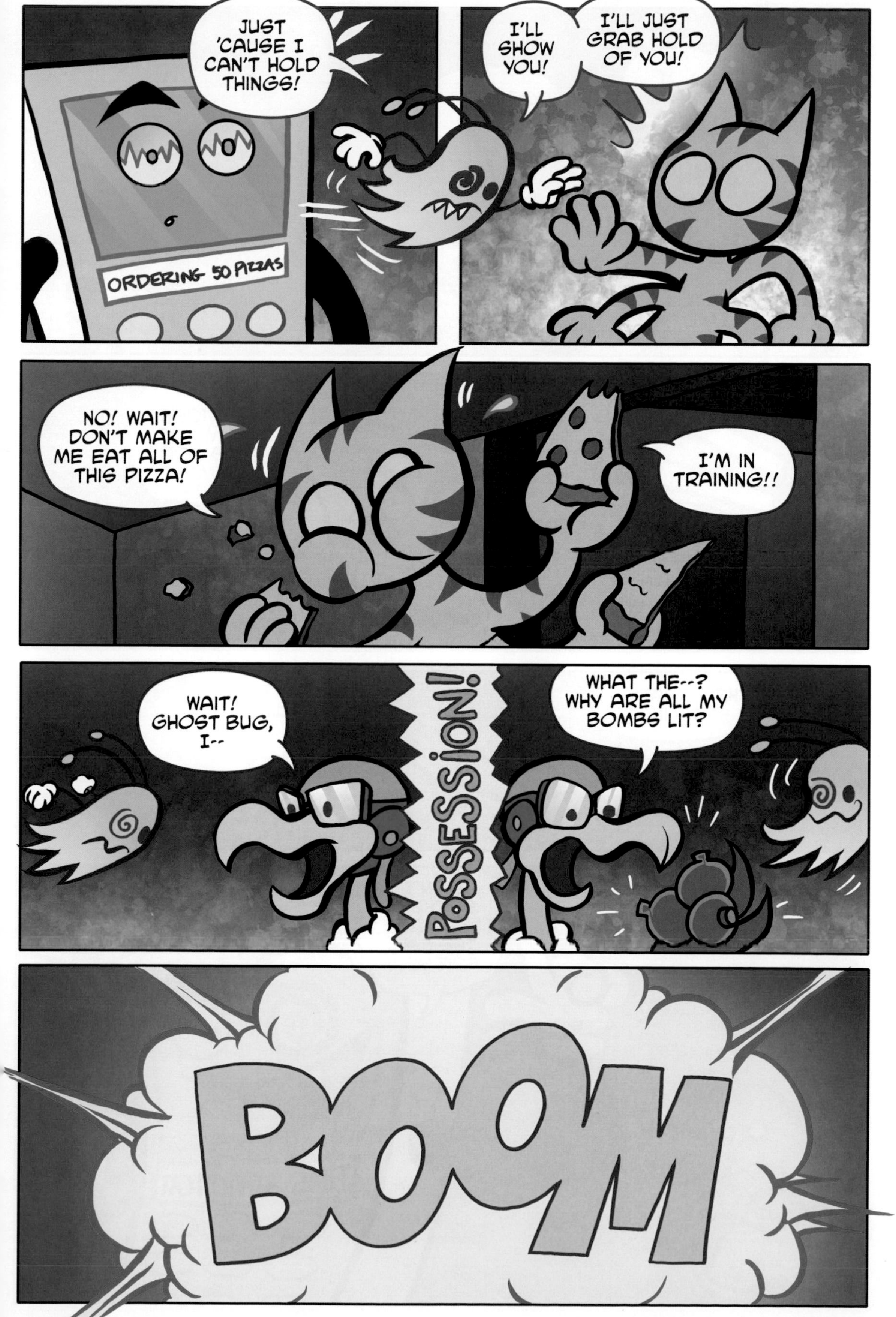
JUST 'CAUSE I CAN'T HOLD THINGS!
ORDERING 50 PIZZAS
I'LL SHOW YOU!
I'LL JUST GRAB HOLD OF YOU!
NO! WAIT! DON'T MAKE ME EAT ALL OF THIS PIZZA!
I'M IN TRAINING!!
WAIT! GHOST BUG, I--
POSSESSION!
WHAT THE--? WHY ARE ALL MY BOMBS LIT?
BOOM

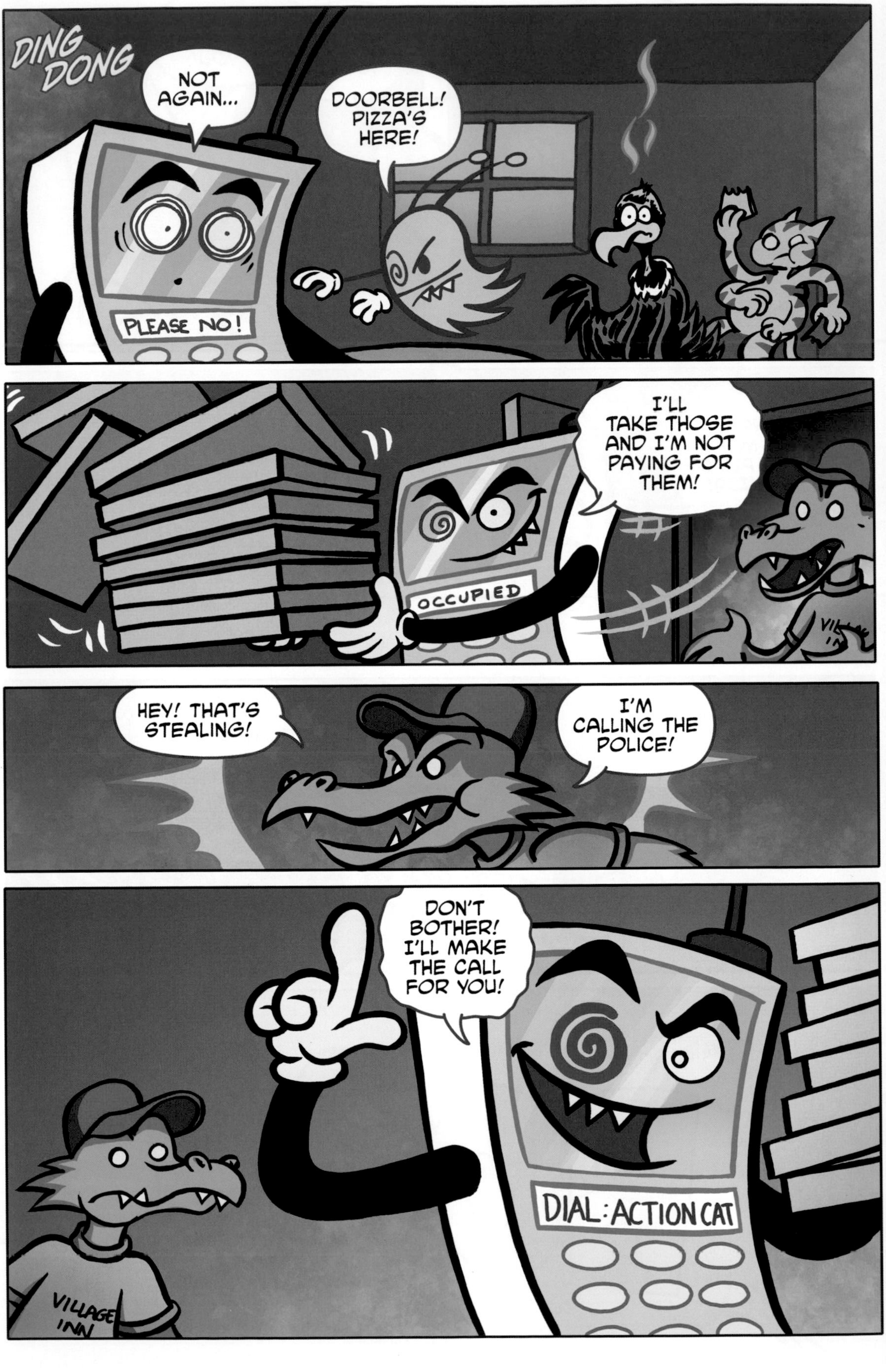
DING DONG
NOT AGAIN...
DOORBELL! PIZZA'S HERE!
PLEASE NO!
I'LL TAKE THOSE AND I'M NOT PAYING FOR THEM!
OCCUPIED
HEY! THAT'S STEALING!
I'M CALLING THE POLICE!
DON'T BOTHER! I'LL MAKE THE CALL FOR YOU!
DIAL: ACTION CAT
VILLAGE INN

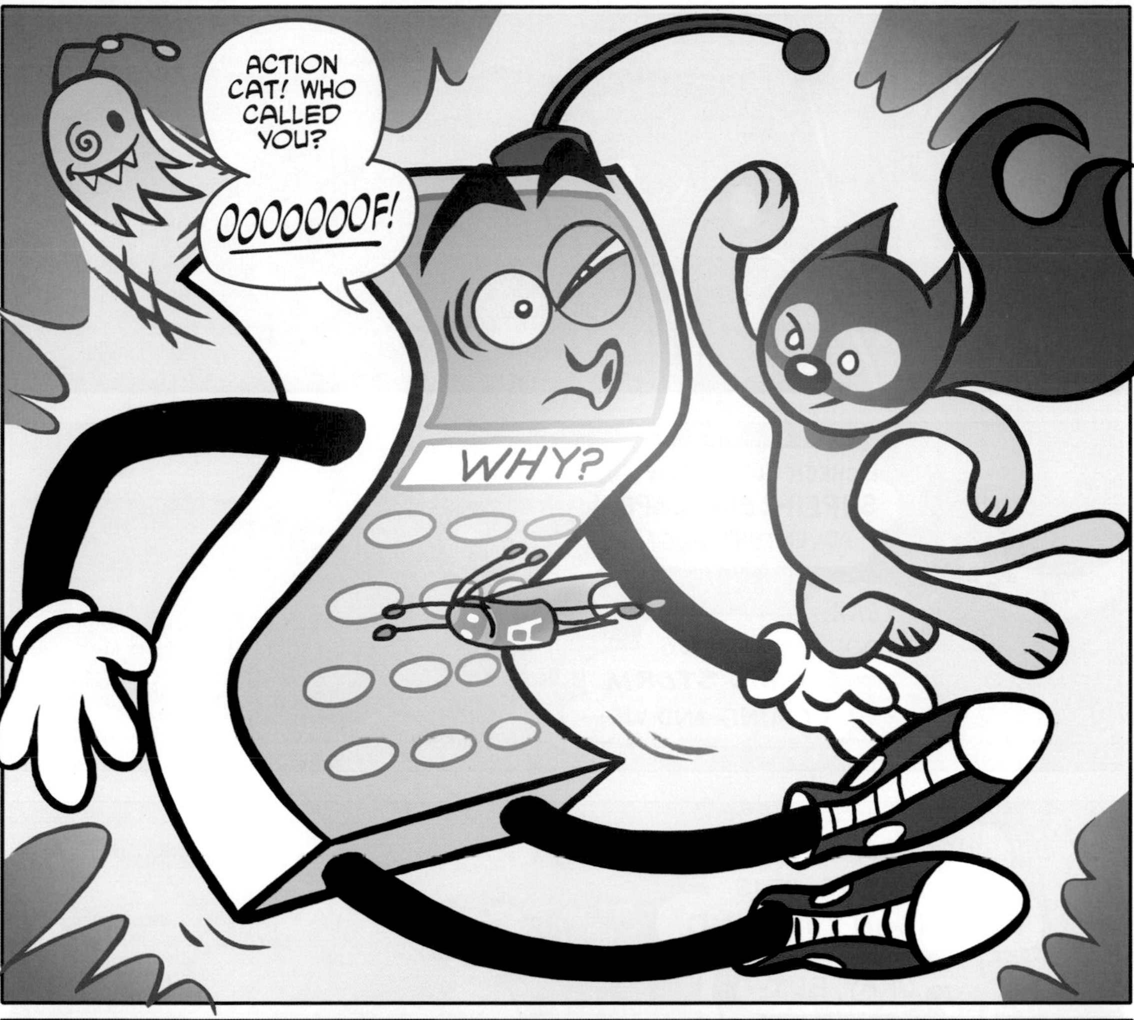
ACTION CAT! WHO CALLED YOU?
OOOOOOOF!
WHY?

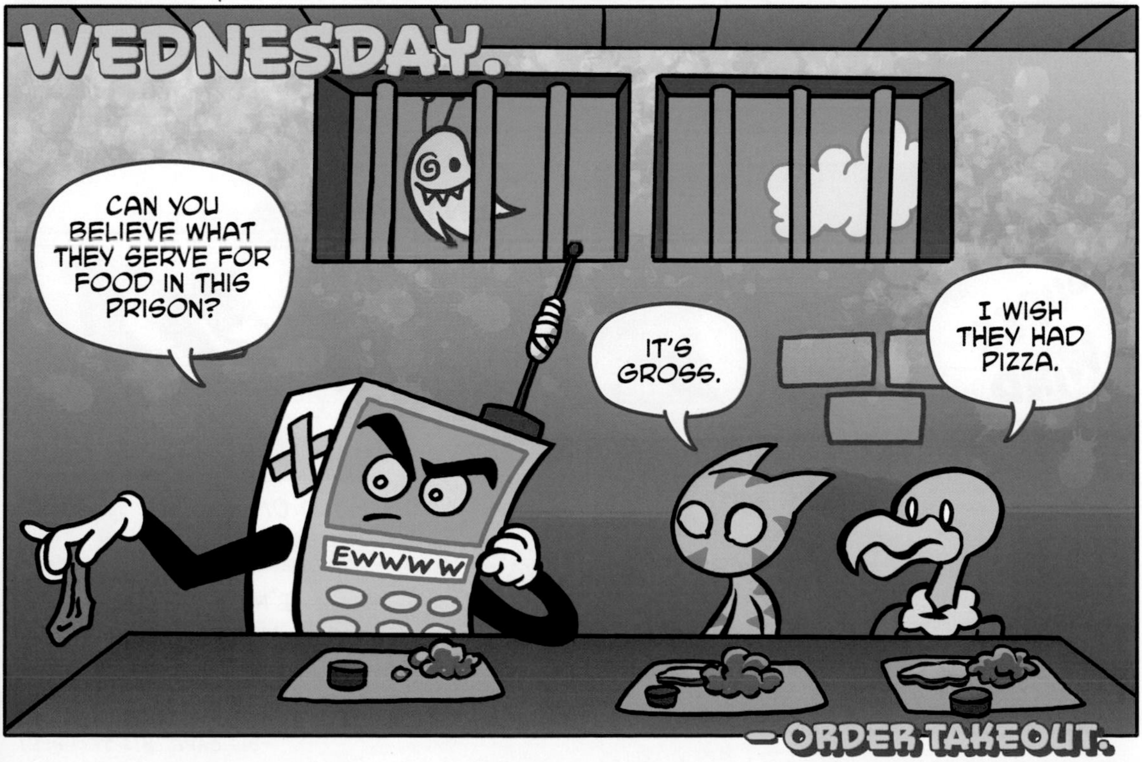
WEDNESDAY.
CAN YOU BELIEVE WHAT THEY SERVE FOR FOOD IN THIS PRISON?
EWWWW
IT'S GROSS.
I WISH THEY HAD PIZZA.
—ORDER TAKEOUT.

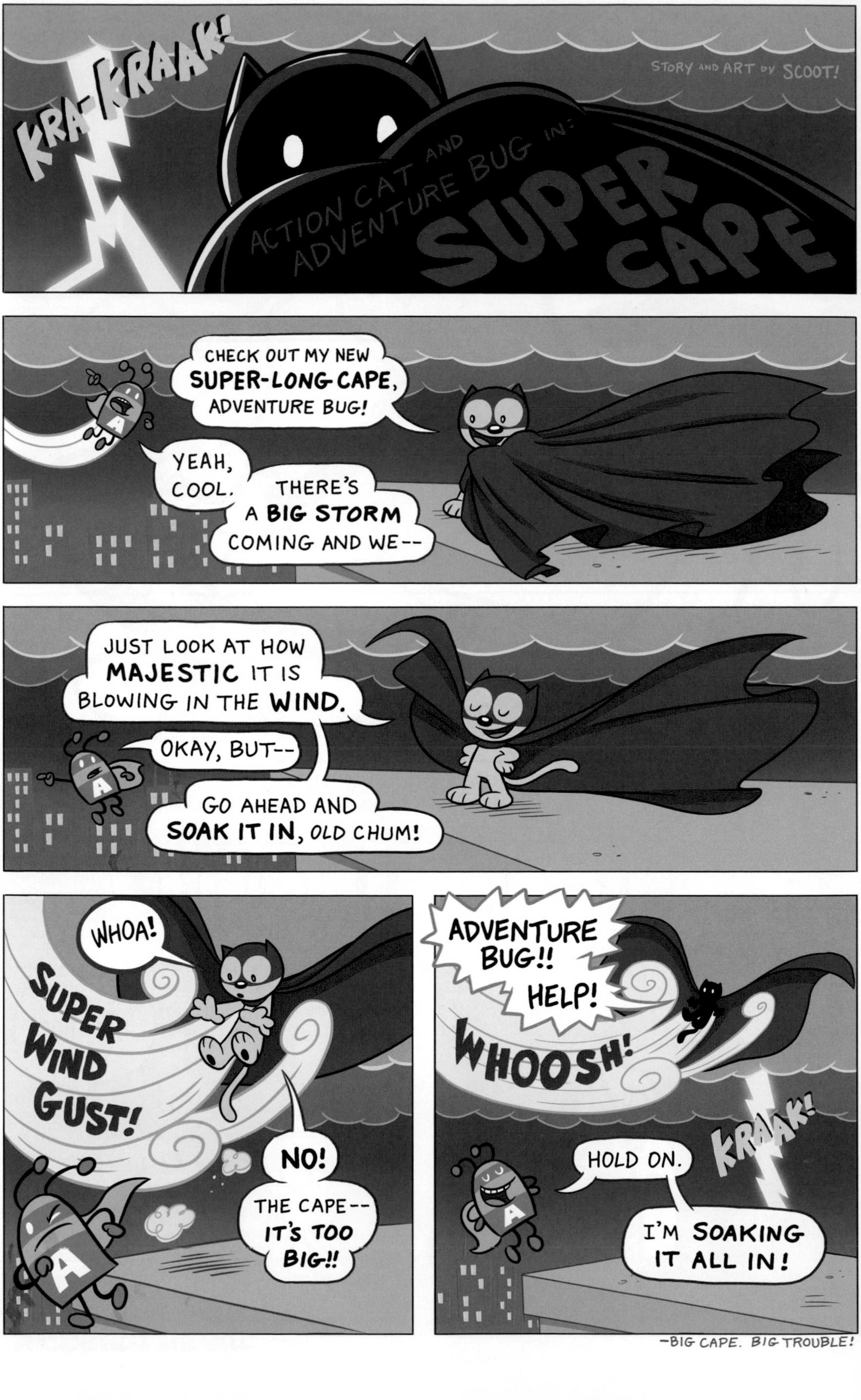
KRA-KRAAK!
STORY AND ART BY SCOOT!
ACTION CAT AND ADVENTURE BUG IN:
SUPER CAPE
CHECK OUT MY NEW SUPER-LONG CAPE, ADVENTURE BUG!
YEAH, COOL.
THERE'S A BIG STORM COMING AND WE--
JUST LOOK AT HOW MAJESTIC IT IS BLOWING IN THE WIND.
OKAY, BUT--
GO AHEAD AND SOAK IT IN, OLD CHUM!
WHOA!
SUPER WIND GUST!
NO!
THE CAPE-- IT'S TOO BIG!!
ADVENTURE BUG!!
HELP!
WHOOSH!
KRAAK!
HOLD ON.
I'M SOAKING IT ALL IN!
-BIG CAPE. BIG TROUBLE!

OH NO CAT! BY ALEJANDRO ROSADO

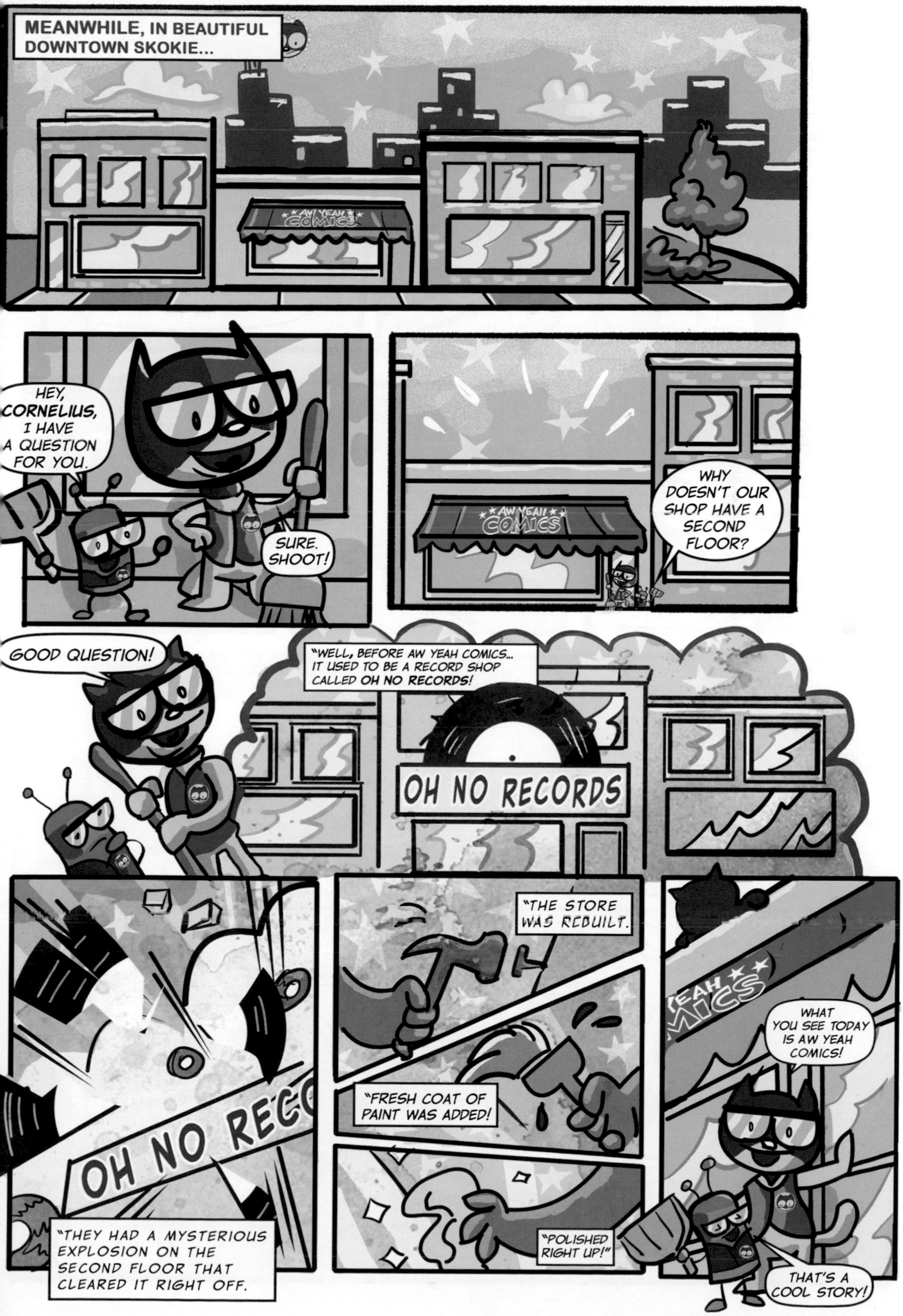
MEANWHILE, IN BEAUTIFUL DOWNTOWN SKOKIE...
AW YEAH COMICS
HEY, CORNELIUS, I HAVE A QUESTION FOR YOU.
SURE. SHOOT!
AW YEAH COMICS
WHY DOESN'T OUR SHOP HAVE A SECOND FLOOR?
GOOD QUESTION!
"WELL, BEFORE AW YEAH COMICS... IT USED TO BE A RECORD SHOP CALLED OH NO RECORDS!
OH NO RECORDS
OH NO RECO
"THEY HAD A MYSTERIOUS EXPLOSION ON THE SECOND FLOOR THAT CLEARED IT RIGHT OFF.
"THE STORE WAS REBUILT.
"FRESH COAT OF PAINT WAS ADDED!
"POLISHED RIGHT UP!"
YEAH MICS
WHAT YOU SEE TODAY IS AW YEAH COMICS!
THAT'S A COOL STORY!

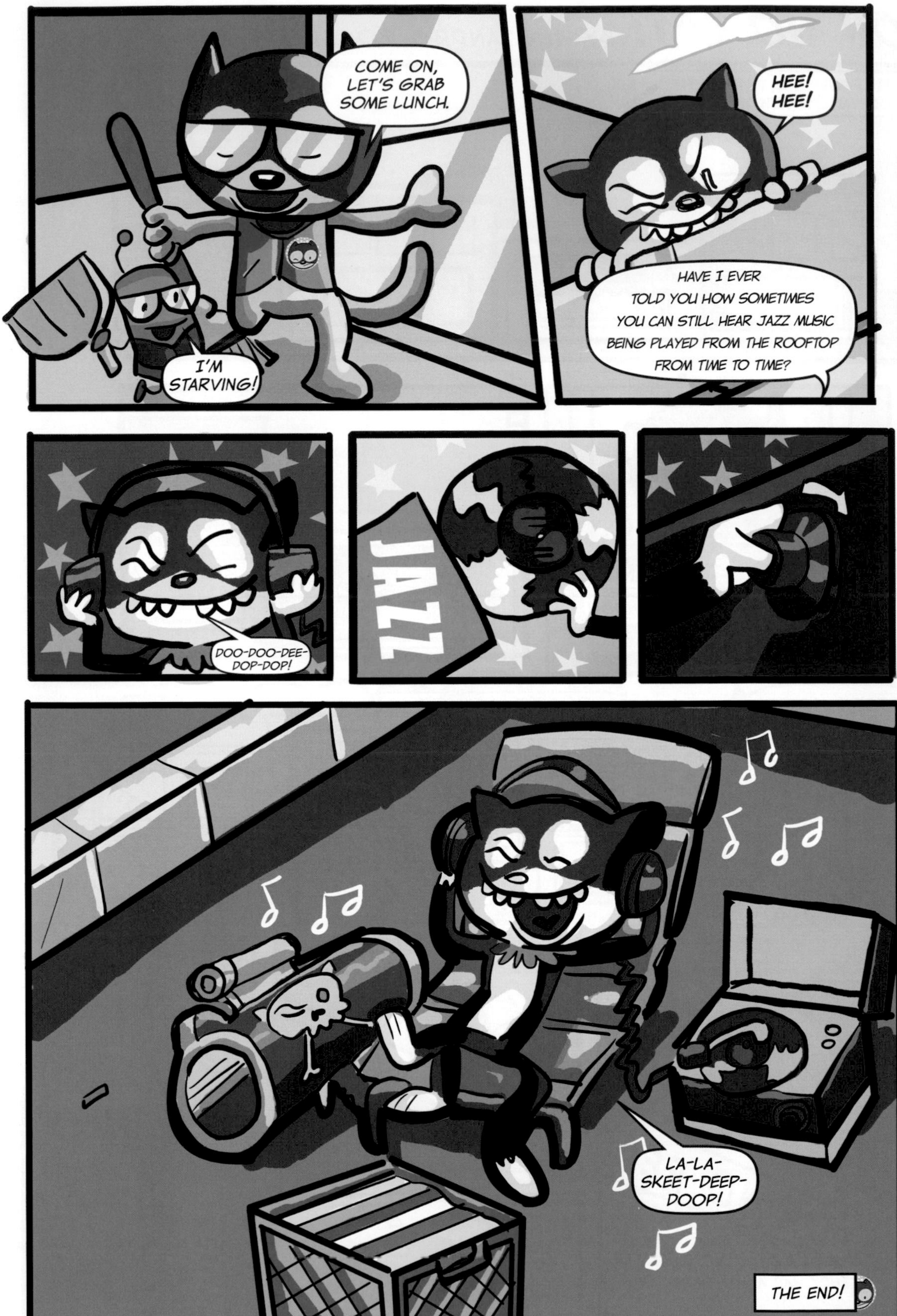
COME ON, LET'S GRAB SOME LUNCH.
I'M STARVING!
HEE! HEE!
HAVE I EVER TOLD YOU HOW SOMETIMES YOU CAN STILL HEAR JAZZ MUSIC BEING PLAYED FROM THE ROOFTOP FROM TIME TO TIME?
DOO-DOO-DEE-DOP-DOP!
JAZZ
LA-LA-SKEET-DEEP-DOOP!
THE END!

ADVENTURE BUG in: GHOST BUGGED! by: SCOOT

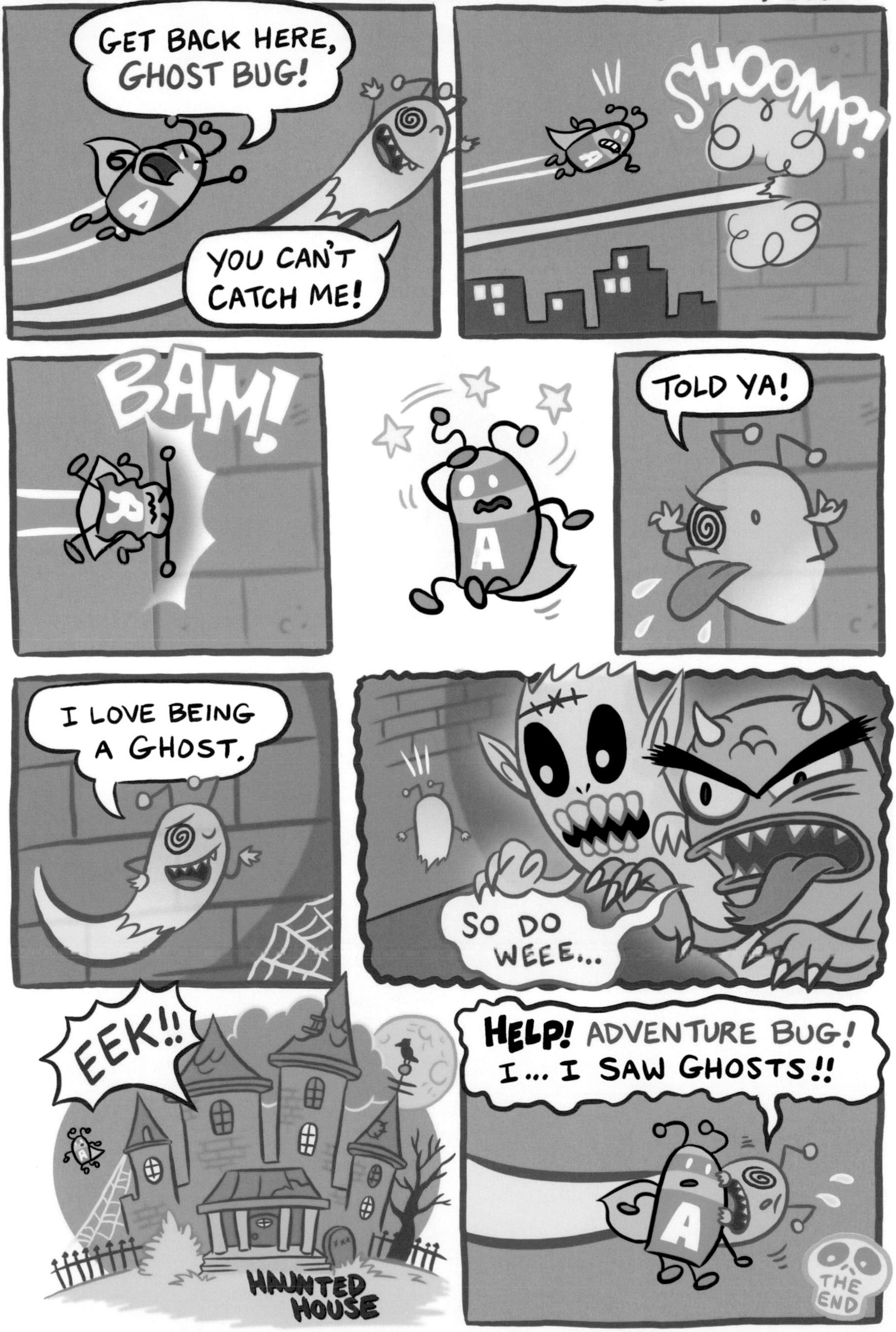
GET BACK HERE, GHOST BUG!
YOU CAN'T CATCH ME!
SHOOMP!
BAM!
TOLD YA!
I LOVE BEING A GHOST.
SO DO WEEE...
EEK!!
HAUNTED HOUSE
HELP! ADVENTURE BUG! I... I SAW GHOSTS!!
THE END

★ CHAPTER FOUR ★

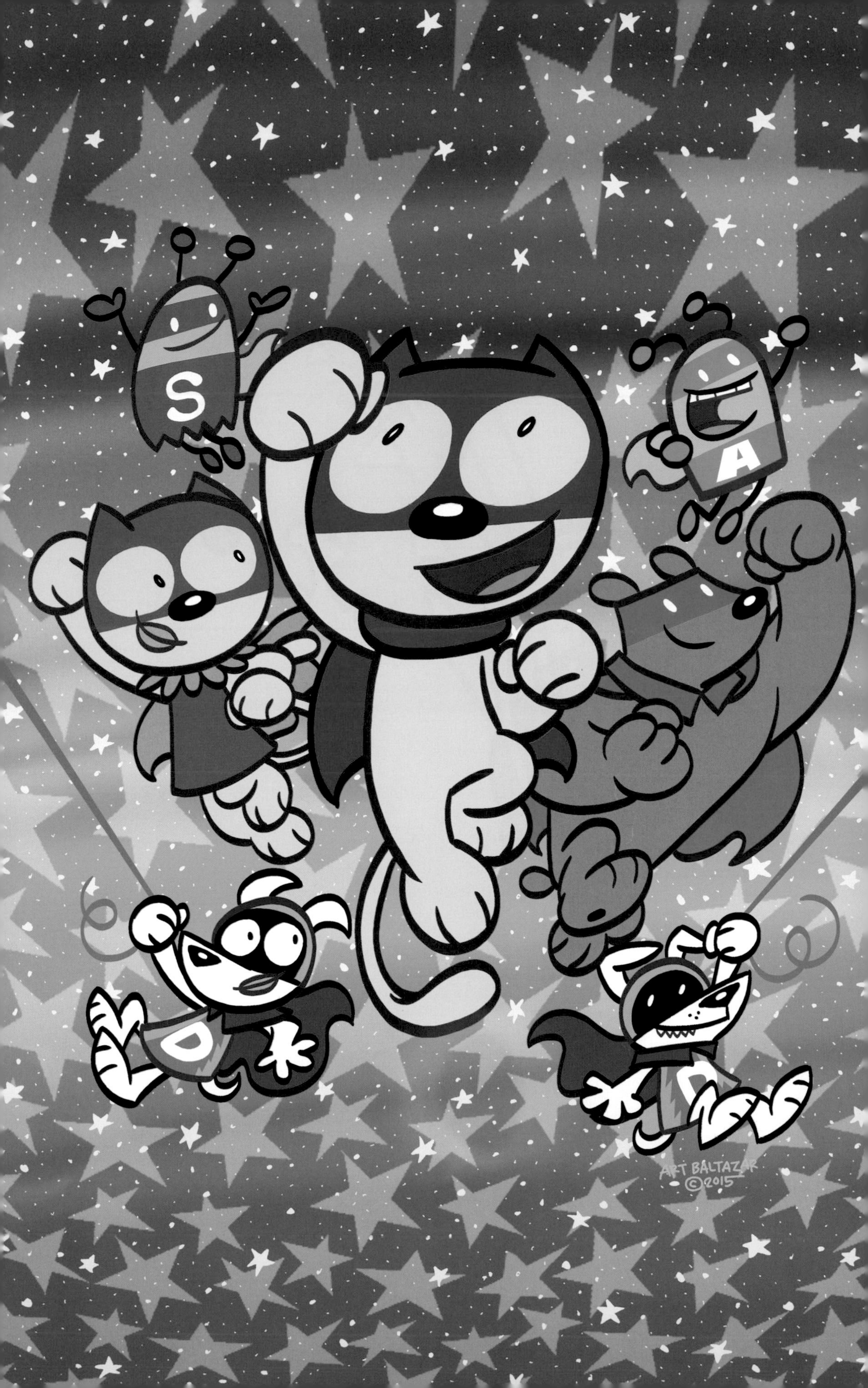
S
A
D
D
ART BALTAZAR
©2015

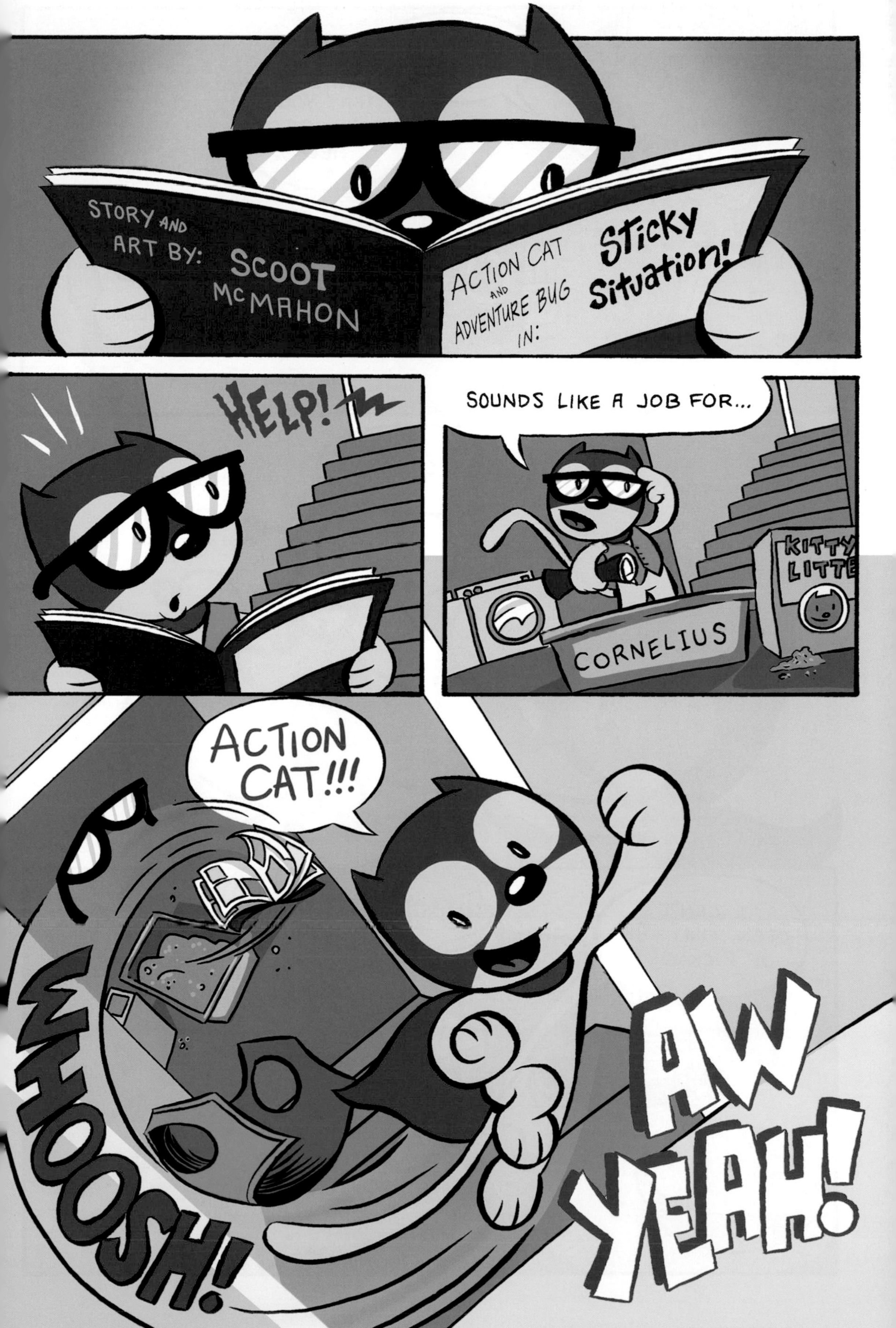
STORY AND ART BY: SCOOT McMAHON
ACTION CAT AND ADVENTURE BUG IN:
Sticky Situation!
HELP!
SOUNDS LIKE A JOB FOR...
CORNELIUS
ACTION CAT!!!
WHOOOSH!
AW YEAH!

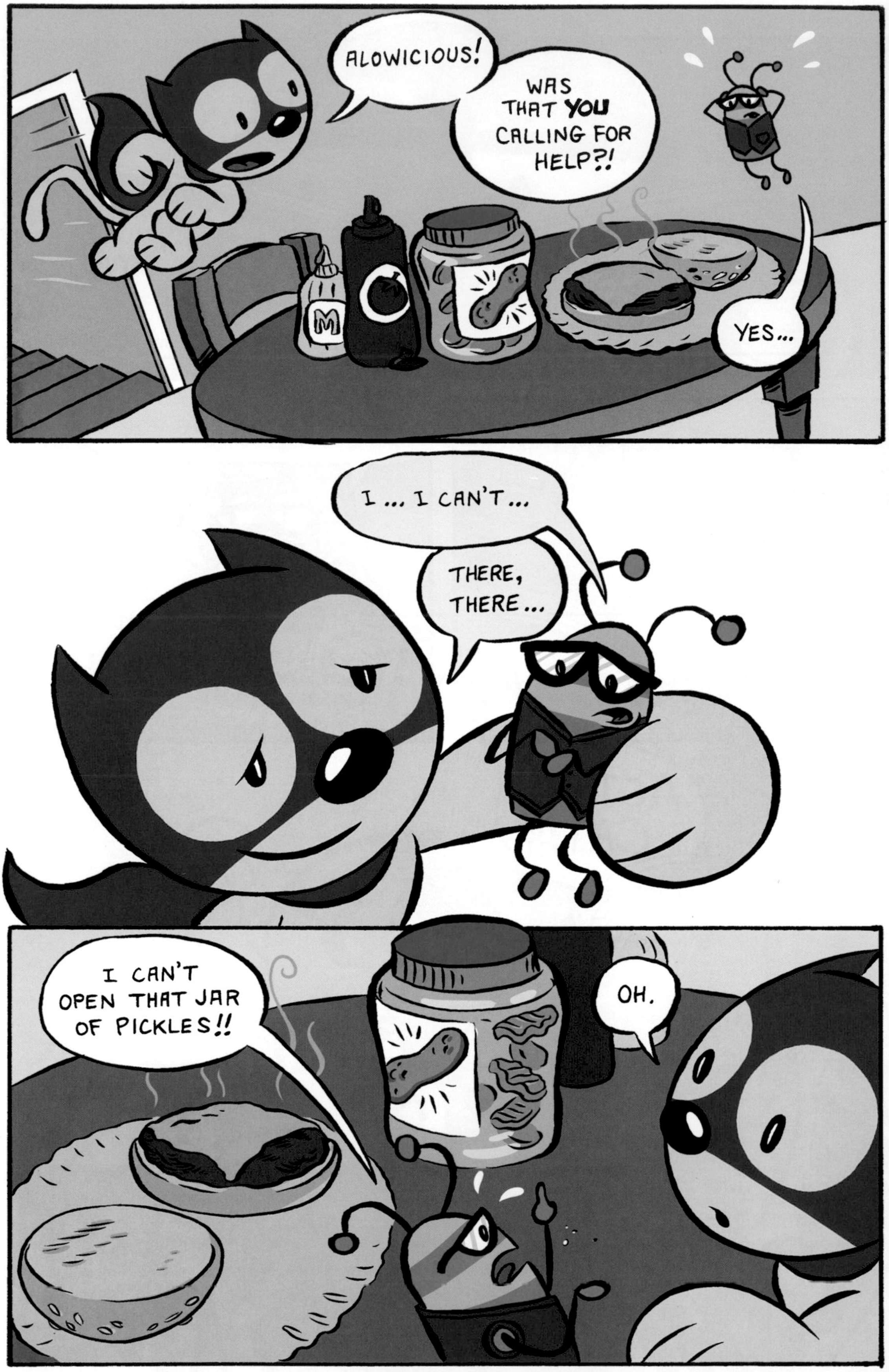
ALOWICIOUS!
WAS THAT YOU CALLING FOR HELP?!
YES...
I ... I CAN'T ...
THERE, THERE ...
I CAN'T OPEN THAT JAR OF PICKLES!!
OH.

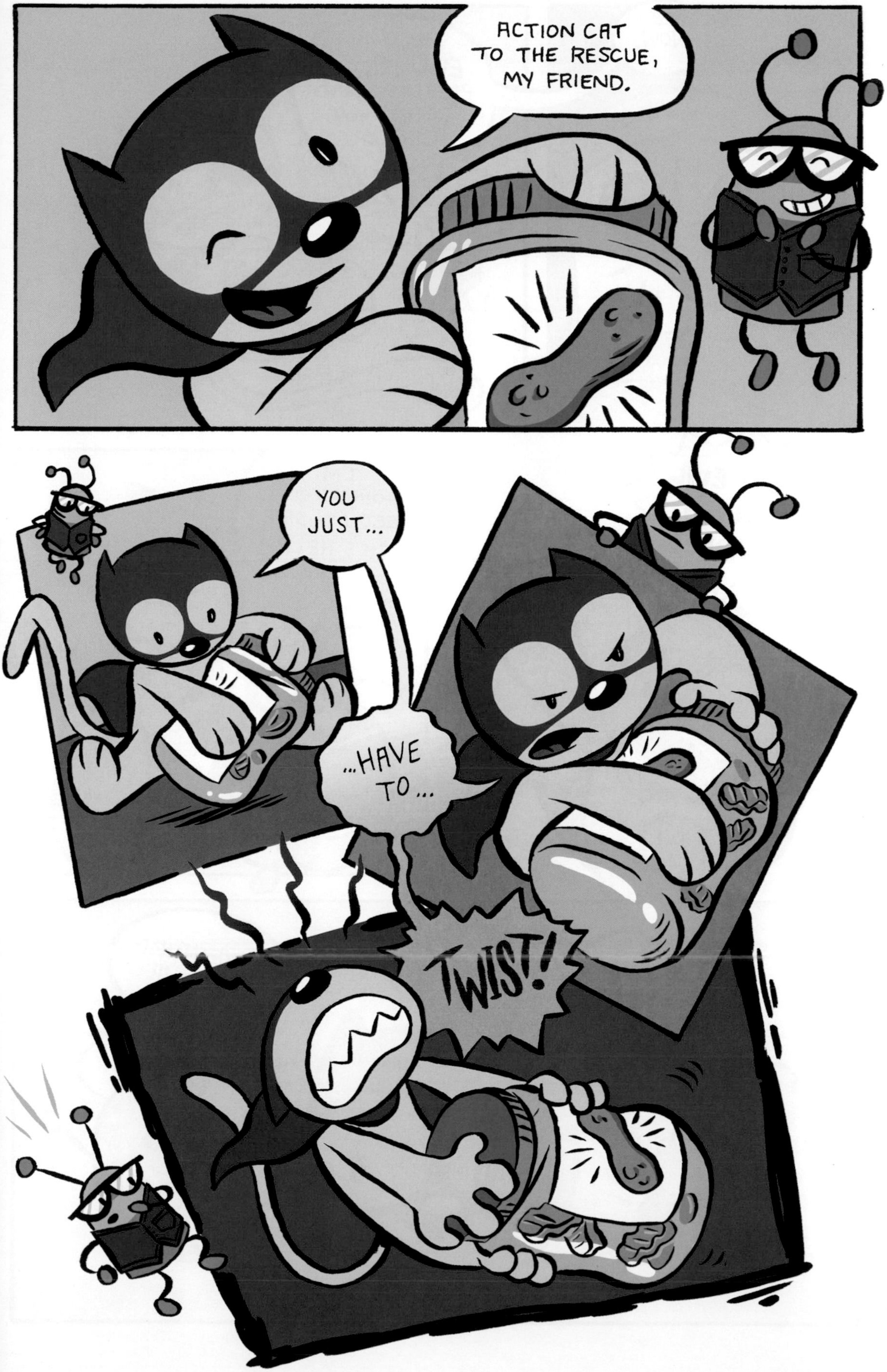
ACTION CAT TO THE RESCUE, MY FRIEND.
YOU JUST...
...HAVE TO...
TWIST!

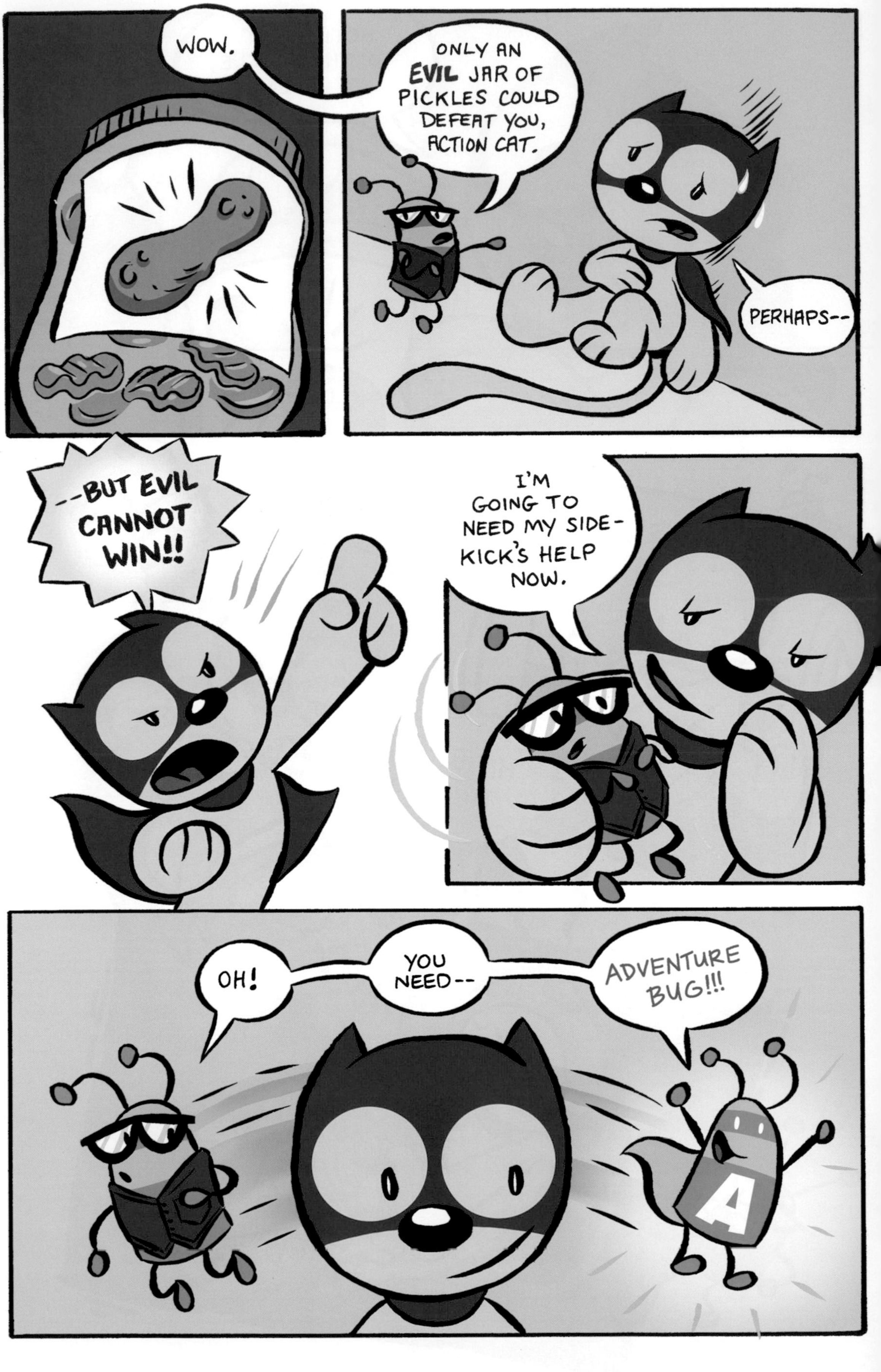
WOW.
ONLY AN EVIL JAR OF PICKLES COULD DEFEAT YOU, ACTION CAT.
PERHAPS--
--BUT EVIL CANNOT WIN!!
I'M GOING TO NEED MY SIDE-KICK'S HELP NOW.
OH!
YOU NEED--
ADVENTURE BUG!!!

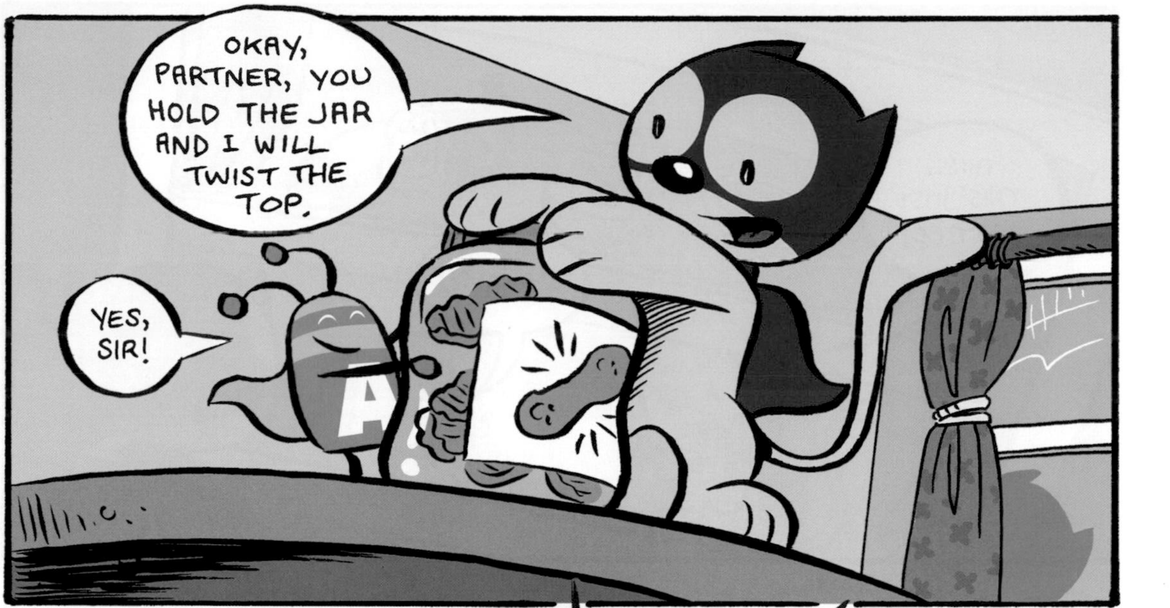
OKAY, PARTNER, YOU HOLD THE JAR AND I WILL TWIST THE TOP.
YES, SIR!

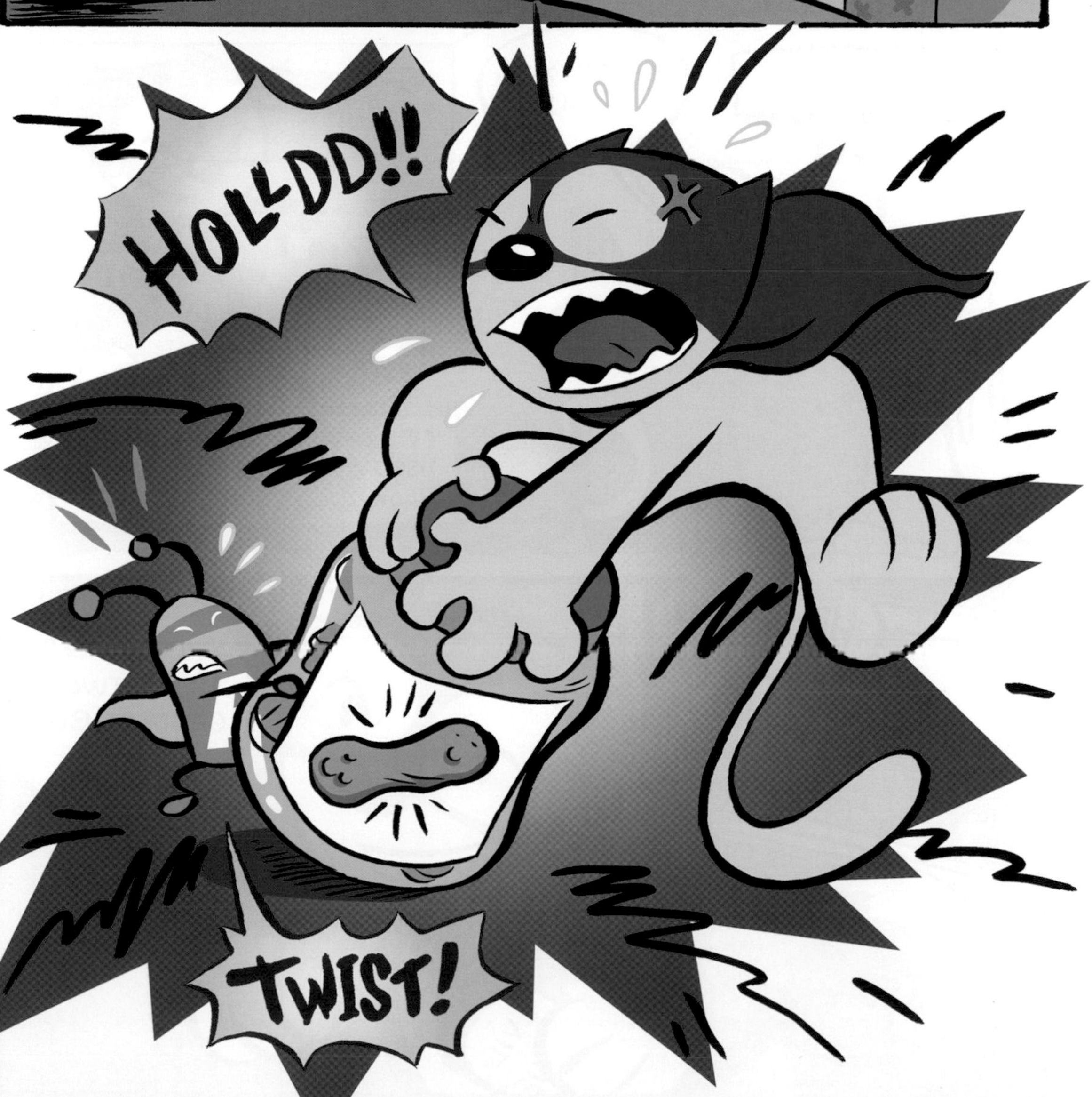
HOLLDD!!
TWIST!

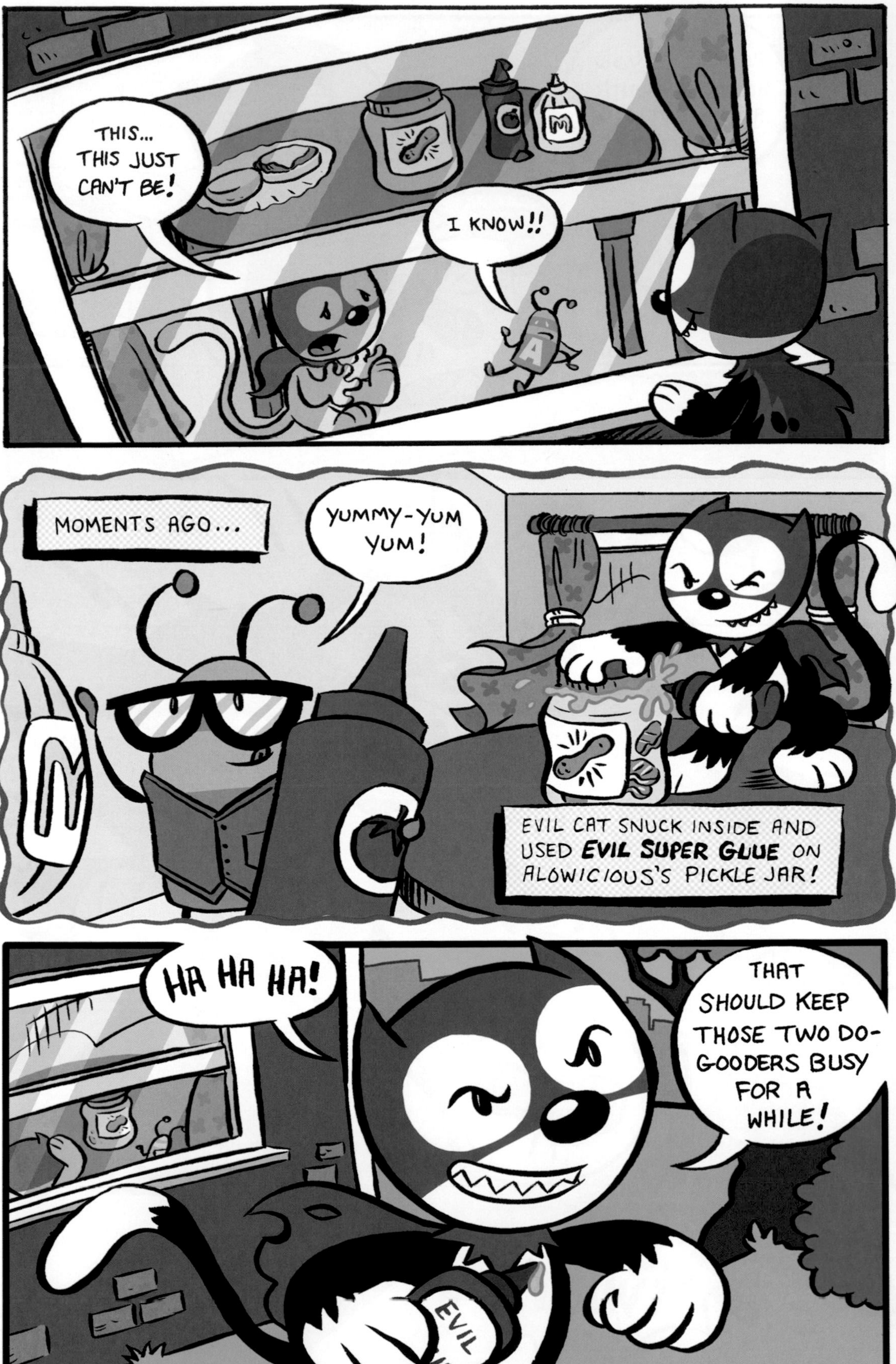
THIS... THIS JUST CAN'T BE!
I KNOW!!
MOMENTS AGO...
YUMMY-YUM YUM!
EVIL CAT SNUCK INSIDE AND USED **EVIL SUPER GLUE** ON ALOWICIOUS'S PICKLE JAR!
HA HA HA!
THAT SHOULD KEEP THOSE TWO DO-GOODERS BUSY FOR A WHILE!

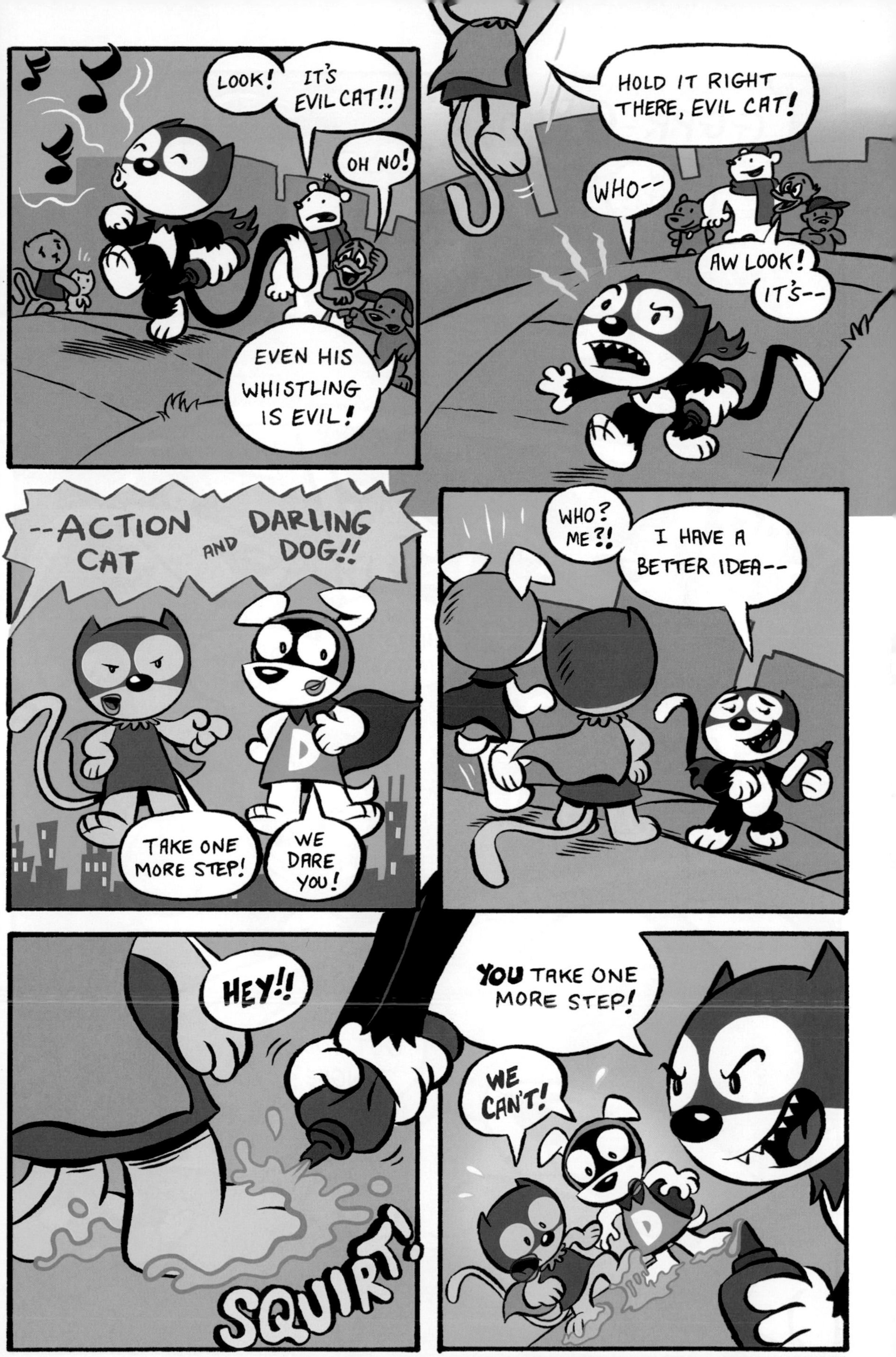
LOOK! IT'S EVIL CAT!!
OH NO!
EVEN HIS WHISTLING IS EVIL!
HOLD IT RIGHT THERE, EVIL CAT!
WHO--
AW LOOK! IT'S--
--ACTION CAT AND DARLING DOG!!
TAKE ONE MORE STEP!
WE DARE YOU!
WHO? ME?!
I HAVE A BETTER IDEA--
HEY!!
SQUIRT!
YOU TAKE ONE MORE STEP!
WE CAN'T!

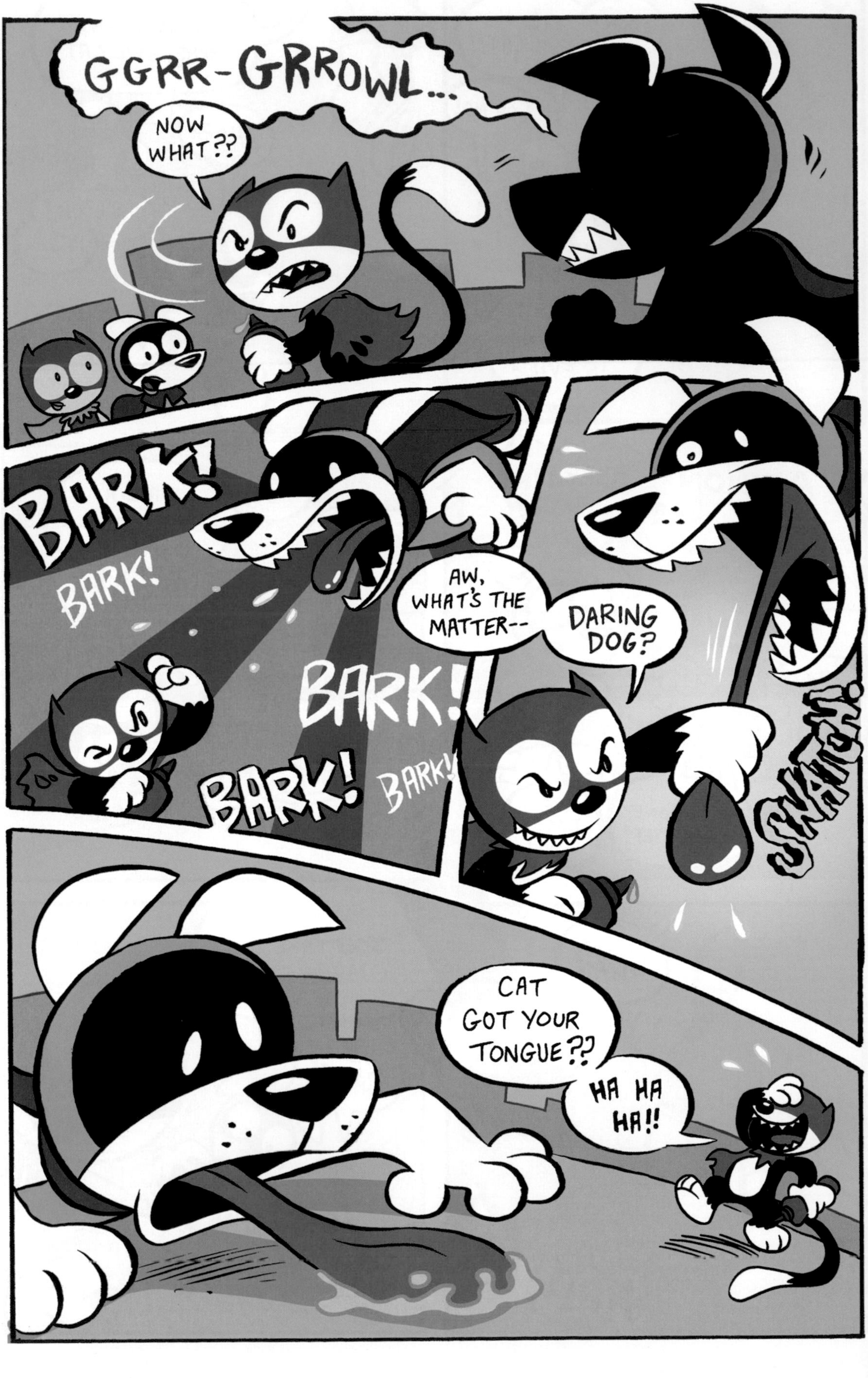
GGRR-GRROWL...
NOW WHAT??
BARK!
BARK!
BARK!
BARK!
BARK!
AW, WHAT'S THE MATTER--
DARING DOG?
SNATCH!
CAT GOT YOUR TONGUE??
HA HA HA!!

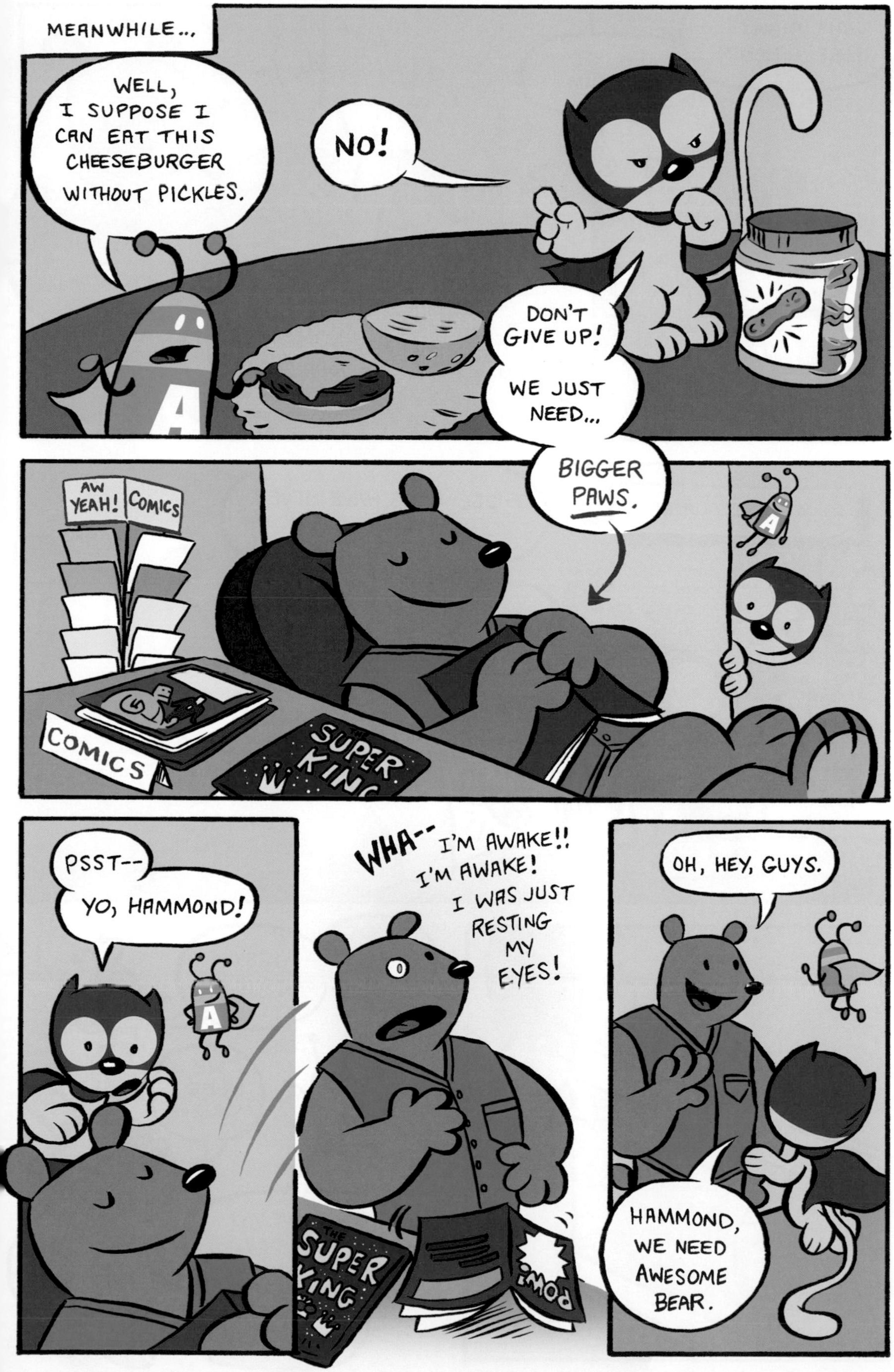
MEANWHILE...
WELL, I SUPPOSE I CAN EAT THIS CHEESEBURGER WITHOUT PICKLES.
NO!
DON'T GIVE UP!
WE JUST NEED...
BIGGER PAWS.
AW YEAH! COMICS
COMICS
THE SUPER KING
PSST--
YO, HAMMOND!
WHA--
I'M AWAKE!! I'M AWAKE! I WAS JUST RESTING MY EYES!
THE SUPER KING
POW!
OH, HEY, GUYS.
HAMMOND, WE NEED AWESOME BEAR.

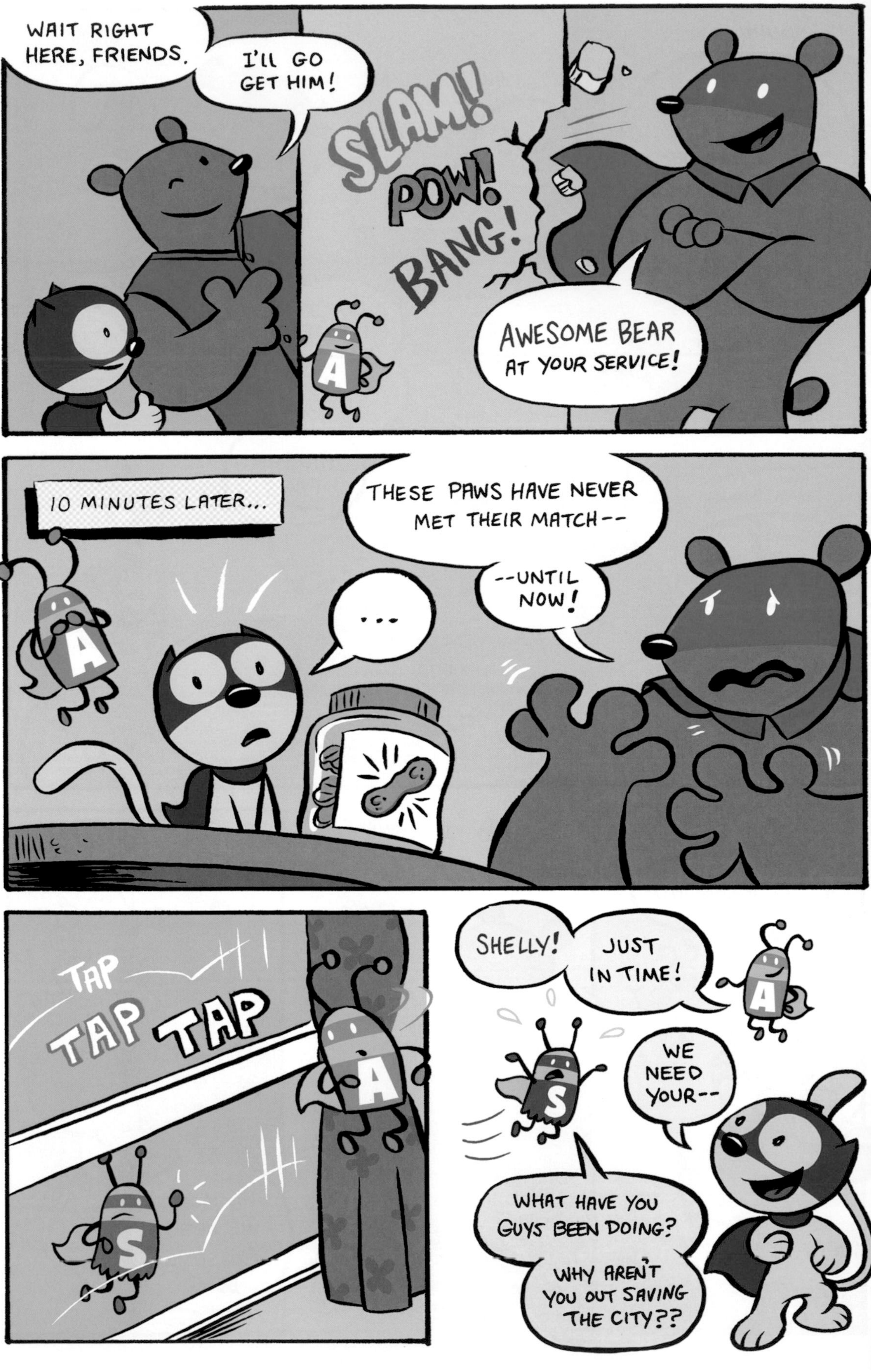

WAIT RIGHT HERE, FRIENDS.
I'LL GO GET HIM!
SLAM!
POW!
BANG!
AWESOME BEAR AT YOUR SERVICE!
10 MINUTES LATER...
THESE PAWS HAVE NEVER MET THEIR MATCH--
--UNTIL NOW!
...
TAP
TAP
TAP
SHELLY!
JUST IN TIME!
WE NEED YOUR--
WHAT HAVE YOU GUYS BEEN DOING?
WHY AREN'T YOU OUT SAVING THE CITY??

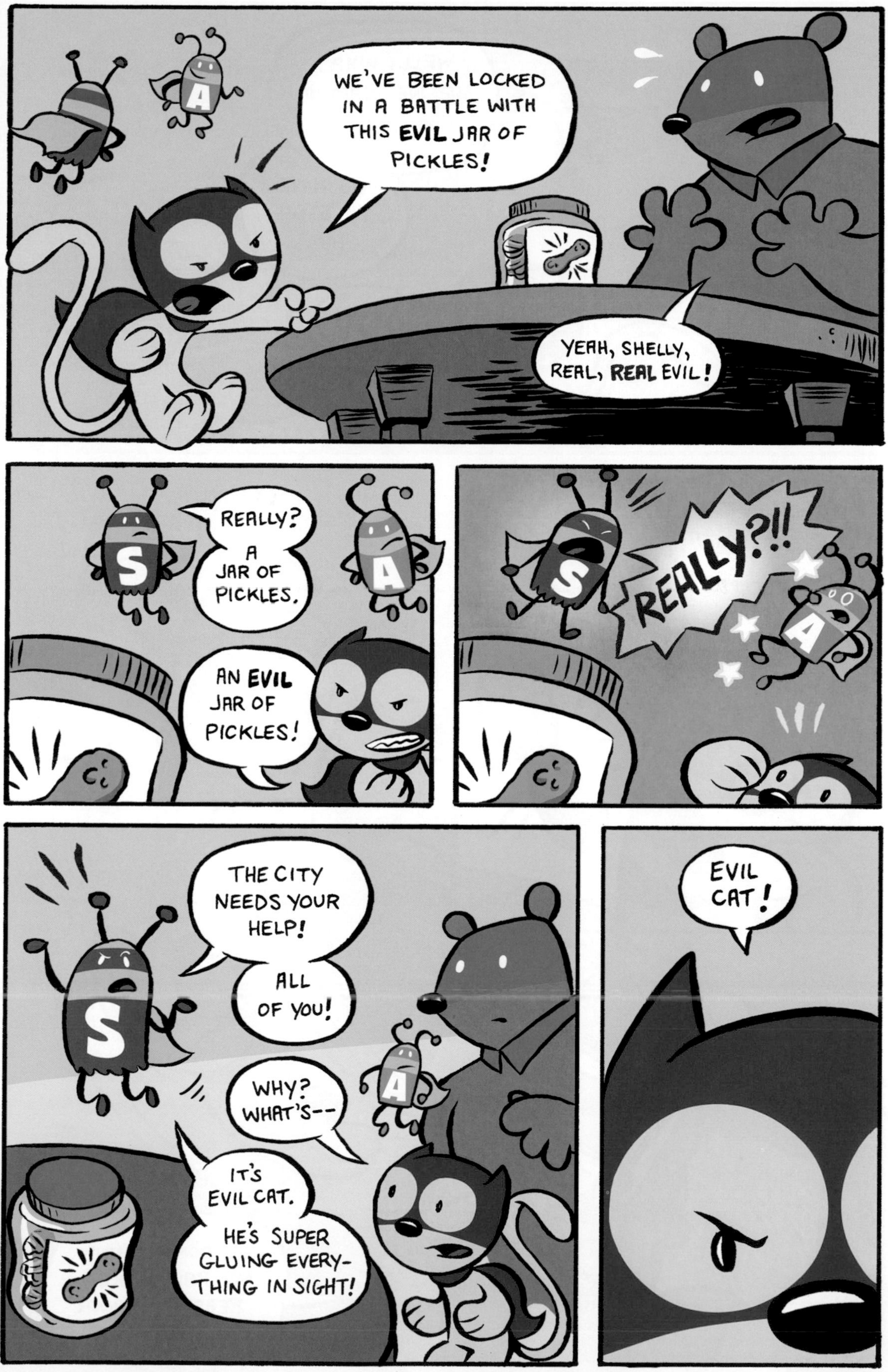
WE'VE BEEN LOCKED IN A BATTLE WITH THIS **EVIL** JAR OF PICKLES!
YEAH, SHELLY, REAL, **REAL** EVIL!
REALLY? A JAR OF PICKLES.
AN **EVIL** JAR OF PICKLES!
REALLY?!!
THE CITY NEEDS YOUR HELP!
ALL OF YOU!
WHY? WHAT'S--
IT'S EVIL CAT.
HE'S SUPER GLUING EVERY-THING IN SIGHT!
EVIL CAT!

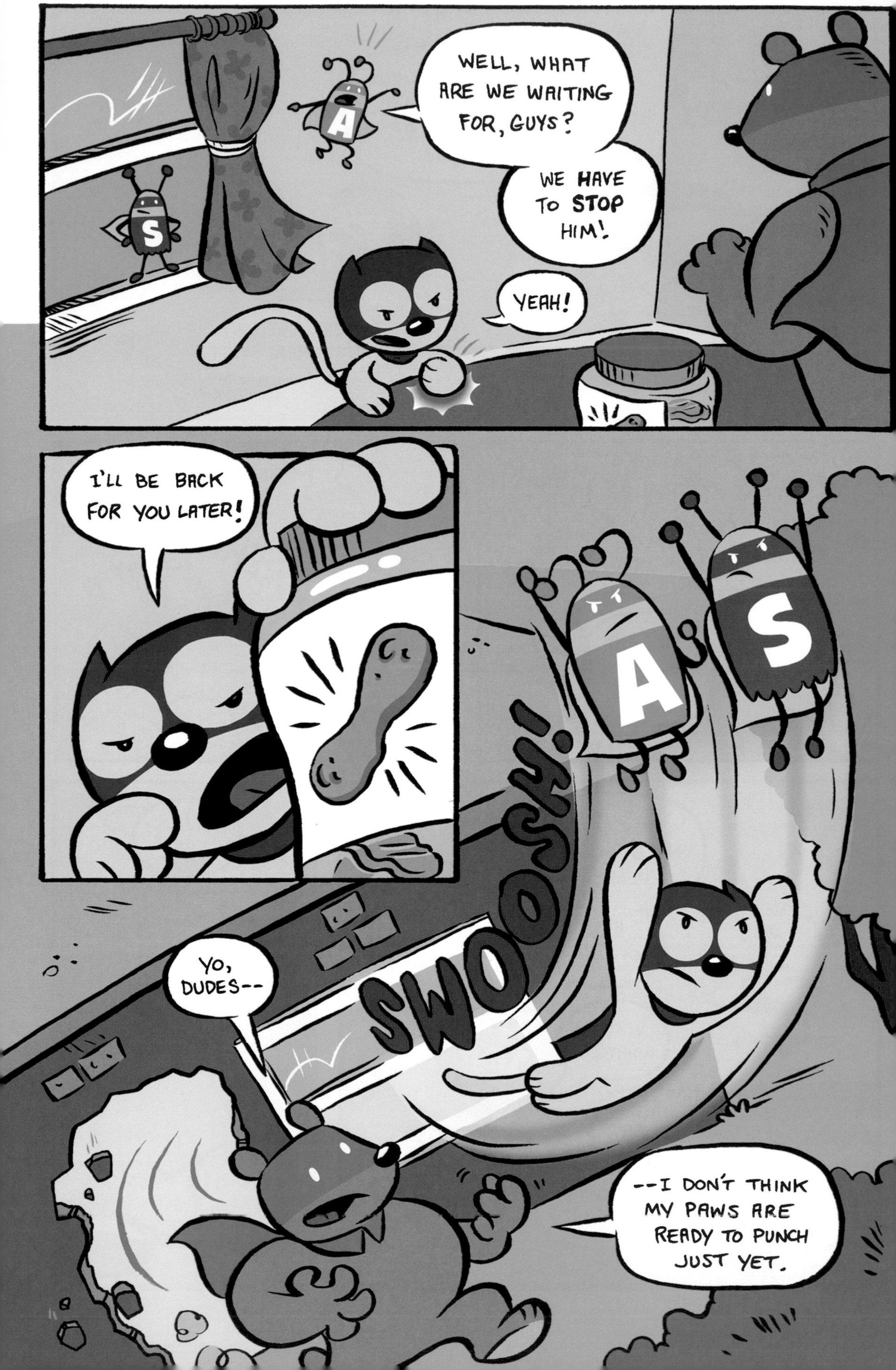
WELL, WHAT ARE WE WAITING FOR, GUYS?
WE HAVE TO STOP HIM!
YEAH!
I'LL BE BACK FOR YOU LATER!
SWOOSH!
YO, DUDES--
--I DON'T THINK MY PAWS ARE READY TO PUNCH JUST YET.

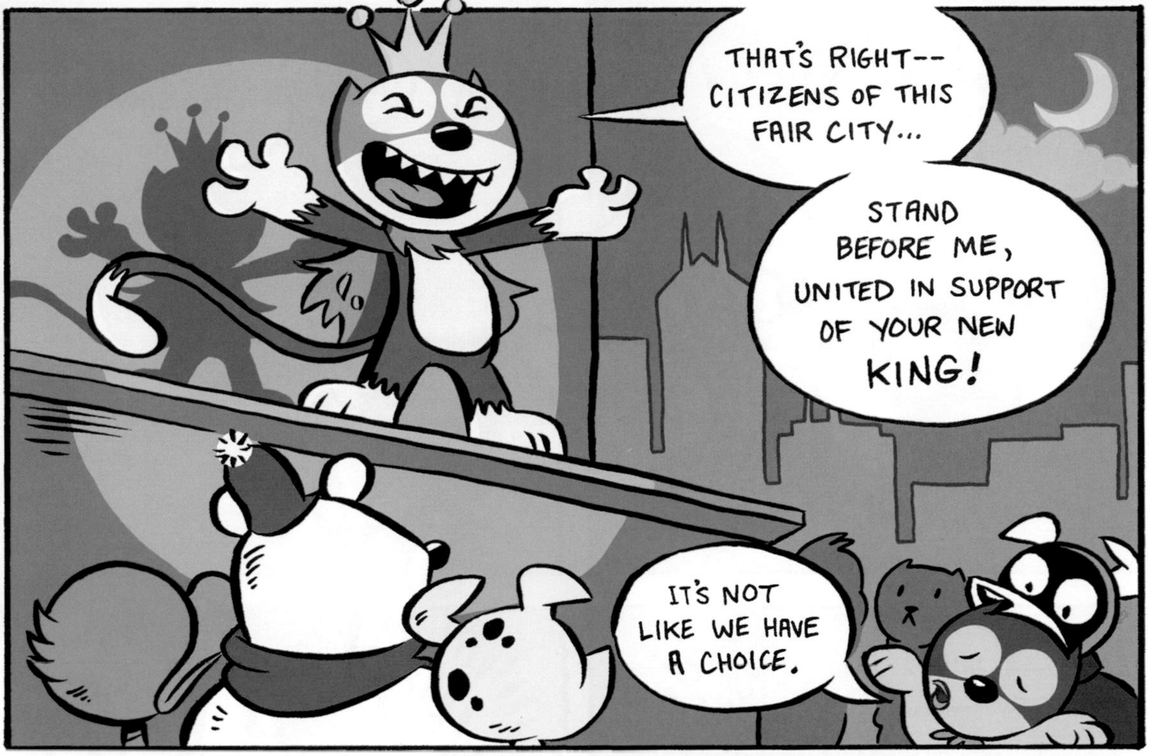
THAT'S RIGHT-- CITIZENS OF THIS FAIR CITY...
STAND BEFORE ME, UNITED IN SUPPORT OF YOUR NEW KING!
IT'S NOT LIKE WE HAVE A CHOICE.

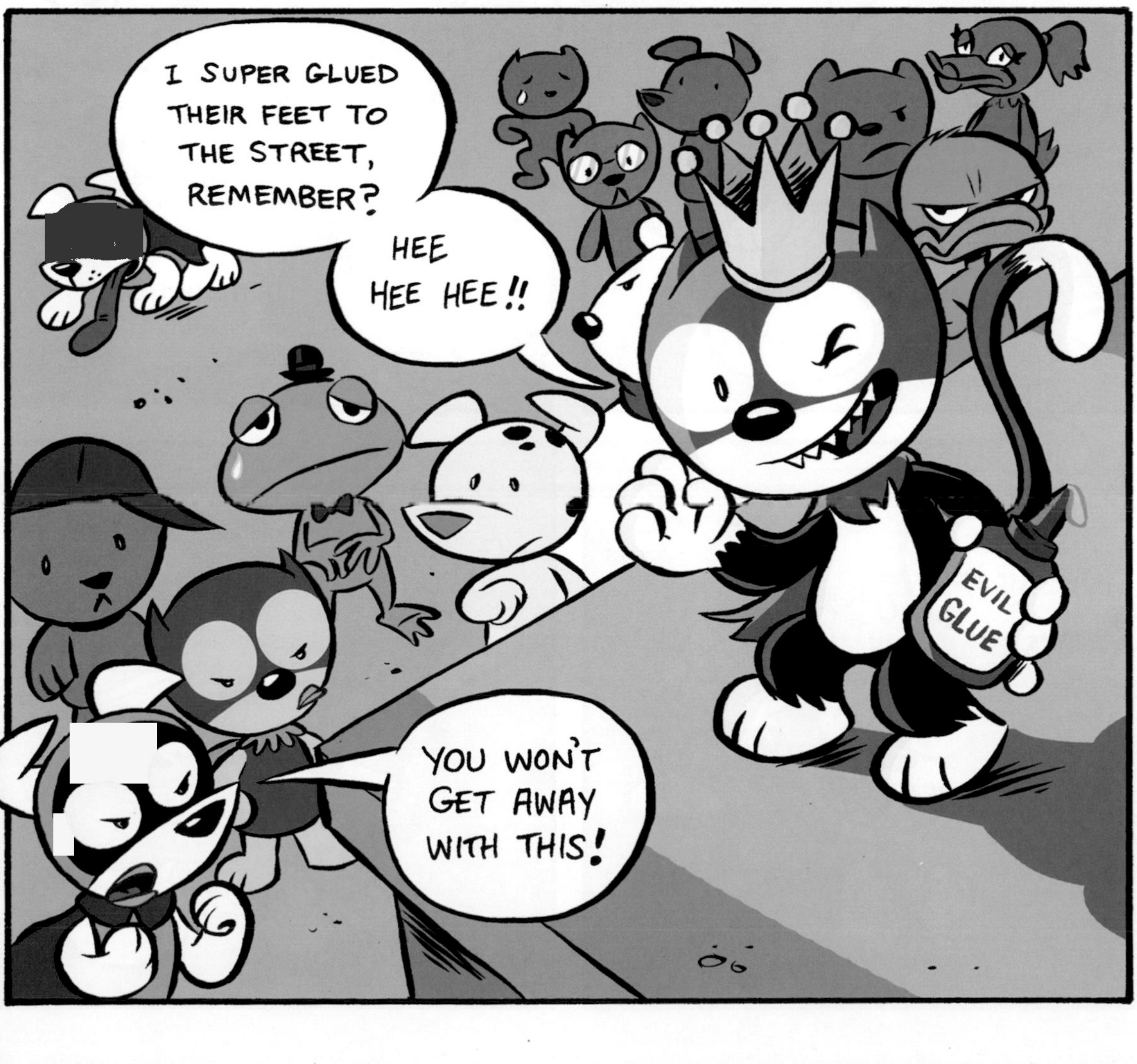
I SUPER GLUED THEIR FEET TO THE STREET, REMEMBER?
HEE HEE HEE!!
EVIL GLUE
YOU WON'T GET AWAY WITH THIS!

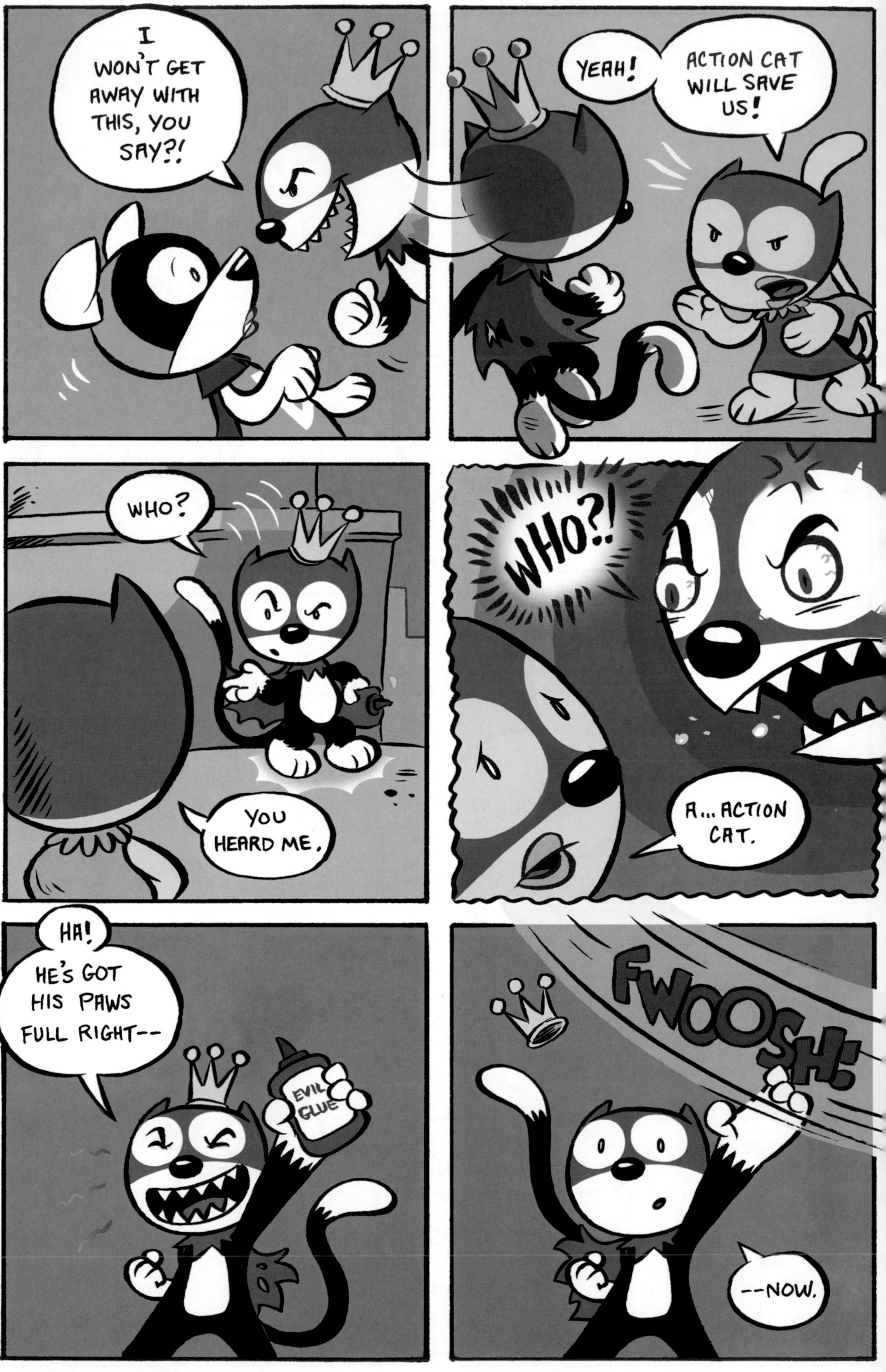
I WON'T GET AWAY WITH THIS, YOU SAY?!
YEAH!
ACTION CAT WILL SAVE US!
WHO?
YOU HEARD ME.
WHO?!
A... ACTION CAT.
HA!
HE'S GOT HIS PAWS FULL RIGHT--
EVIL GLUE
FWOOSH!
--NOW.

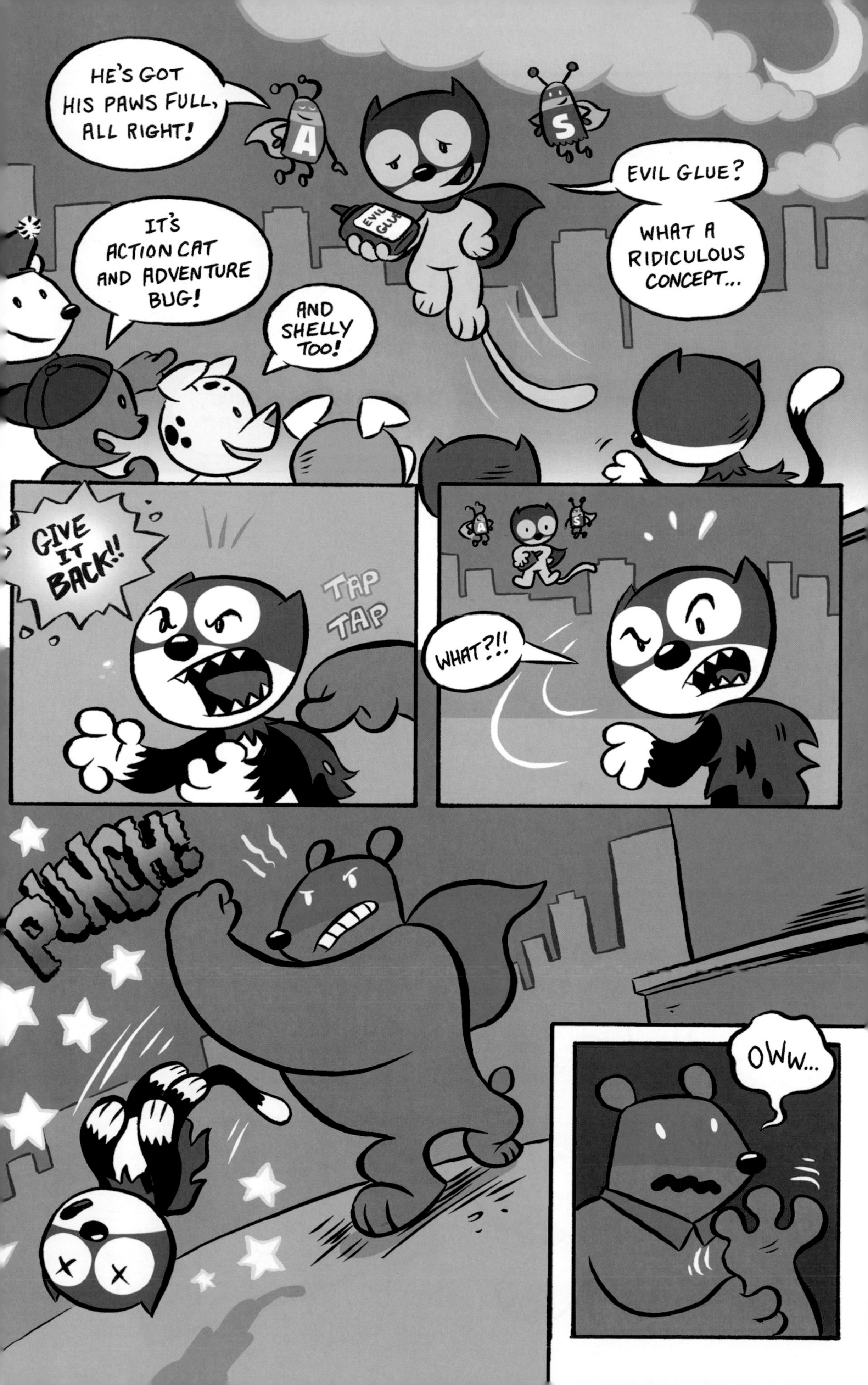
HE'S GOT HIS PAWS FULL, ALL RIGHT!
EVIL GLUE
EVIL GLUE?
WHAT A RIDICULOUS CONCEPT...
IT'S ACTION CAT AND ADVENTURE BUG!
AND SHELLY TOO!
GIVE IT BACK!!
TAP TAP
WHAT?!!
PUNCH!
OWW...

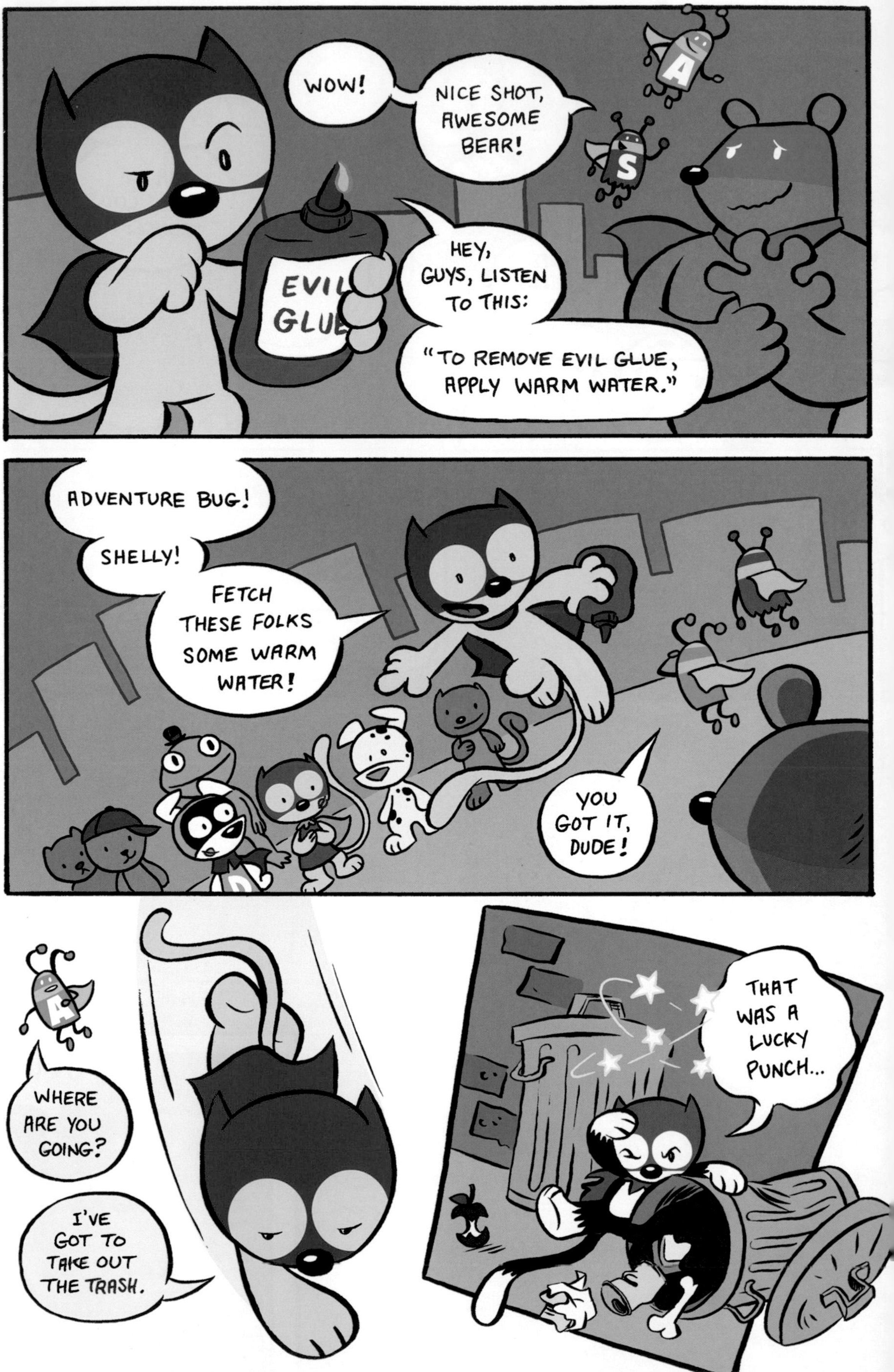
WOW!
NICE SHOT, AWESOME BEAR!
EVIL GLUE
HEY, GUYS, LISTEN TO THIS:
"TO REMOVE EVIL GLUE, APPLY WARM WATER."
ADVENTURE BUG!
SHELLY!
FETCH THESE FOLKS SOME WARM WATER!
YOU GOT IT, DUDE!
WHERE ARE YOU GOING?
I'VE GOT TO TAKE OUT THE TRASH.
THAT WAS A LUCKY PUNCH...

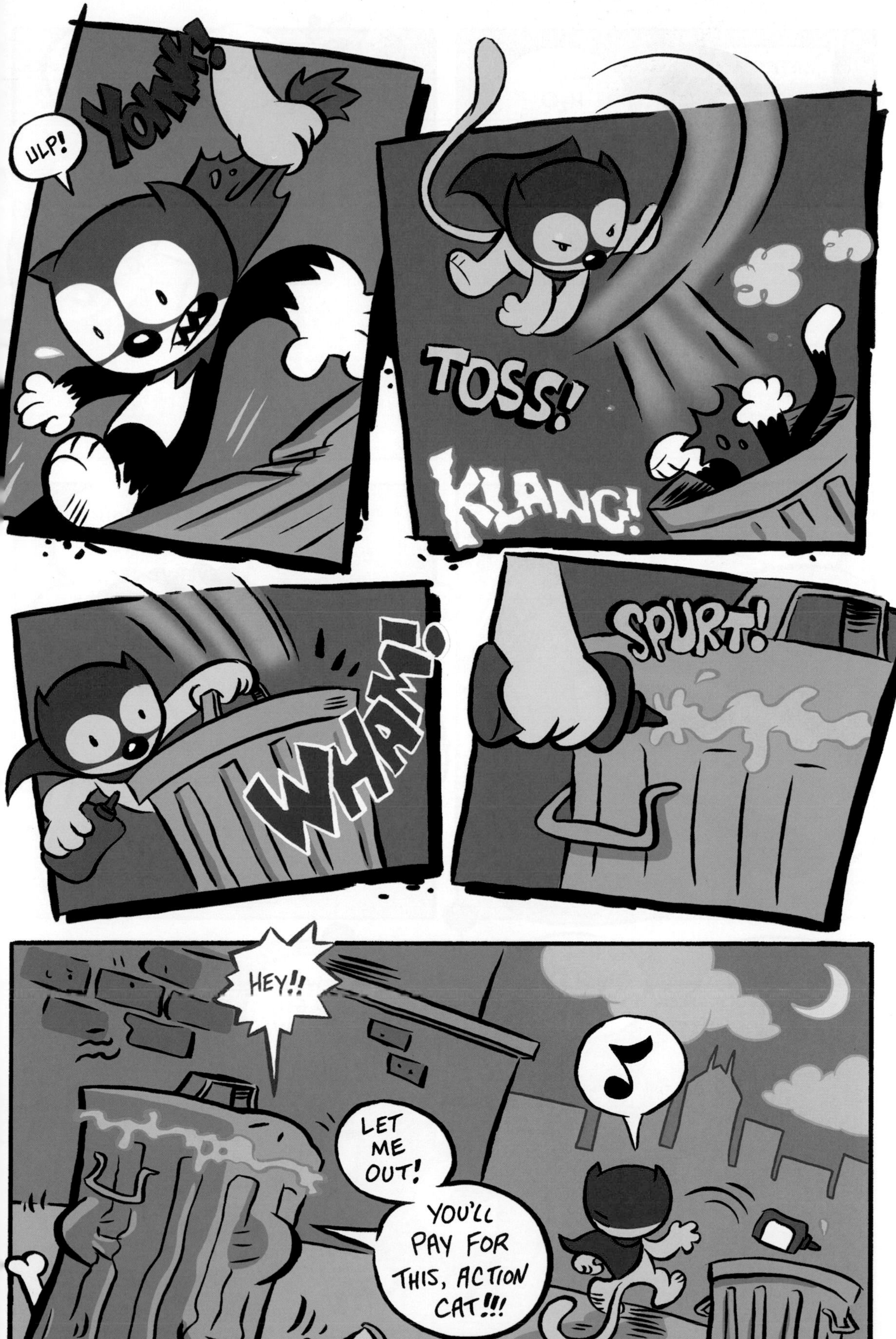
ULP!
YOINK!
TOSS!
KLANG!
WHAM!
SPURT!
HEY!!
LET ME OUT!
YOU'LL PAY FOR THIS, ACTION CAT!!!

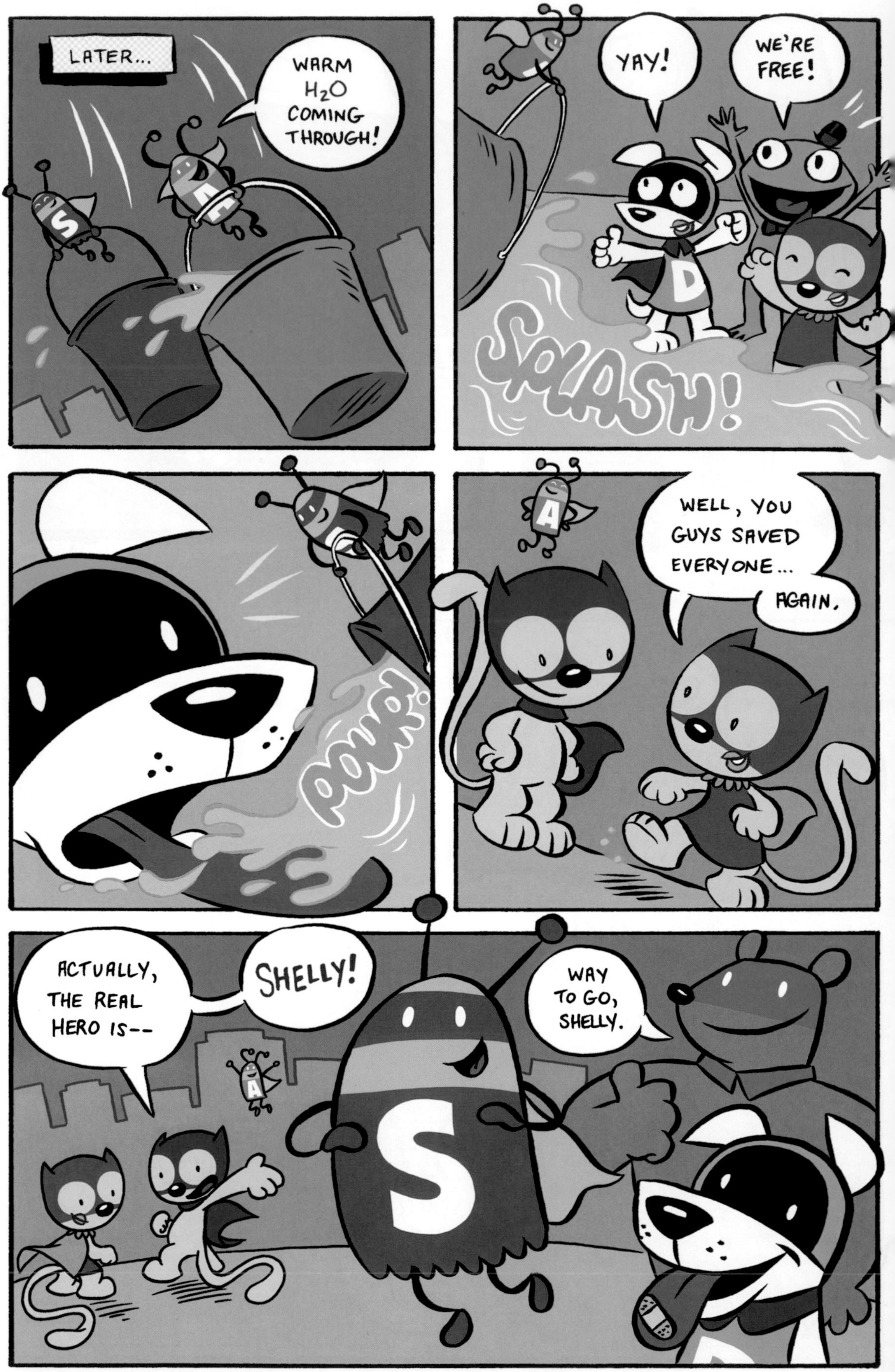
LATER...
WARM H_2O COMING THROUGH!
YAY!
WE'RE FREE!
SPLASH!
POUR!
WELL, YOU GUYS SAVED EVERYONE...
AGAIN.
ACTUALLY, THE REAL HERO IS--
SHELLY!
WAY TO GO, SHELLY.

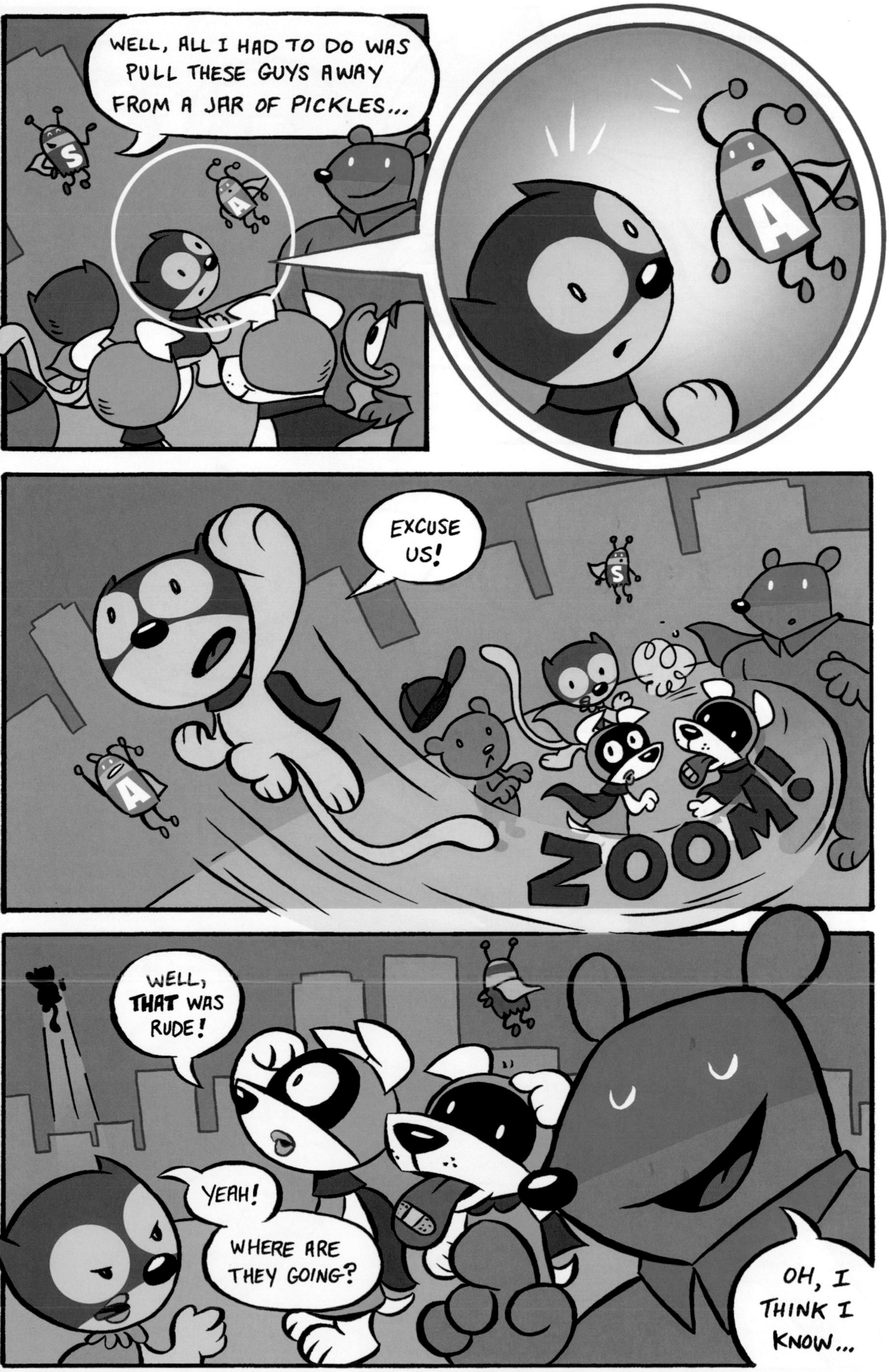

WELL, ALL I HAD TO DO WAS PULL THESE GUYS AWAY FROM A JAR OF PICKLES...
S
A
EXCUSE US!
ZOOM!
WELL, THAT WAS RUDE!
YEAH!
WHERE ARE THEY GOING?
OH, I THINK I KNOW...

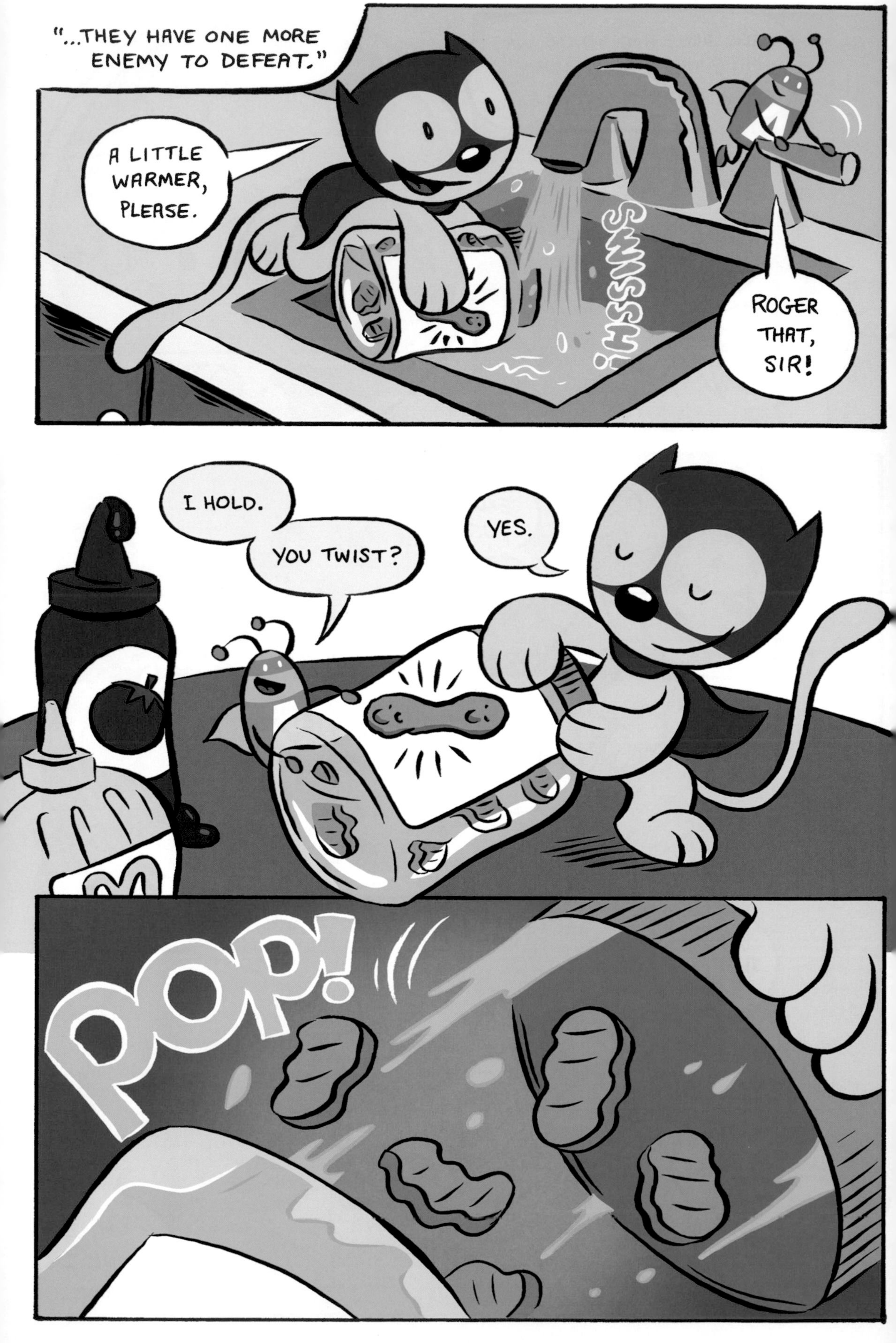
"...THEY HAVE ONE MORE ENEMY TO DEFEAT."
A LITTLE WARMER, PLEASE.
SWISSH!
ROGER THAT, SIR!
I HOLD.
YOU TWIST?
YES.
POP!

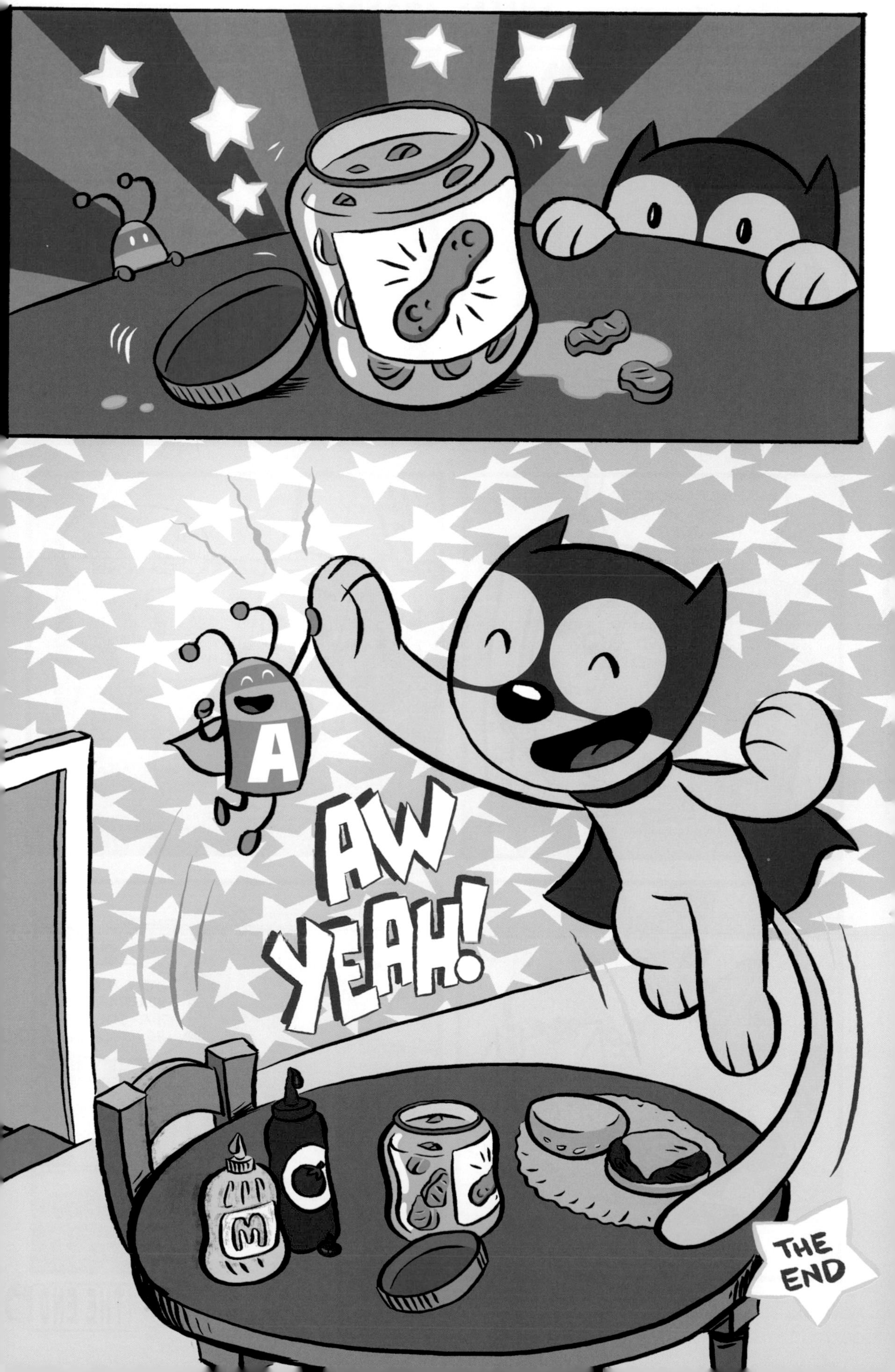

AW YEAH!
THE END

COFFEE SMACK!

WORDS BY **SHARIFF MUSALLAM** ART BY **ALEJANDRO ROSADO**

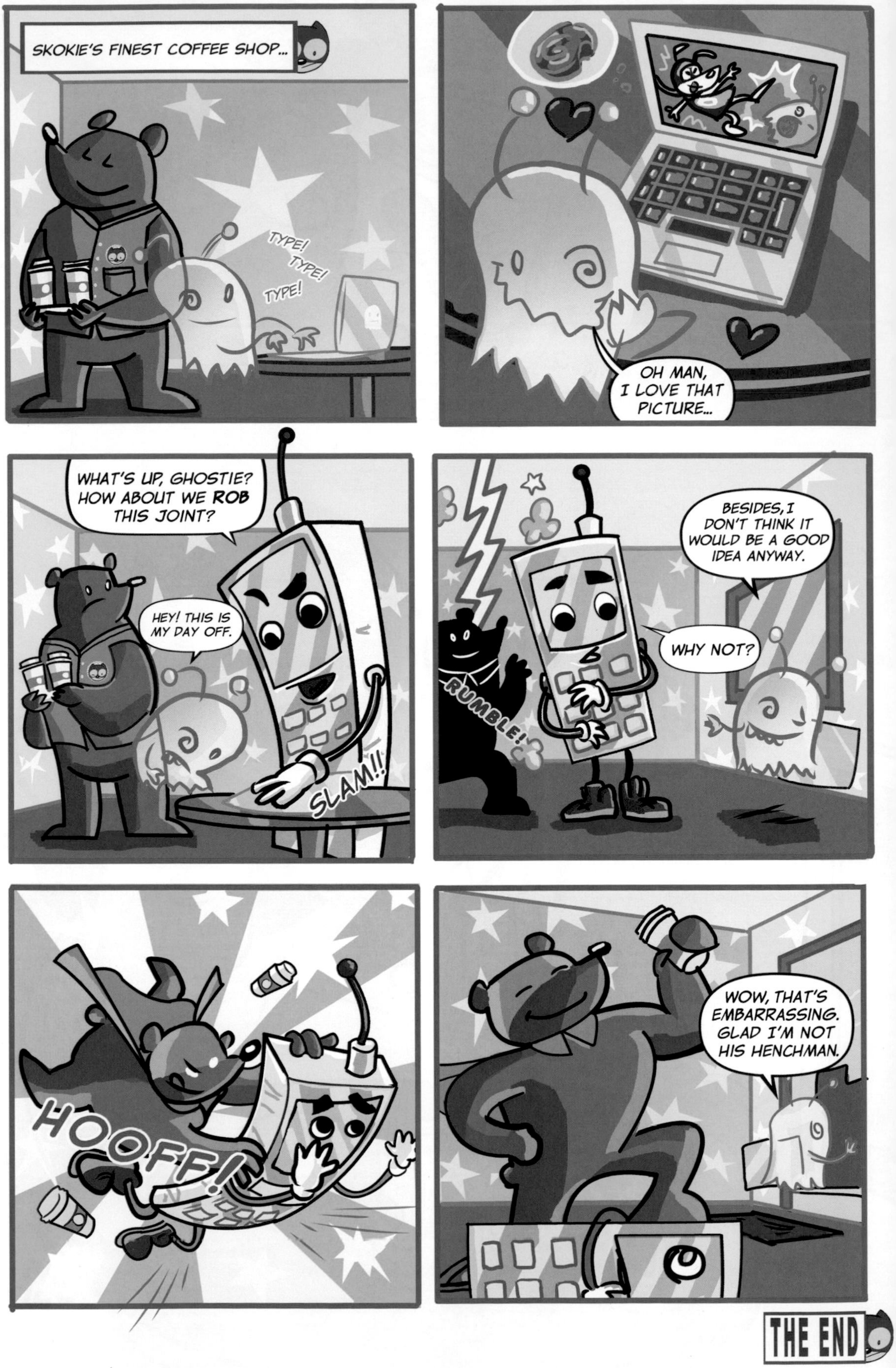

SKOKIE'S FINEST COFFEE SHOP...
TYPE! TYPE! TYPE!
OH MAN, I LOVE THAT PICTURE...
WHAT'S UP, GHOSTIE? HOW ABOUT WE **ROB** THIS JOINT?
HEY! THIS IS MY DAY OFF.
SLAM!!
WHY NOT?
BESIDES, I DON'T THINK IT WOULD BE A GOOD IDEA ANYWAY.
RUMBLE!
HOOFF!
WOW, THAT'S EMBARRASSING. GLAD I'M NOT HIS HENCHMAN.
THE END

AW YEAH COMICS: GONE CAMPING BY KURT WOOD

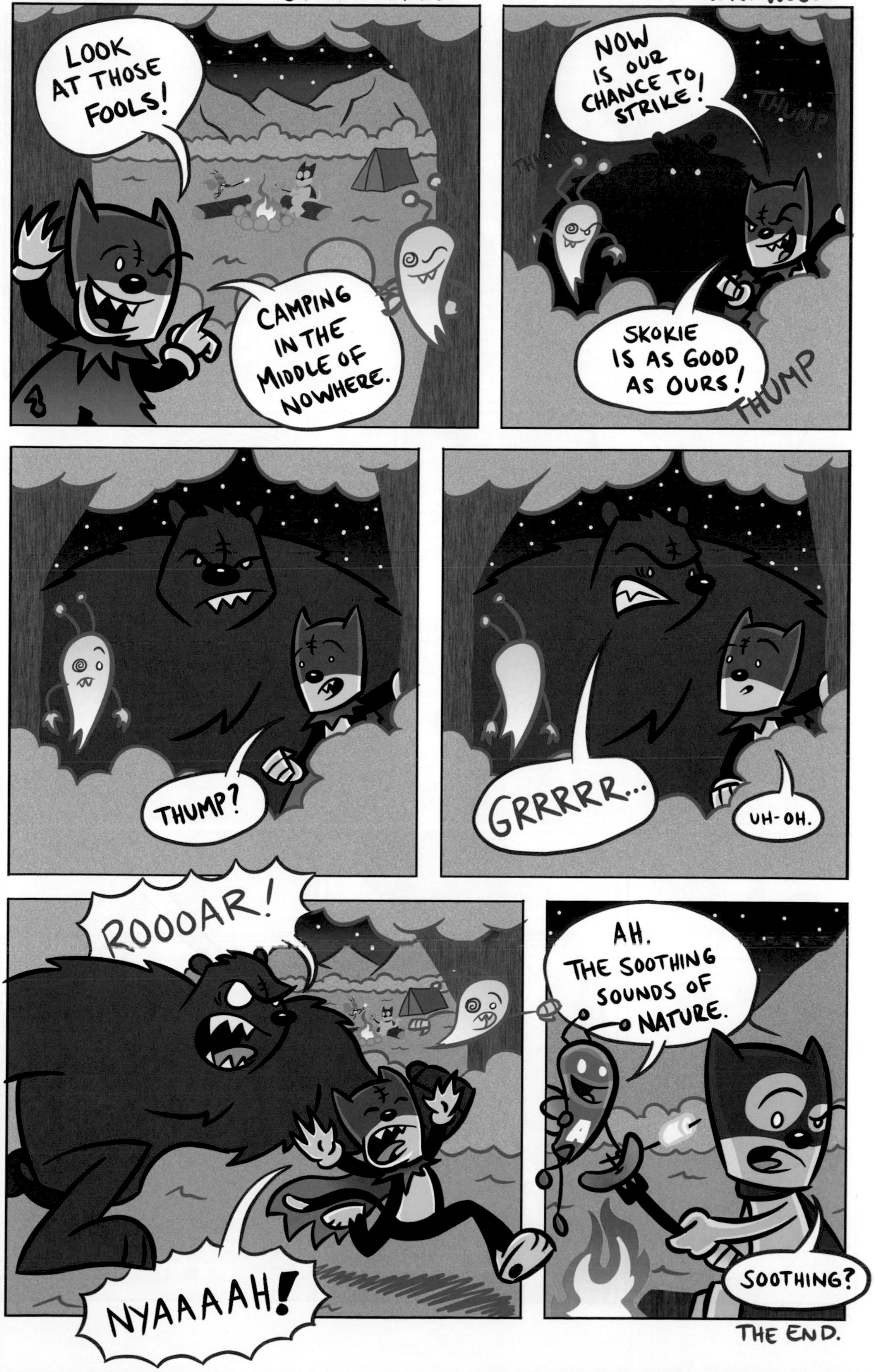
LOOK AT THOSE FOOLS!
CAMPING IN THE MIDDLE OF NOWHERE.
NOW IS OUR CHANCE TO STRIKE!
THUMP
SKOKIE IS AS GOOD AS OURS!
THUMP
THUMP?
GRRRRR...
UH-OH.
ROOOAR!
NYAAAAH!
AH. THE SOOTHING SOUNDS OF NATURE.
SOOTHING?
THE END.

"THE LUNCHTIME HORROR" WRITTEN BY DAVE SCHEIDT ILLUSTRATED BY ALISE GLUŠKOVA

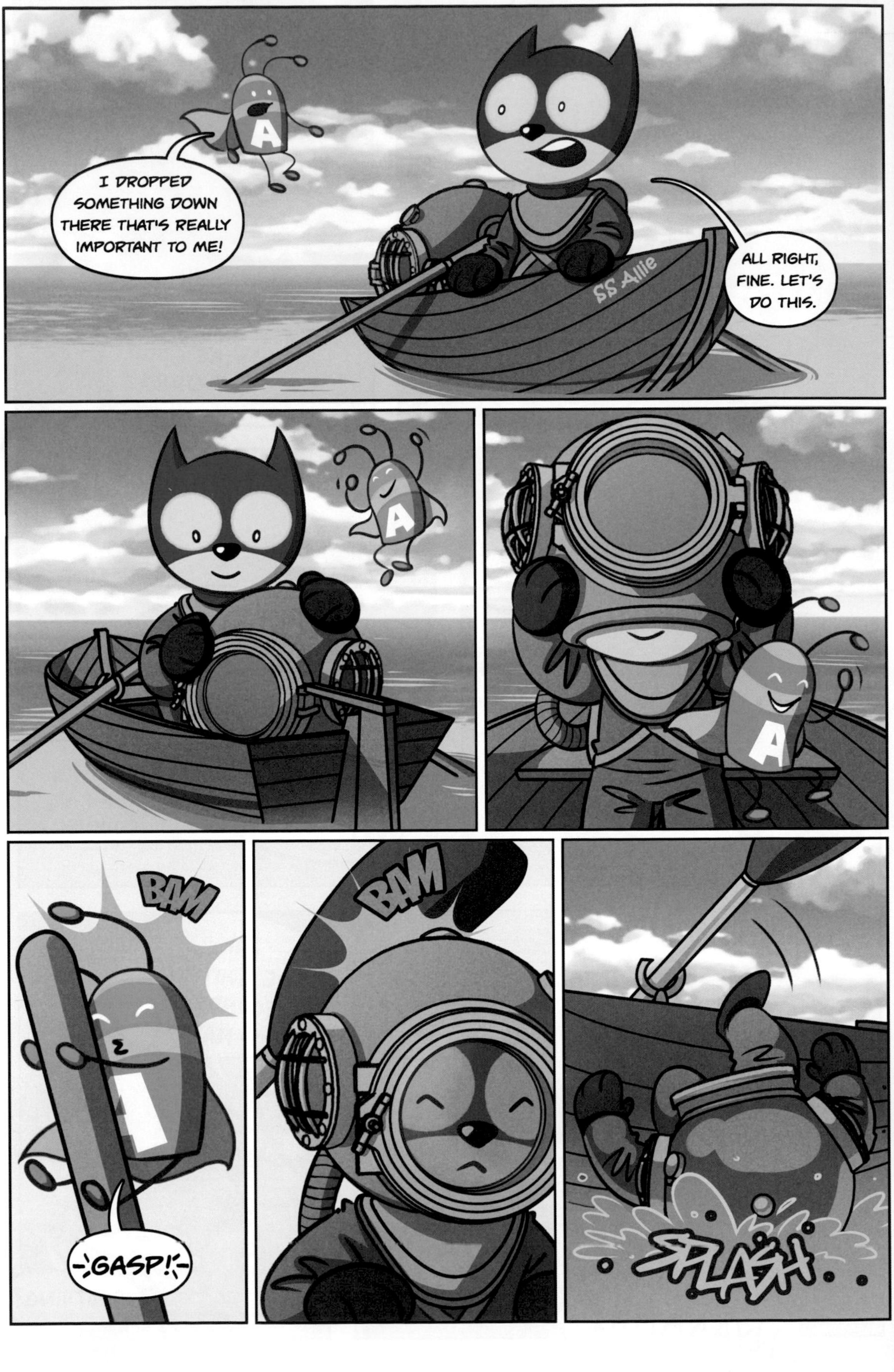
I DROPPED SOMETHING DOWN THERE THAT'S REALLY IMPORTANT TO ME!
SS Allie
ALL RIGHT, FINE. LET'S DO THIS.
BAM
-GASP!-
BAM
SPLASH

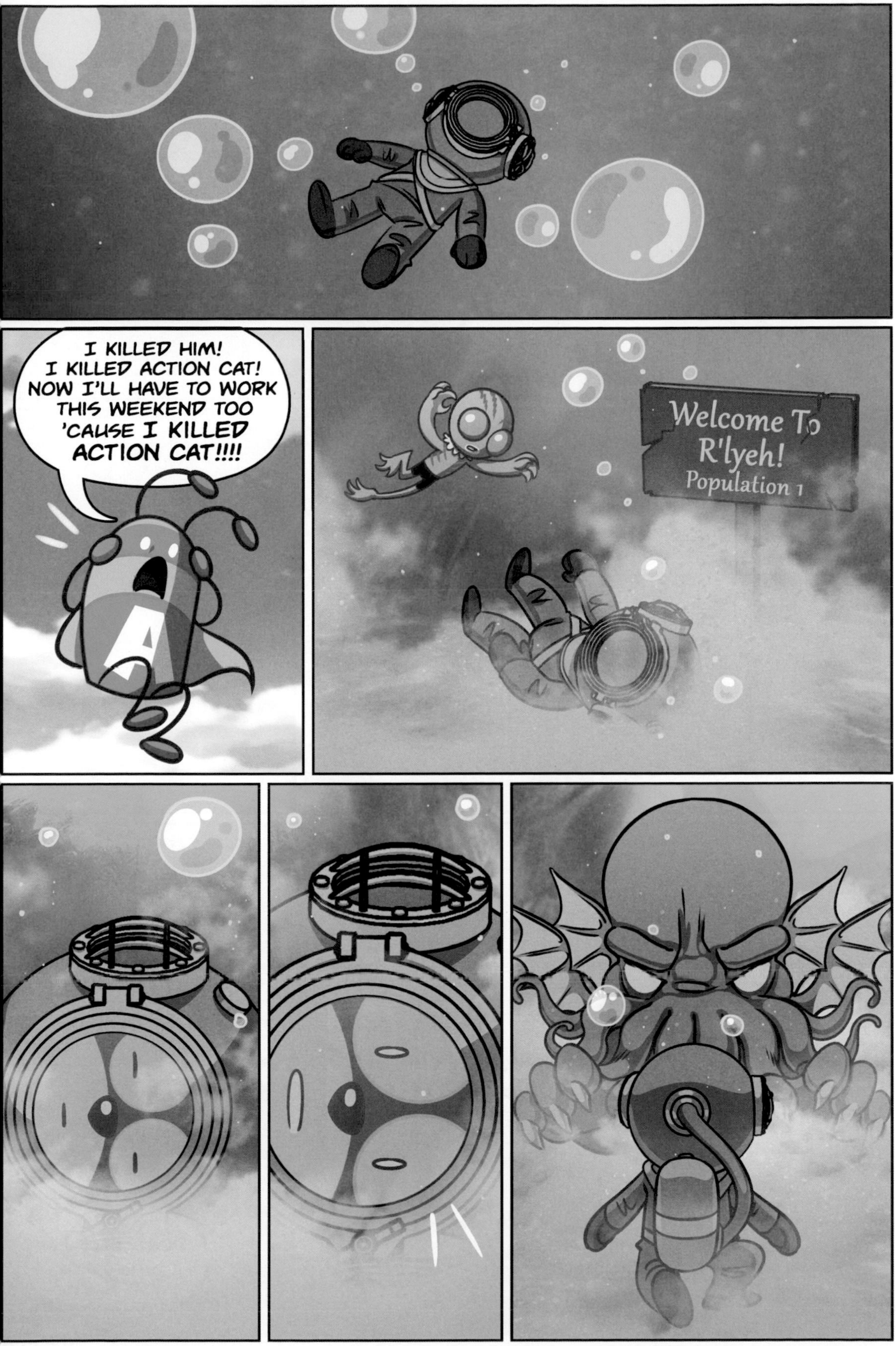
I KILLED HIM! I KILLED ACTION CAT! NOW I'LL HAVE TO WORK THIS WEEKEND TOO 'CAUSE I KILLED ACTION CAT!!!!
Welcome To R'lyeh! Population 1

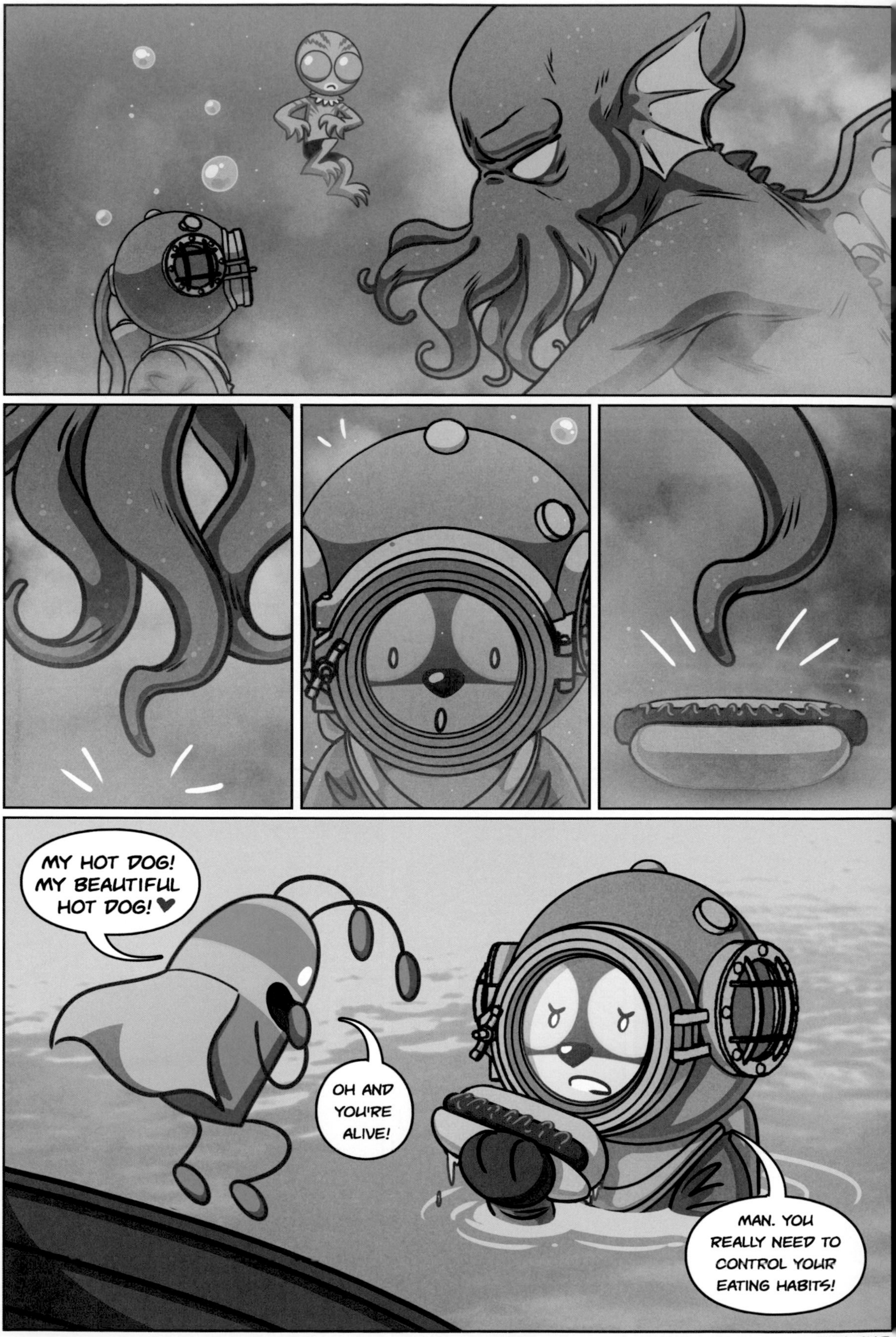
MY HOT DOG! MY BEAUTIFUL HOT DOG! ♥
OH AND YOU'RE ALIVE!
MAN. YOU REALLY NEED TO CONTROL YOUR EATING HABITS!

THE END.

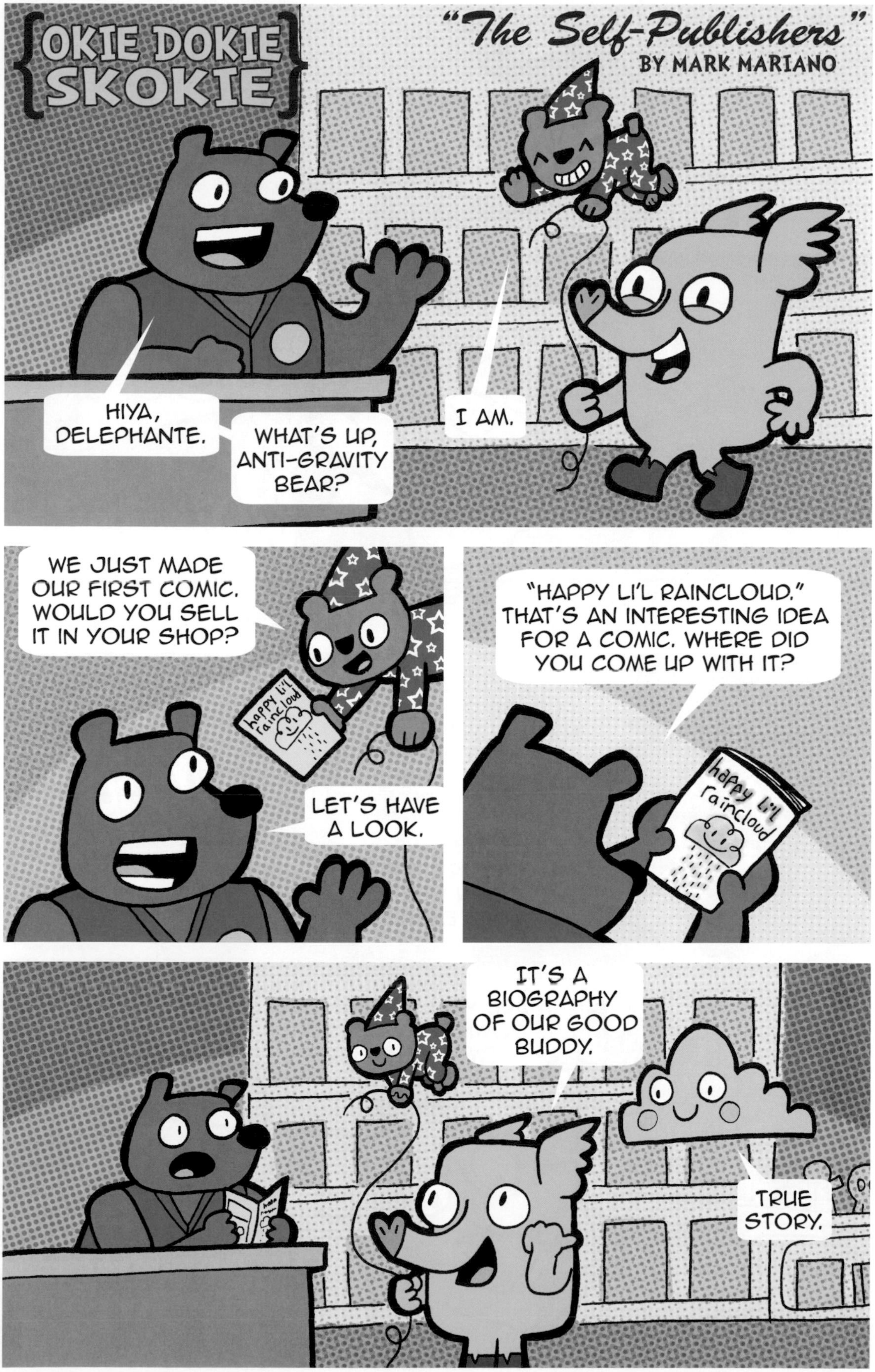
OKIE DOKIE SKOKIE
"The Self-Publishers"
BY MARK MARIANO
HIYA, DELEPHANTE.
WHAT'S UP, ANTI-GRAVITY BEAR?
I AM.
WE JUST MADE OUR FIRST COMIC. WOULD YOU SELL IT IN YOUR SHOP?
happy li'l raincloud
LET'S HAVE A LOOK.
"HAPPY LI'L RAINCLOUD." THAT'S AN INTERESTING IDEA FOR A COMIC. WHERE DID YOU COME UP WITH IT?
happy li'l raincloud
IT'S A BIOGRAPHY OF OUR GOOD BUDDY.
TRUE STORY.

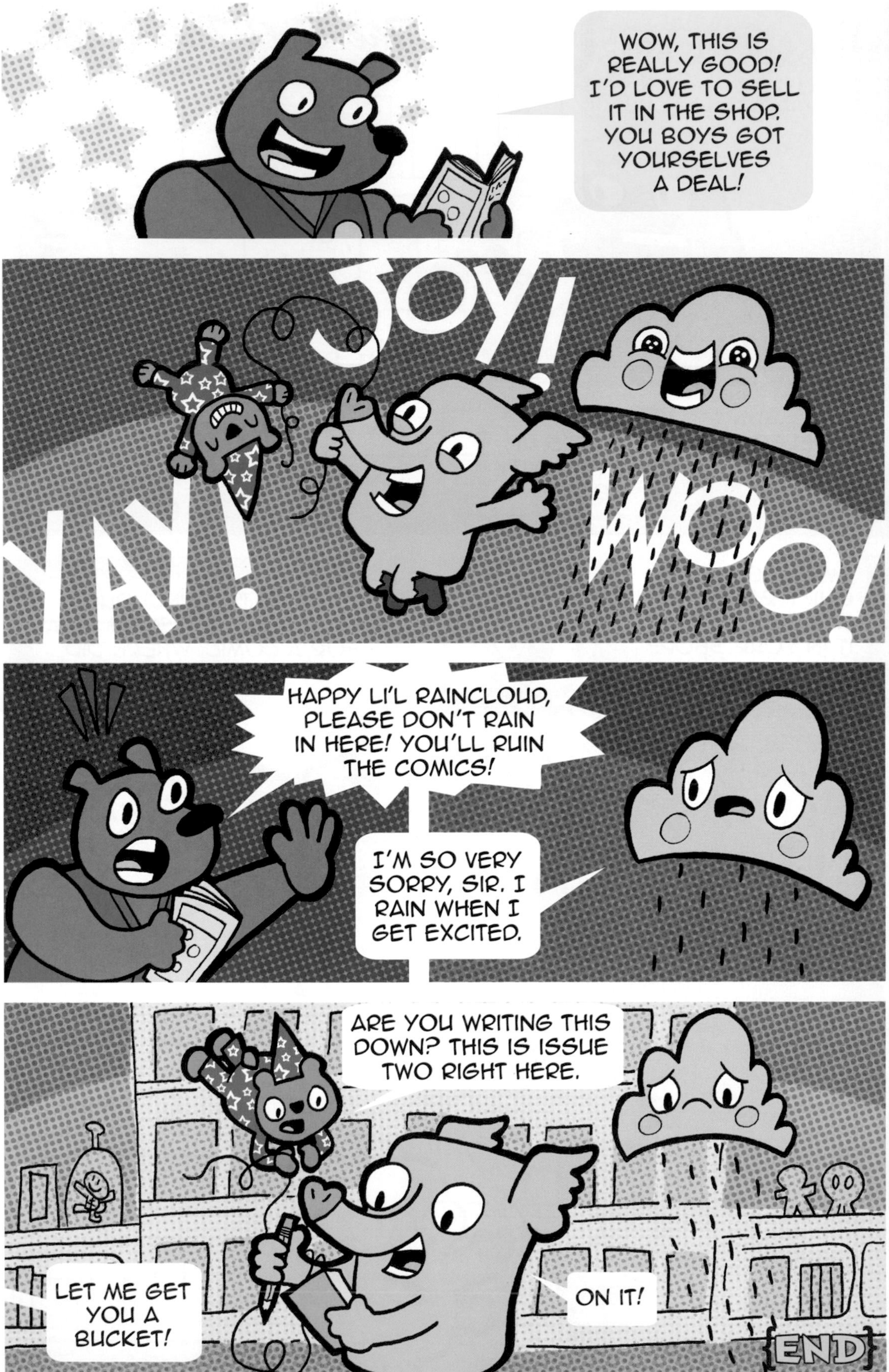
WOW, THIS IS REALLY GOOD! I'D LOVE TO SELL IT IN THE SHOP. YOU BOYS GOT YOURSELVES A DEAL!
JOY!
YAY!
WOO!
HAPPY LI'L RAINCLOUD, PLEASE DON'T RAIN IN HERE! YOU'LL RUIN THE COMICS!
I'M SO VERY SORRY, SIR. I RAIN WHEN I GET EXCITED.
ARE YOU WRITING THIS DOWN? THIS IS ISSUE TWO RIGHT HERE.
LET ME GET YOU A BUCKET!
ON IT!
END

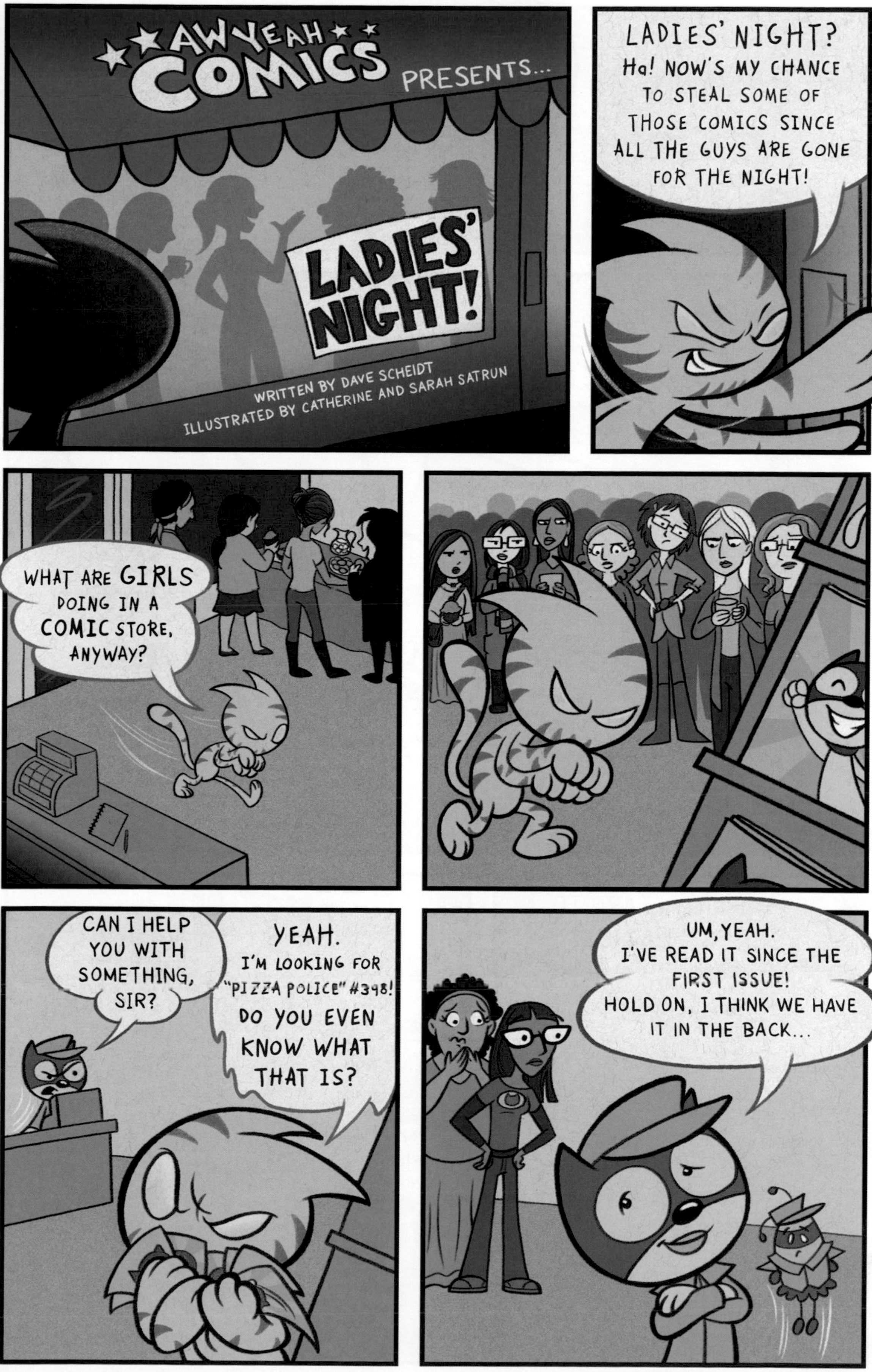
AW YEAH COMICS
PRESENTS...
LADIES' NIGHT!
WRITTEN BY DAVE SCHEIDT
ILLUSTRATED BY CATHERINE AND SARAH SATRUN
LADIES' NIGHT? Ha! NOW'S MY CHANCE TO STEAL SOME OF THOSE COMICS SINCE ALL THE GUYS ARE GONE FOR THE NIGHT!
WHAT ARE GIRLS DOING IN A COMIC STORE, ANYWAY?
CAN I HELP YOU WITH SOMETHING, SIR?
YEAH. I'M LOOKING FOR "PIZZA POLICE" #348! DO YOU EVEN KNOW WHAT THAT IS?
UM, YEAH. I'VE READ IT SINCE THE FIRST ISSUE! HOLD ON, I THINK WE HAVE IT IN THE BACK...

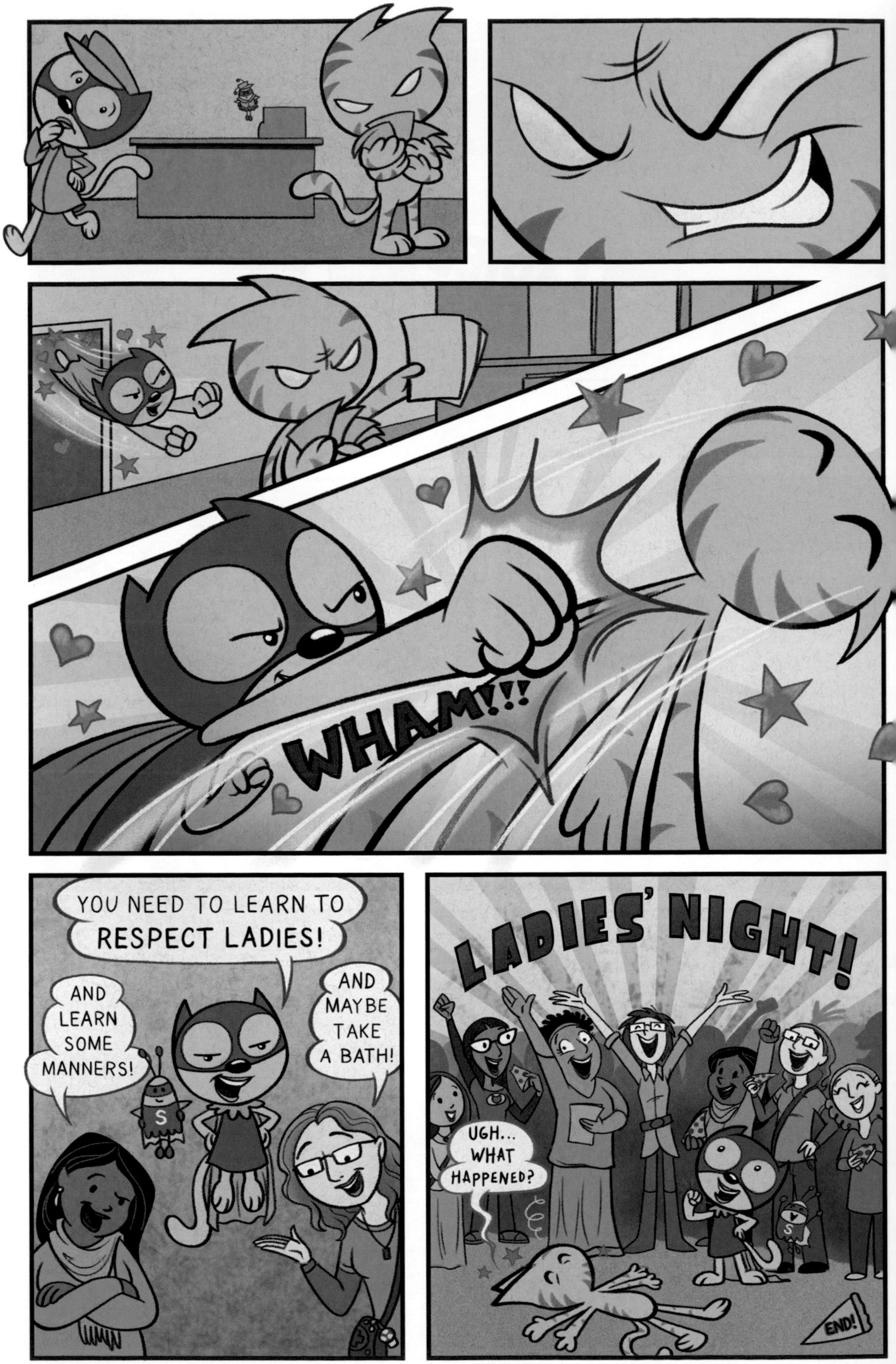
WHAM!!!
YOU NEED TO LEARN TO RESPECT LADIES!
AND LEARN SOME MANNERS!
AND MAYBE TAKE A BATH!
LADIES' NIGHT!
UGH... WHAT HAPPENED?
END!

AW YEAH COMICS! PRESENTS...

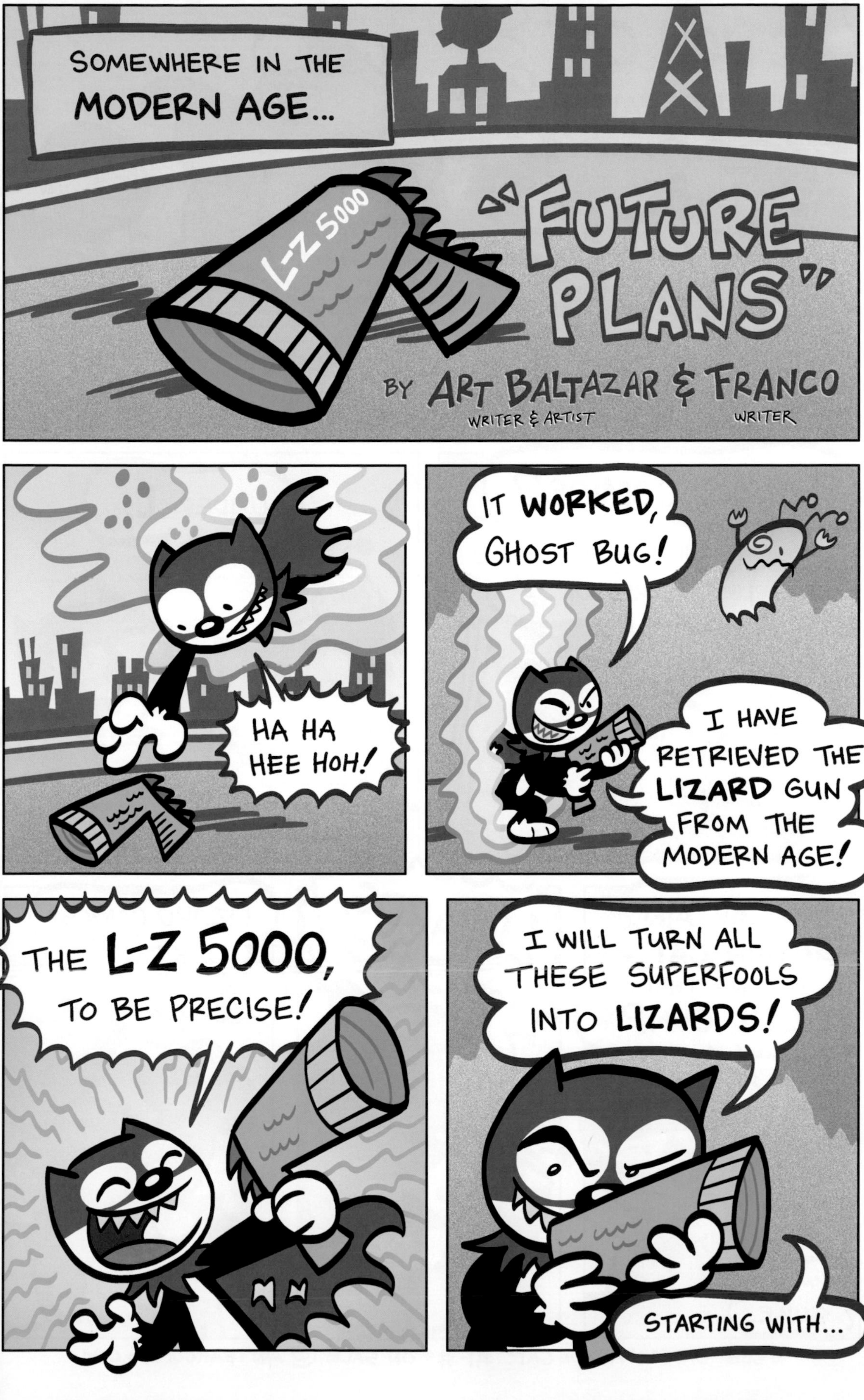
SOMEWHERE IN THE MODERN AGE...
L-Z 5000
"FUTURE PLANS"
BY ART BALTAZAR & FRANCO
WRITER & ARTIST
WRITER
HA HA HEE HOH!
IT **WORKED**, GHOST BUG!
I HAVE RETRIEVED THE **LIZARD** GUN FROM THE MODERN AGE!
THE **L-Z 5000**, TO BE PRECISE!
I WILL TURN ALL THESE SUPERFOOLS INTO **LIZARDS**!
STARTING WITH...

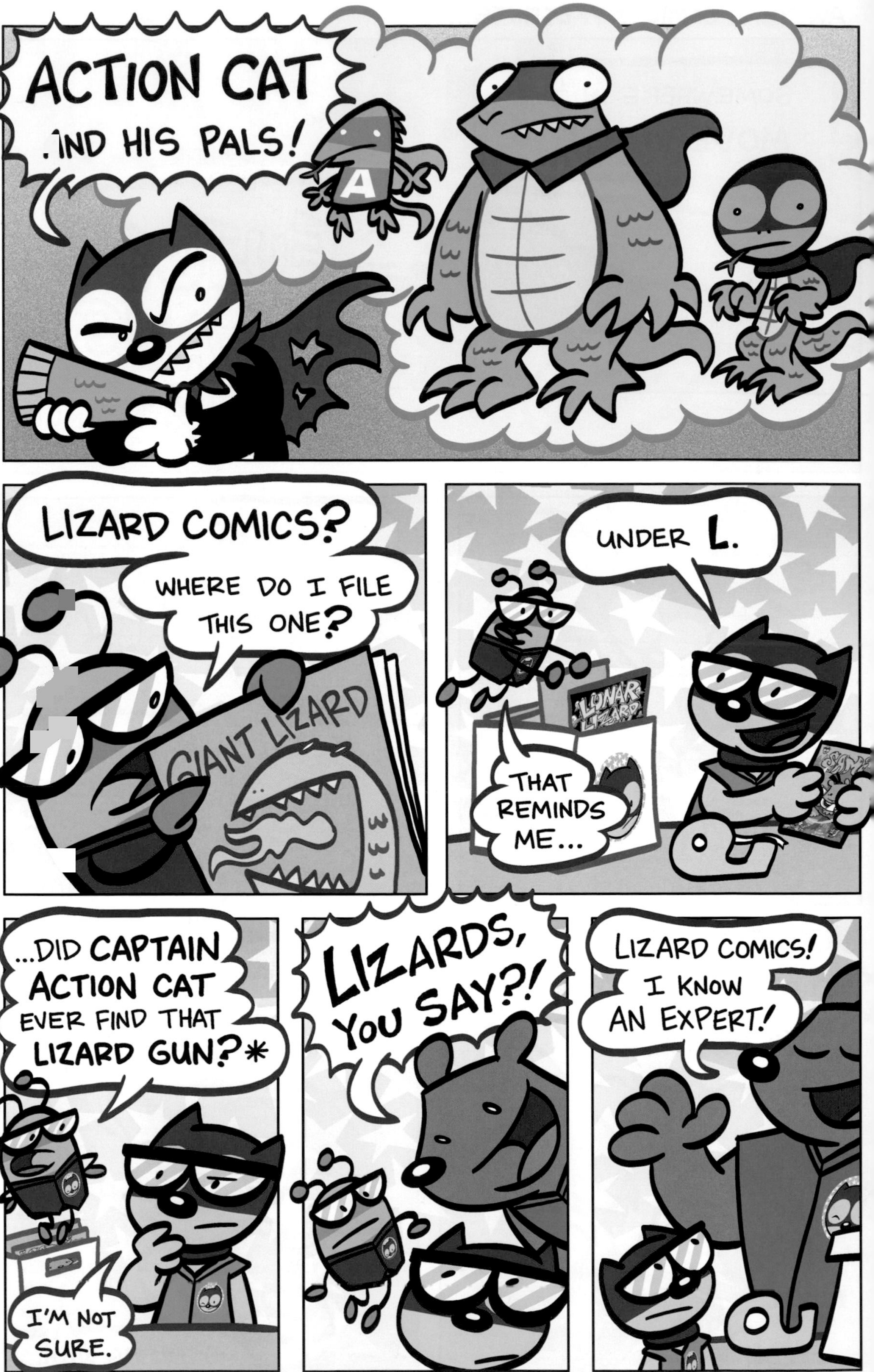
ACTION CAT AND HIS PALS!
LIZARD COMICS?
WHERE DO I FILE THIS ONE?
GIANT LIZARD
UNDER L.
LUNAR LIZARD
THAT REMINDS ME...
...DID CAPTAIN ACTION CAT EVER FIND THAT LIZARD GUN?*
I'M NOT SURE.
LIZARDS, YOU SAY?!
LIZARD COMICS! I KNOW AN EXPERT!

* SEE "CAPTAIN ACTION CAT" #1-#4 ON SALE @ AWYEAHCOMICS.COM.

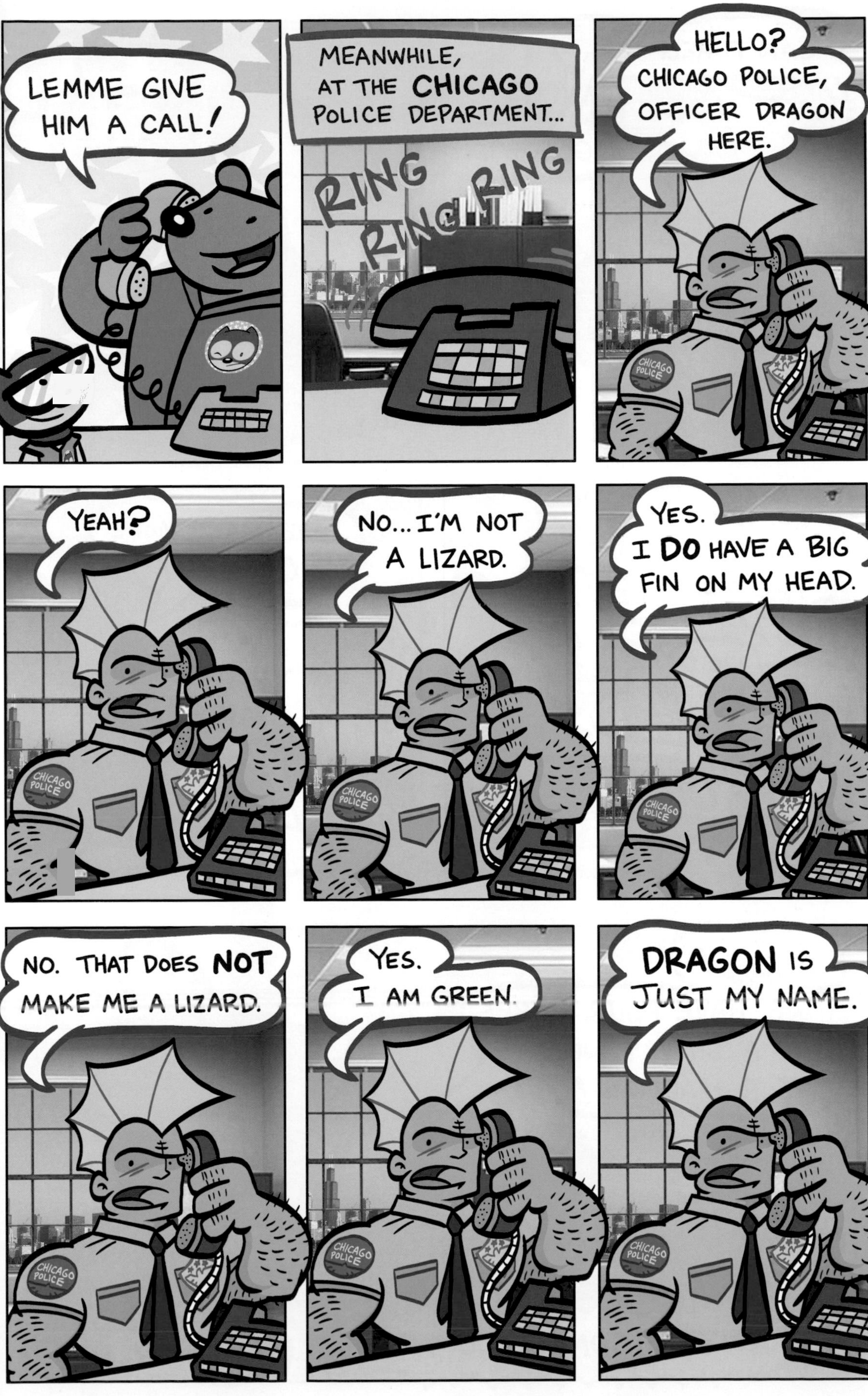
LEMME GIVE HIM A CALL!
MEANWHILE, AT THE CHICAGO POLICE DEPARTMENT...
RING RING RING
HELLO? CHICAGO POLICE, OFFICER DRAGON HERE.
CHICAGO POLICE
YEAH?
NO... I'M NOT A LIZARD.
YES. I DO HAVE A BIG FIN ON MY HEAD.
NO. THAT DOES NOT MAKE ME A LIZARD.
YES. I AM GREEN.
DRAGON IS JUST MY NAME.

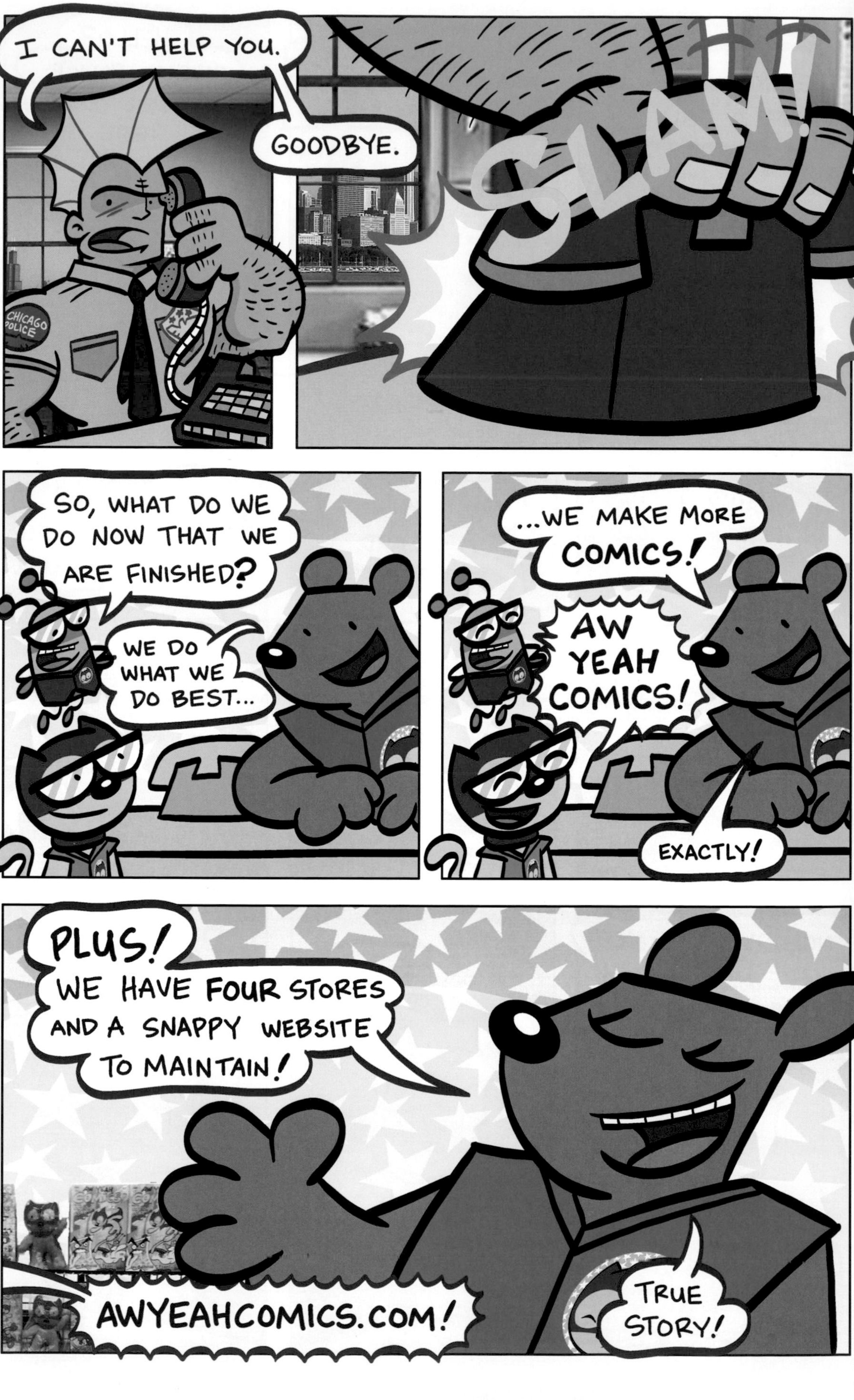
I CAN'T HELP YOU.
GOODBYE.
CHICAGO POLICE
SLAM!
SO, WHAT DO WE DO NOW THAT WE ARE FINISHED?
WE DO WHAT WE DO BEST...
...WE MAKE MORE COMICS!
AW YEAH COMICS!
EXACTLY!
PLUS! WE HAVE FOUR STORES AND A SNAPPY WEBSITE TO MAINTAIN!
AWYEAHCOMICS.COM!
TRUE STORY!

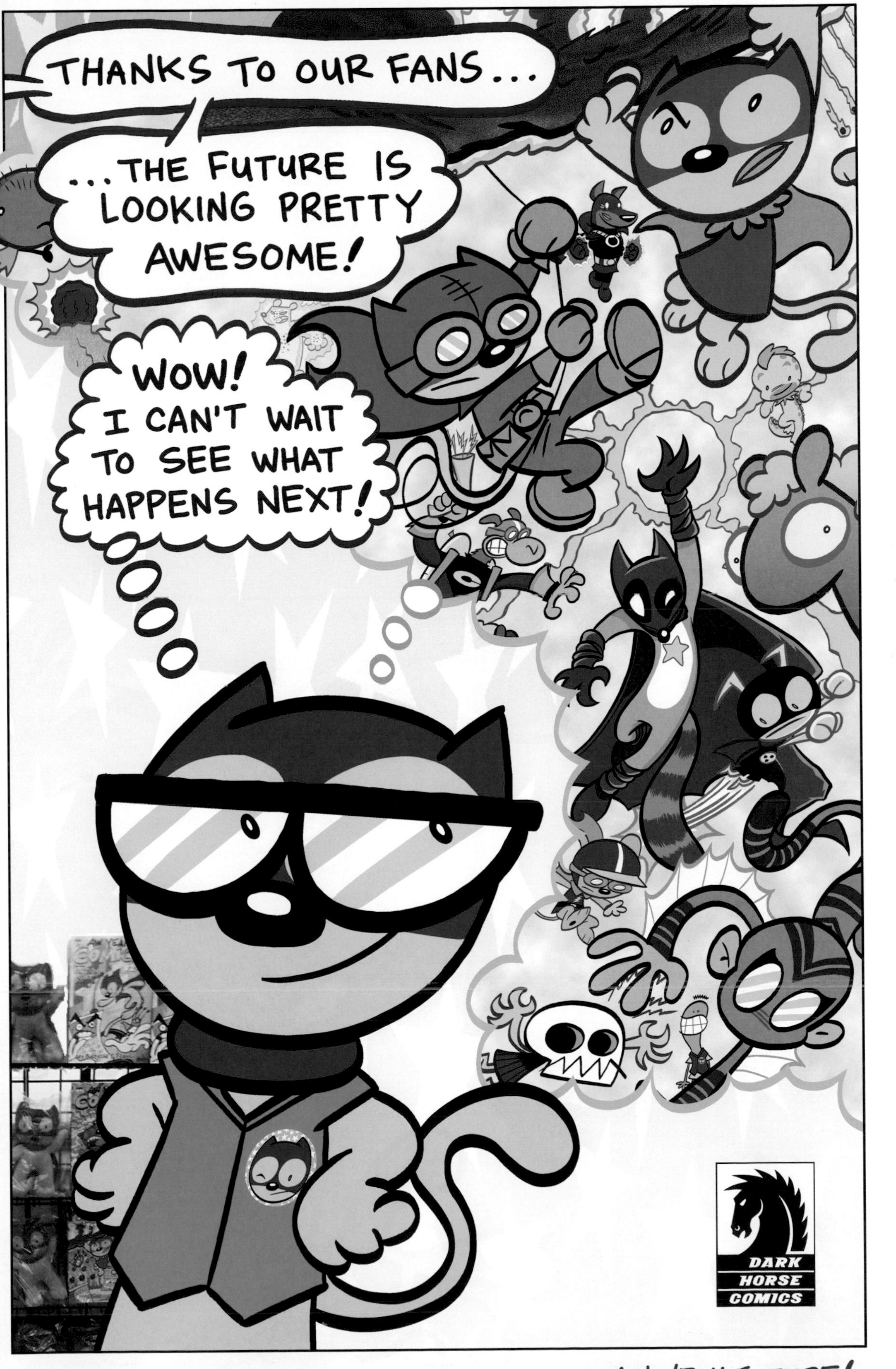
THANKS TO OUR FANS...
...THE FUTURE IS LOOKING PRETTY AWESOME!
WOW! I CAN'T WAIT TO SEE WHAT HAPPENS NEXT!
DARK HORSE COMICS

-AW YEAH FUTURE!

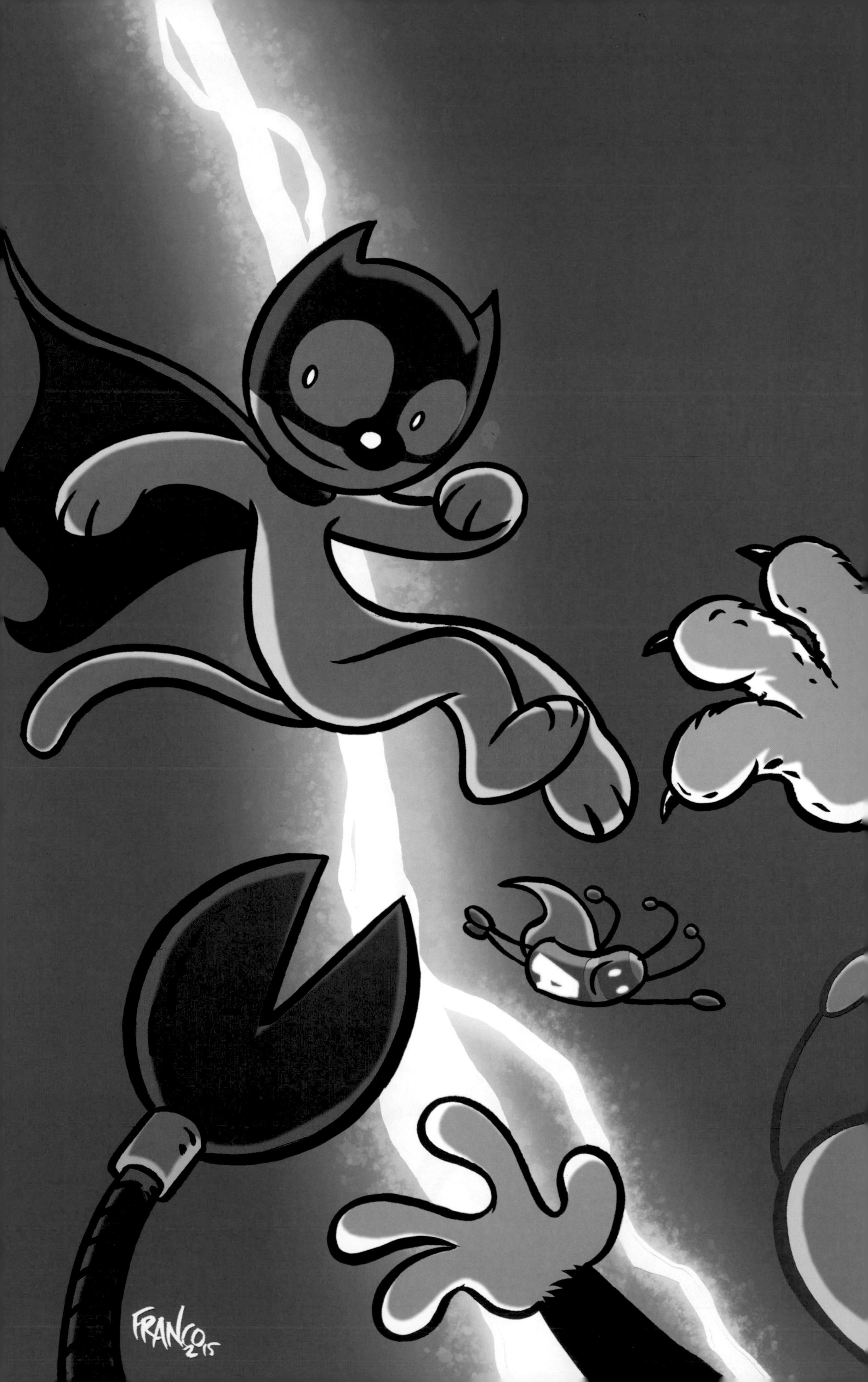

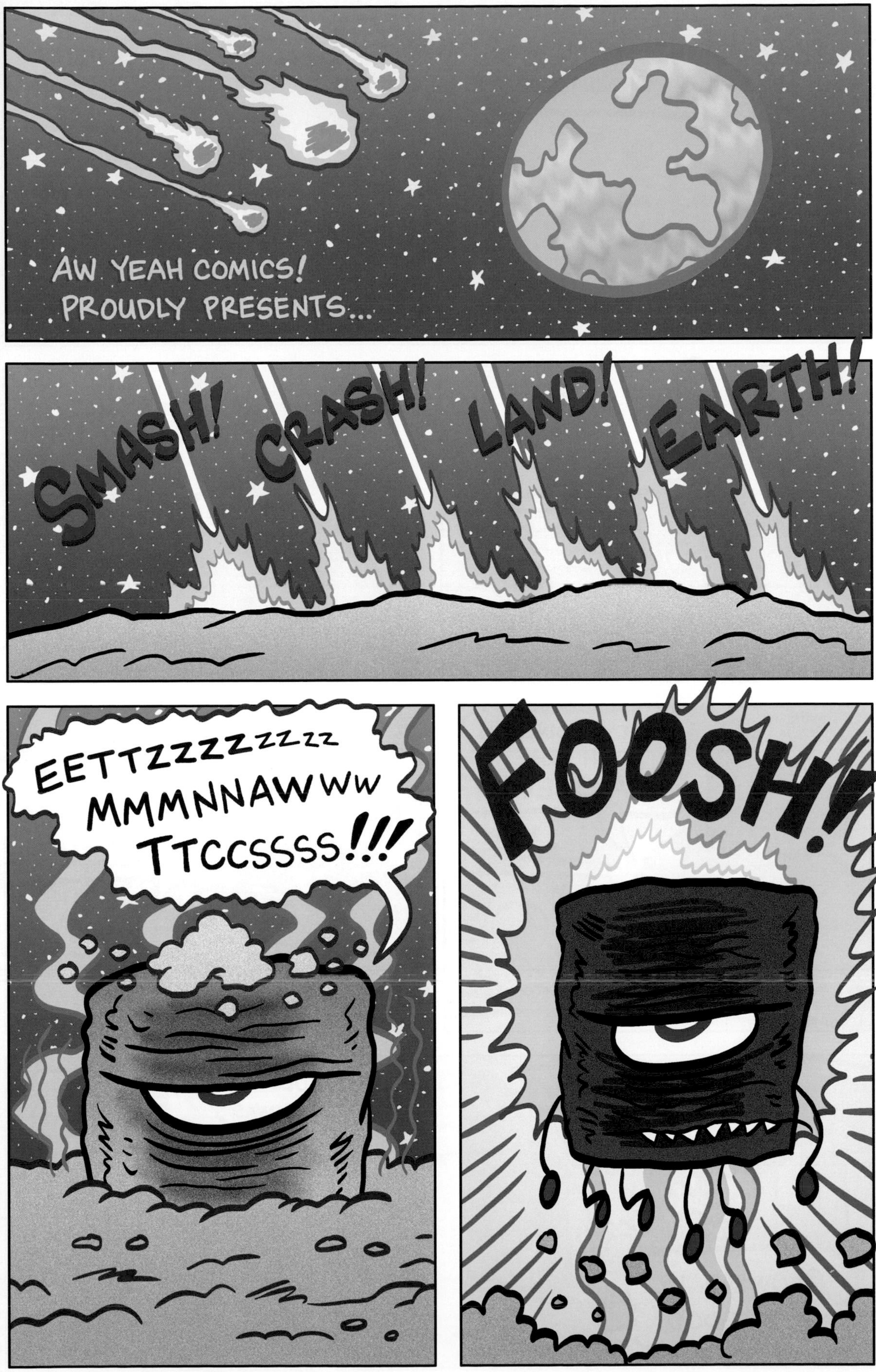
AW YEAH COMICS! PROUDLY PRESENTS...
SMASH! CRASH! LAND! EARTH!
EETTZZZZZZZZ MMMNNAWWW TTCCSSSS!!!
FOOSH!

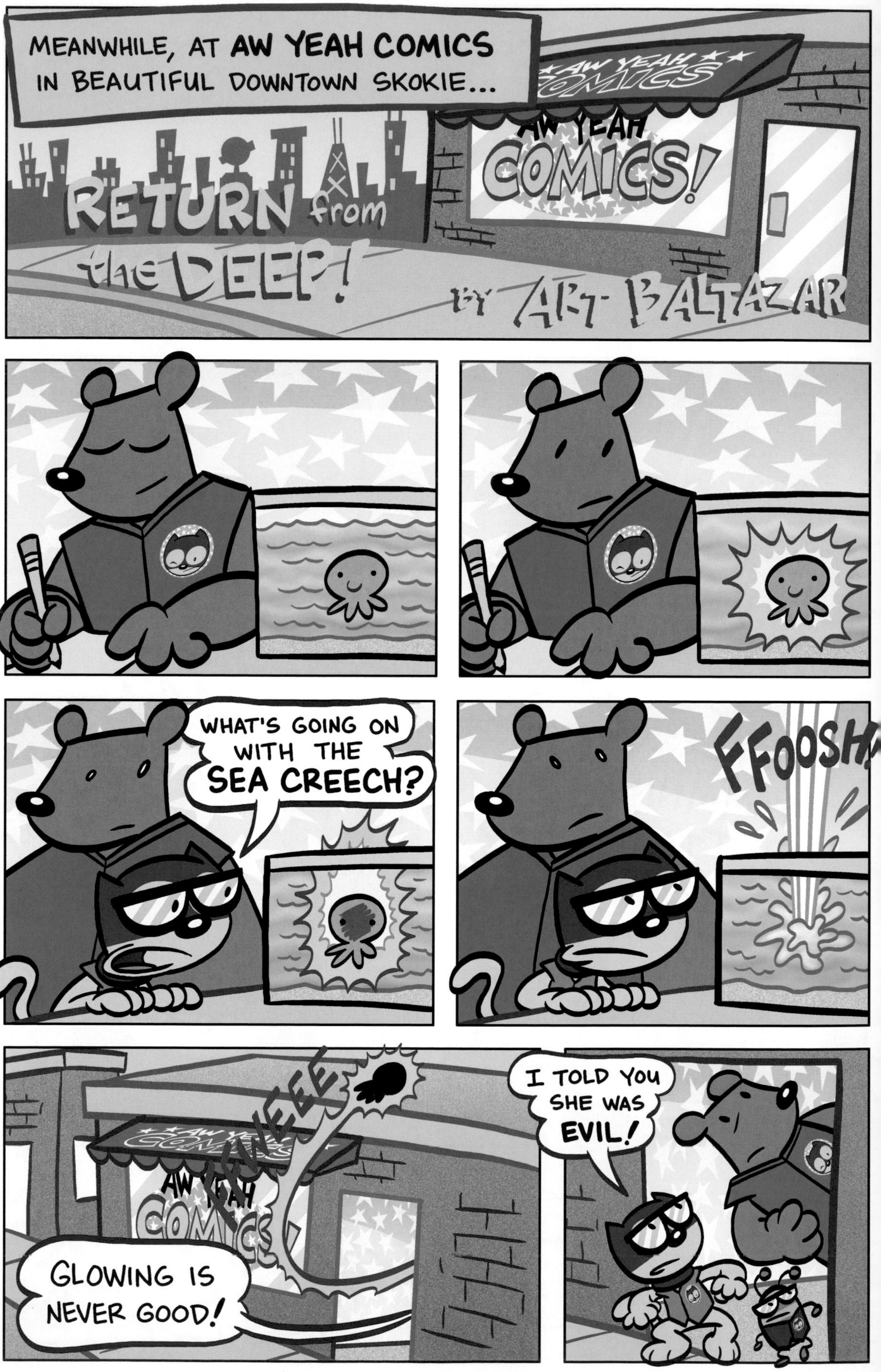
MEANWHILE, AT AW YEAH COMICS IN BEAUTIFUL DOWNTOWN SKOKIE...
AW YEAH COMICS
AW YEAH COMICS!
RETURN from the DEEP!
BY ART BALTAZAR
WHAT'S GOING ON WITH THE SEA CREECH?
FFOOSH!
AW YEAH COMICS
GLOWING IS NEVER GOOD!
I TOLD YOU SHE WAS EVIL!

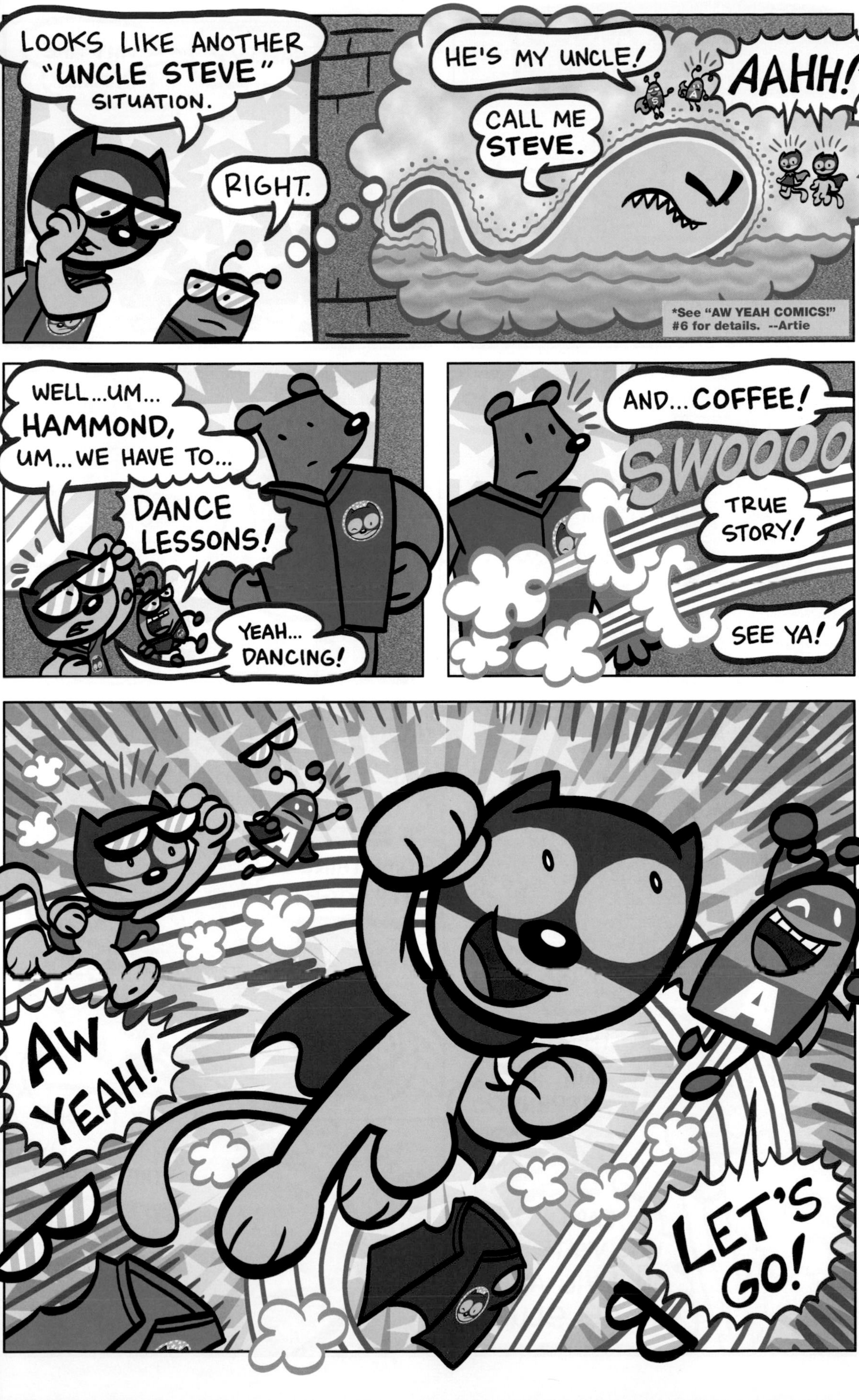
LOOKS LIKE ANOTHER "UNCLE STEVE" SITUATION.
RIGHT.
HE'S MY UNCLE!
CALL ME STEVE.
AAHH!*
*See "AW YEAH COMICS!" #6 for details. --Artie
WELL...UM... HAMMOND, UM...WE HAVE TO...
DANCE LESSONS!
YEAH... DANCING!
AND...COFFEE!
SWOOOO
TRUE STORY!
SEE YA!
AW YEAH!
LET'S GO!

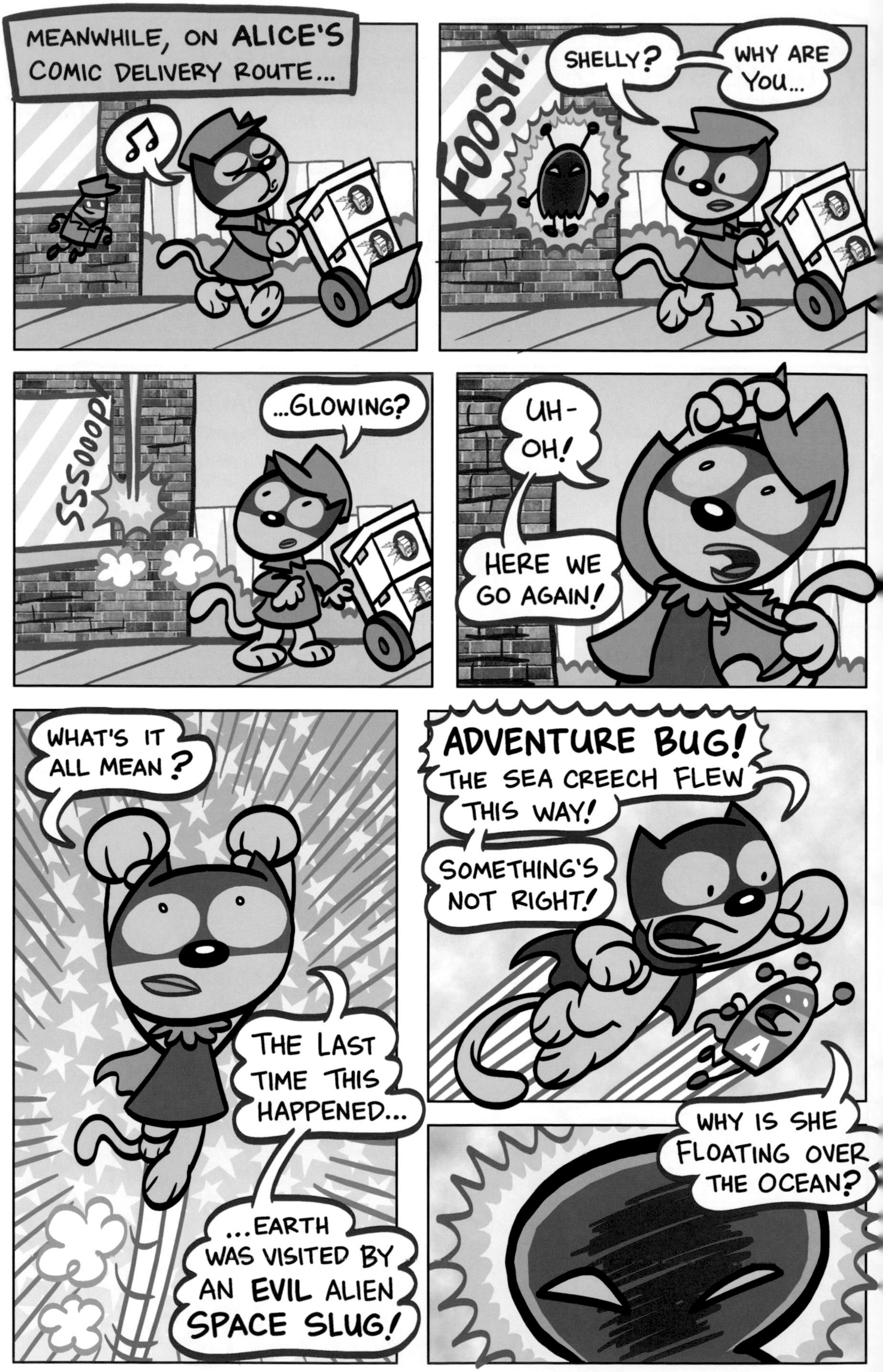
MEANWHILE, ON ALICE'S COMIC DELIVERY ROUTE...
FOOSH!
SHELLY?
WHY ARE YOU...
SSSOOOP!
...GLOWING?
UH-OH!
HERE WE GO AGAIN!
WHAT'S IT ALL MEAN?
THE LAST TIME THIS HAPPENED...
...EARTH WAS VISITED BY AN EVIL ALIEN SPACE SLUG!
ADVENTURE BUG! THE SEA CREECH FLEW THIS WAY!
SOMETHING'S NOT RIGHT!
WHY IS SHE FLOATING OVER THE OCEAN?

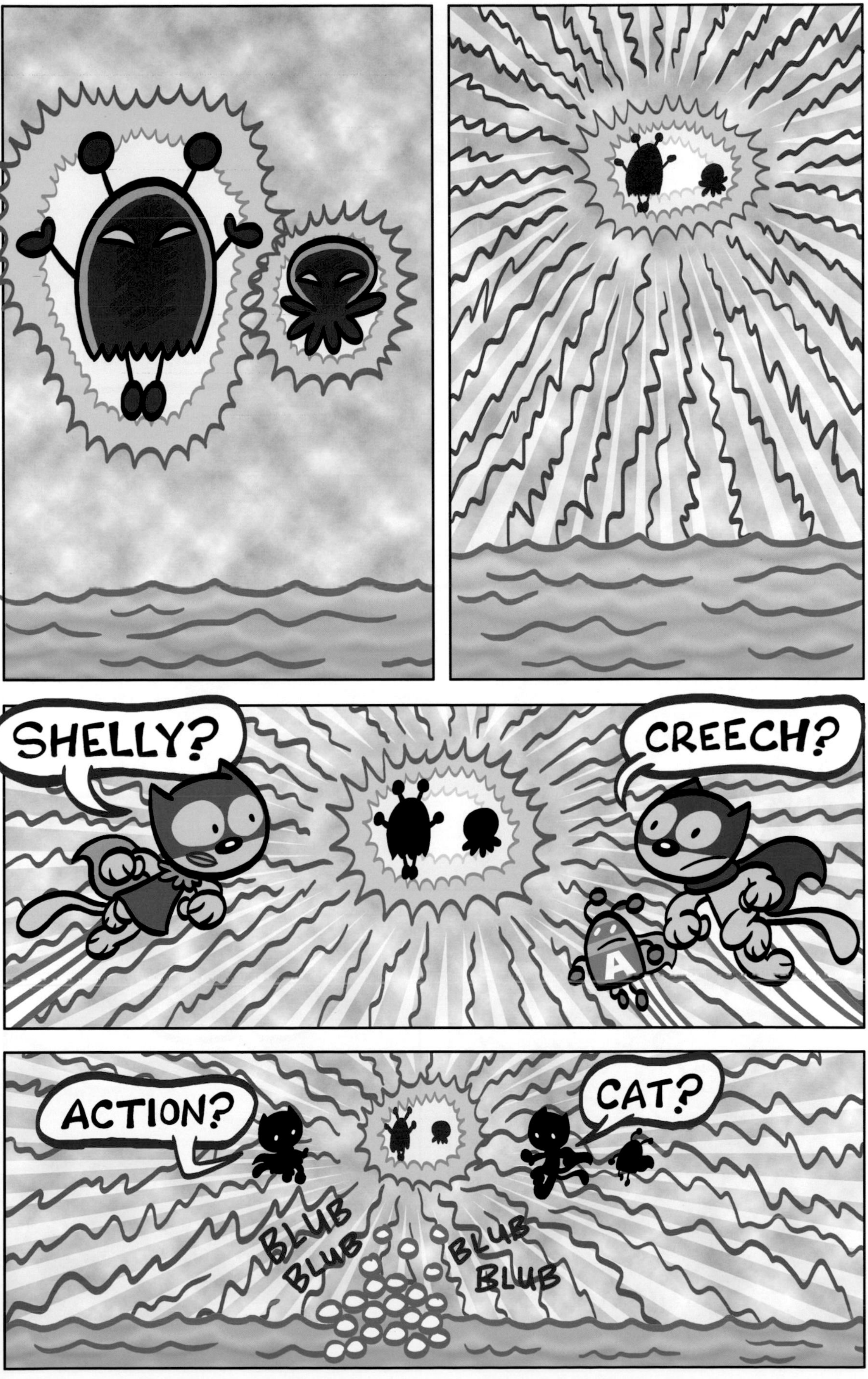
SHELLY?
CREECH?
ACTION?
CAT?
BLUB BLUB
BLUB BLUB

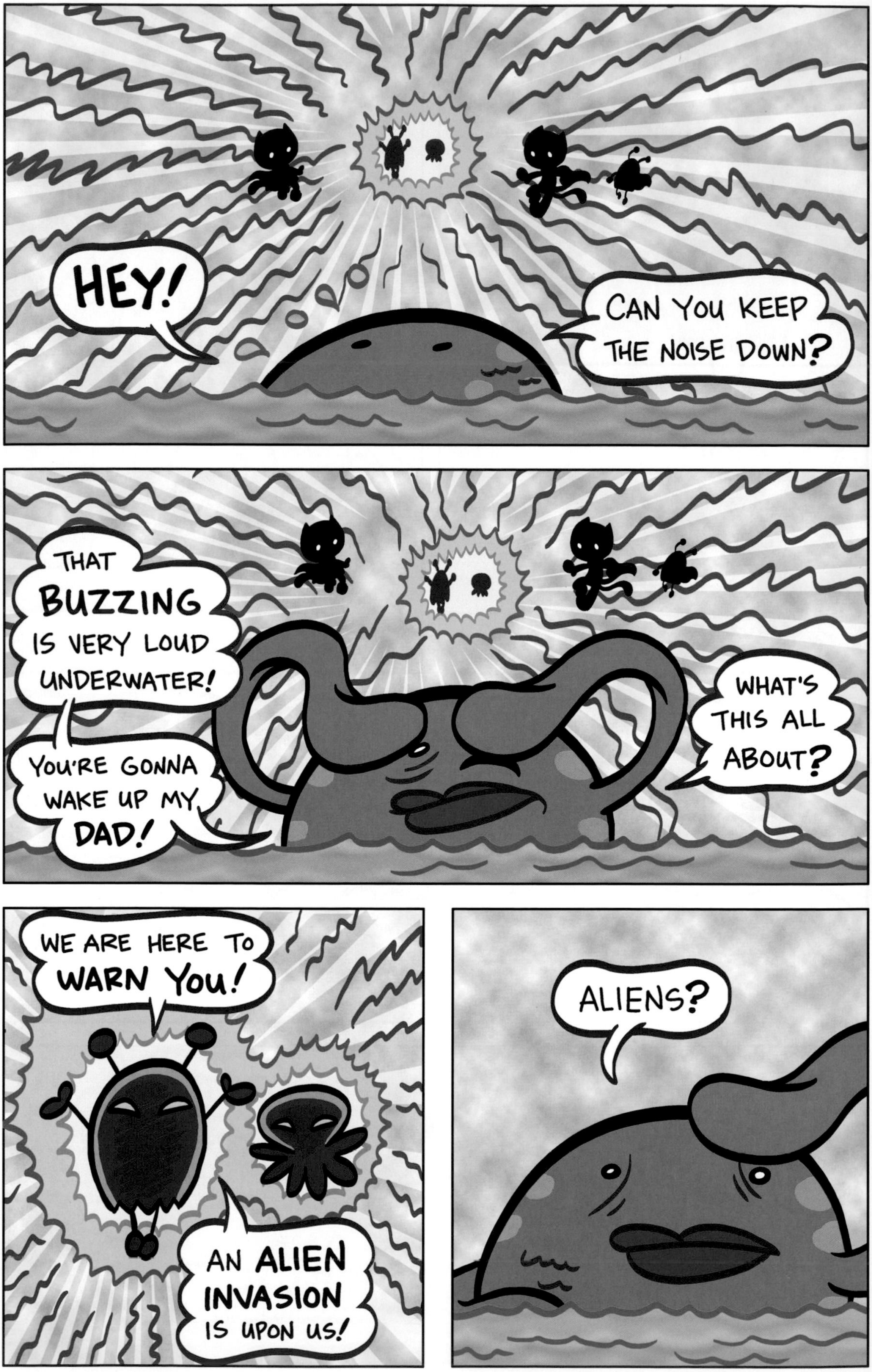
HEY!
CAN YOU KEEP THE NOISE DOWN?
THAT BUZZING IS VERY LOUD UNDERWATER!
YOU'RE GONNA WAKE UP MY DAD!
WHAT'S THIS ALL ABOUT?
WE ARE HERE TO WARN YOU!
AN ALIEN INVASION IS UPON US!
ALIENS?

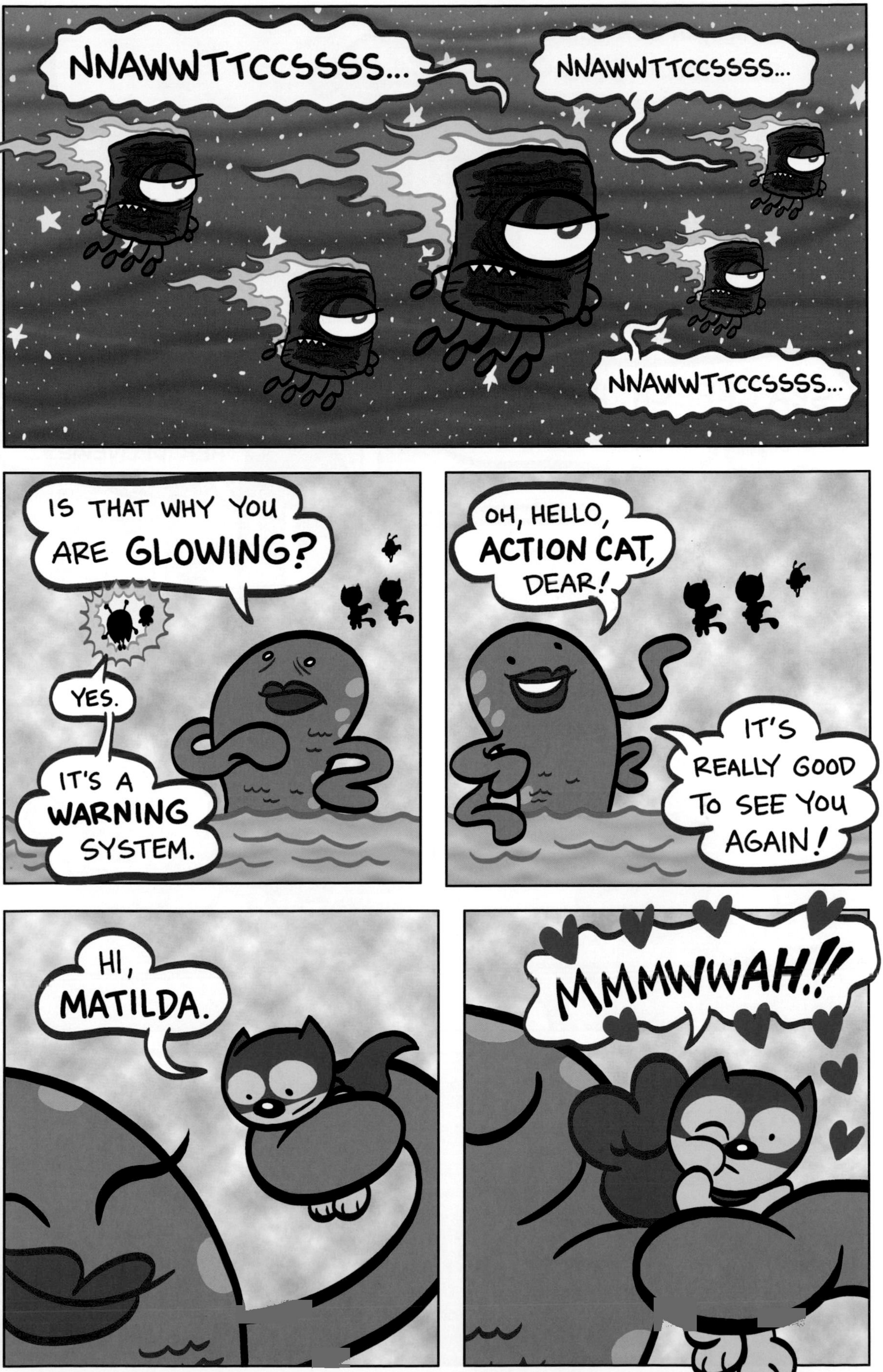
NNAWWTTCCSSSS...
NNAWWTTCCSSSS...
NNAWWTTCCSSSS...
IS THAT WHY YOU ARE GLOWING?
YES.
IT'S A WARNING SYSTEM.
OH, HELLO, ACTION CAT, DEAR!
IT'S REALLY GOOD TO SEE YOU AGAIN!
HI, MATILDA.
MMMWWAH!!

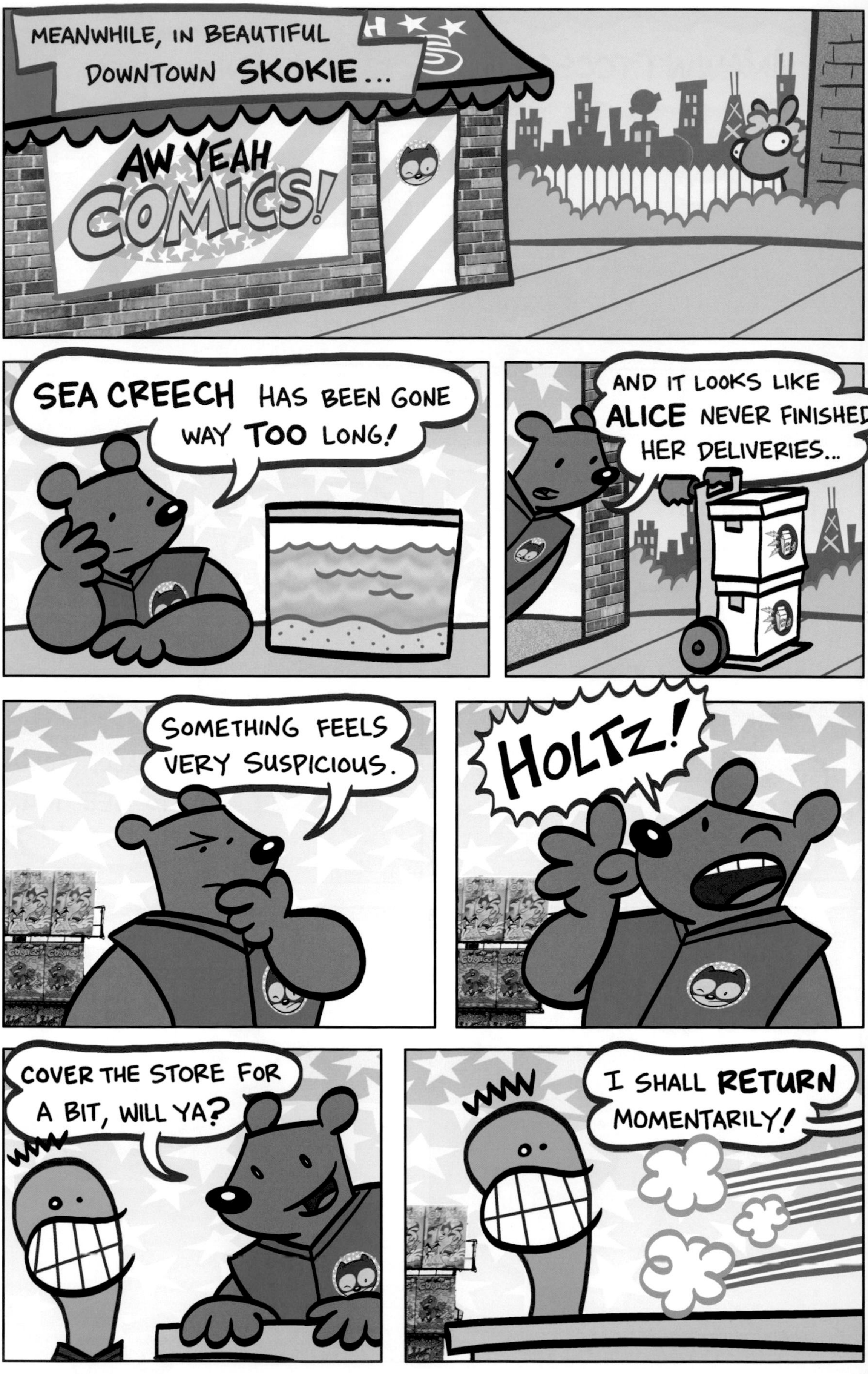
MEANWHILE, IN BEAUTIFUL DOWNTOWN SKOKIE...
AW YEAH COMICS!
SEA CREECH HAS BEEN GONE WAY TOO LONG!
AND IT LOOKS LIKE ALICE NEVER FINISHED HER DELIVERIES...
SOMETHING FEELS VERY SUSPICIOUS.
HOLTZ!
COVER THE STORE FOR A BIT, WILL YA?
I SHALL RETURN MOMENTARILY!

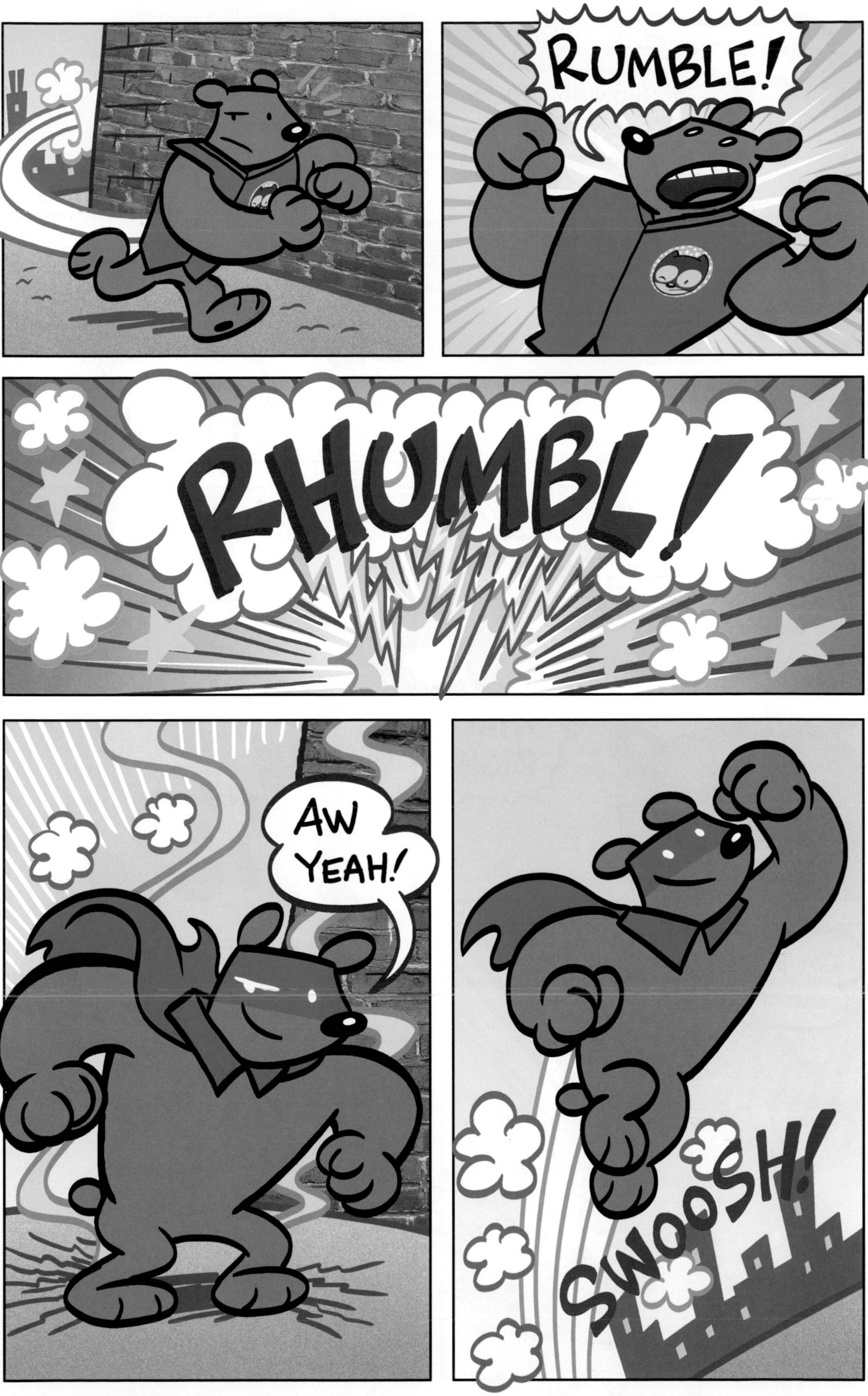
RUMBLE!
RHUMBL!
AW YEAH!
SWOOSH!

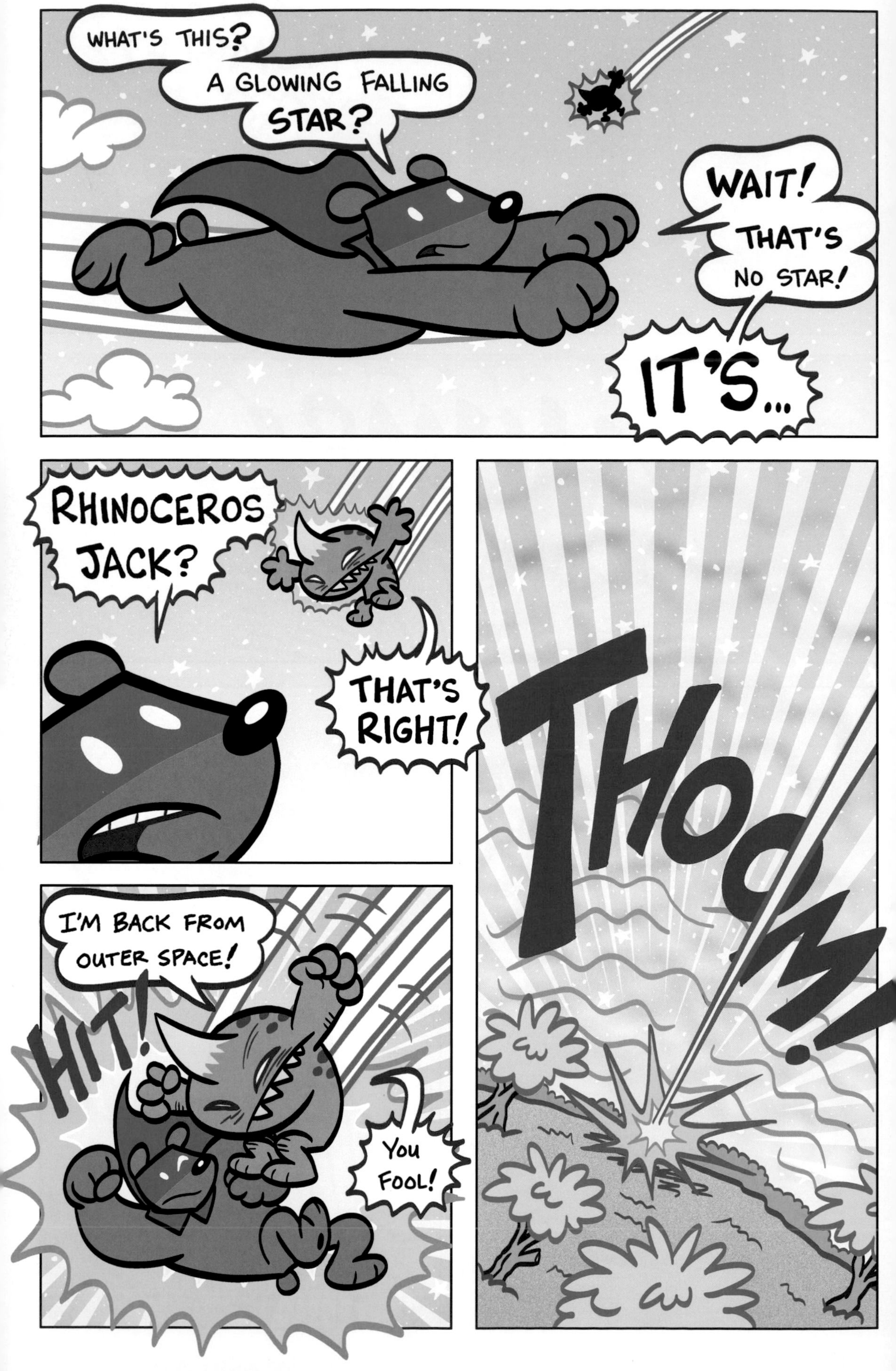

WHAT'S THIS?
A GLOWING FALLING STAR?
WAIT! THAT'S NO STAR!
IT'S...
RHINOCEROS JACK?
THAT'S RIGHT!
I'M BACK FROM OUTER SPACE!
HIT!
YOU FOOL!
THOOM!!

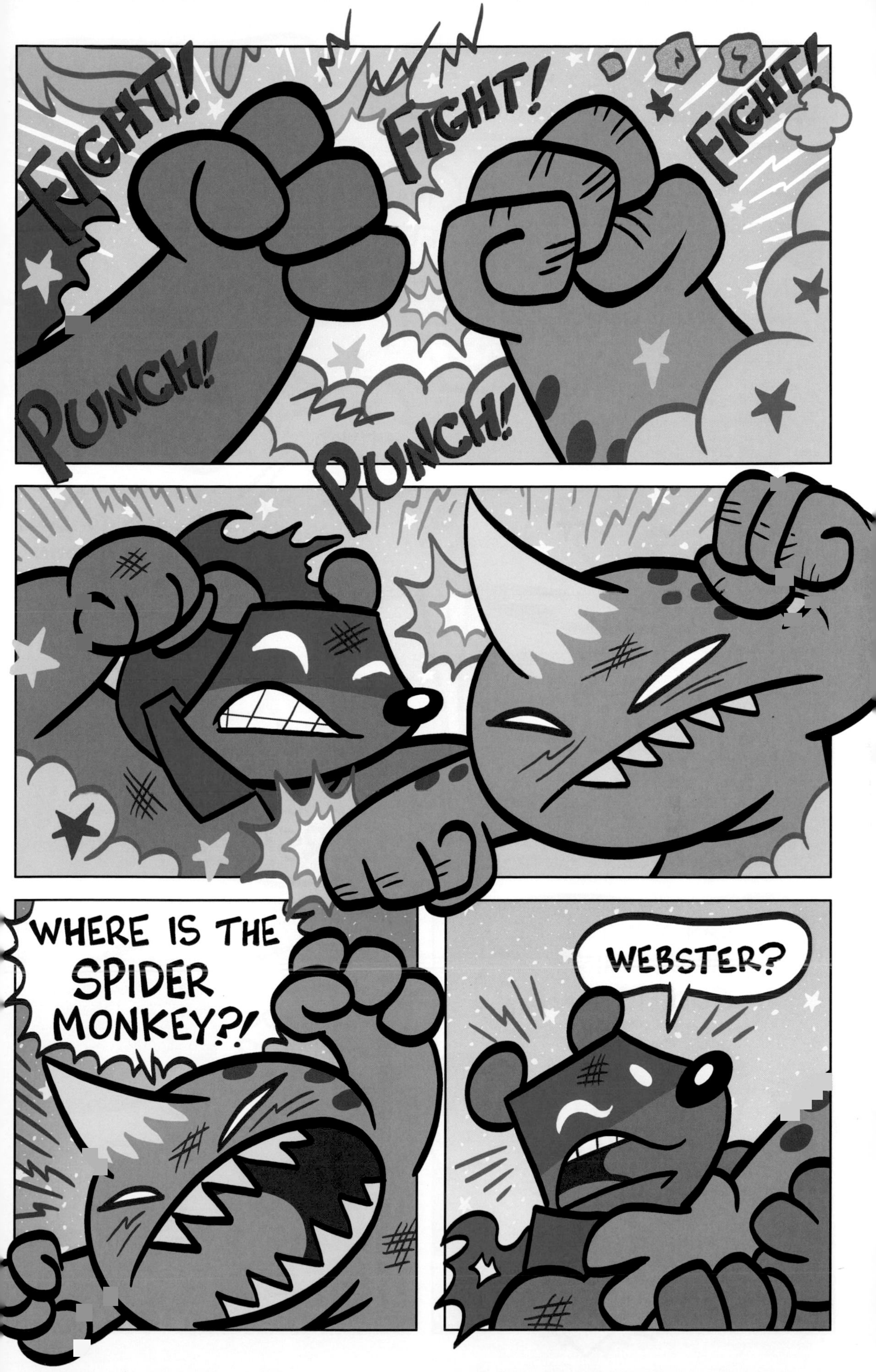
FIGHT!
FIGHT!
FIGHT!
PUNCH!
PUNCH!
WHERE IS THE SPIDER MONKEY?!
WEBSTER?

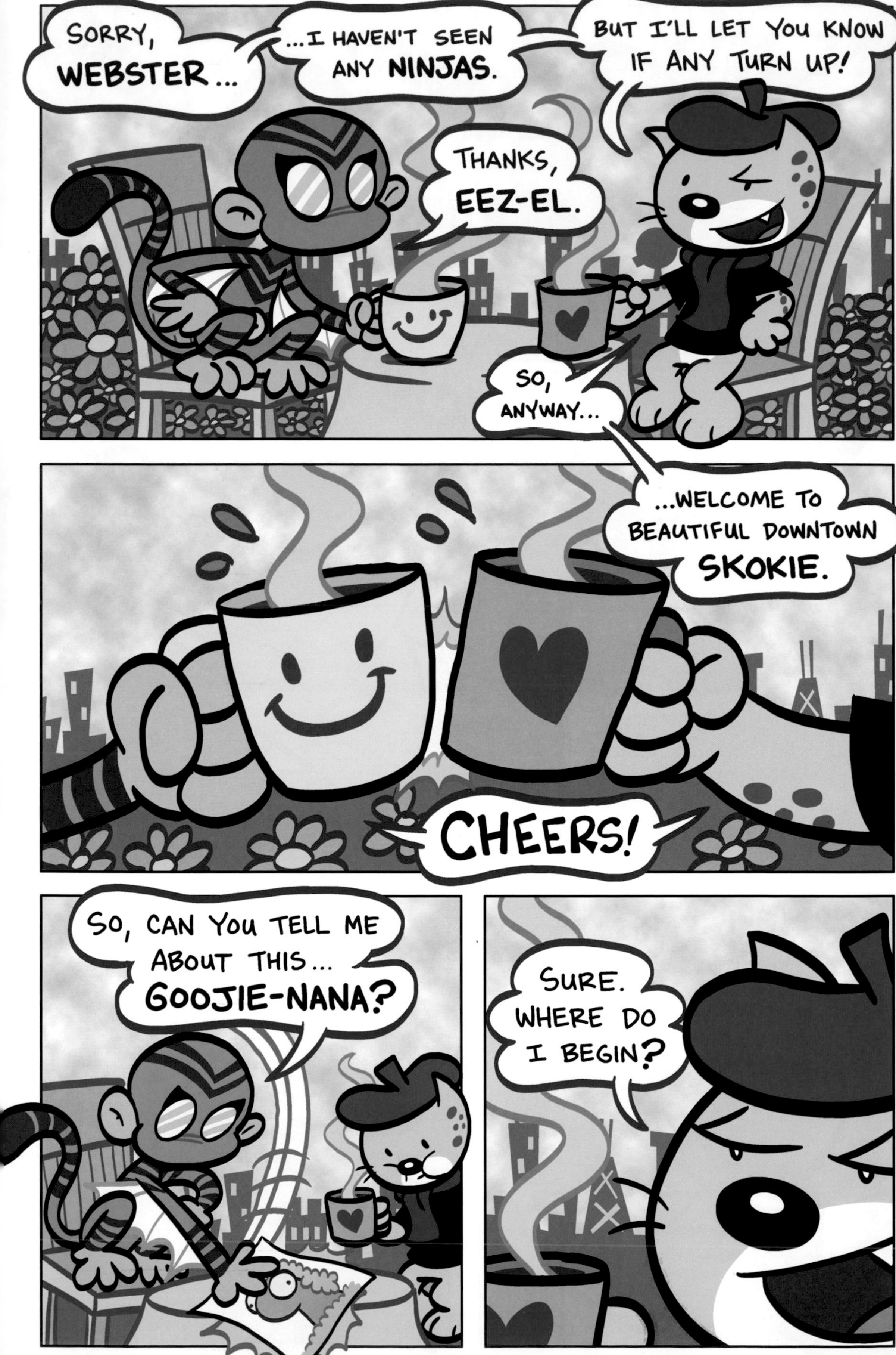
SORRY, WEBSTER...
...I HAVEN'T SEEN ANY NINJAS.
BUT I'LL LET YOU KNOW IF ANY TURN UP!
THANKS, EEZ-EL.
SO, ANYWAY...
...WELCOME TO BEAUTIFUL DOWNTOWN SKOKIE.
CHEERS!
SO, CAN YOU TELL ME ABOUT THIS... GOOJIE-NANA?
SURE. WHERE DO I BEGIN?

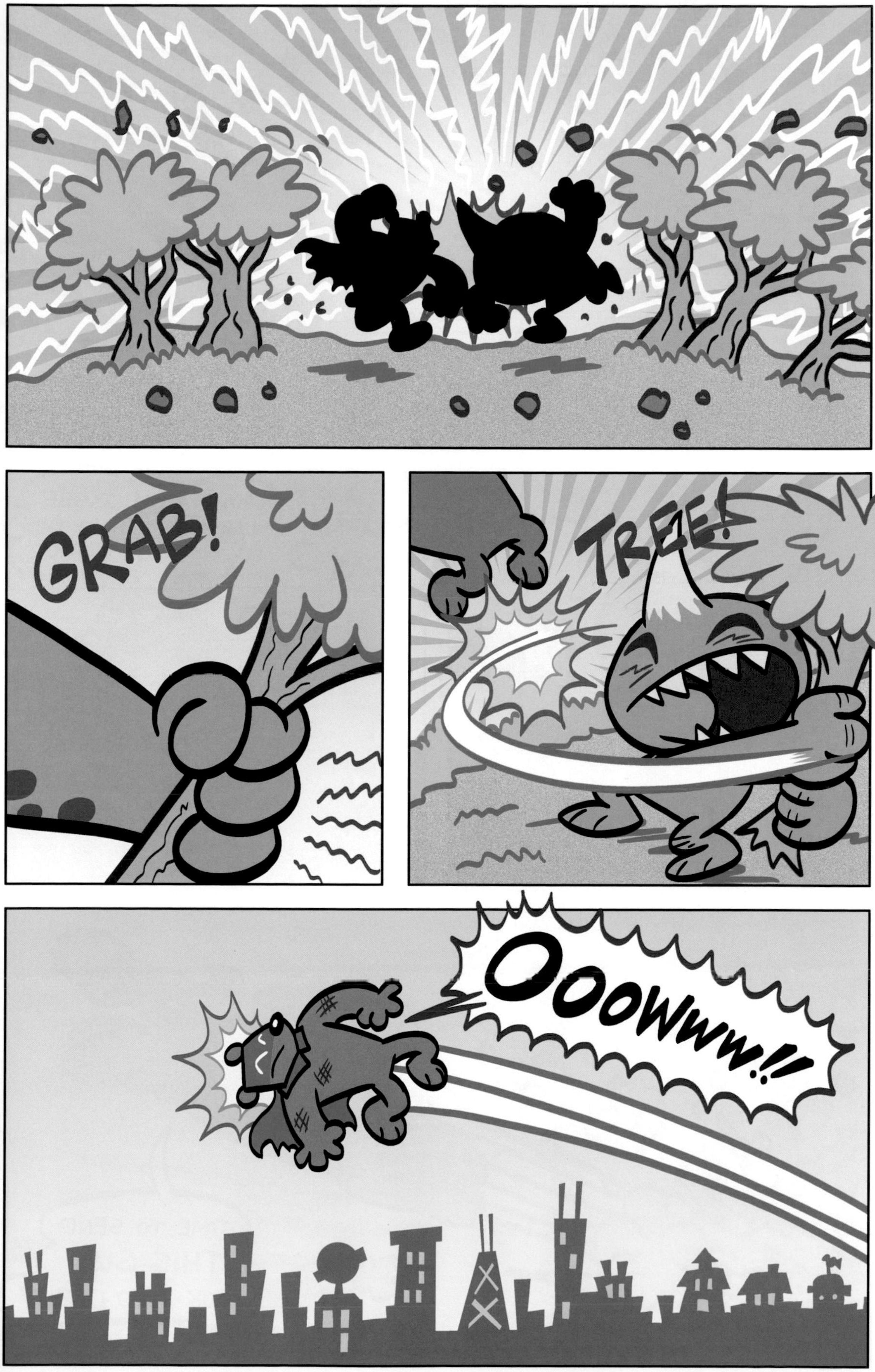
GRAB!
TREE!
OOOWWW!!

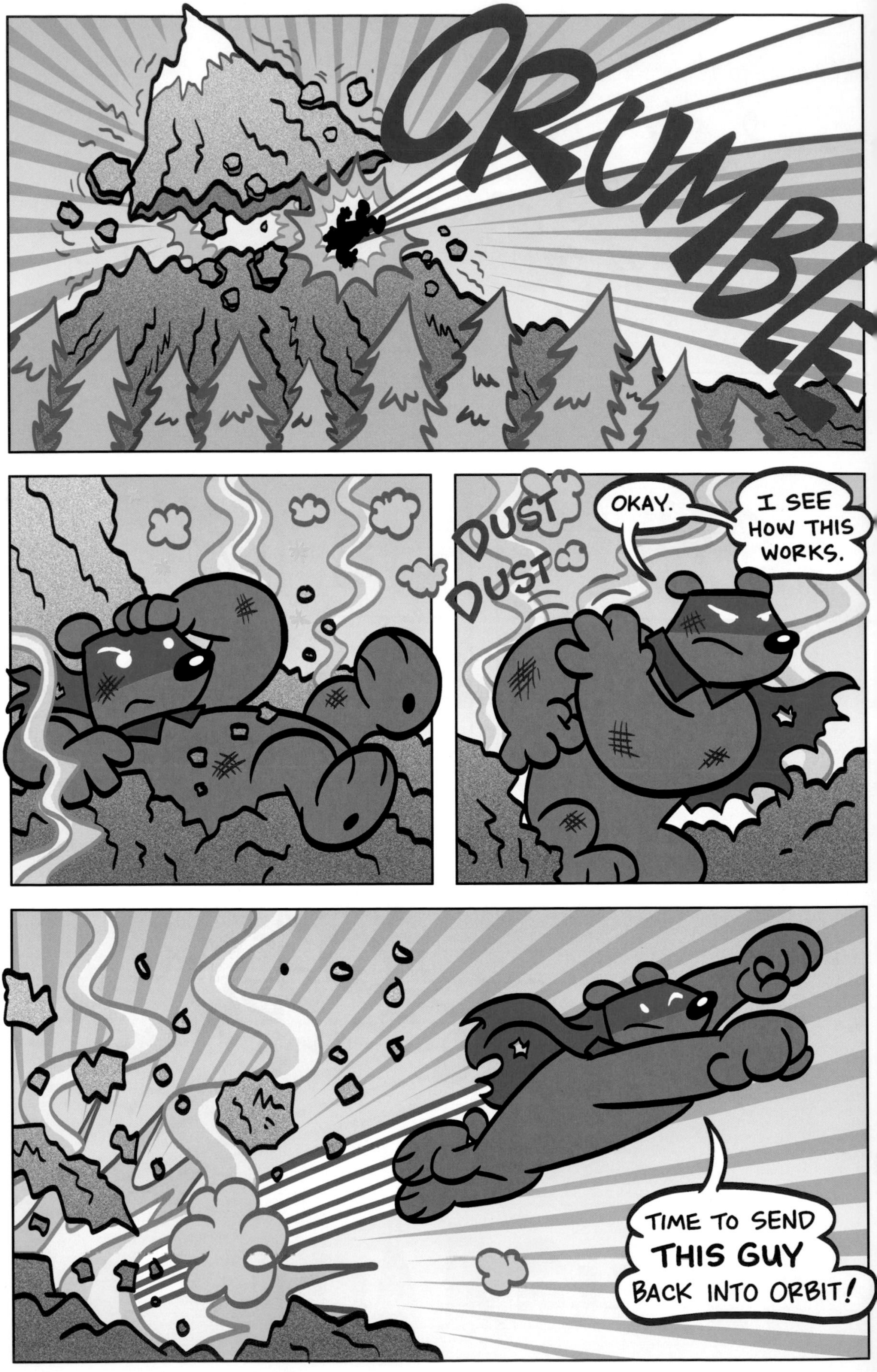
CRUMBLE
DUST
DUST
OKAY.
I SEE HOW THIS WORKS.
TIME TO SEND THIS GUY BACK INTO ORBIT!

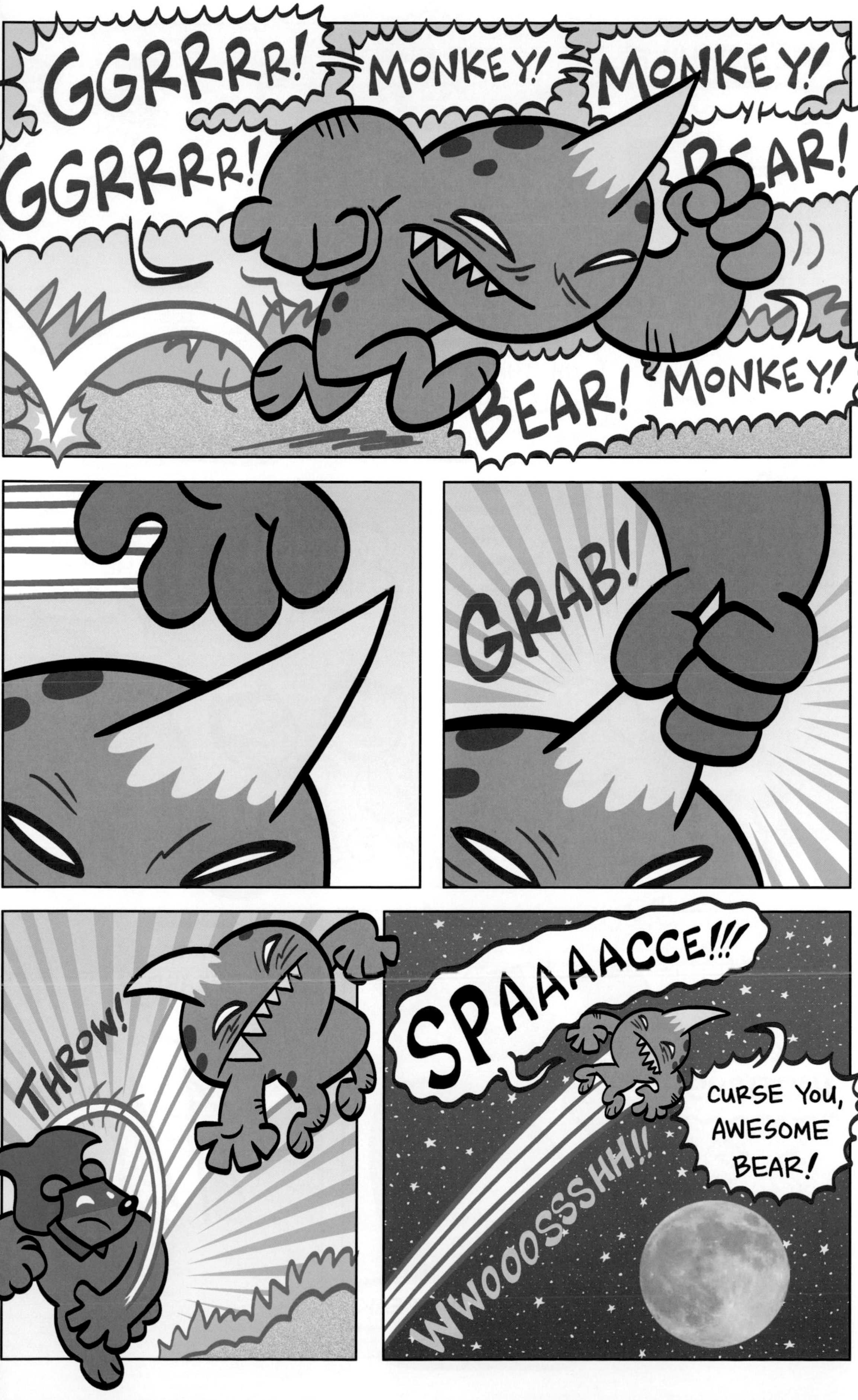
GGRRRRR!
MONKEY!
MONKEY!
GGRRRRR!
BEAR!
BEAR!
MONKEY!
GRAB!
THROW!
SPAAAACCE!!!
CURSE YOU, AWESOME BEAR!
WWOOOSSSHH!!

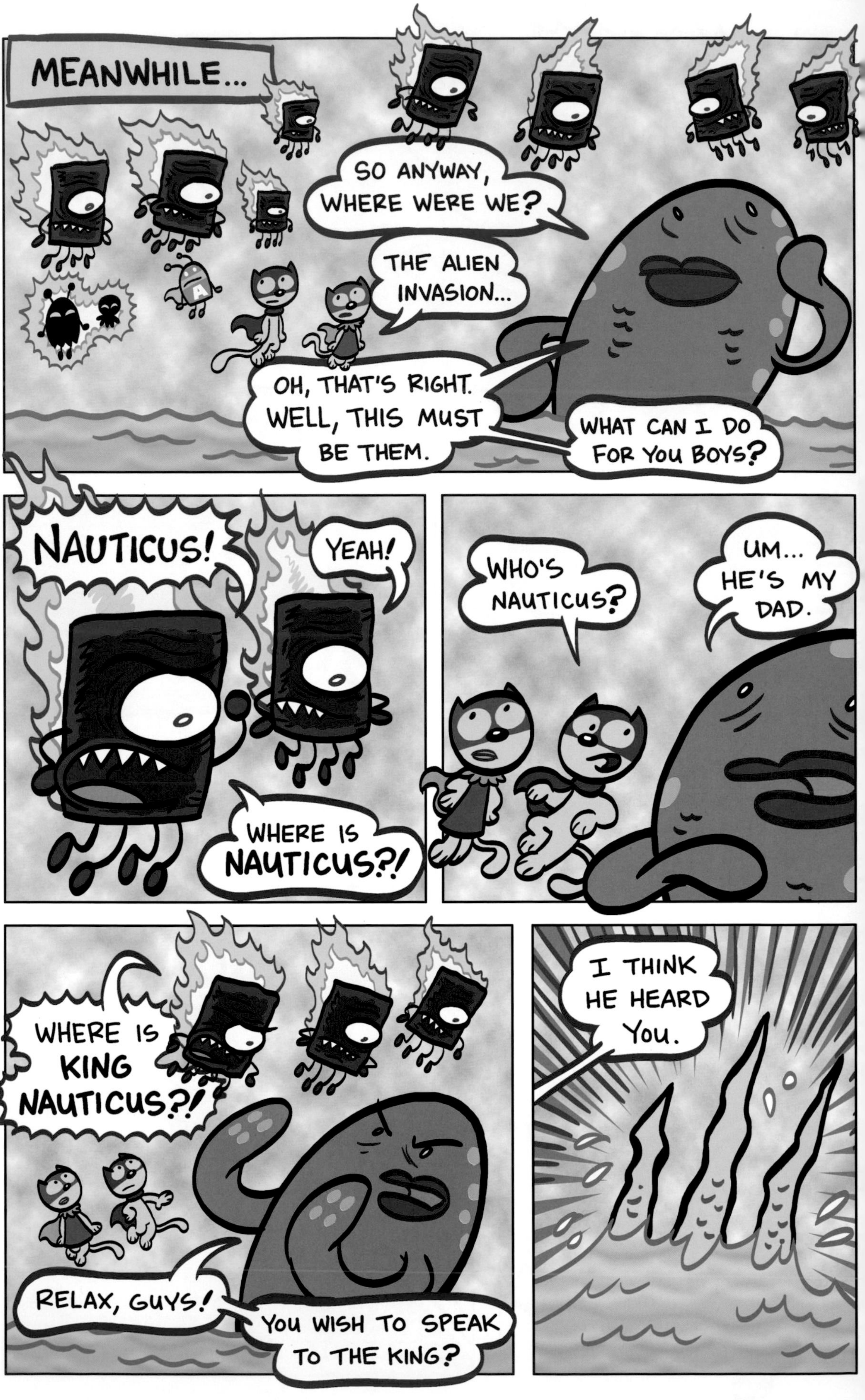
MEANWHILE...
SO ANYWAY, WHERE WERE WE?
THE ALIEN INVASION...
OH, THAT'S RIGHT. WELL, THIS MUST BE THEM.
WHAT CAN I DO FOR YOU BOYS?
NAUTICUS!
YEAH!
WHERE IS NAUTICUS?!
WHO'S NAUTICUS?
UM... HE'S MY DAD.
WHERE IS KING NAUTICUS?!
RELAX, GUYS!
YOU WISH TO SPEAK TO THE KING?
I THINK HE HEARD YOU.

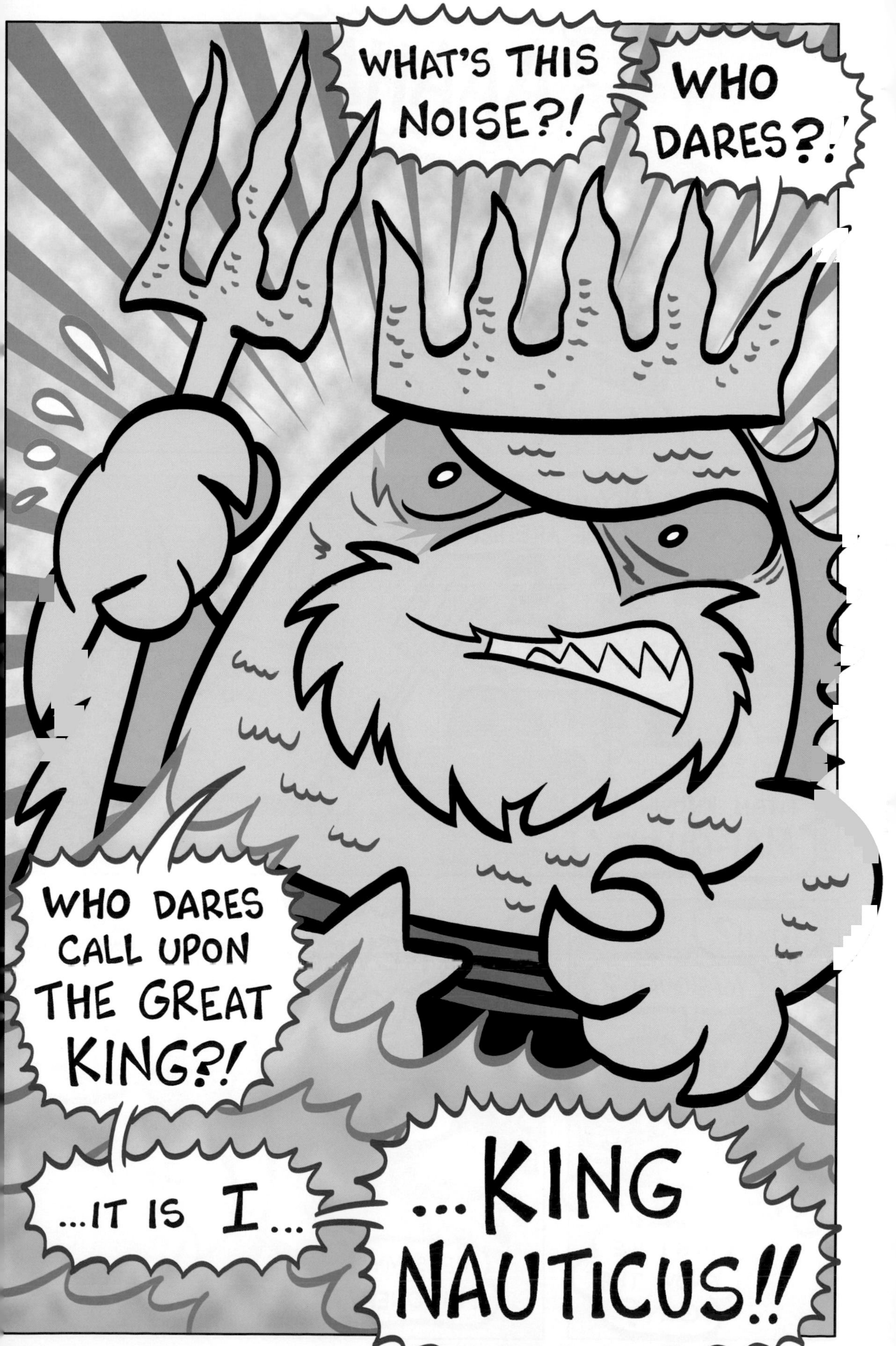
WHAT'S THIS NOISE?!
WHO DARES?!
WHO DARES CALL UPON THE GREAT KING?!
...IT IS I...
...KING NAUTICUS!!

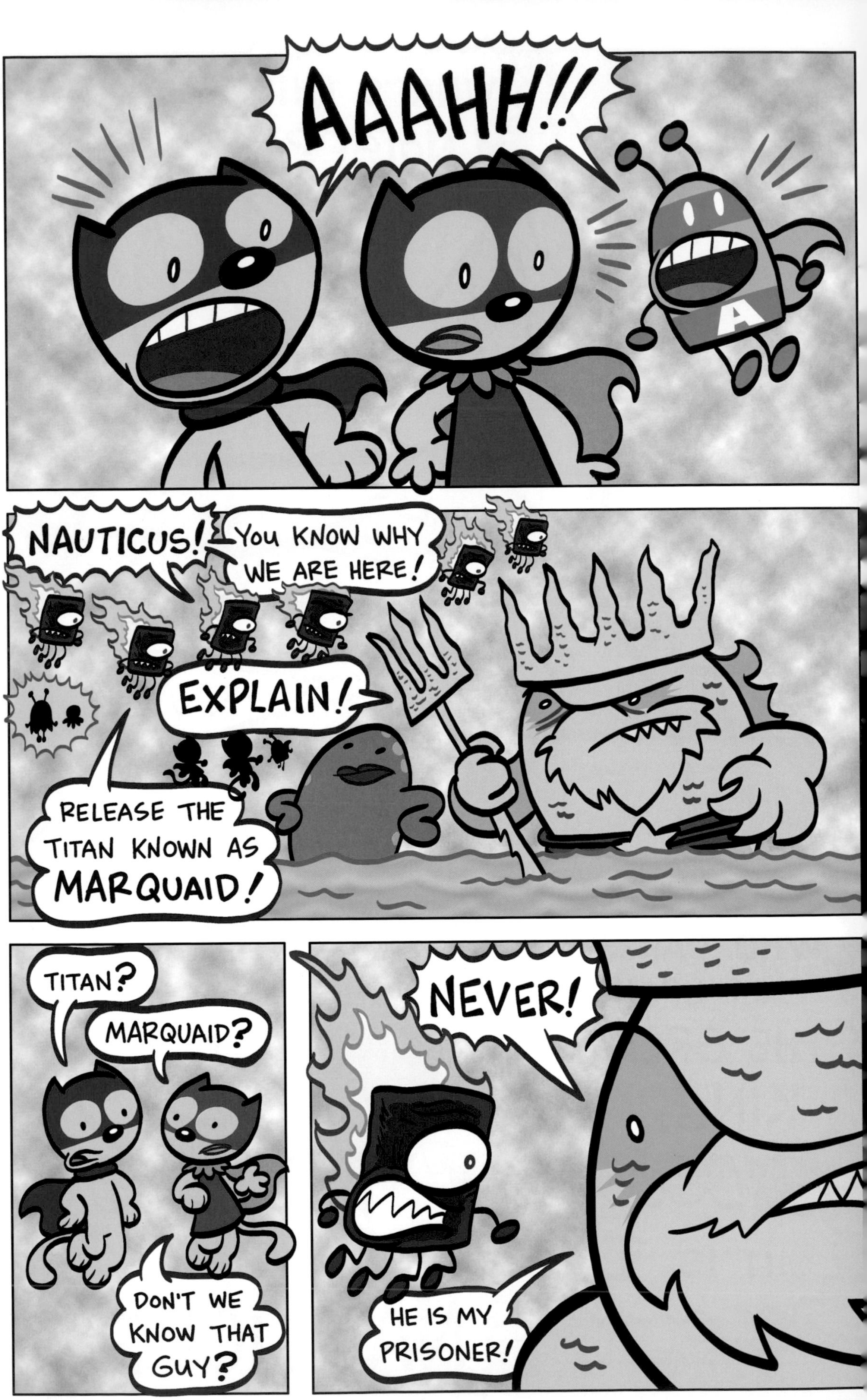
AAAHH!!
NAUTICUS!
You KNOW WHY WE ARE HERE!
EXPLAIN!
RELEASE THE TITAN KNOWN AS MARQUAID!
TITAN?
MARQUAID?
DON'T WE KNOW THAT GUY?
NEVER!
HE IS MY PRISONER!

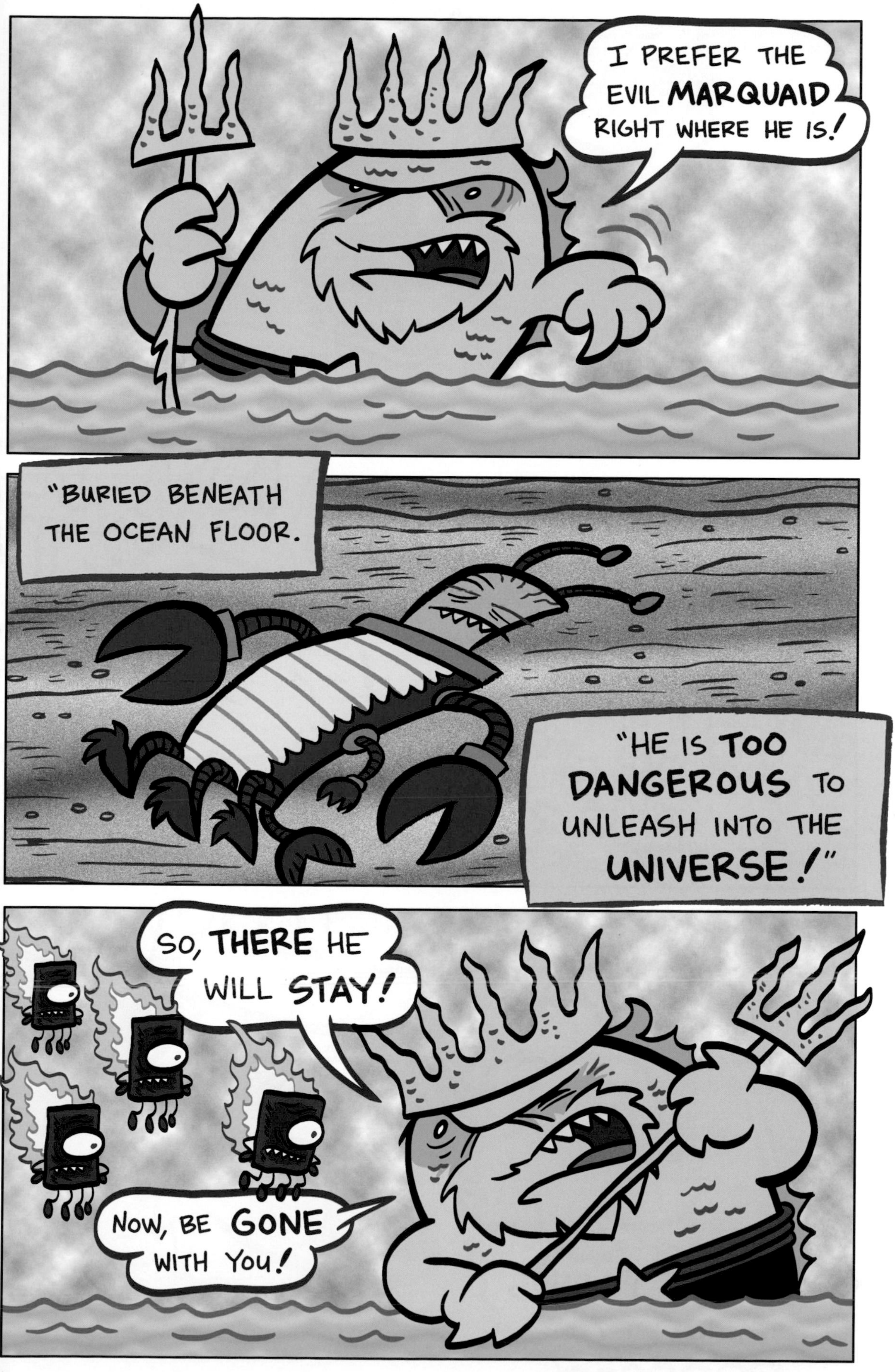
I PREFER THE EVIL MARQUAID RIGHT WHERE HE IS!
"BURIED BENEATH THE OCEAN FLOOR.
"HE IS TOO DANGEROUS TO UNLEASH INTO THE UNIVERSE!"
SO, THERE HE WILL STAY!
NOW, BE GONE WITH YOU!

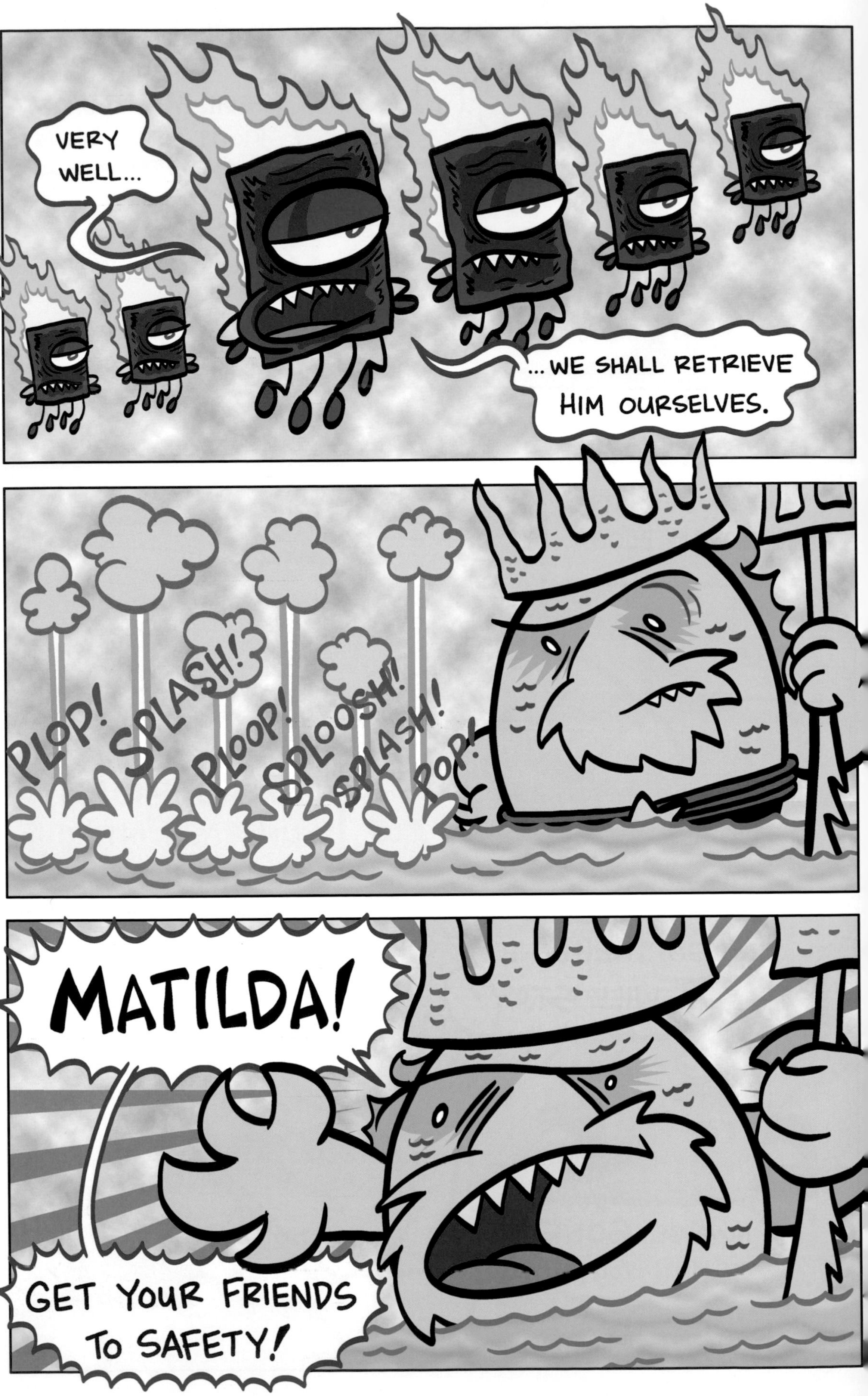
VERY WELL...
...WE SHALL RETRIEVE HIM OURSELVES.
PLOP!
SPLASH!
PLOOP!
SPLOOSH!
SPLASH!
POP!
MATILDA!
GET YOUR FRIENDS TO SAFETY!

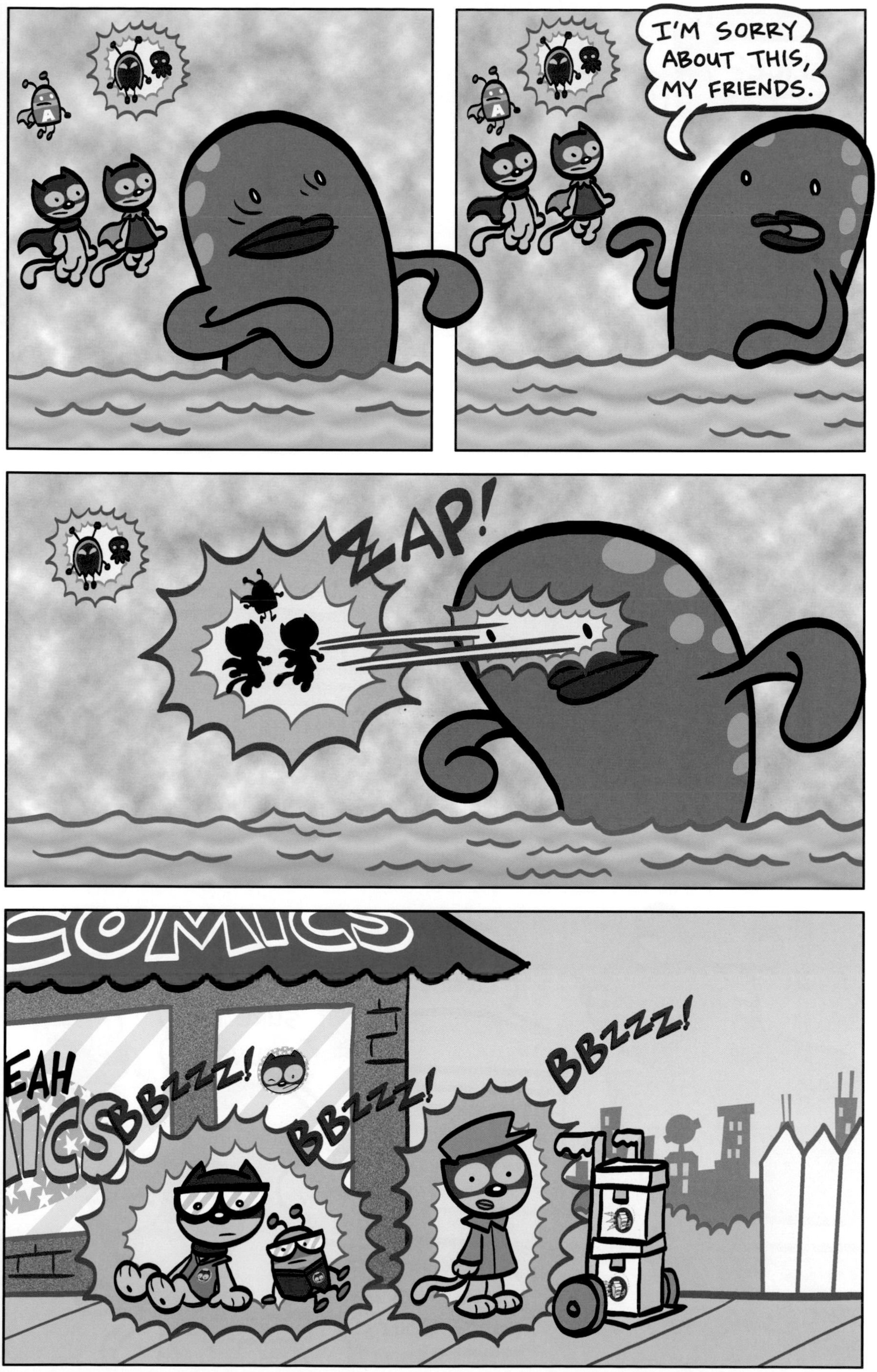
I'M SORRY ABOUT THIS, MY FRIENDS.
ZAP!
COMICS
BBzzz!
BBzzz!
BBzzz!

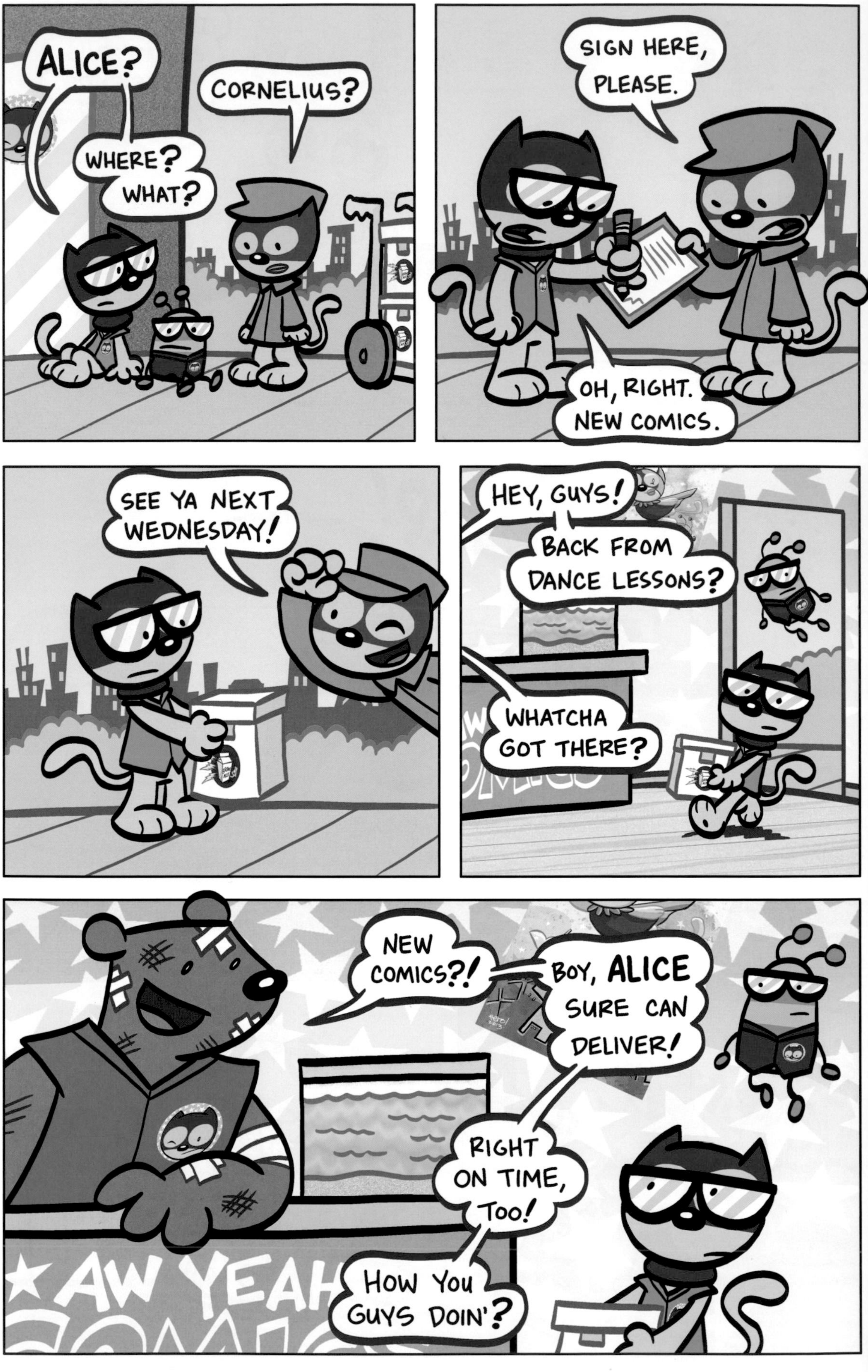
ALICE?
CORNELIUS?
WHERE? WHAT?
SIGN HERE, PLEASE.
OH, RIGHT. NEW COMICS.
SEE YA NEXT WEDNESDAY!
HEY, GUYS!
BACK FROM DANCE LESSONS?
WHATCHA GOT THERE?
NEW COMICS?!
BOY, ALICE SURE CAN DELIVER!
RIGHT ON TIME, TOO!
HOW YOU GUYS DOIN'?
AW YEAH

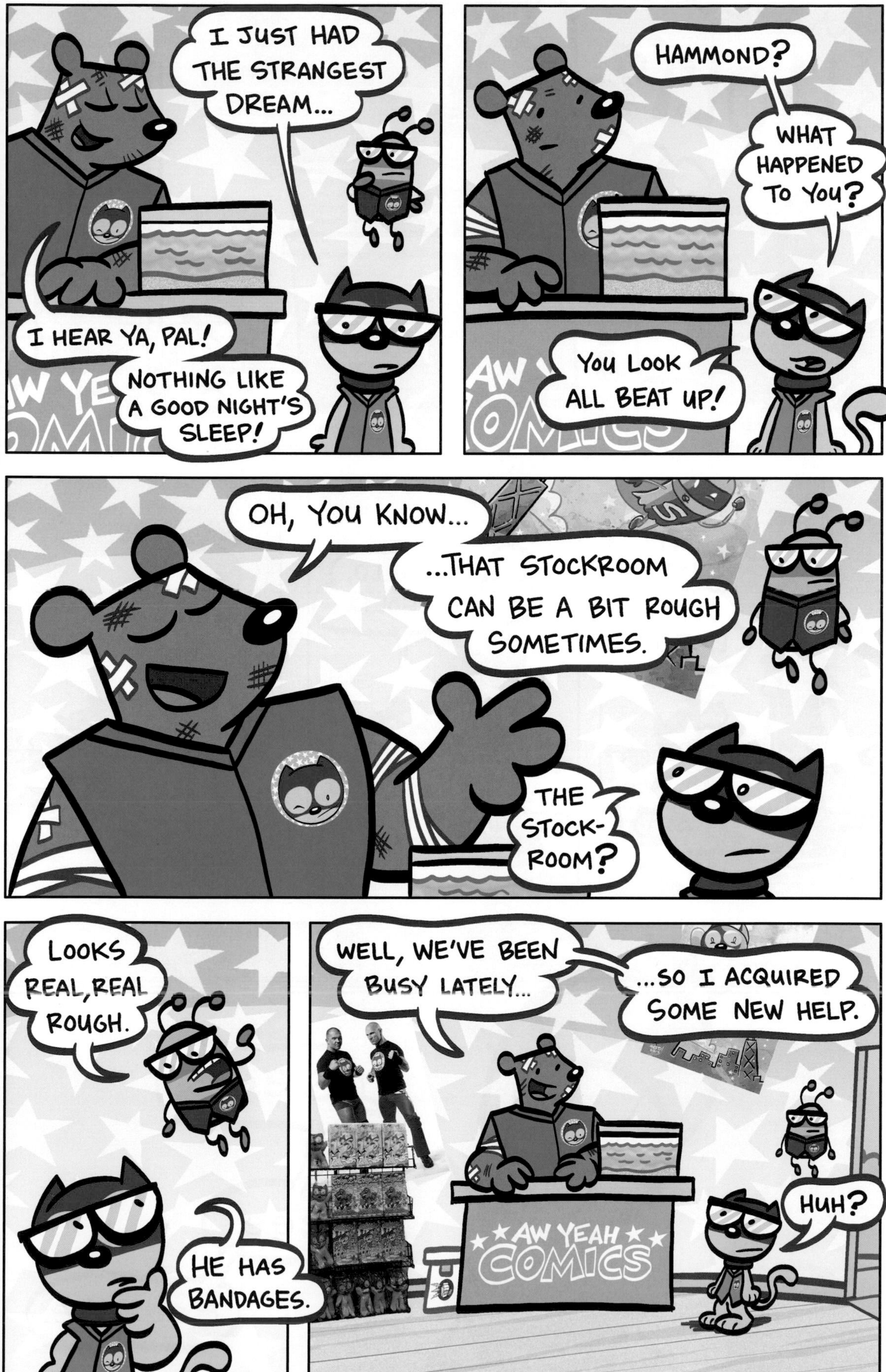

I JUST HAD THE STRANGEST DREAM...
I HEAR YA, PAL!
NOTHING LIKE A GOOD NIGHT'S SLEEP!
HAMMOND?
WHAT HAPPENED TO YOU?
YOU LOOK ALL BEAT UP!
OH, YOU KNOW...
...THAT STOCKROOM CAN BE A BIT ROUGH SOMETIMES.
THE STOCK-ROOM?
LOOKS REAL, REAL ROUGH.
HE HAS BANDAGES.
WELL, WE'VE BEEN BUSY LATELY...
...SO I ACQUIRED SOME NEW HELP.
HUH?
AW YEAH COMICS

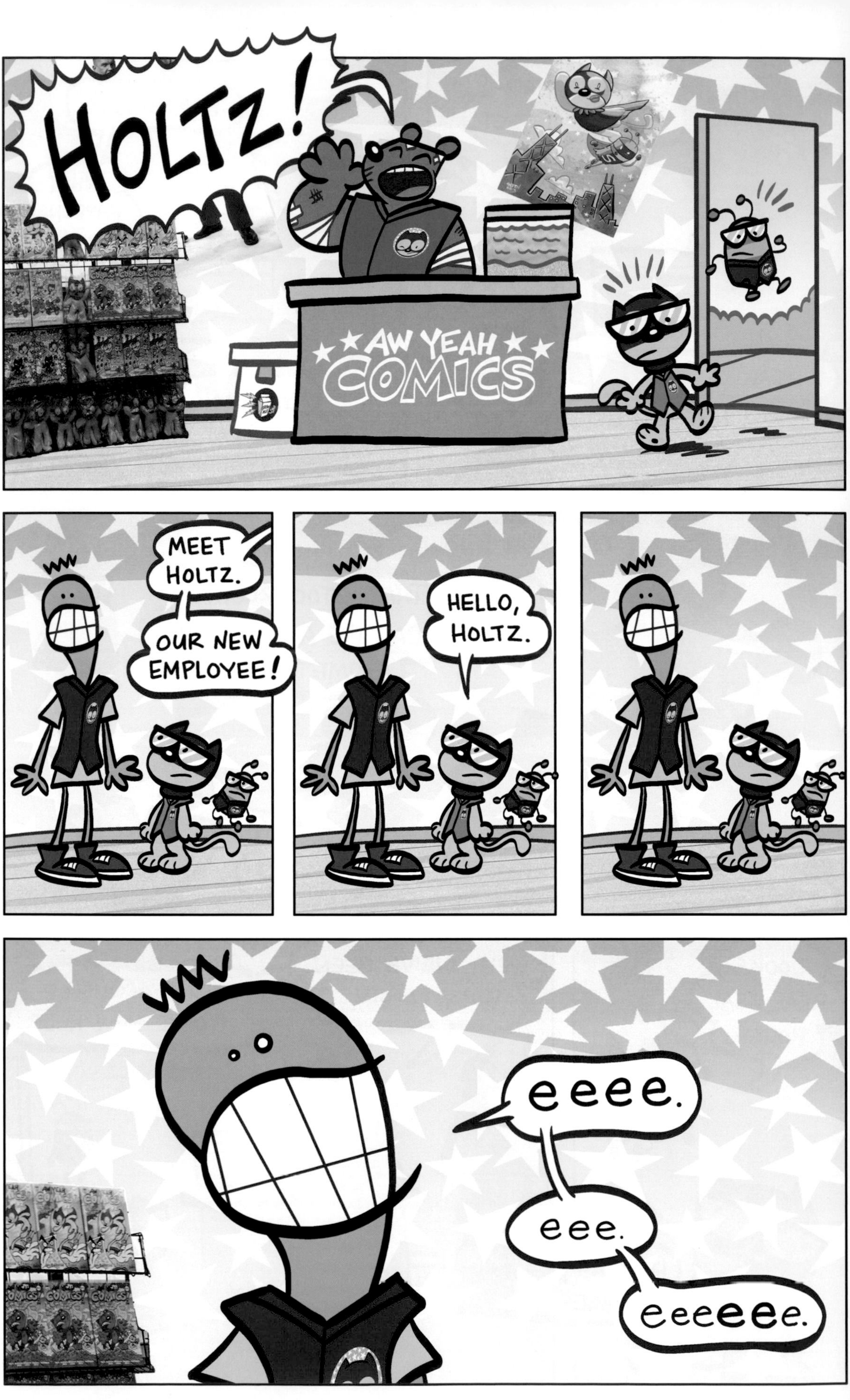
HOLTZ!
AW YEAH COMICS
MEET HOLTZ.
OUR NEW EMPLOYEE!
HELLO, HOLTZ.
eeee.
eee.
eeeeee.

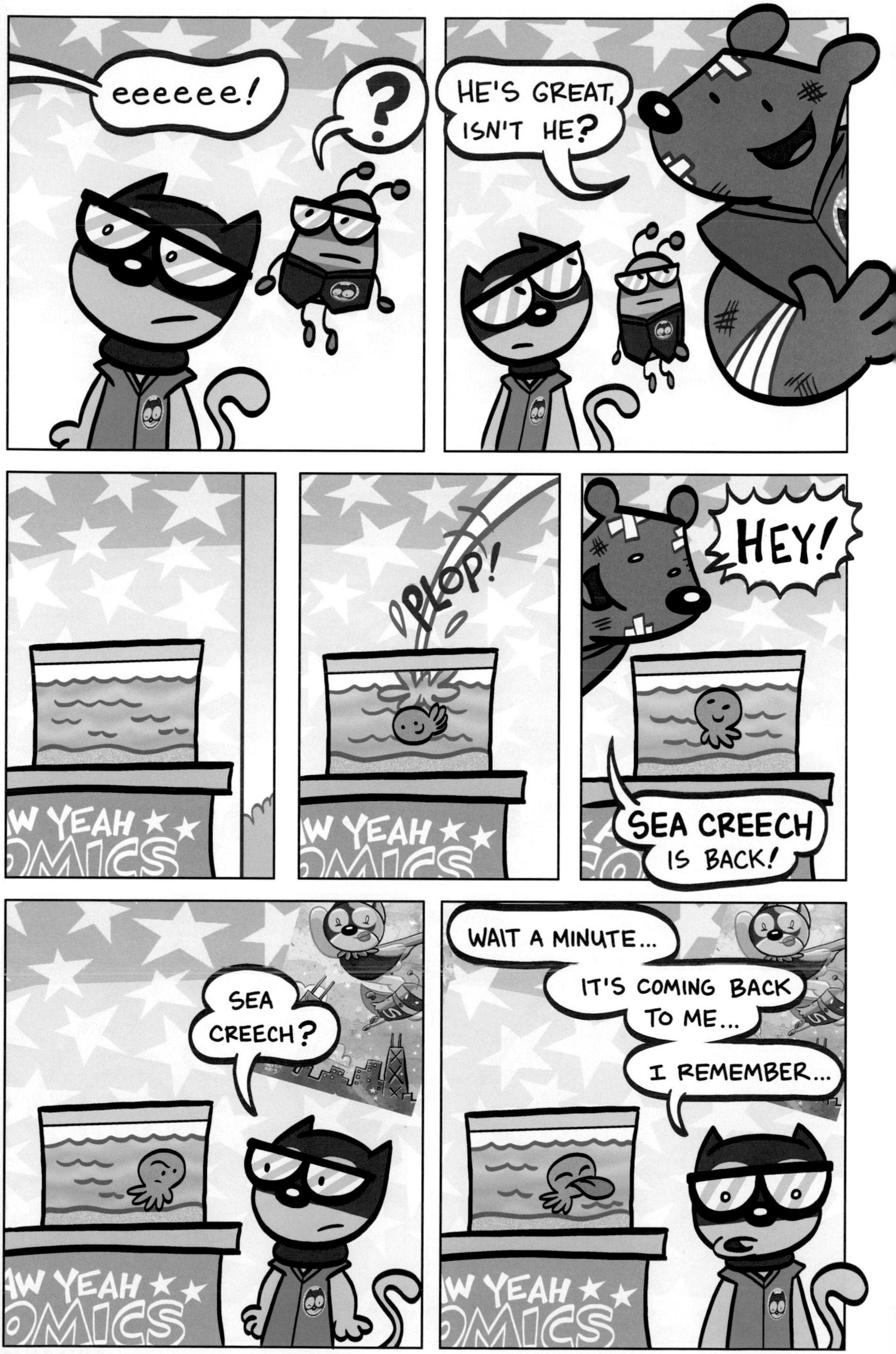
eeeeee!
?
HE'S GREAT, ISN'T HE?
PLOP!
HEY!
SEA CREECH IS BACK!
AW YEAH ★★
SEA CREECH?
WAIT A MINUTE...
IT'S COMING BACK TO ME...
I REMEMBER...

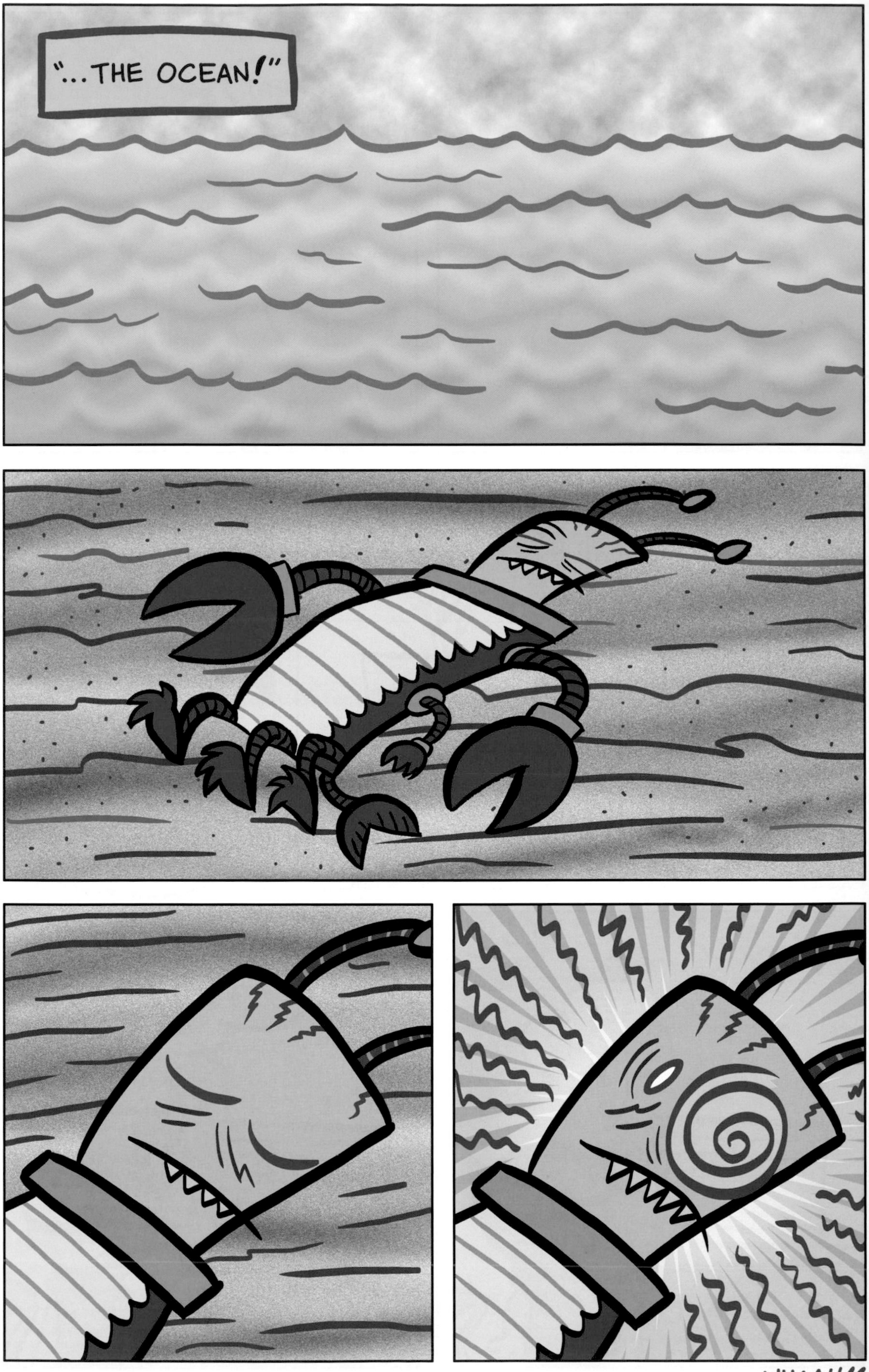
"...THE OCEAN!"
-WHAAH!!

EVIL CAT & GHOST BUG in: THE MONSTER MUTT by: SCOOT

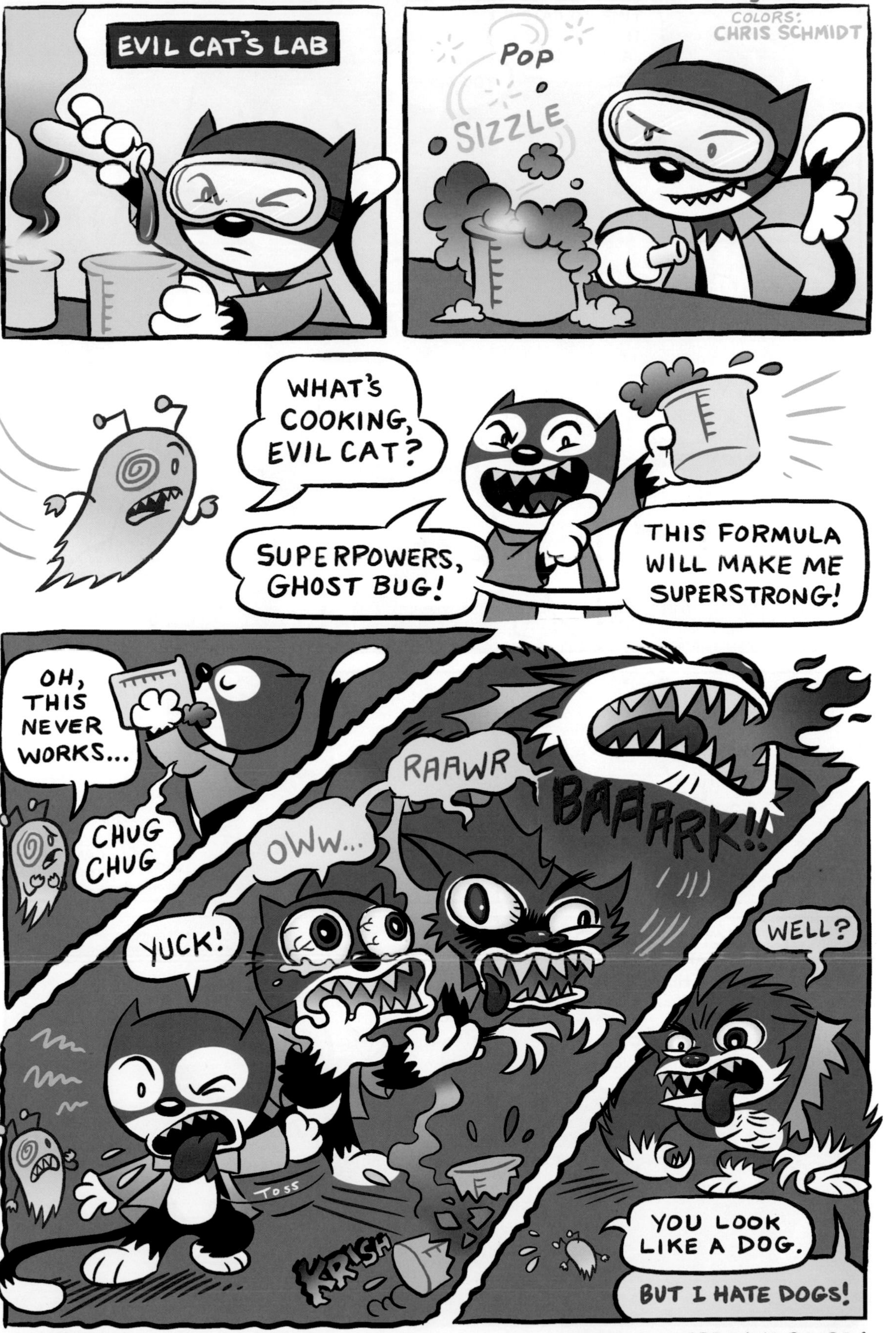

EVIL CAT'S LAB
COLORS: CHRIS SCHMIDT
POP
SIZZLE
WHAT'S COOKING, EVIL CAT?
SUPERPOWERS, GHOST BUG!
THIS FORMULA WILL MAKE ME SUPERSTRONG!
OH, THIS NEVER WORKS...
CHUG CHUG
RAAWR
BAAARK!!
OWW...
YUCK!
TOSS
KRISH
WELL?
YOU LOOK LIKE A DOG.
BUT I HATE DOGS!

-BACK TO THE DRAWING BOARD!

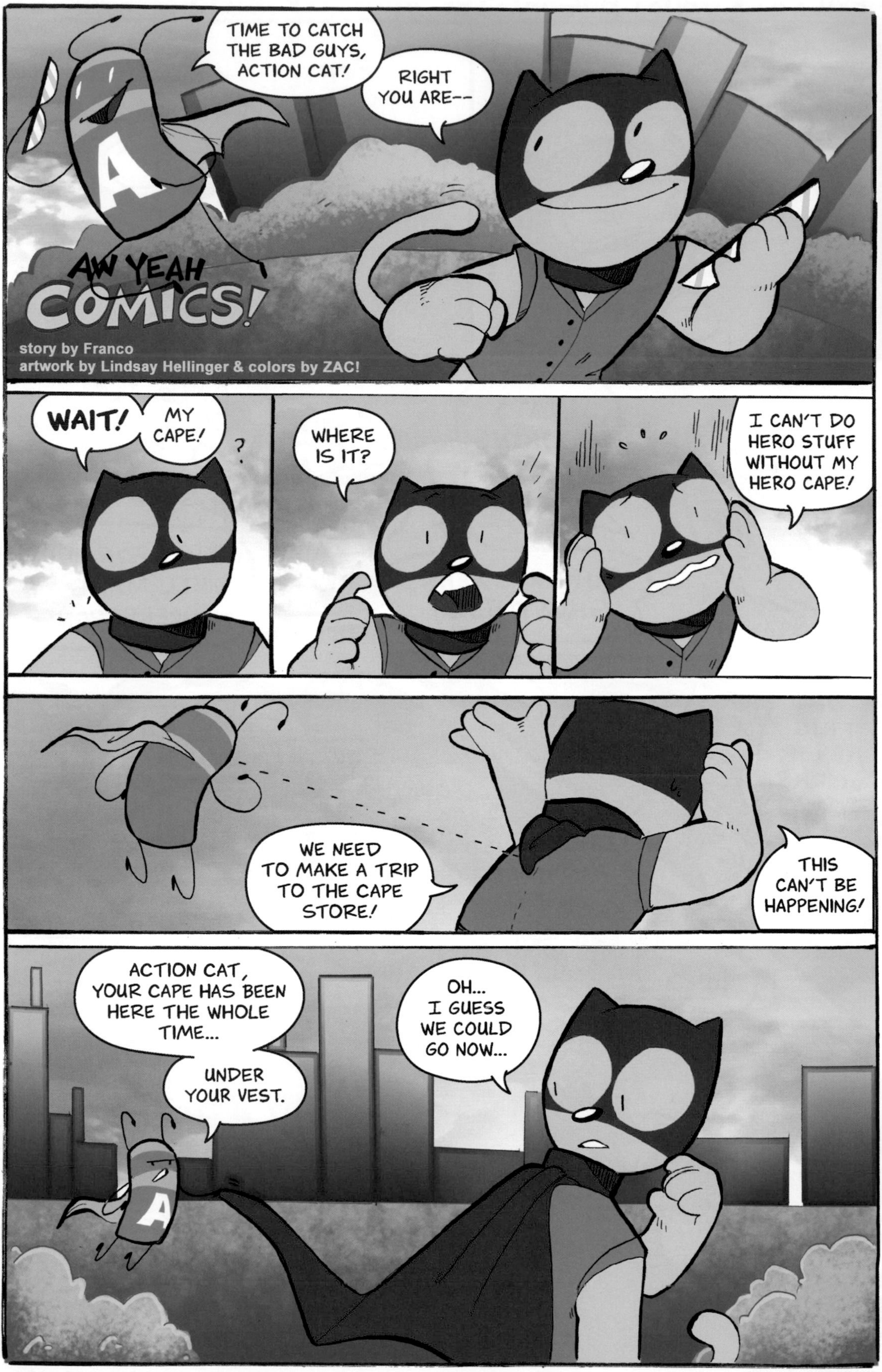
AW YEAH COMICS!
story by Franco
artwork by Lindsay Hellinger & colors by ZAC!
TIME TO CATCH THE BAD GUYS, ACTION CAT!
RIGHT YOU ARE--
WAIT!
MY CAPE!
?
WHERE IS IT?
I CAN'T DO HERO STUFF WITHOUT MY HERO CAPE!
WE NEED TO MAKE A TRIP TO THE CAPE STORE!
THIS CAN'T BE HAPPENING!
ACTION CAT, YOUR CAPE HAS BEEN HERE THE WHOLE TIME...
UNDER YOUR VEST.
OH... I GUESS WE COULD GO NOW...

--AW YEAH WARDROBE!

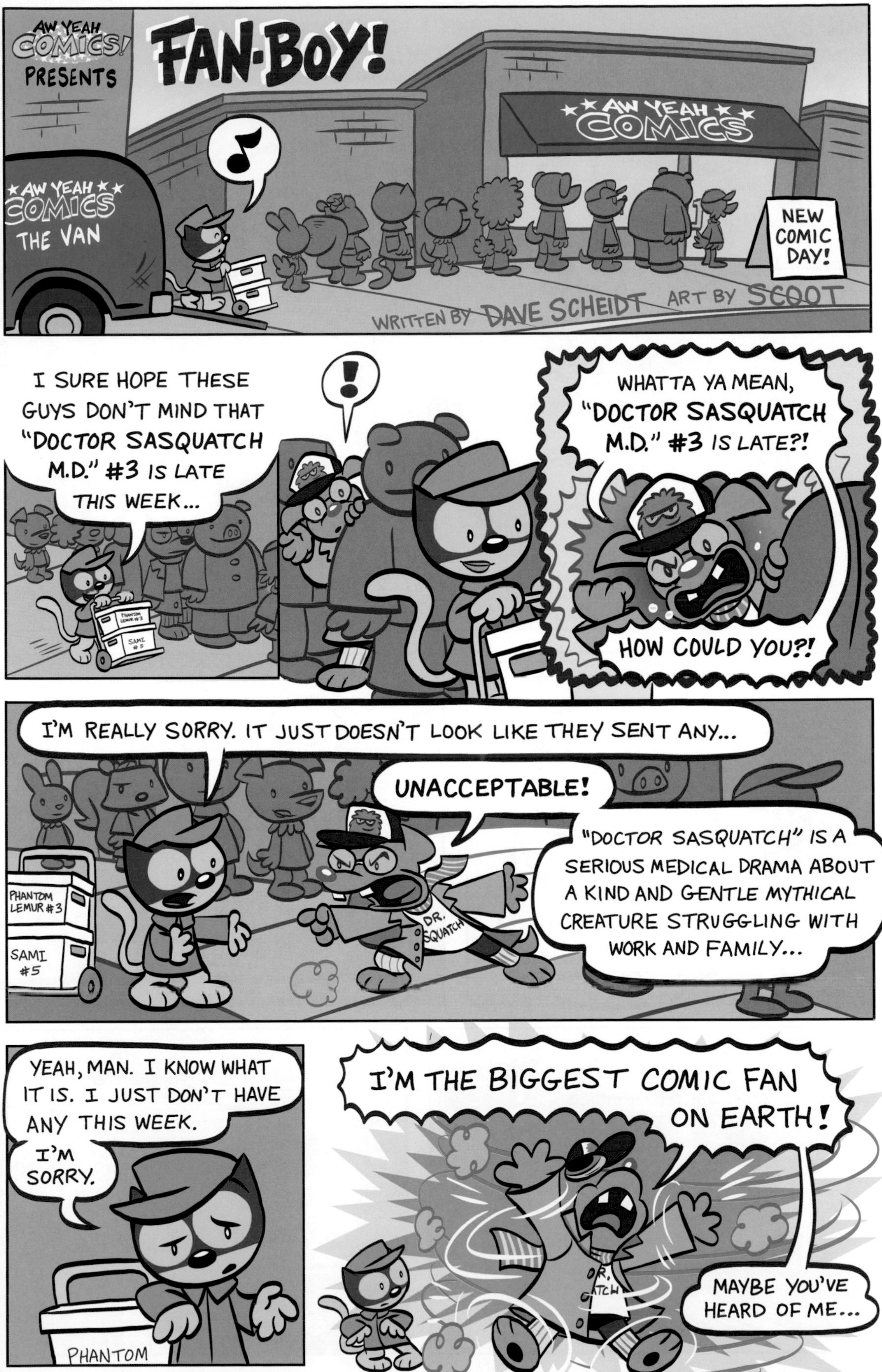
AW YEAH COMICS! PRESENTS
FAN-BOY!
AW YEAH COMICS
AW YEAH COMICS THE VAN
NEW COMIC DAY!
WRITTEN BY DAVE SCHEIDT ART BY SCOOT
I SURE HOPE THESE GUYS DON'T MIND THAT "DOCTOR SASQUATCH M.D." #3 IS LATE THIS WEEK...
PHANTOM LEMUR #3
SAMI #5
!
WHATTA YA MEAN, "DOCTOR SASQUATCH M.D." #3 IS LATE?!
HOW COULD YOU?!
I'M REALLY SORRY. IT JUST DOESN'T LOOK LIKE THEY SENT ANY...
UNACCEPTABLE!
"DOCTOR SASQUATCH" IS A SERIOUS MEDICAL DRAMA ABOUT A KIND AND GENTLE MYTHICAL CREATURE STRUGGLING WITH WORK AND FAMILY...
PHANTOM LEMUR #3
SAMI #5
DR. SQUATCH
YEAH, MAN. I KNOW WHAT IT IS. I JUST DON'T HAVE ANY THIS WEEK.
I'M SORRY.
PHANTOM
I'M THE BIGGEST COMIC FAN ON EARTH!
MAYBE YOU'VE HEARD OF ME...

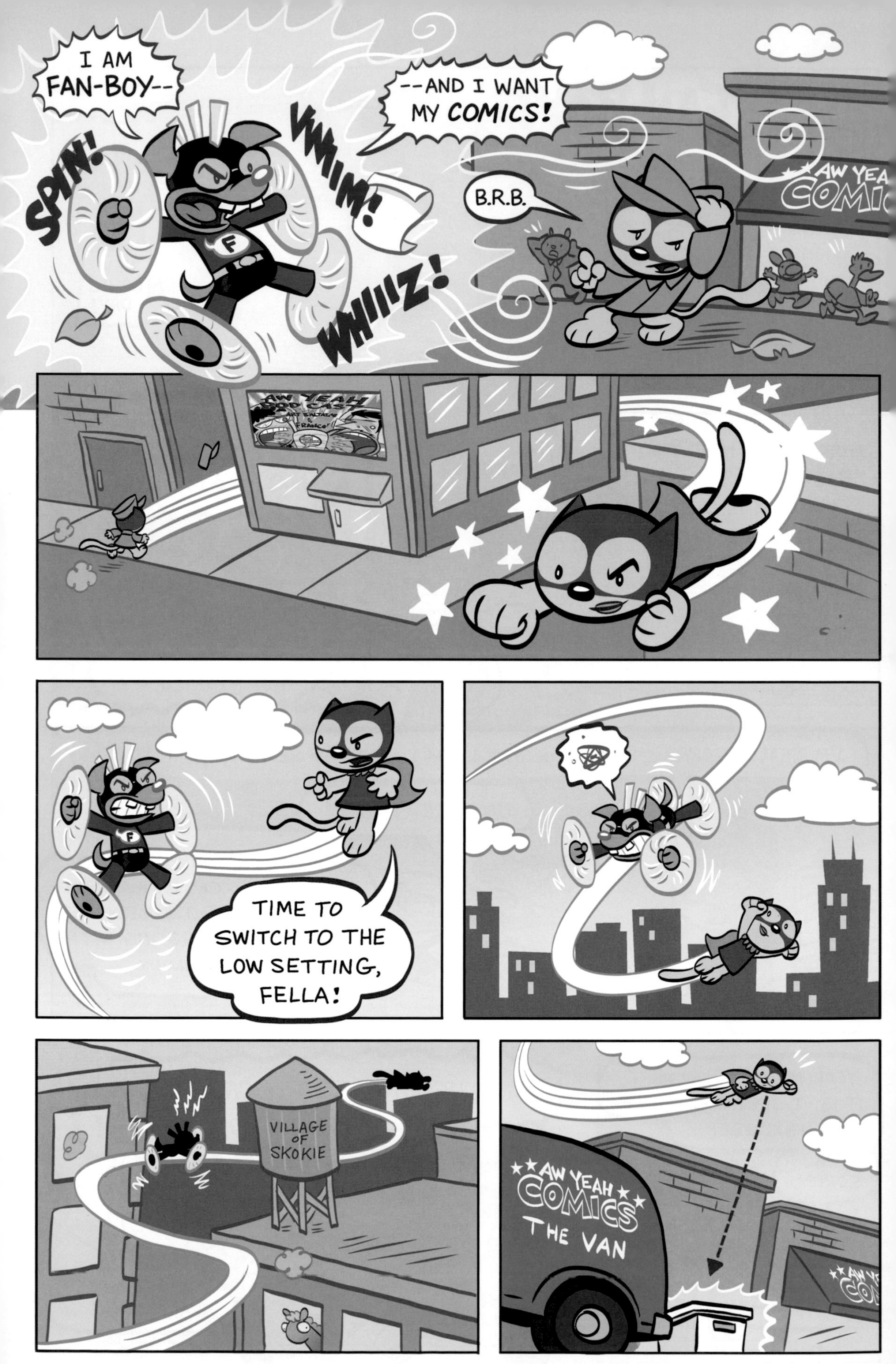
I AM FAN-BOY--
SPIN!
VWMM!
WHIIIZ!
--AND I WANT MY COMICS!
B.R.B.
AW YEAH COMICS
AW YEAH
TIME TO SWITCH TO THE LOW SETTING, FELLA!
VILLAGE OF SKOKIE
AW YEAH COMICS THE VAN
AW YEAH COMICS

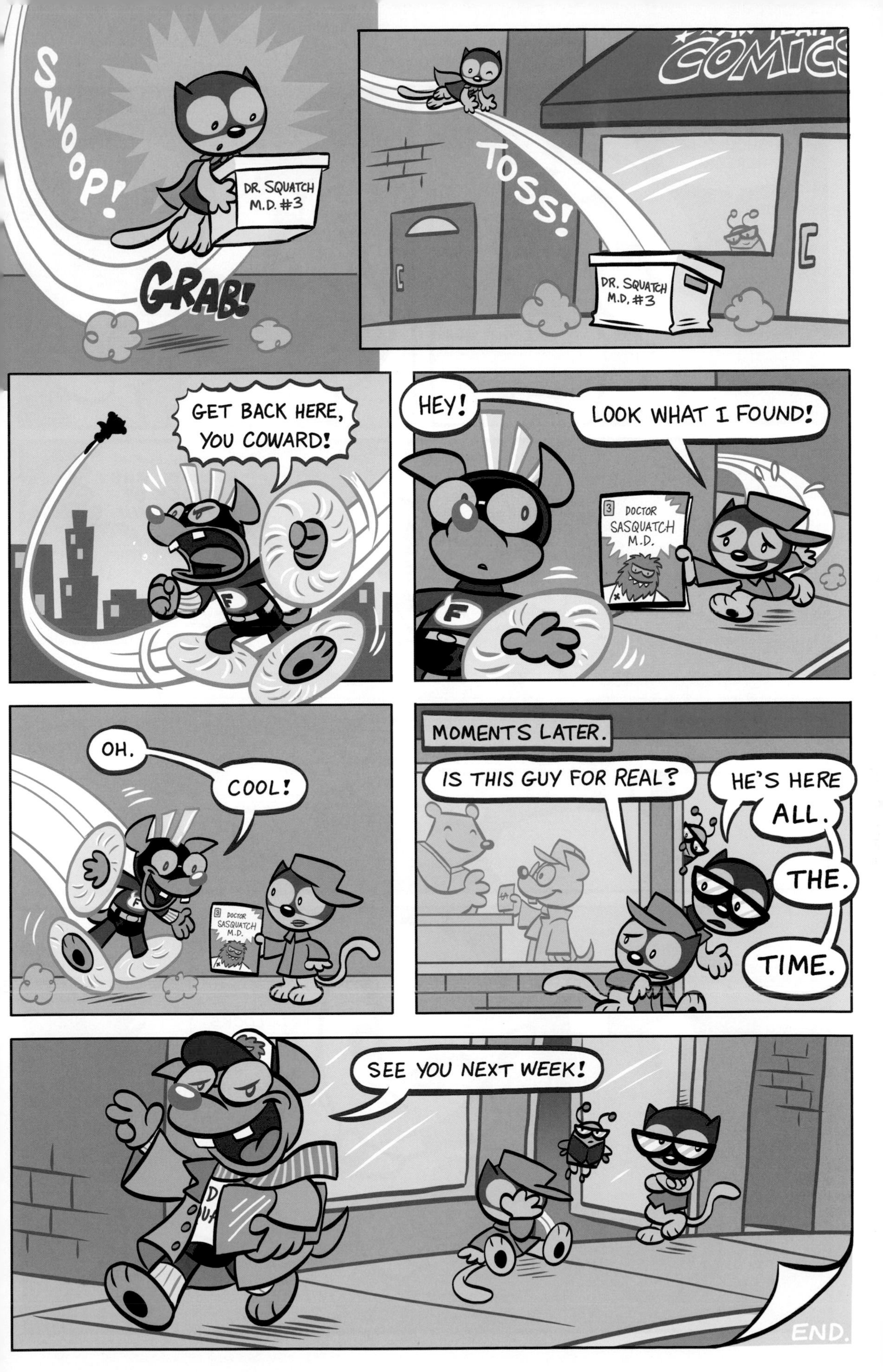
SWOOP!
DR. SQUATCH M.D. #3
GRAB!
COMICS
TOSS!
DR. SQUATCH M.D. #3
GET BACK HERE, YOU COWARD!
HEY!
LOOK WHAT I FOUND!
3 DOCTOR SASQUATCH M.D.
OH.
COOL!
MOMENTS LATER.
IS THIS GUY FOR REAL?
HE'S HERE
ALL.
THE.
TIME.
SEE YOU NEXT WEEK!
END.

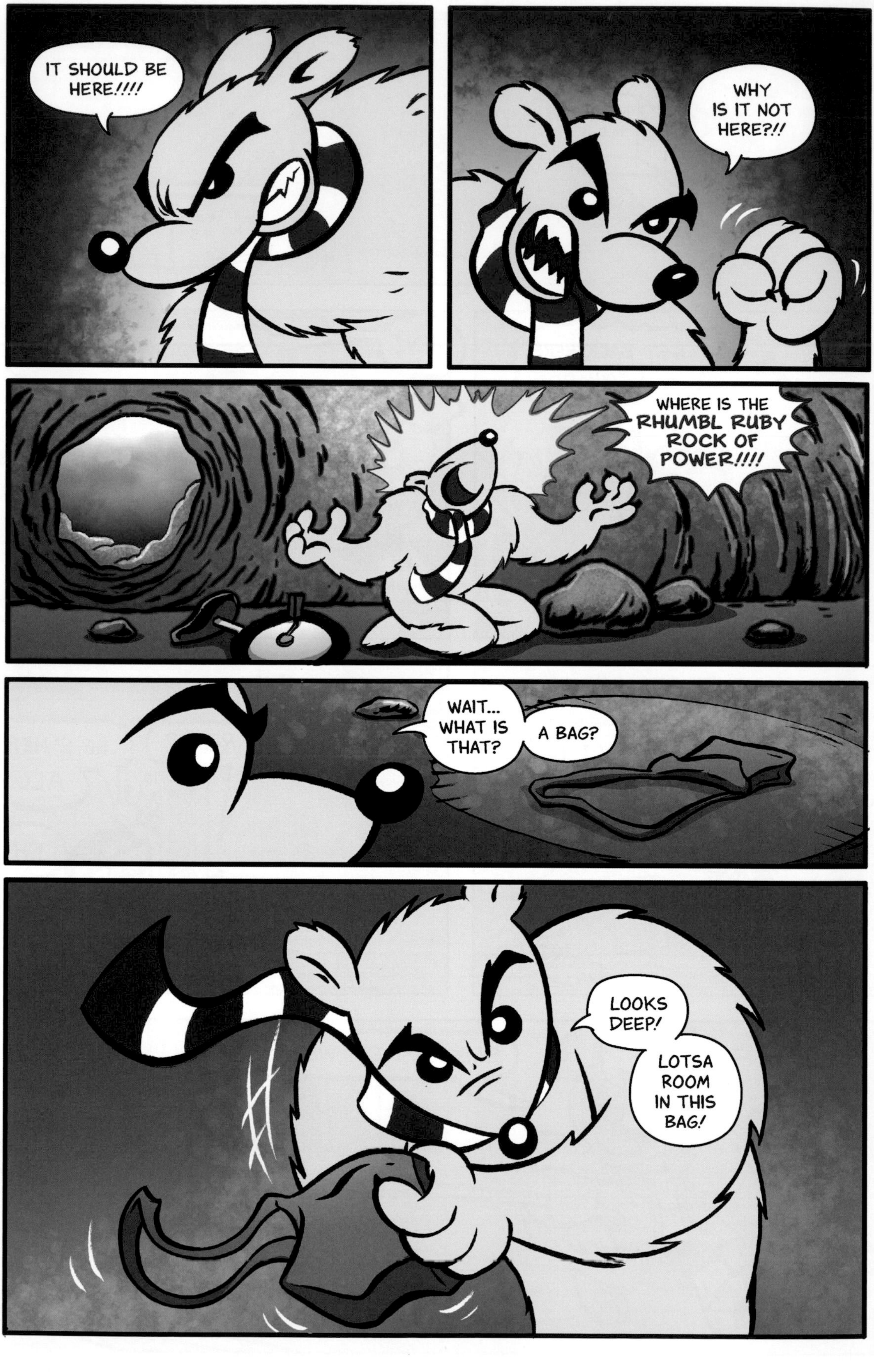
IT SHOULD BE HERE!!!!
WHY IS IT NOT HERE?!!
WHERE IS THE RHUMBL RUBY ROCK OF POWER!!!!
WAIT... WHAT IS THAT?
A BAG?
LOOKS DEEP!
LOTSA ROOM IN THIS BAG!

ROYAL RUMBLE PHONY

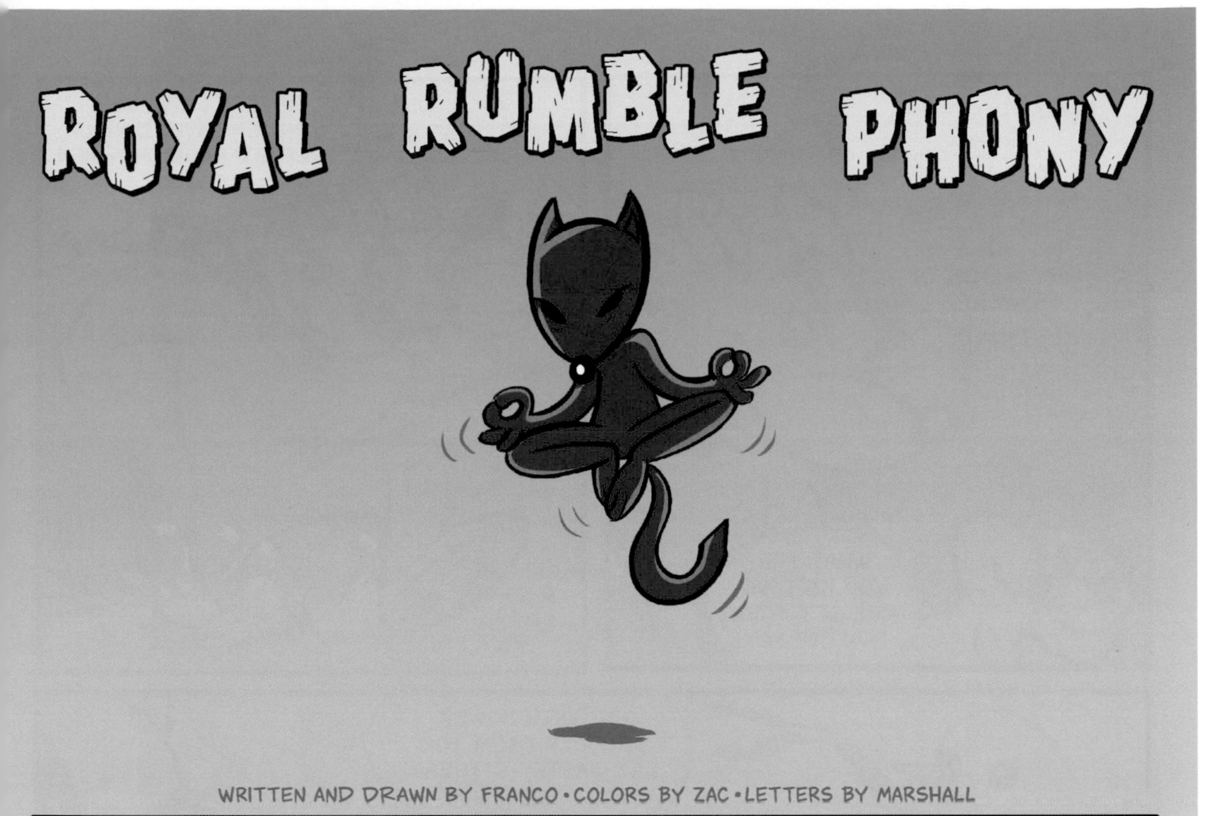

WRITTEN AND DRAWN BY FRANCO • COLORS BY ZAC • LETTERS BY MARSHALL

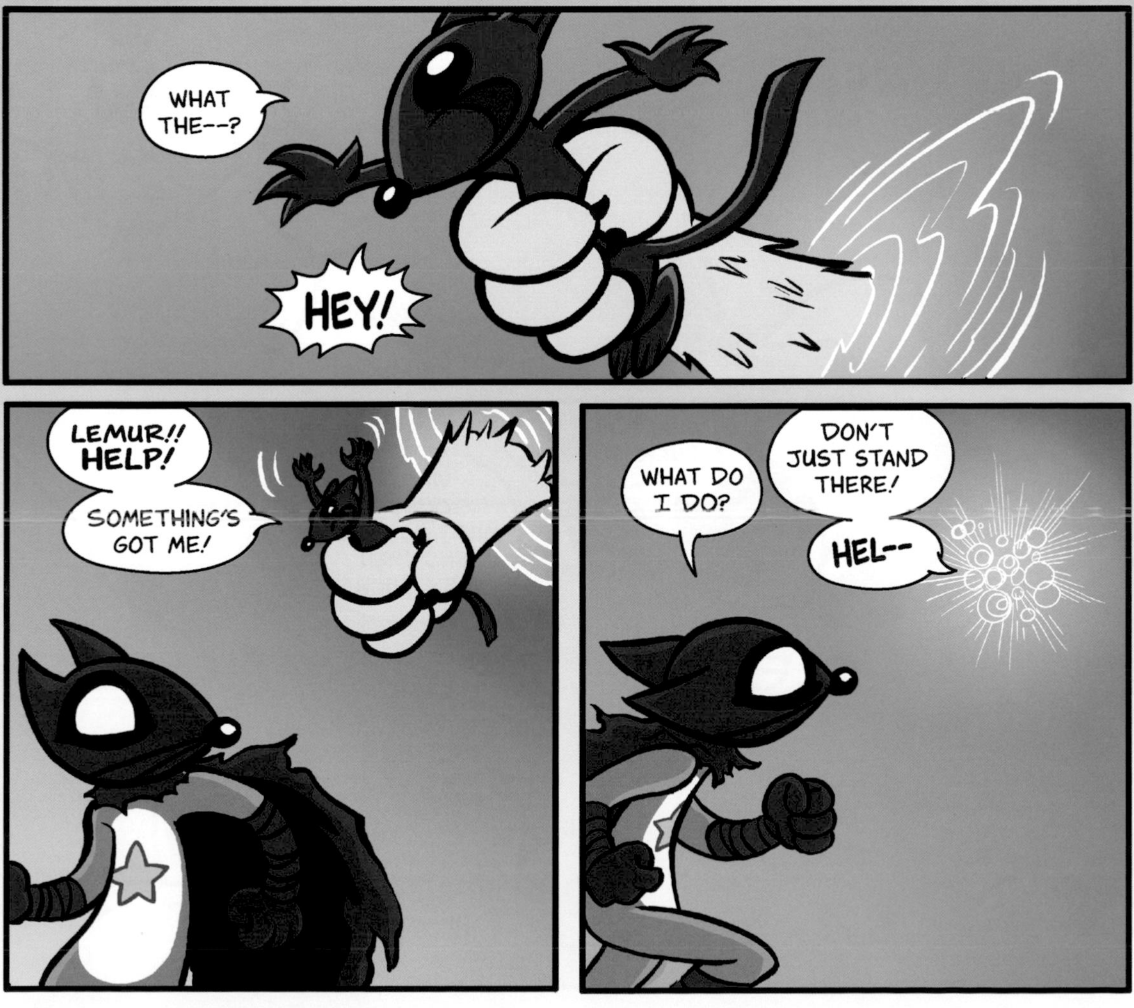
WHAT THE--?
HEY!
LEMUR!! HELP!
SOMETHING'S GOT ME!
WHAT DO I DO?
DON'T JUST STAND THERE!
HEL--

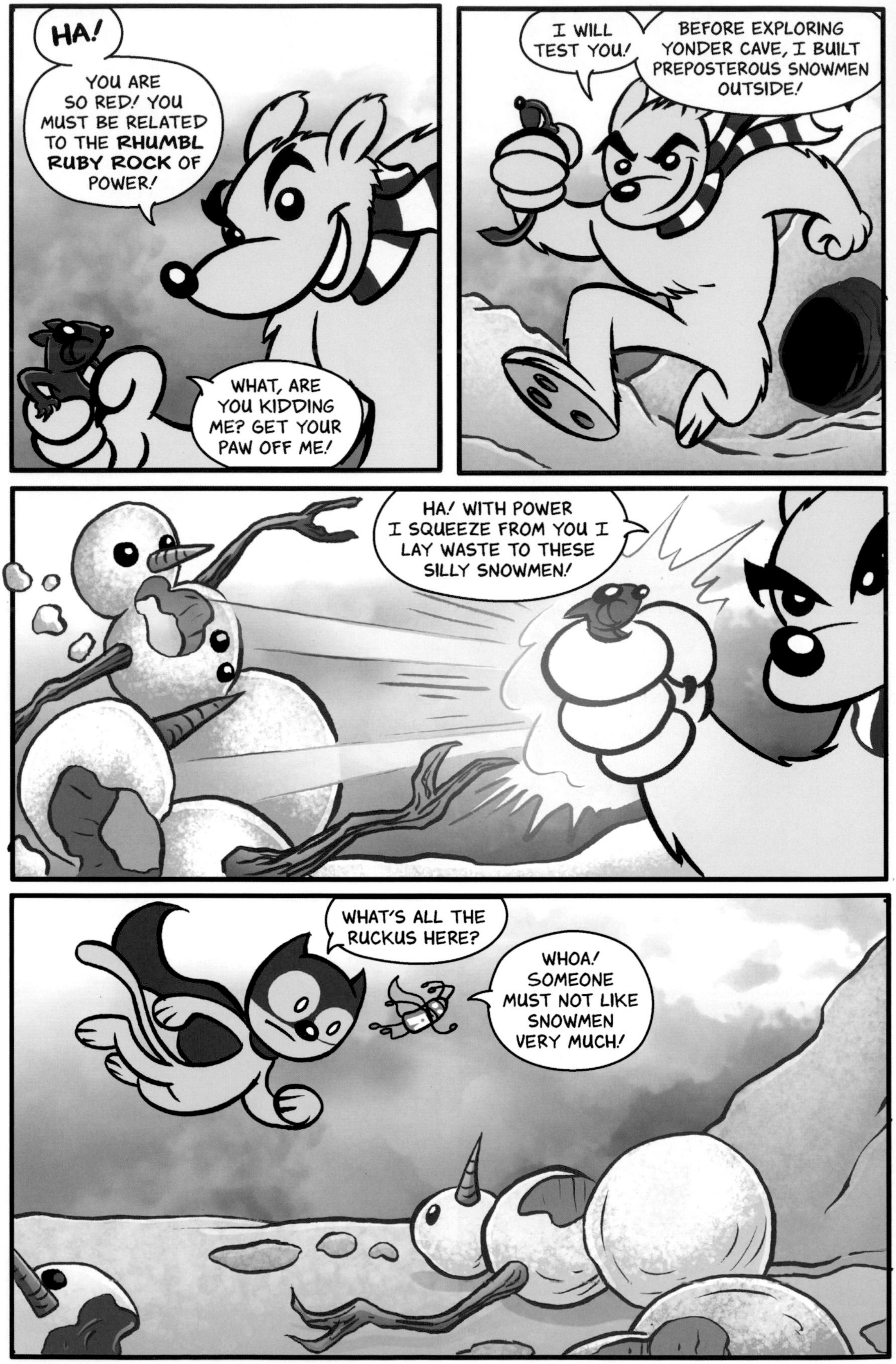
HA!
YOU ARE SO RED! YOU MUST BE RELATED TO THE **RHUMBL RUBY ROCK** OF POWER!
WHAT, ARE YOU KIDDING ME? GET YOUR PAW OFF ME!
I WILL TEST YOU!
BEFORE EXPLORING YONDER CAVE, I BUILT PREPOSTEROUS SNOWMEN OUTSIDE!
HA! WITH POWER I SQUEEZE FROM YOU I LAY WASTE TO THESE SILLY SNOWMEN!
WHAT'S ALL THE RUCKUS HERE?
WHOA! SOMEONE MUST NOT LIKE SNOWMEN VERY MUCH!

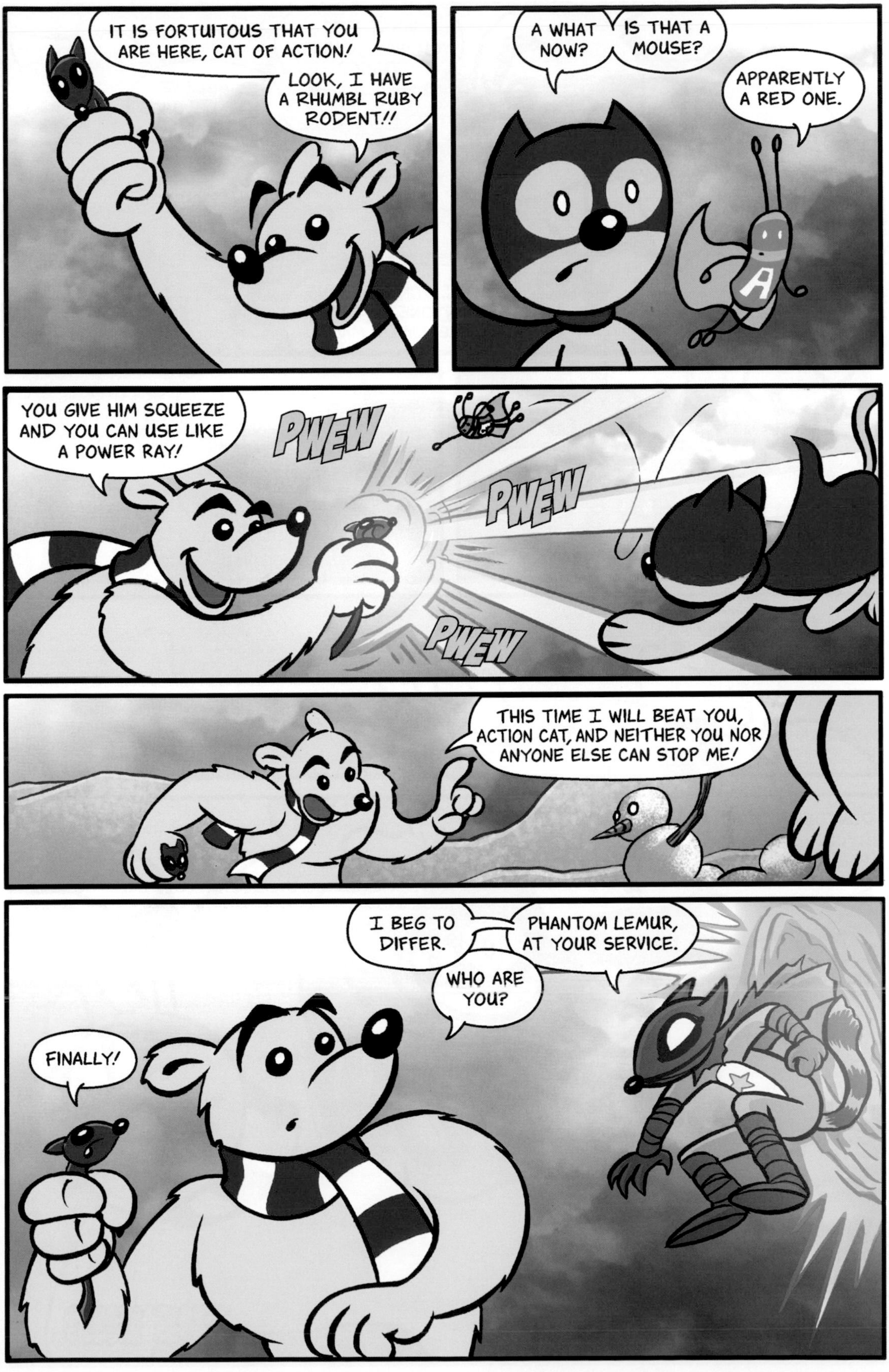
IT IS FORTUITOUS THAT YOU ARE HERE, CAT OF ACTION!
LOOK, I HAVE A RHUMBL RUBY RODENT!!
A WHAT NOW?
IS THAT A MOUSE?
APPARENTLY A RED ONE.
YOU GIVE HIM SQUEEZE AND YOU CAN USE LIKE A POWER RAY!
PWEW
PWEW
PWEW
THIS TIME I WILL BEAT YOU, ACTION CAT, AND NEITHER YOU NOR ANYONE ELSE CAN STOP ME!
I BEG TO DIFFER.
WHO ARE YOU?
PHANTOM LEMUR, AT YOUR SERVICE.
FINALLY!

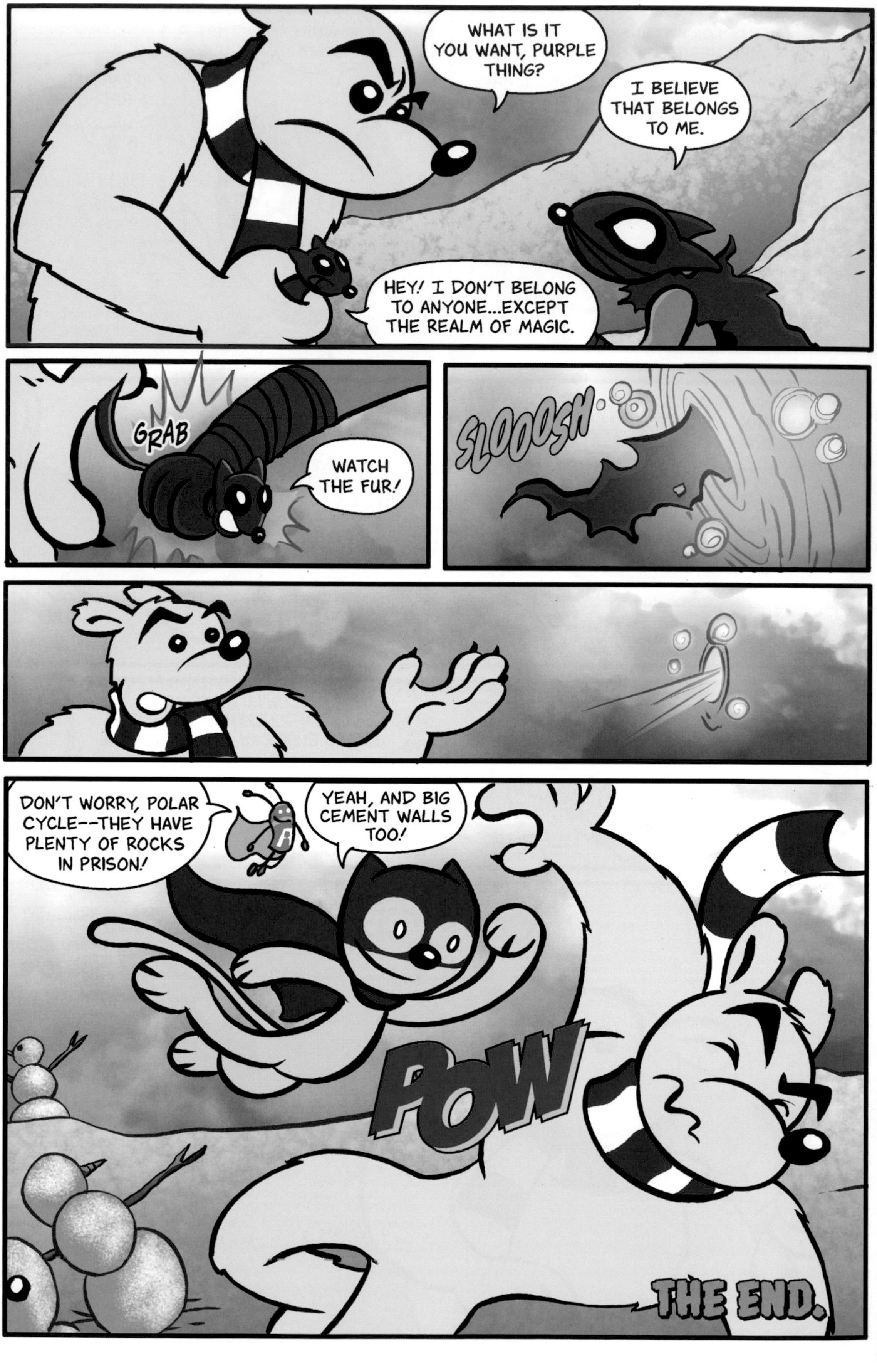
WHAT IS IT YOU WANT, PURPLE THING?
I BELIEVE THAT BELONGS TO ME.
HEY! I DON'T BELONG TO ANYONE...EXCEPT THE REALM OF MAGIC.
GRAB
WATCH THE FUR!
SLOOOSH
DON'T WORRY, POLAR CYCLE--THEY HAVE PLENTY OF ROCKS IN PRISON!
YEAH, AND BIG CEMENT WALLS TOO!
POW
THE END.

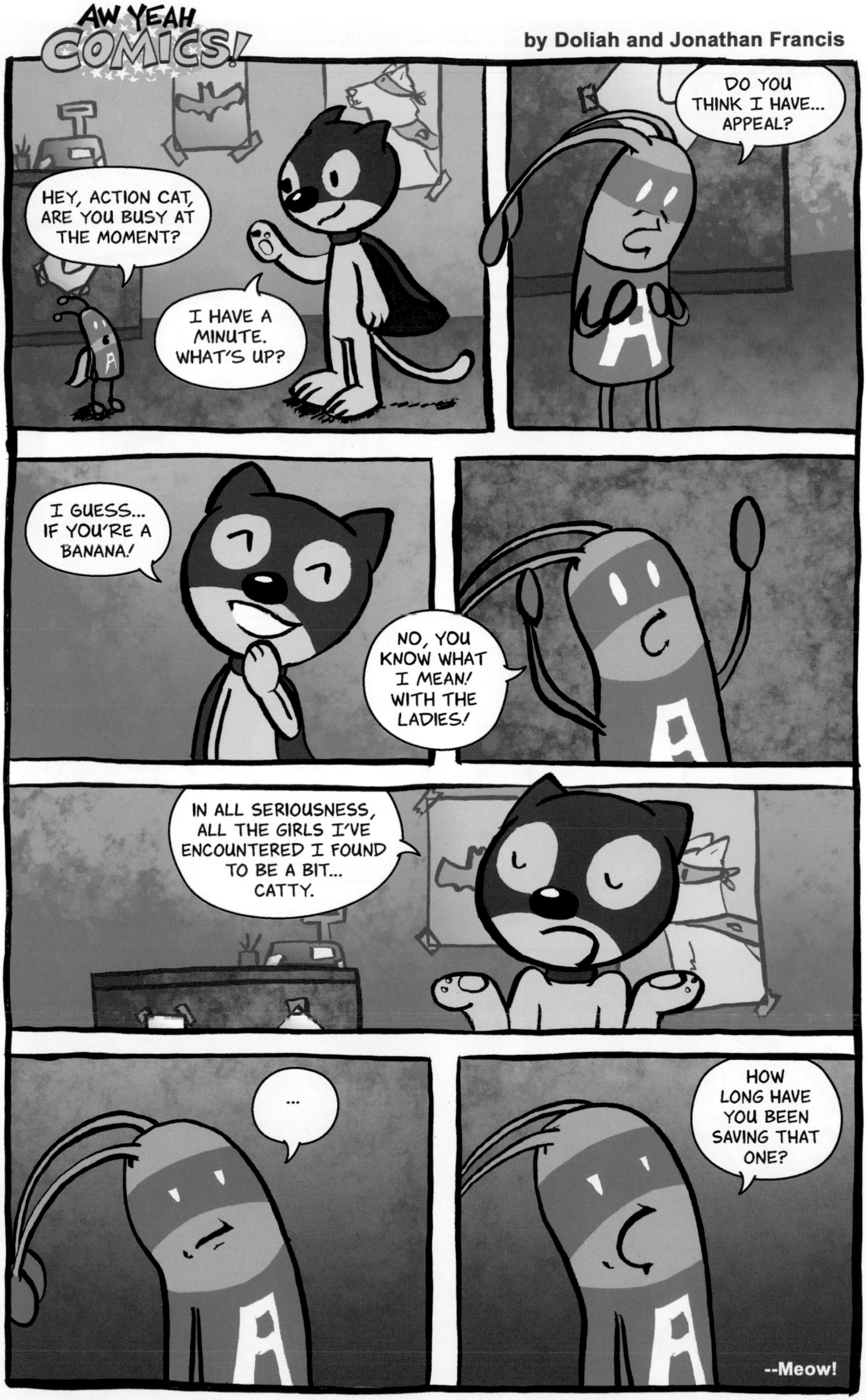
AW YEAH COMICS!
by Doliah and Jonathan Francis
HEY, ACTION CAT, ARE YOU BUSY AT THE MOMENT?
I HAVE A MINUTE. WHAT'S UP?
DO YOU THINK I HAVE... APPEAL?
I GUESS... IF YOU'RE A BANANA!
NO, YOU KNOW WHAT I MEAN! WITH THE LADIES!
IN ALL SERIOUSNESS, ALL THE GIRLS I'VE ENCOUNTERED I FOUND TO BE A BIT... CATTY.
...
HOW LONG HAVE YOU BEEN SAVING THAT ONE?
--Meow!

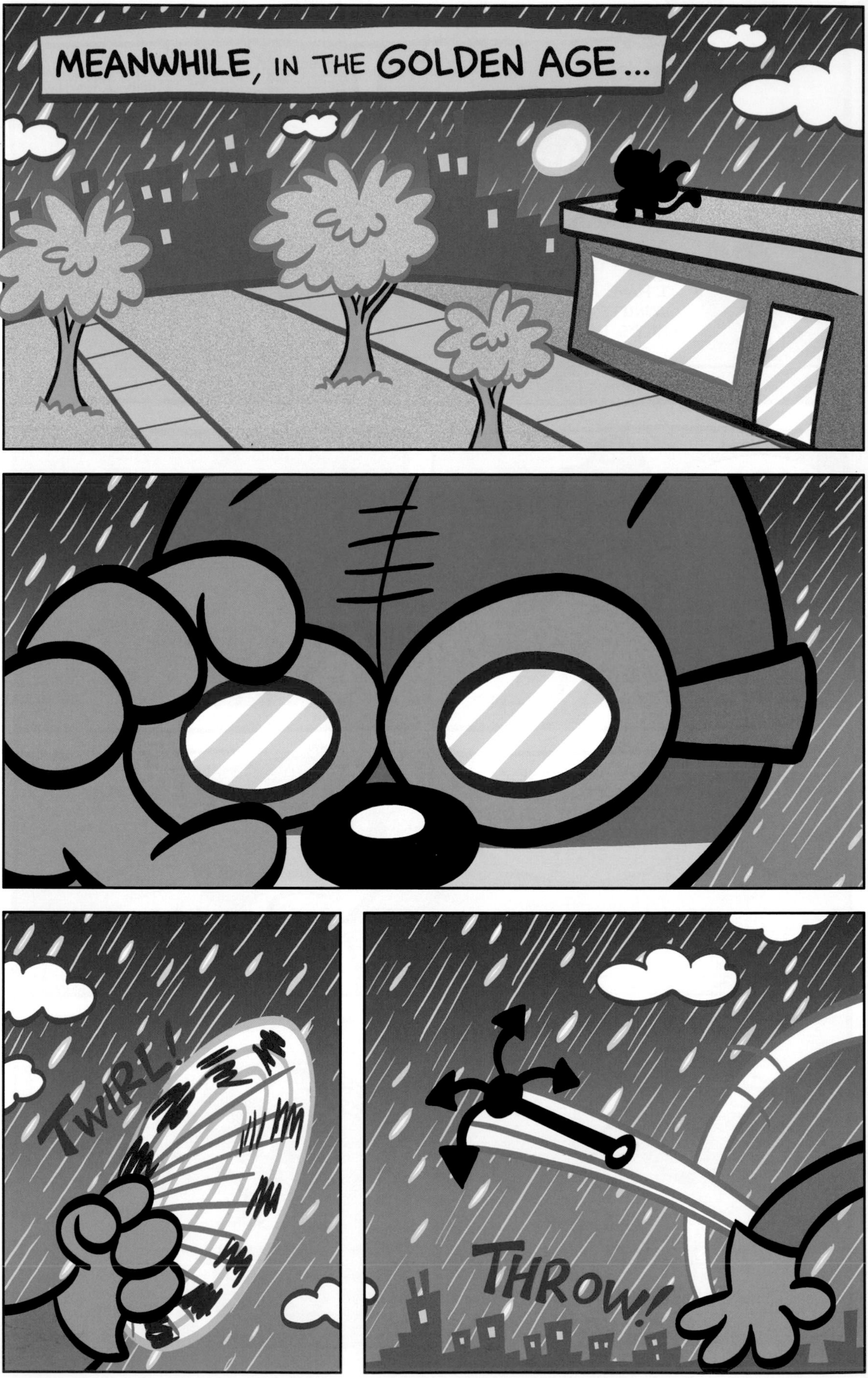
MEANWHILE, IN THE GOLDEN AGE...
TWIRL!
THROW!

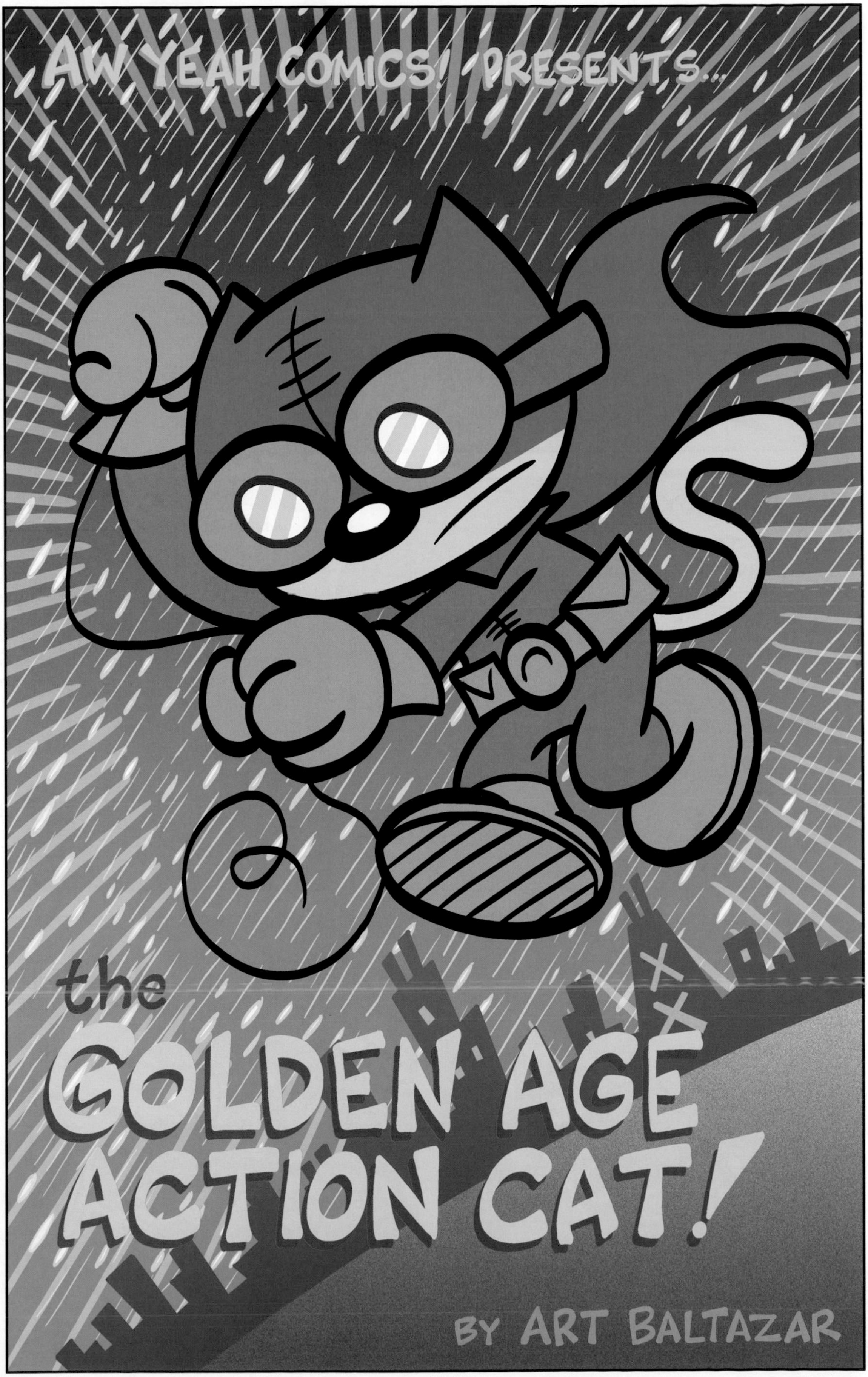
AW YEAH COMICS! PRESENTS...
the GOLDEN AGE ACTION CAT!
BY ART BALTAZAR

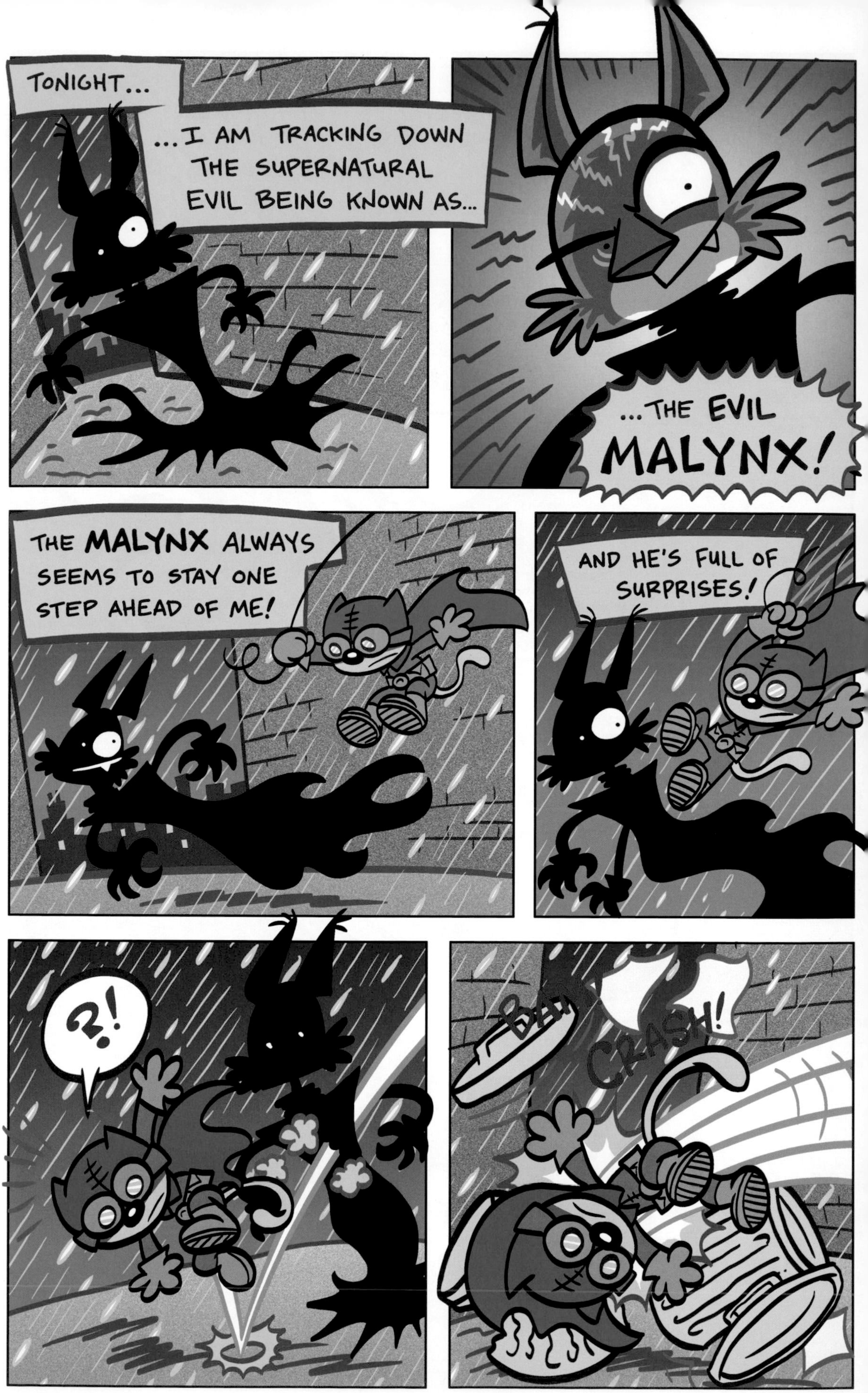
TONIGHT...
...I AM TRACKING DOWN THE SUPERNATURAL EVIL BEING KNOWN AS...
...THE EVIL MALYNX!
THE MALYNX ALWAYS SEEMS TO STAY ONE STEP AHEAD OF ME!
AND HE'S FULL OF SURPRISES!
?!
CRASH!

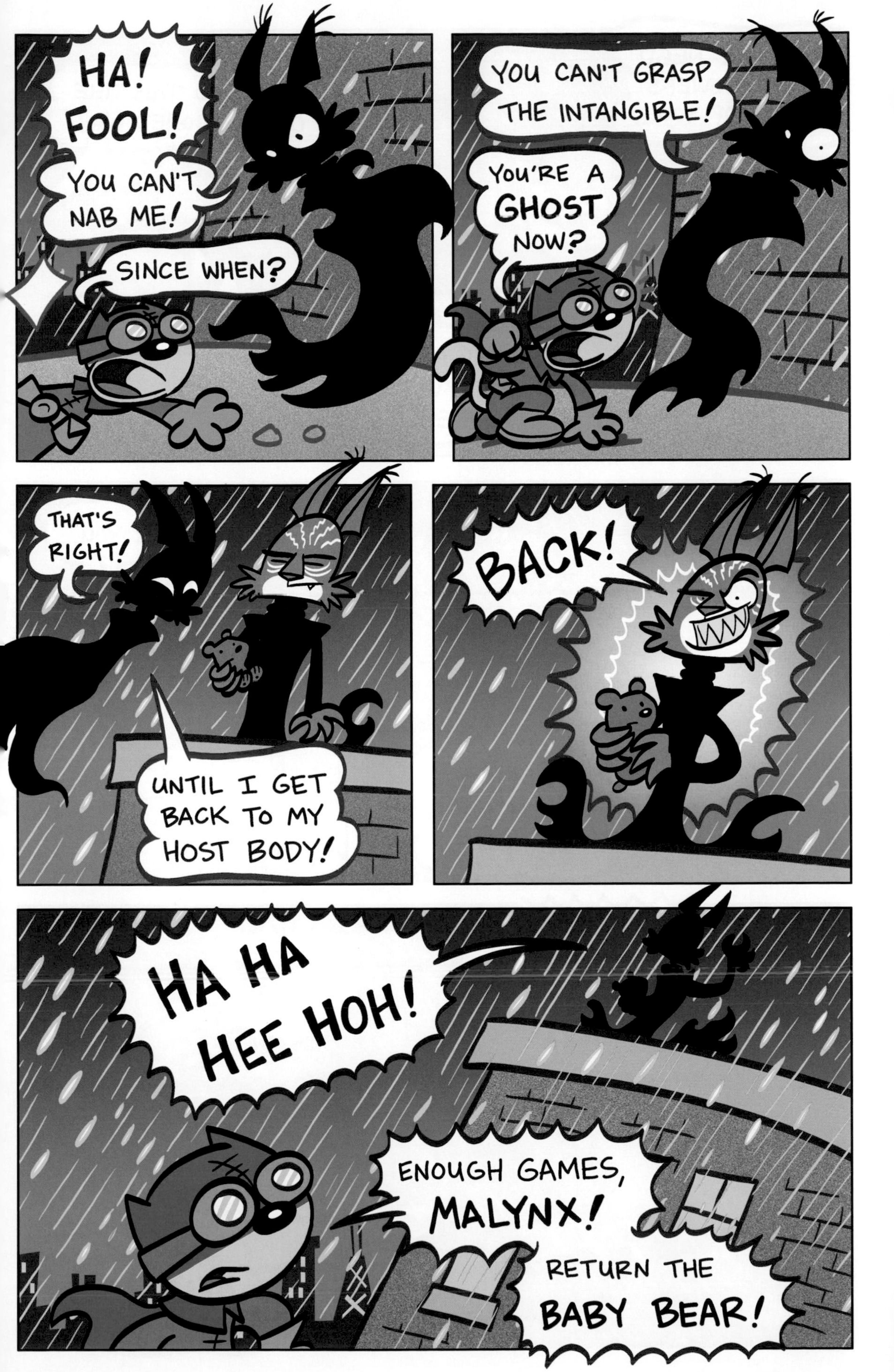
HA! FOOL!
YOU CAN'T NAB ME!
SINCE WHEN?
YOU CAN'T GRASP THE INTANGIBLE!
YOU'RE A GHOST NOW?
THAT'S RIGHT!
UNTIL I GET BACK TO MY HOST BODY!
BACK!
HA HA HEE HOH!
ENOUGH GAMES, MALYNX!
RETURN THE BABY BEAR!

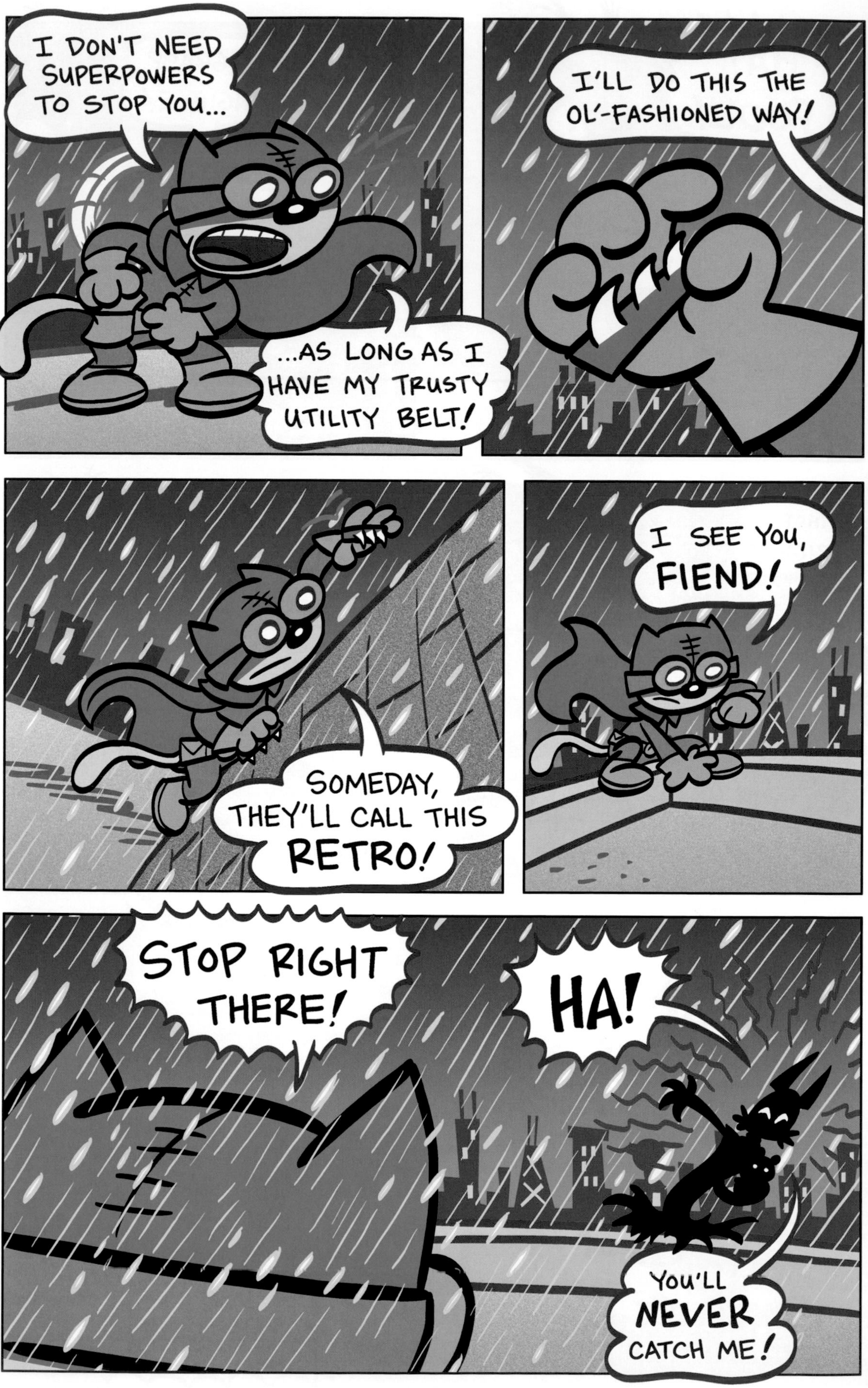
I DON'T NEED SUPERPOWERS TO STOP YOU...
...AS LONG AS I HAVE MY TRUSTY UTILITY BELT!
I'LL DO THIS THE OL'-FASHIONED WAY!
SOMEDAY, THEY'LL CALL THIS RETRO!
I SEE YOU, FIEND!
STOP RIGHT THERE!
HA!
YOU'LL NEVER CATCH ME!

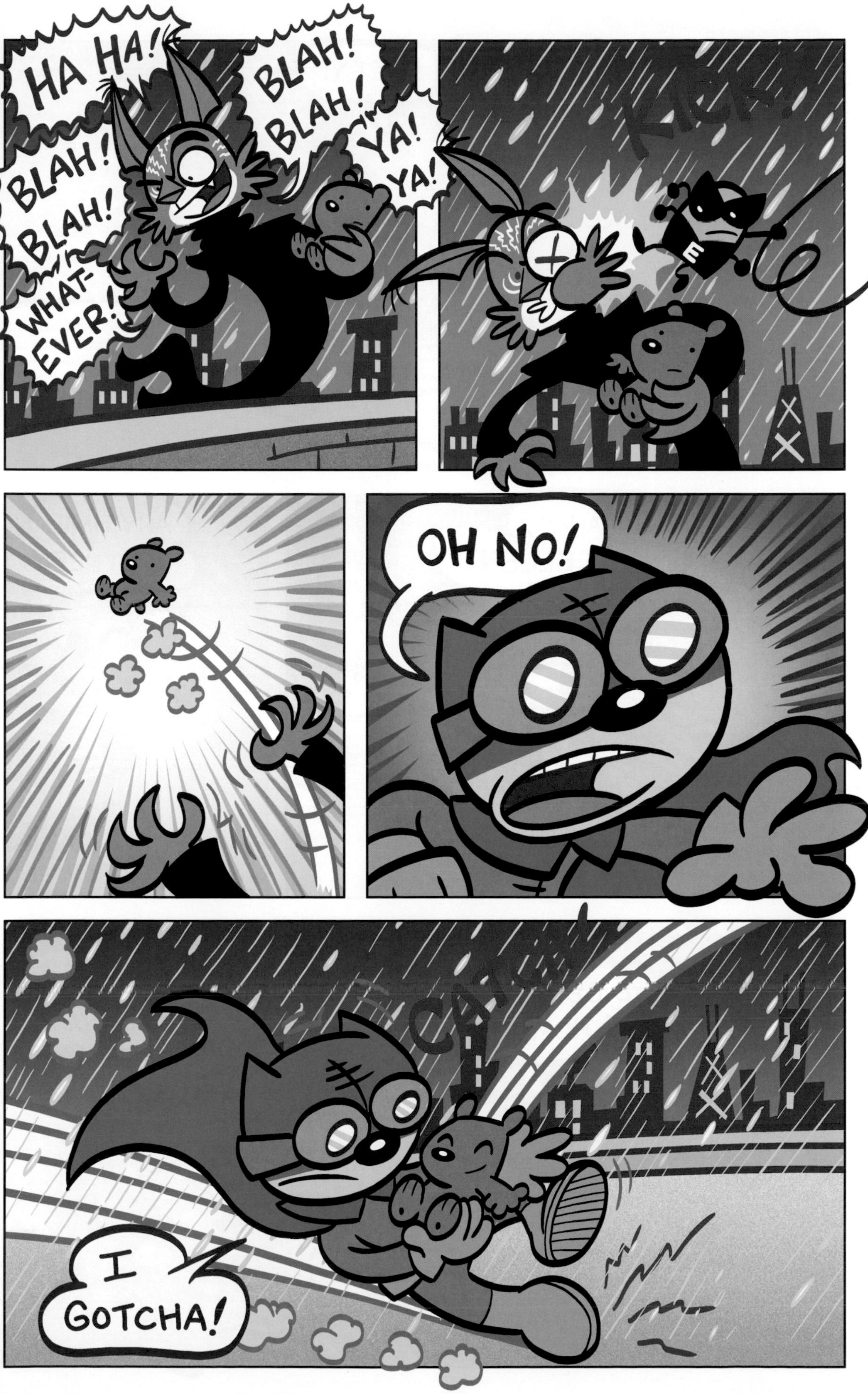
HA HA!
BLAH! BLAH! WHAT-EVER!
BLAH! BLAH!
YA! YA!
KICK!
OH NO!
CATCH!
I GOTCHA!

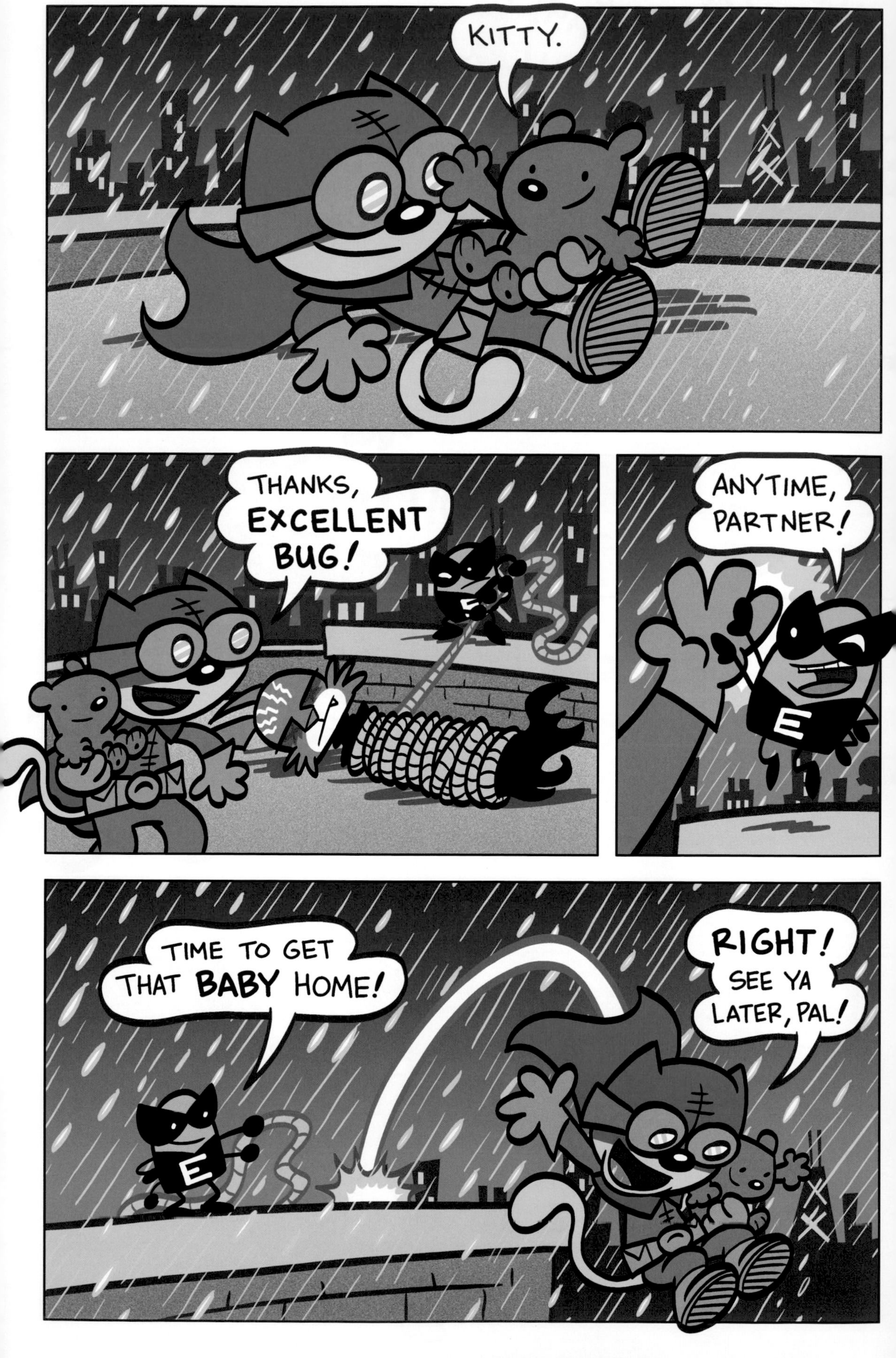
KITTY.
THANKS, EXCELLENT BUG!
ANYTIME, PARTNER!
TIME TO GET THAT BABY HOME!
RIGHT! SEE YA LATER, PAL!

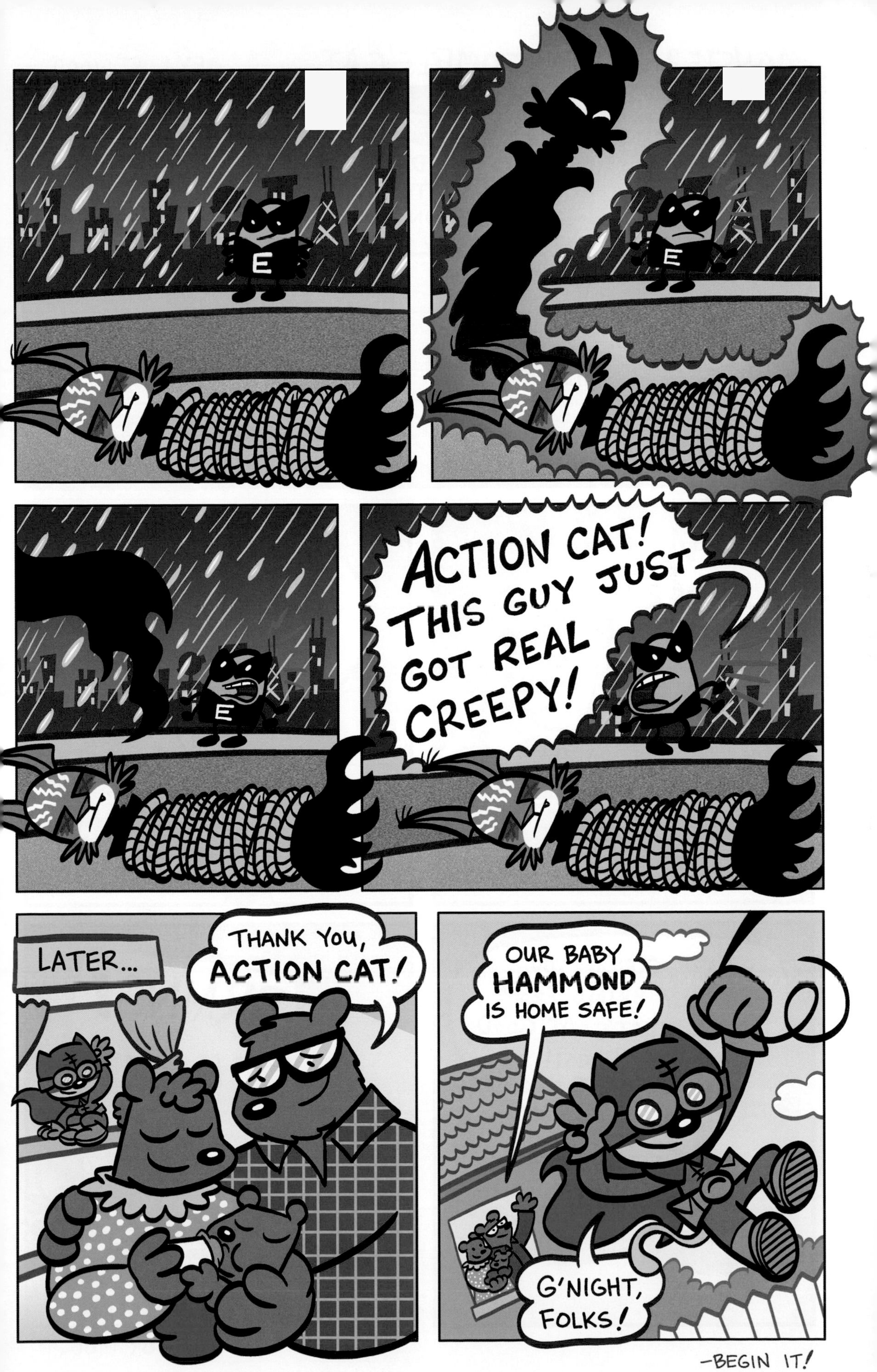
ACTION CAT! THIS GUY JUST GOT REAL CREEPY!
LATER...
THANK YOU, ACTION CAT!
OUR BABY HAMMOND IS HOME SAFE!
G'NIGHT, FOLKS!

—BEGIN IT!

MONSTER CAT AND ZOMBIE CAT BY KURT WOOD

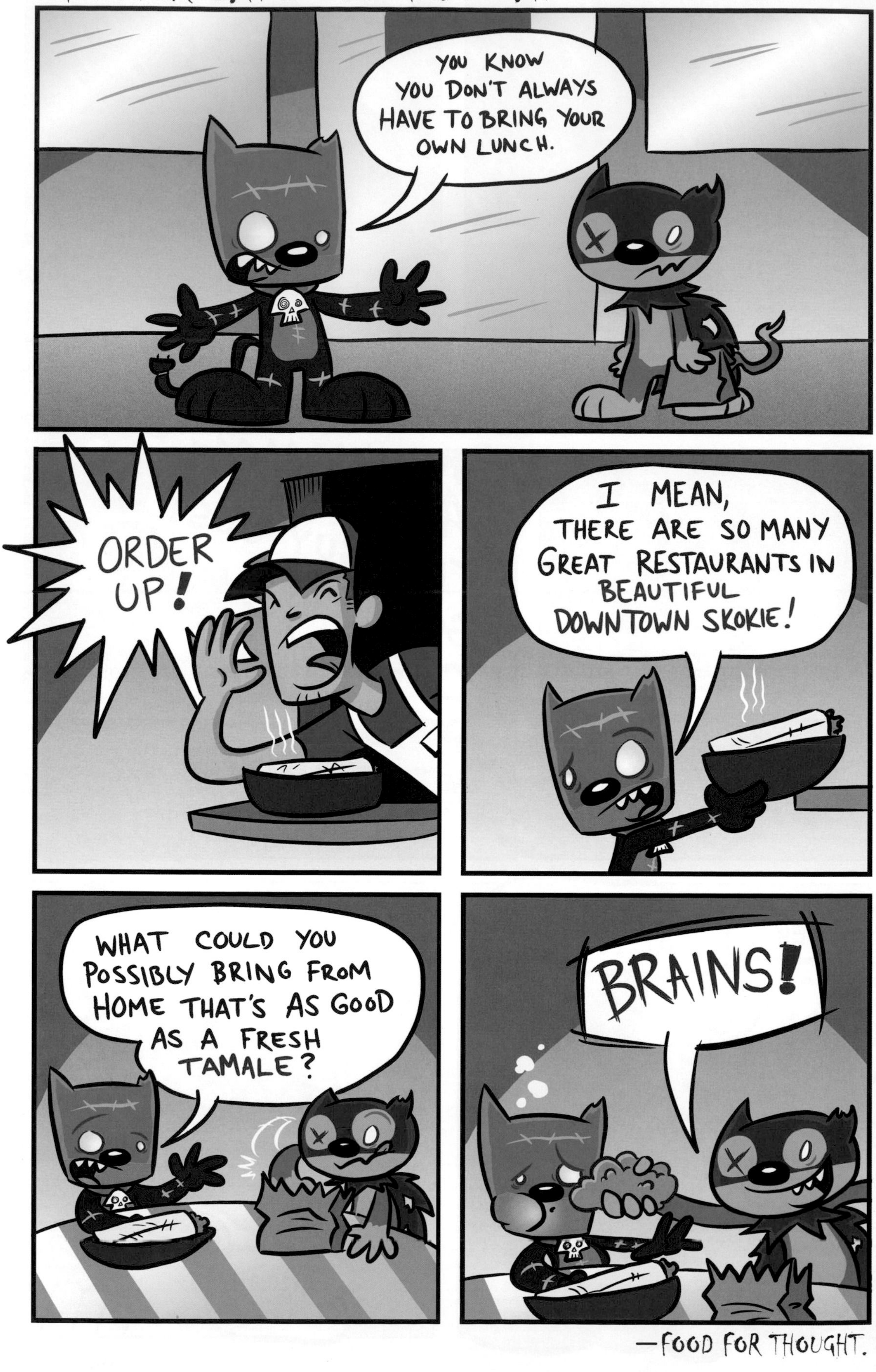
YOU KNOW YOU DON'T ALWAYS HAVE TO BRING YOUR OWN LUNCH.
ORDER UP!
I MEAN, THERE ARE SO MANY GREAT RESTAURANTS IN BEAUTIFUL DOWNTOWN SKOKIE!
WHAT COULD YOU POSSIBLY BRING FROM HOME THAT'S AS GOOD AS A FRESH TAMALE?
BRAINS!

—FOOD FOR THOUGHT.

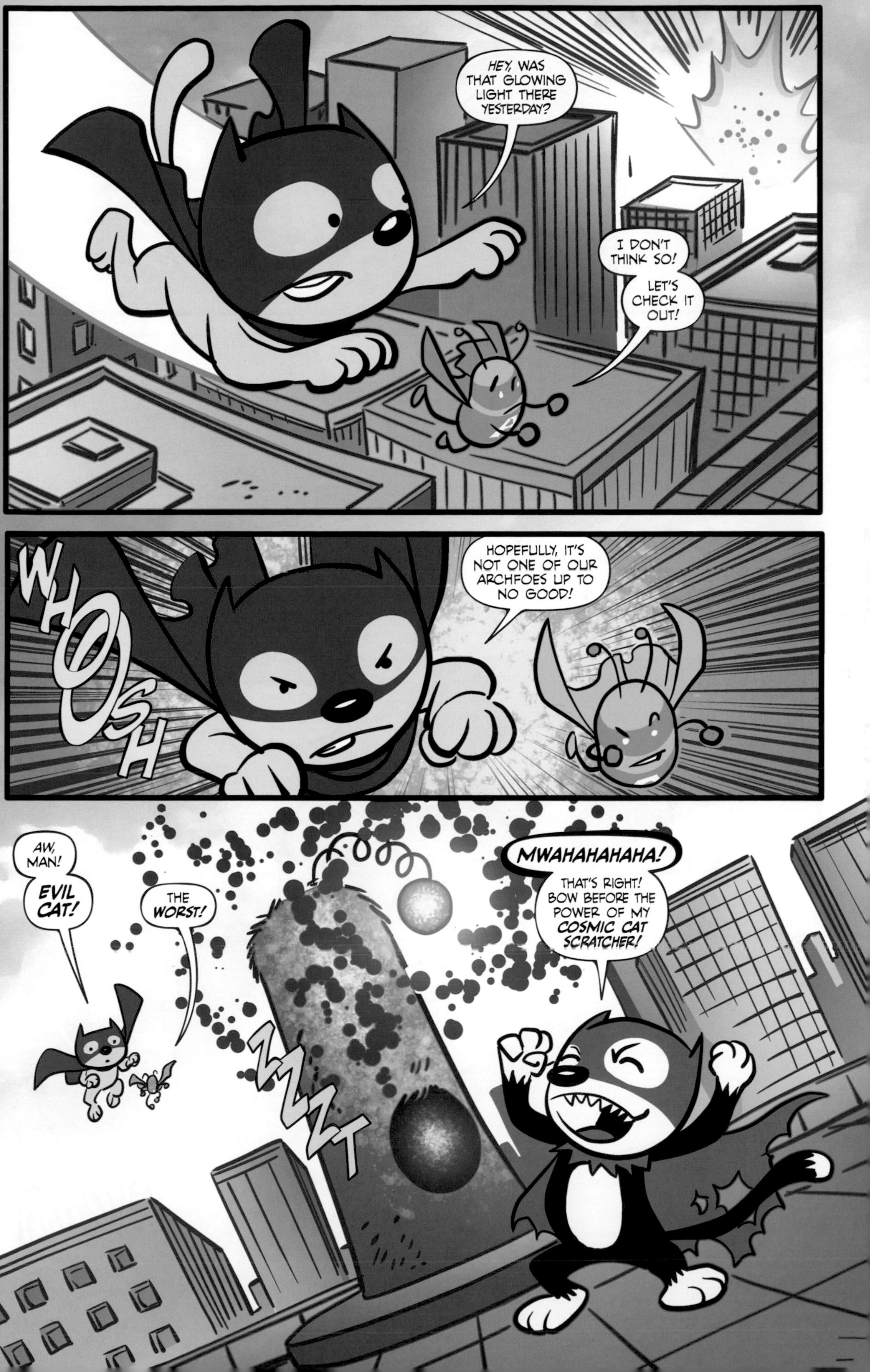
HEY, WAS THAT GLOWING LIGHT THERE YESTERDAY?
I DON'T THINK SO!
LET'S CHECK IT OUT!
WHOOSH
HOPEFULLY, IT'S NOT ONE OF OUR ARCHFOES UP TO NO GOOD!
AW, MAN!
EVIL CAT!
THE WORST!
MWAHAHAHAHA!
THAT'S RIGHT! BOW BEFORE THE POWER OF MY COSMIC CAT SCRATCHER!
ZZZZT

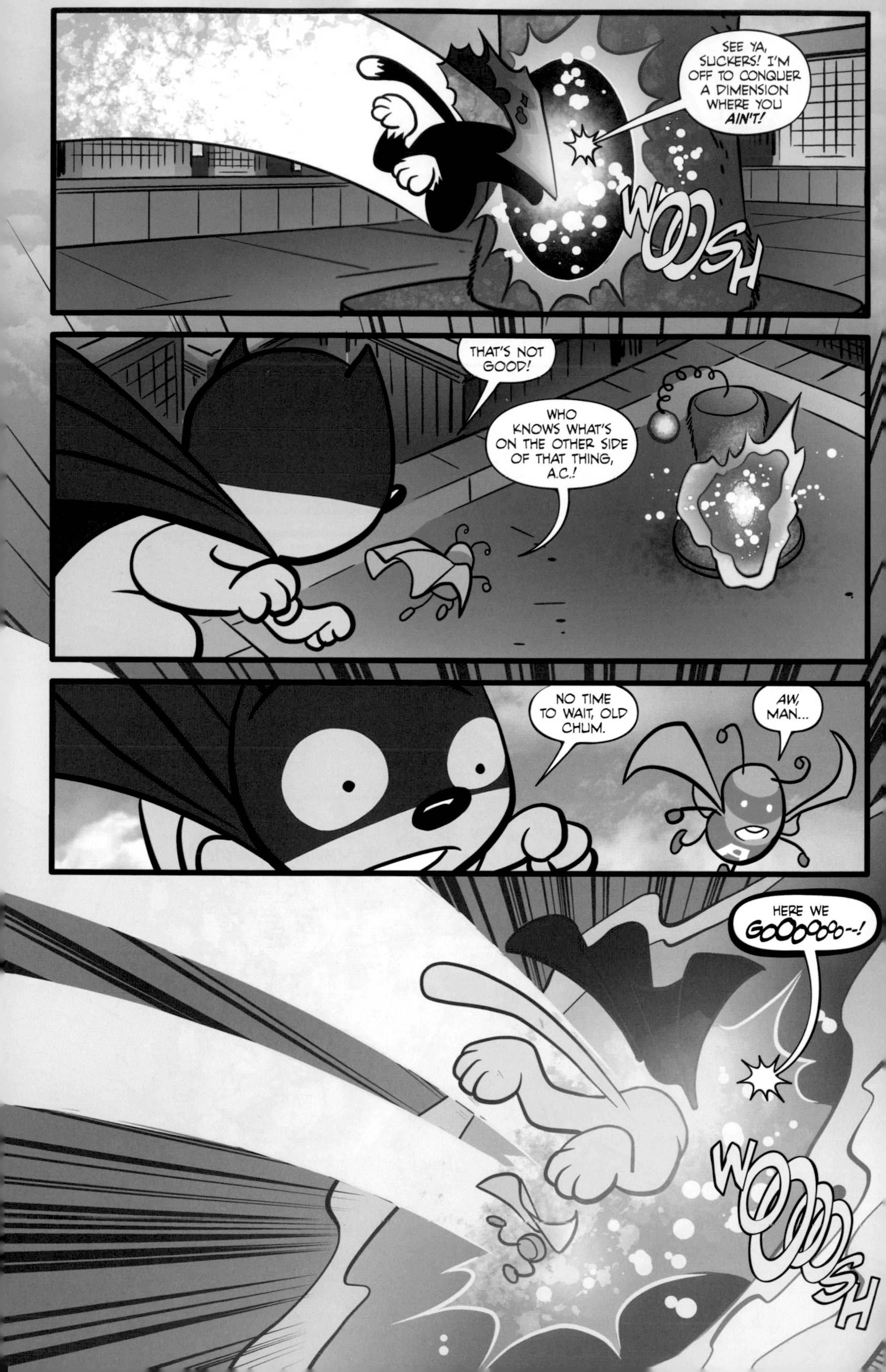
SEE YA, SUCKERS! I'M OFF TO CONQUER A DIMENSION WHERE YOU AIN'T!
WOOSH
THAT'S NOT GOOD!
WHO KNOWS WHAT'S ON THE OTHER SIDE OF THAT THING, A.C.!
NO TIME TO WAIT, OLD CHUM.
AW, MAN...
HERE WE GOOOOOOO--!
WOOOOSH

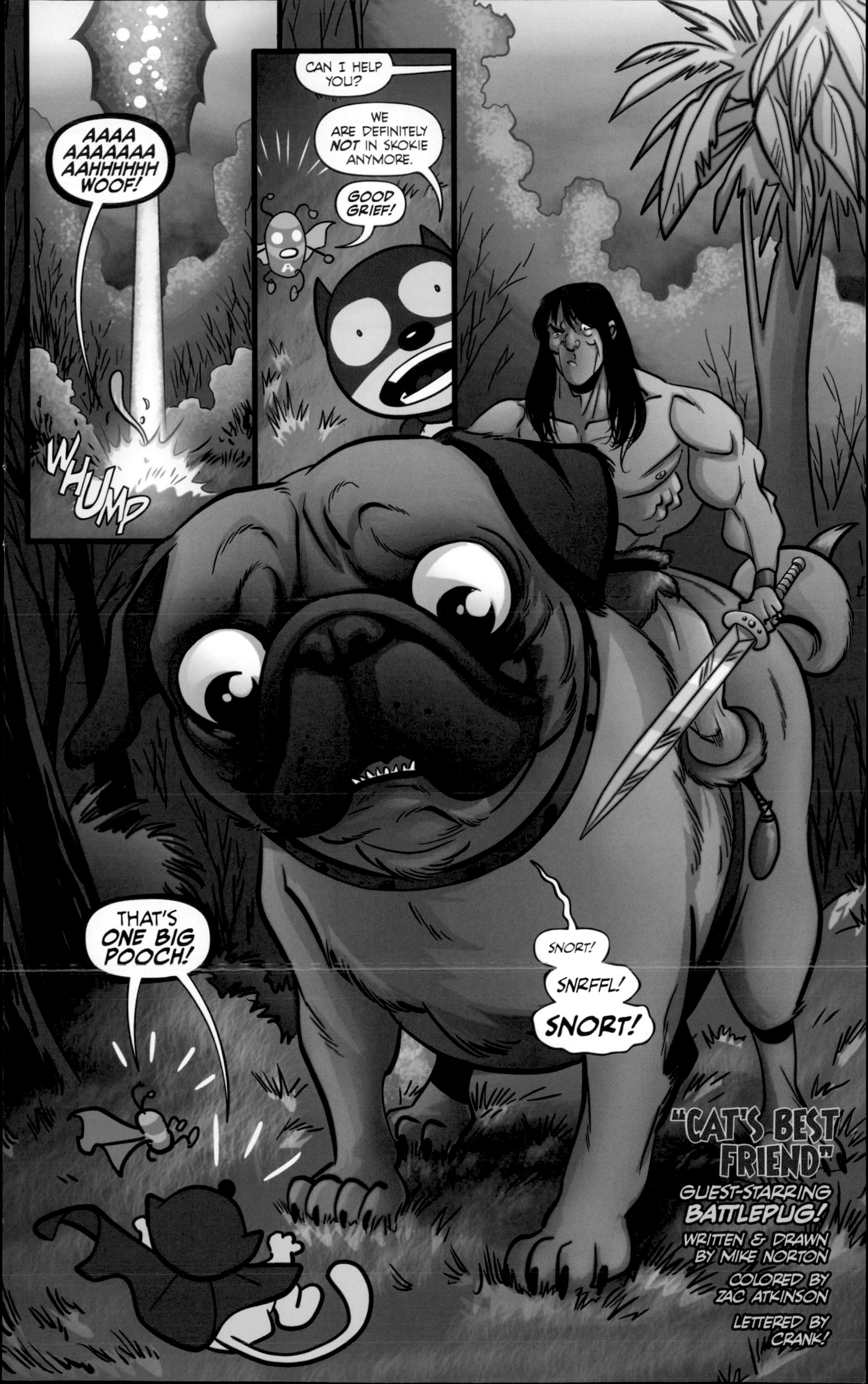
AAAA AAAAAAA AAHHHHHH WOOF!
WHUMP
CAN I HELP YOU?
WE ARE DEFINITELY NOT IN SKOKIE ANYMORE.
GOOD GRIEF!
THAT'S ONE BIG POOCH!
SNORT!
SNRFFL!
SNORT!
"CAT'S BEST FRIEND"
GUEST-STARRING BATTLEPUG!
WRITTEN & DRAWN BY MIKE NORTON
COLORED BY ZAC ATKINSON
LETTERED BY CRANK!

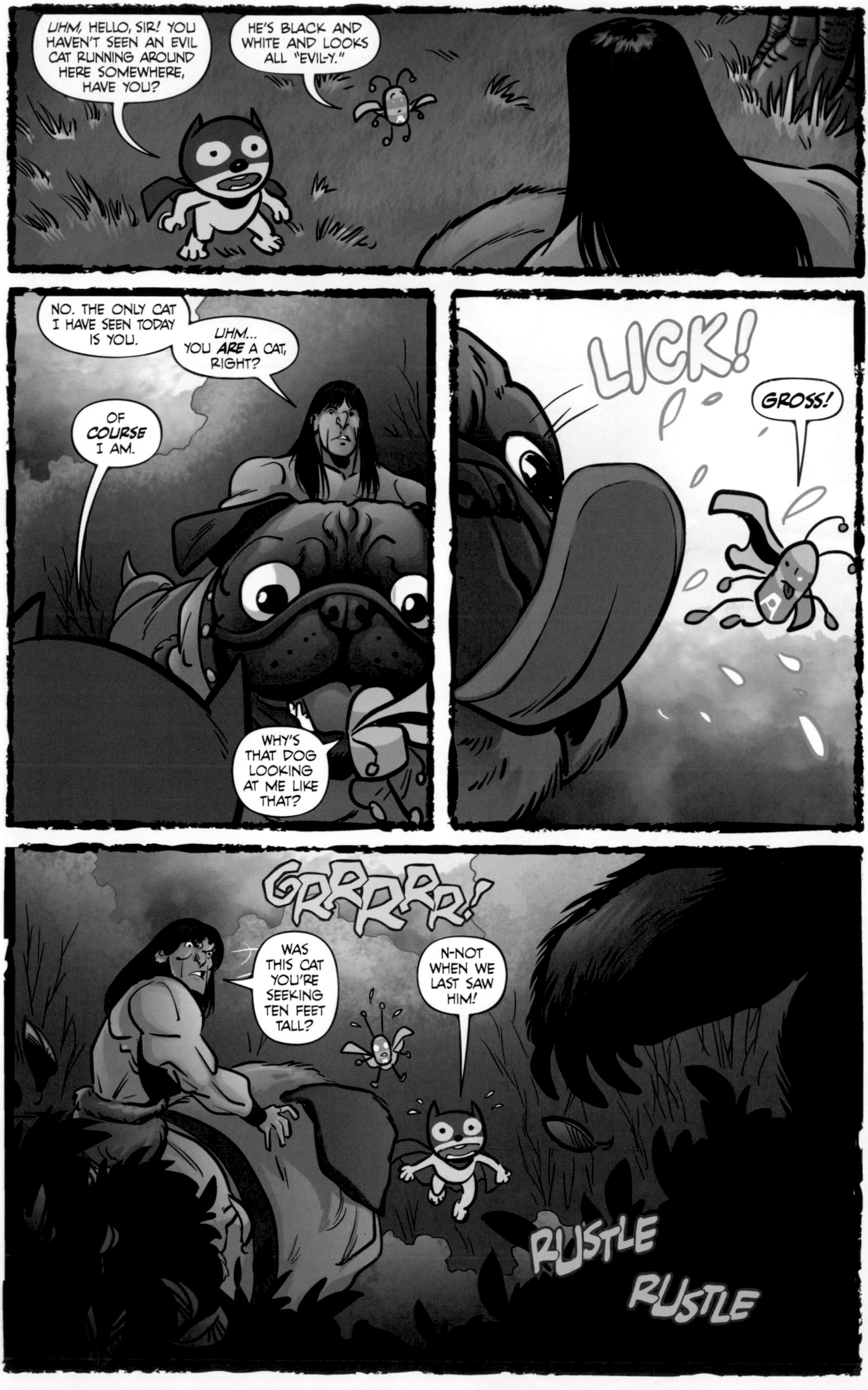
UHM, HELLO, SIR! YOU HAVEN'T SEEN AN EVIL CAT RUNNING AROUND HERE SOMEWHERE, HAVE YOU?
HE'S BLACK AND WHITE AND LOOKS ALL "EVIL-Y."
NO. THE ONLY CAT I HAVE SEEN TODAY IS YOU.
UHM... YOU ARE A CAT, RIGHT?
OF COURSE I AM.
WHY'S THAT DOG LOOKING AT ME LIKE THAT?
LICK!
GROSS!
GRRRRR!
WAS THIS CAT YOU'RE SEEKING TEN FEET TALL?
N-NOT WHEN WE LAST SAW HIM!
RUSTLE
RUSTLE

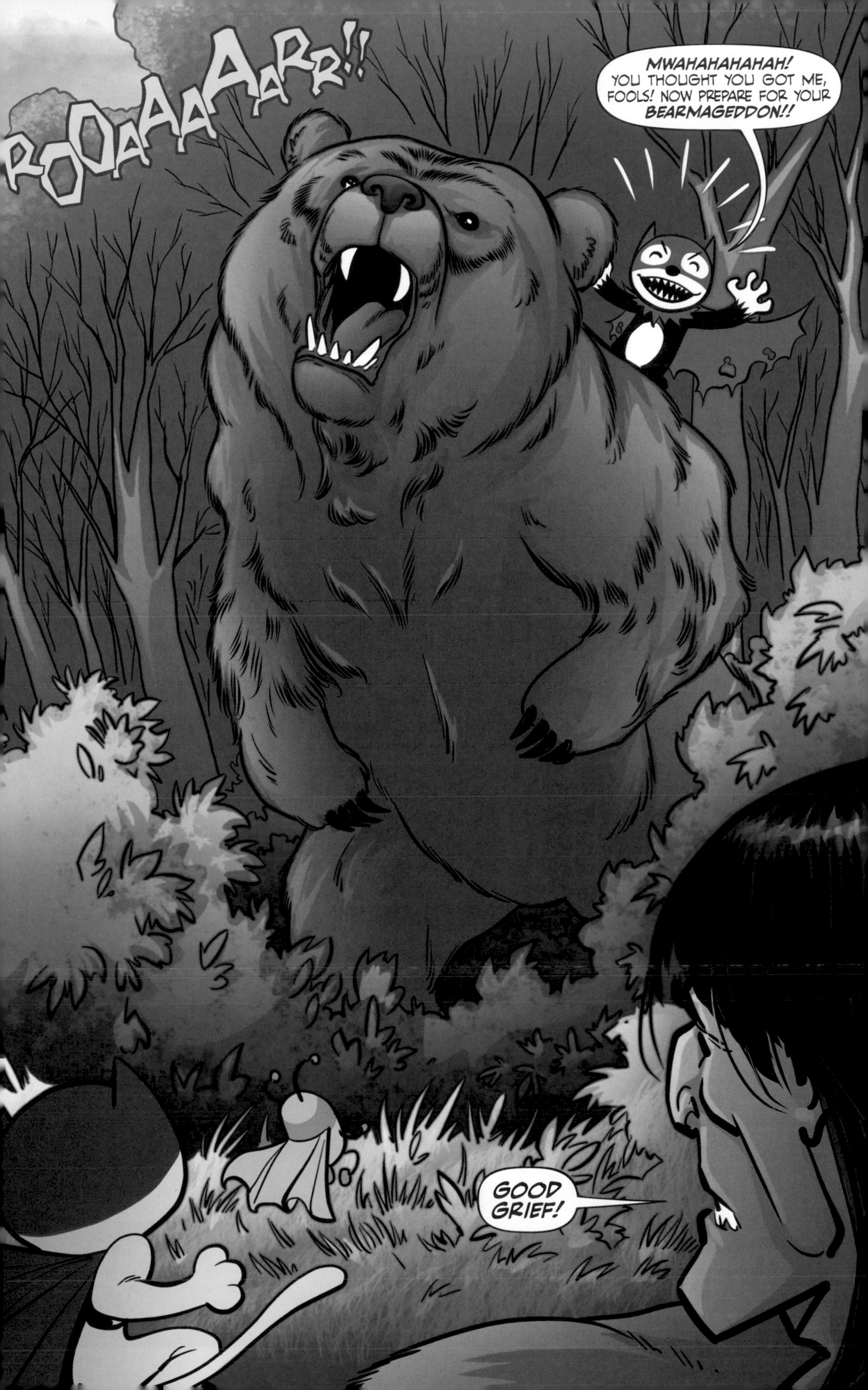
ROOAAAAAARR!!
MWAHAHAHAHAH! YOU THOUGHT YOU GOT ME, FOOLS! NOW PREPARE FOR YOUR BEARMAGEDDON!!
GOOD GRIEF!

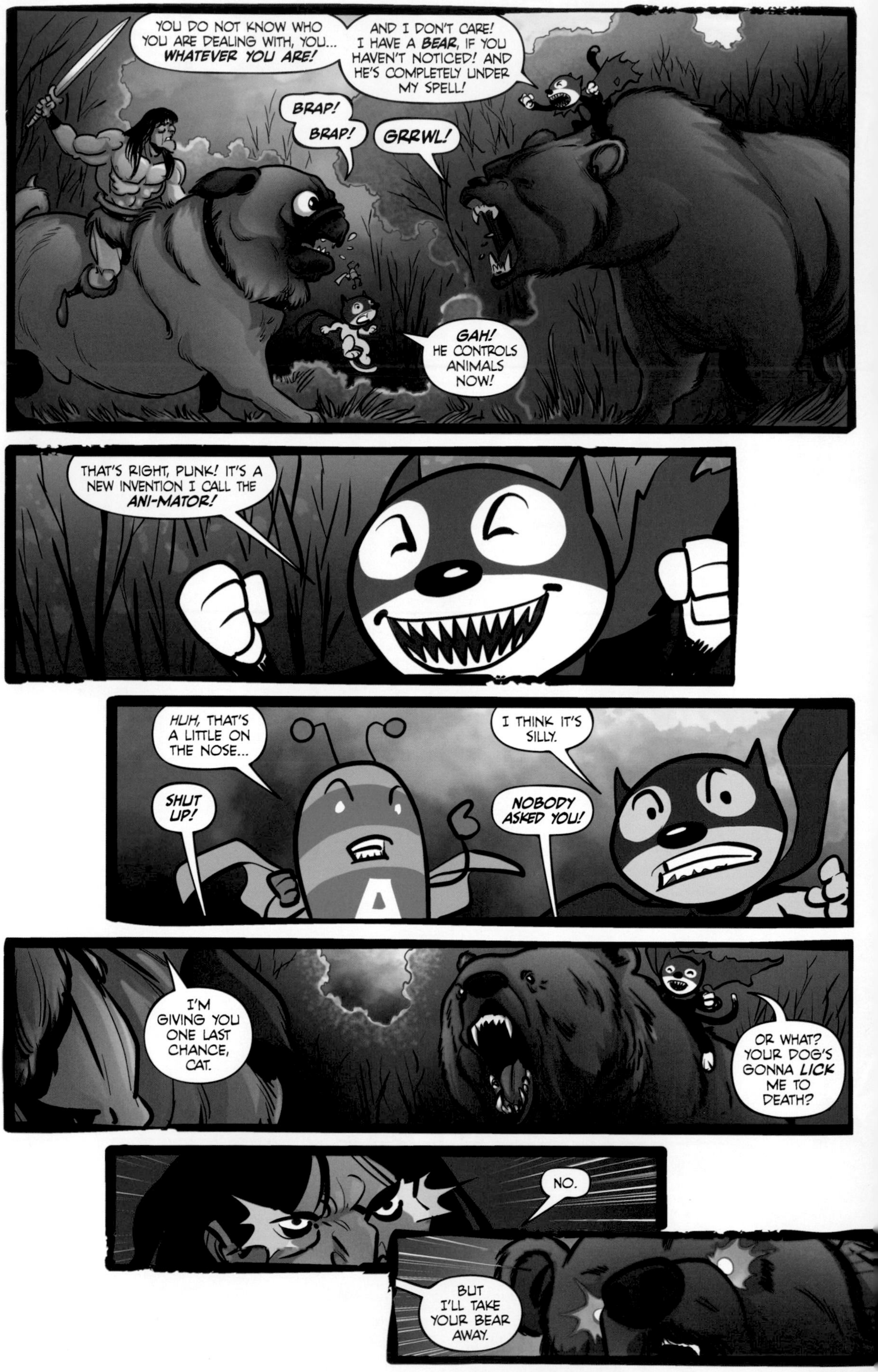
YOU DO NOT KNOW WHO YOU ARE DEALING WITH, YOU... WHATEVER YOU ARE!
AND I DON'T CARE! I HAVE A BEAR, IF YOU HAVEN'T NOTICED! AND HE'S COMPLETELY UNDER MY SPELL!
BRAP!
BRAP!
GRRWL!
GAH! HE CONTROLS ANIMALS NOW!
THAT'S RIGHT, PUNK! IT'S A NEW INVENTION I CALL THE ANI-MATOR!
HUH, THAT'S A LITTLE ON THE NOSE...
I THINK IT'S SILLY.
SHUT UP!
NOBODY ASKED YOU!
I'M GIVING YOU ONE LAST CHANCE, CAT.
OR WHAT? YOUR DOG'S GONNA LICK ME TO DEATH?
NO.
BUT I'LL TAKE YOUR BEAR AWAY.

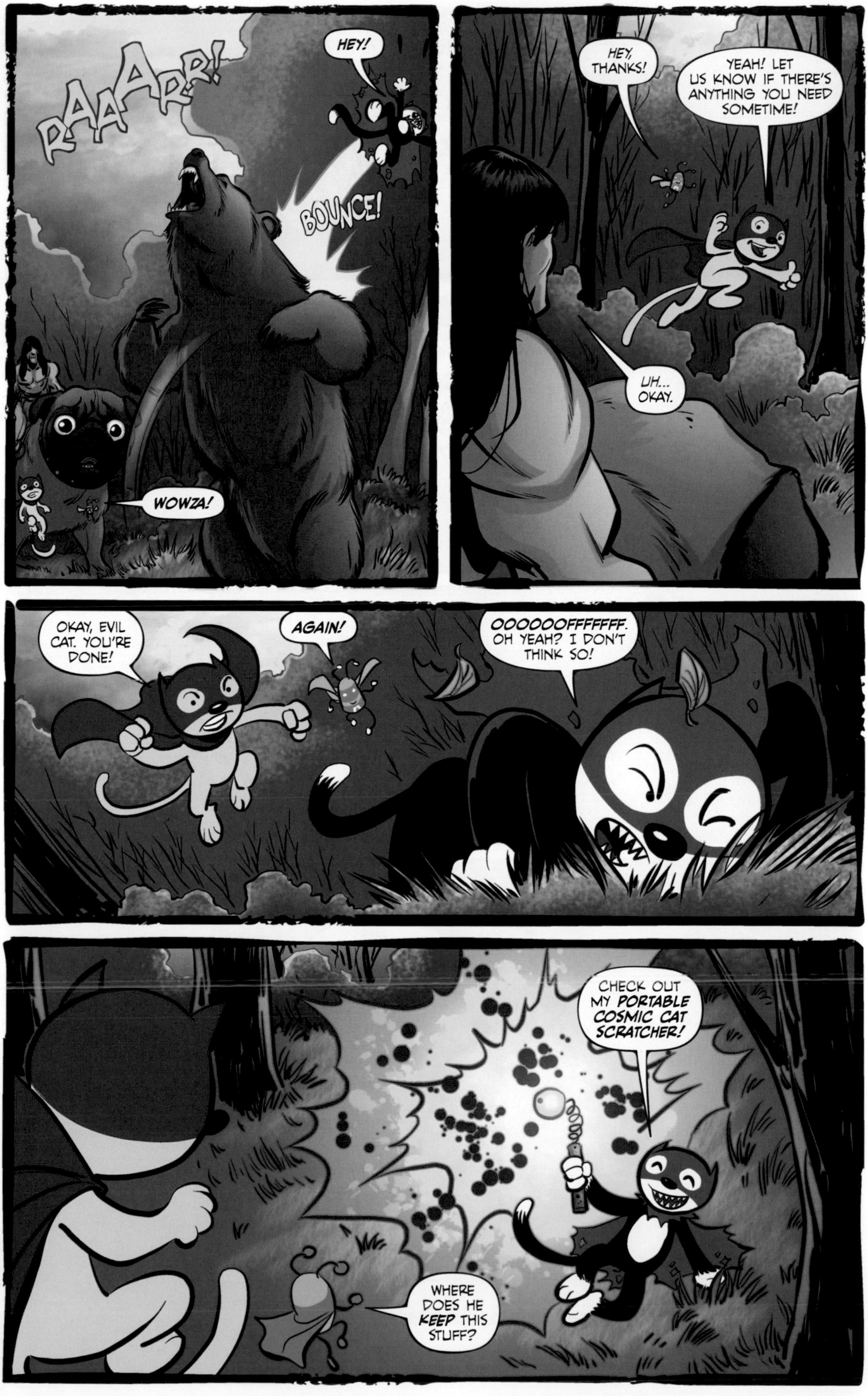
RAAARR!
HEY!
BOUNCE!
WOWZA!
HEY, THANKS!
YEAH! LET US KNOW IF THERE'S ANYTHING YOU NEED SOMETIME!
UH... OKAY.
OKAY, EVIL CAT. YOU'RE DONE!
AGAIN!
OOOOOOFFFFFFF. OH YEAH? I DON'T THINK SO!
CHECK OUT MY PORTABLE COSMIC CAT SCRATCHER!
WHERE DOES HE KEEP THIS STUFF?

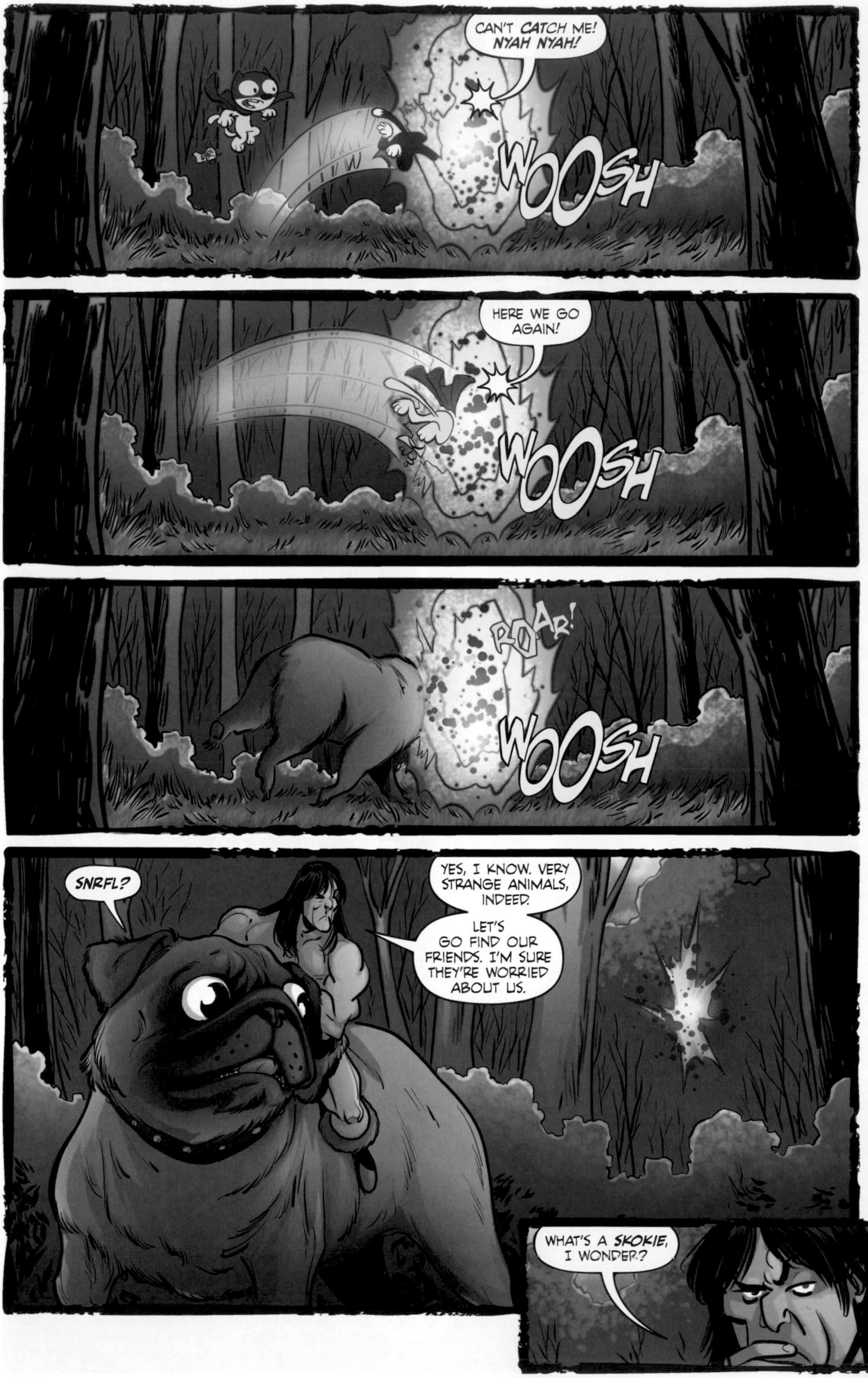
CAN'T CATCH ME! NYAH NYAH!
WOOSH
HERE WE GO AGAIN!
WOOSH
ROAR!
WOOSH
SNRFL?
YES, I KNOW. VERY STRANGE ANIMALS, INDEED.
LET'S GO FIND OUR FRIENDS. I'M SURE THEY'RE WORRIED ABOUT US.
WHAT'S A SKOKIE, I WONDER?

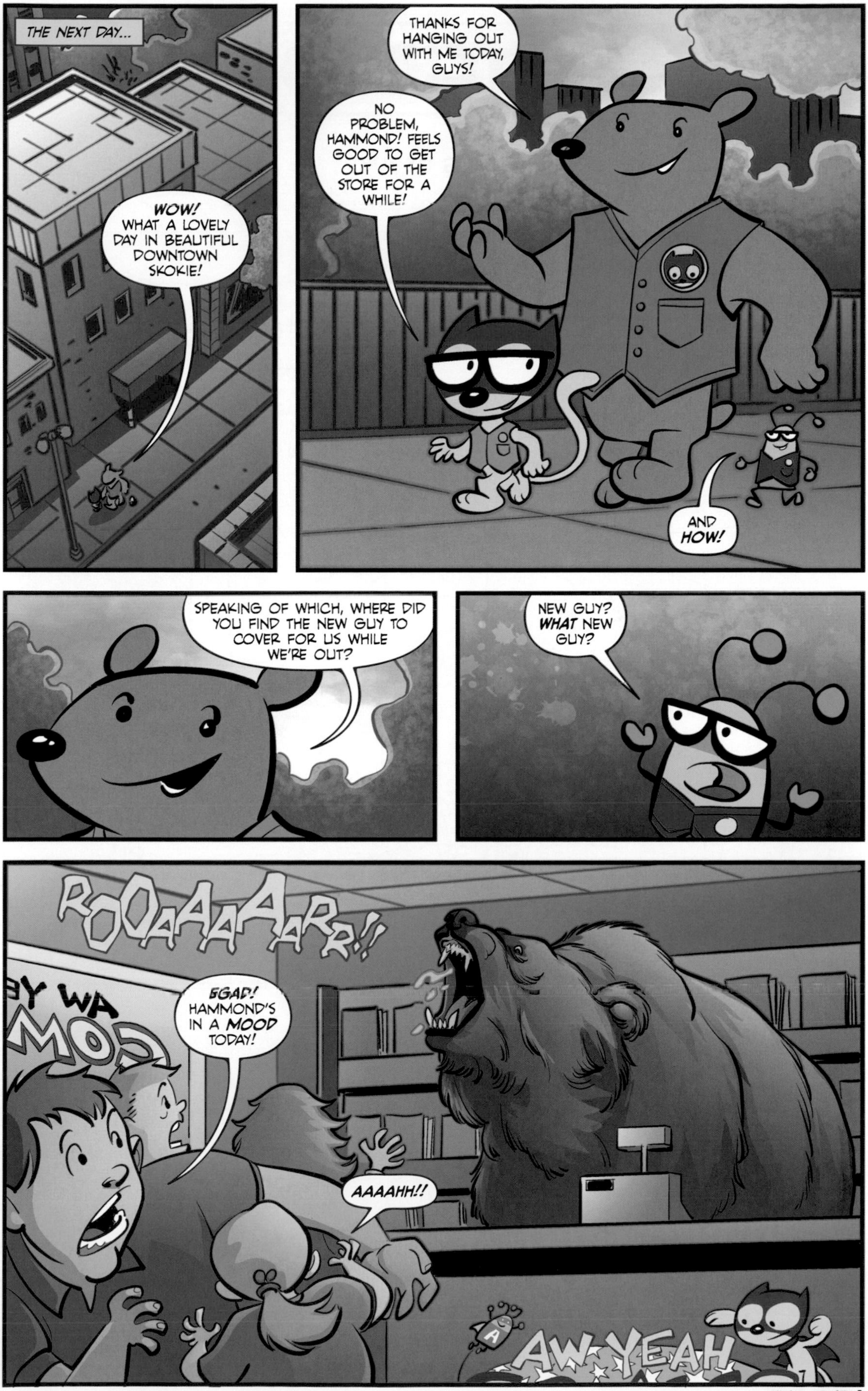
THE NEXT DAY...
WOW! WHAT A LOVELY DAY IN BEAUTIFUL DOWNTOWN SKOKIE!
THANKS FOR HANGING OUT WITH ME TODAY, GUYS!
NO PROBLEM, HAMMOND! FEELS GOOD TO GET OUT OF THE STORE FOR A WHILE!
AND HOW!
SPEAKING OF WHICH, WHERE DID YOU FIND THE NEW GUY TO COVER FOR US WHILE WE'RE OUT?
NEW GUY? WHAT NEW GUY?
ROOAAAAARR!!
EGAD! HAMMOND'S IN A MOOD TODAY!
AAAAHH!!
AW YEAH

THE END!

★ SKETCHBOOK ★

Notes by Art

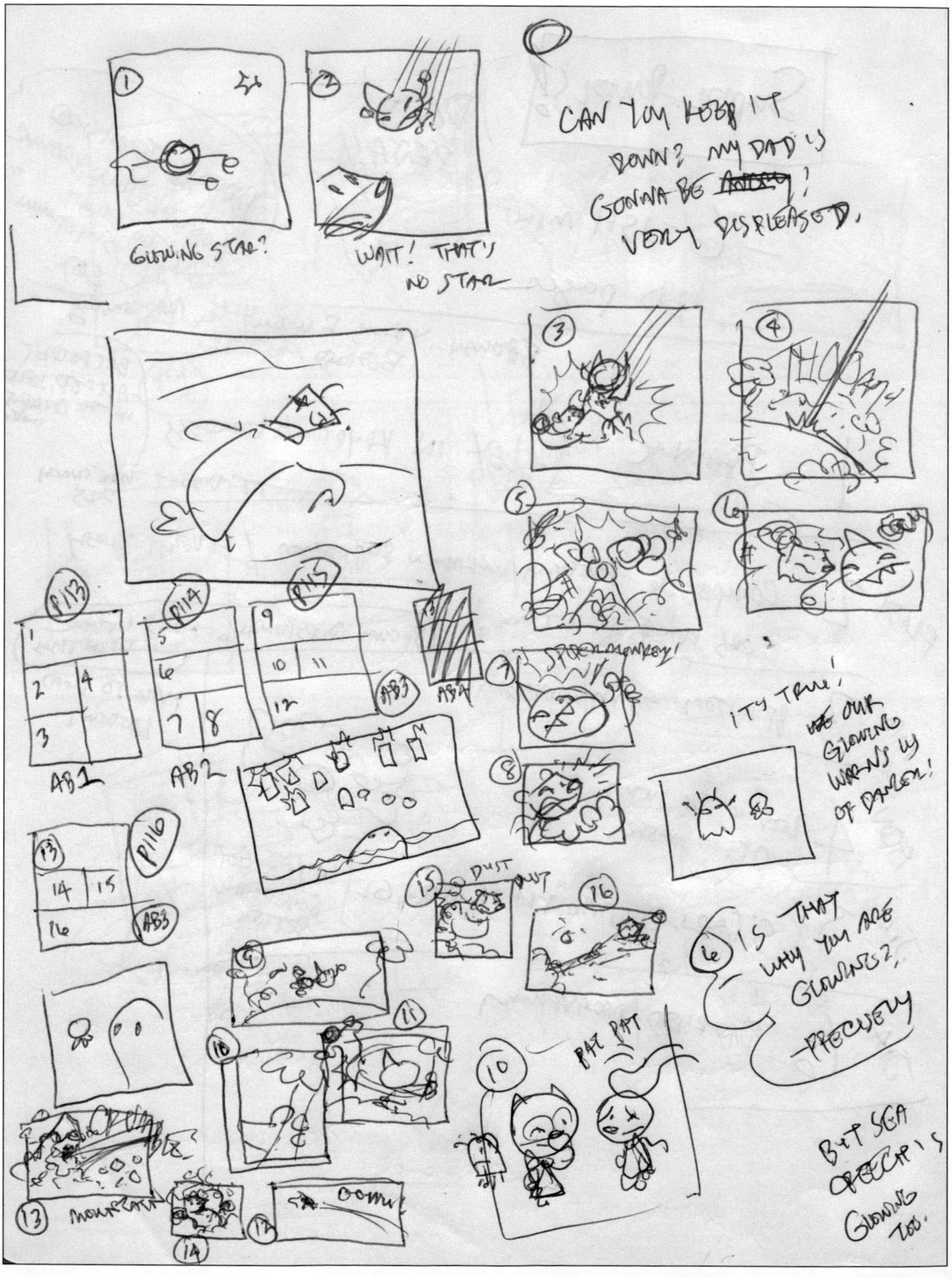
GLOWING STAR?
WAIT! THAT'S NO STAR
CAN YOU KEEP IT DOWN? MY DAD'S GONNA BE VERY DISPLEASED.
IT'S TRUE!
OUR GLOWING WARNS US OF DANGER!
DUST
IS THAT WHY YOU ARE GLOWING?
PRECISELY
PAT PAT
AB1
AB2

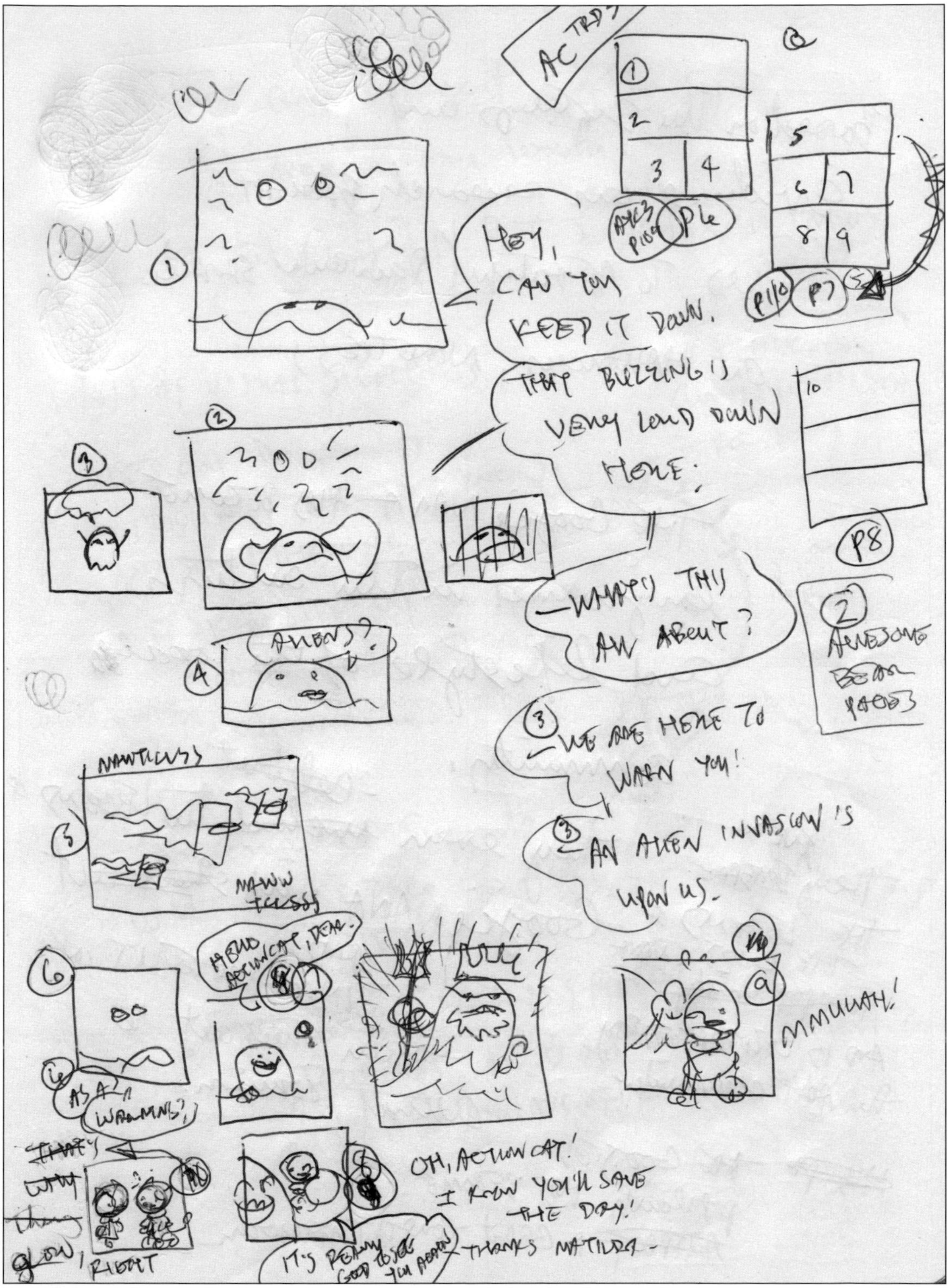
HEY, CAN YOU KEEP IT DOWN.
THAT BUZZING IS VERY LOUD DOWN HERE.
WHAT'S THIS ALL ABOUT?
ALIENS?
WE ARE HERE TO WARN YOU!
AN ALIEN INVASION IS UPON US.
AS A WARNING?
MMUUAH!
OH, ACTION CAT! I KNOW YOU'LL SAVE THE DAY!
IT'S REALLY GOOD TO SEE YOU AGAIN
THANKS MATILDA -

AW YEAH! HERE ARE SOME THUMBNAIL SKETCHES FOR THE NEW STORIES IN THIS BOOK! THIS IS HOW I WRITE COMICS! I THINK OF SCENES AND STORIES AND MAKE LITTLE DRAWINGS. THEN I NUMBER THEM AND PUT THEM TOGETHER. THIS WAS ORIGINALLY AN EVIL MARQUAID STORY. BUT THEN IT GOT MORE EPIC THAN I HAD PAGES FOR. SO I CHANGED THE ENDING AND DECIDED TO USE IT LATER IN *ACTION CAT #4*!

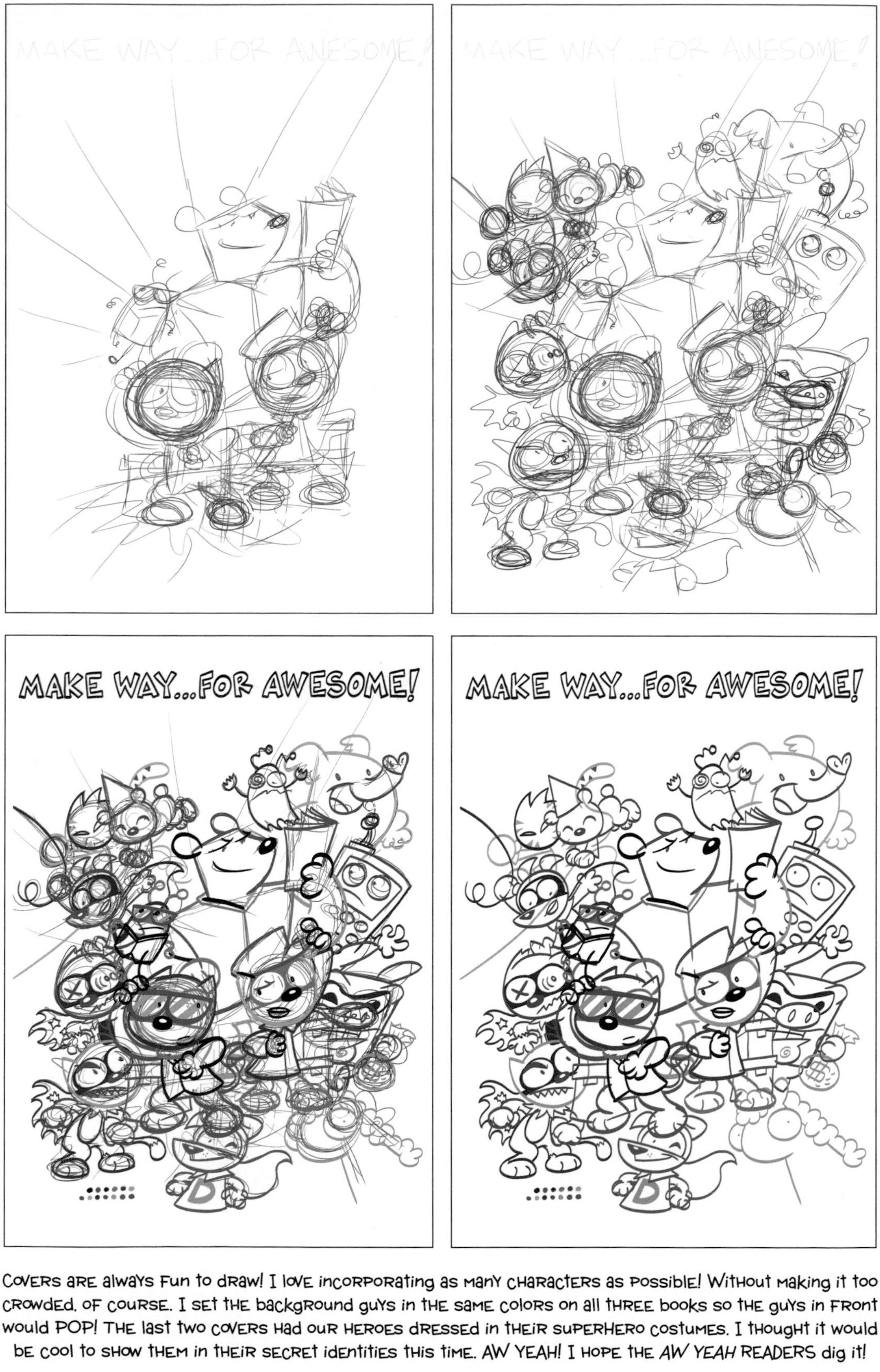
MAKE WAY...FOR AWESOME!
MAKE WAY...FOR AWESOME!
MAKE WAY...FOR AWESOME!
MAKE WAY...FOR AWESOME!

COVERS ARE always FUN to dRAW! I lOVE incORPORating as MANY CHARACTERS as POSSIblE! WitHOUT making it too CROWdEd, OF COURSE. I SET THE backgROUNd gUYS in THE SAME COLORS on all THREE books so THE gUYS in FRONT would POP! THE last two COVERS Had OUR HEROES dRESSEd in THEIR SUPERHERO costumes. I tHOUGHt it would be cool to SHOW THEM in THEIR SECRET idENTITIES THIS TIME. AW YEAH! I HOPE THE *AW YEAH* READERS dig it!

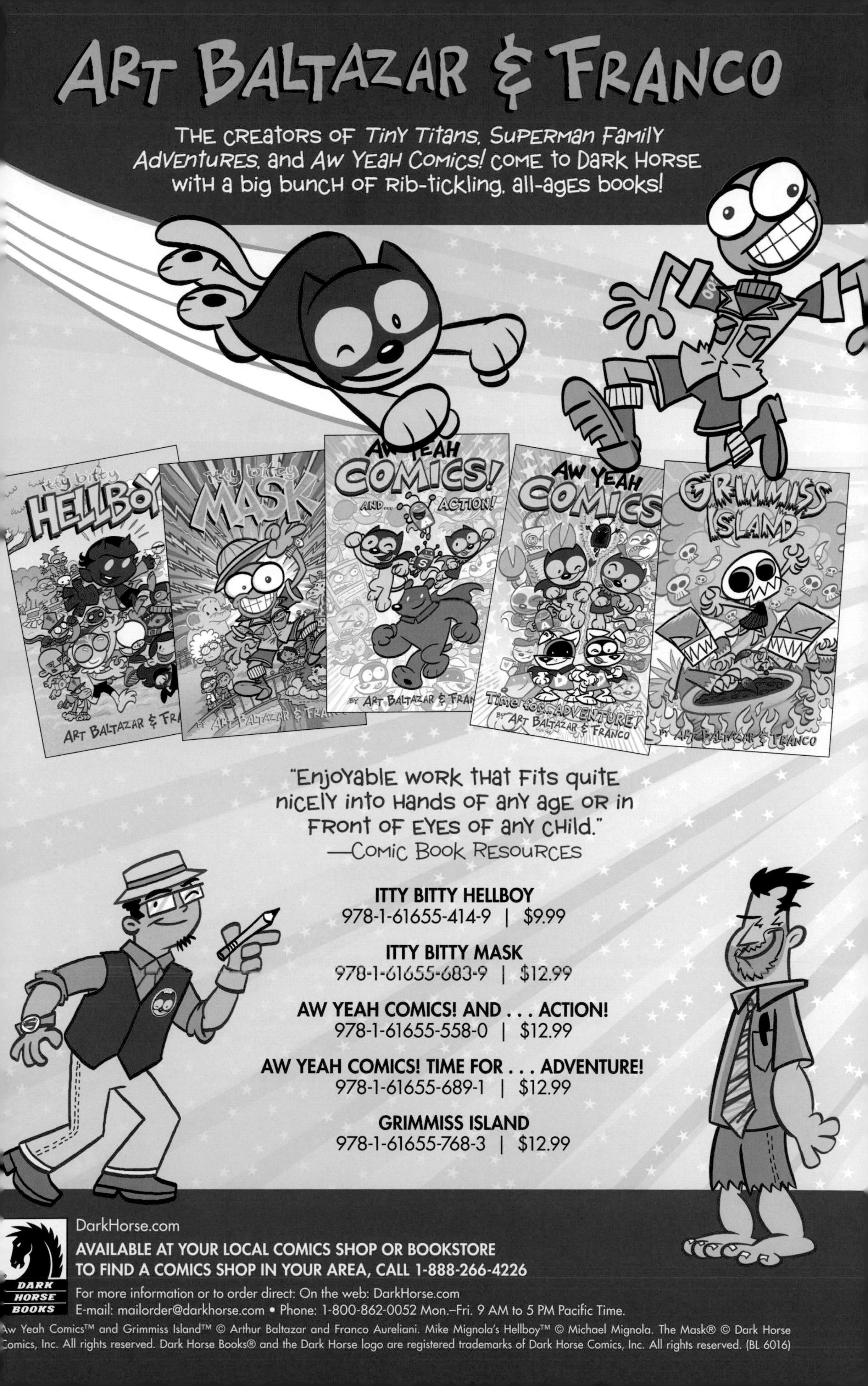
ART BALTAZAR & FRANCO
THE CREATORS OF TINY TITANS, SUPERMAN FAMILY ADVENTURES, AND AW YEAH COMICS! COME TO DARK HORSE WITH A BIG BUNCH OF RIB-TICKLING, ALL-AGES BOOKS!
itty bitty HELLBOY
ART BALTAZAR & FR
itty bitty MASK
AW YEAH COMICS! AND... ACTION!
BY ART BALTAZAR & FRAN
AW YEAH COMICS
TIME FOR... ADVENTURE!
BY ART BALTAZAR & FRANCO
GRIMMISS ISLAND
BY ART BALTAZAR & FRANCO
"Enjoyable work that fits quite nicely into hands of any age or in front of eyes of any child."
—Comic Book Resources
ITTY BITTY HELLBOY
978-1-61655-414-9 | $9.99
ITTY BITTY MASK
978-1-61655-683-9 | $12.99
AW YEAH COMICS! AND . . . ACTION!
978-1-61655-558-0 | $12.99
AW YEAH COMICS! TIME FOR . . . ADVENTURE!
978-1-61655-689-1 | $12.99
GRIMMISS ISLAND
978-1-61655-768-3 | $12.99
DarkHorse.com
AVAILABLE AT YOUR LOCAL COMICS SHOP OR BOOKSTORE
TO FIND A COMICS SHOP IN YOUR AREA, CALL 1-888-266-4226
DARK HORSE BOOKS
For more information or to order direct: On the web: DarkHorse.com
E-mail: mailorder@darkhorse.com • Phone: 1-800-862-0052 Mon.–Fri. 9 AM to 5 PM Pacific Time.
Aw Yeah Comics™ and Grimmiss Island™ © Arthur Baltazar and Franco Aureliani. Mike Mignola's Hellboy™ © Michael Mignola. The Mask® © Dark Horse Comics, Inc. All rights reserved. Dark Horse Books® and the Dark Horse logo are registered trademarks of Dark Horse Comics, Inc. All rights reserved. (BL 6016)

OTHER BOOKS FROM DARK HORSE

ITTY BITTY HELLBOY

Mike Mignola, Art Baltazar, Franco Aureliani

Witness the awesomeness that is *Hellboy*! The characters that sprung from Mike Mignola's imagination, with an AW YEAH Art Baltazar and Franco twist! This book has ALL the FUN, adventure, and AW YEAHNESS in one itty bitty package! That's a true story right there.

Volume 1: 978-1-61655-414-9 | $9.99
Volume 2: The Search for the Were-Jaguar! 978-1-61655-801-7 | $12.99

AVATAR: THE LAST AIRBENDER

Gene Luen Yang, Gurihiru

The wait is over! Ever since the conclusion of *Avatar: The Last Airbender*, its millions of fans have been hungry for more—and it's finally here! This series of digests rejoins Aang and friends for exciting new adventures, beginning with a face-off against the Fire Nation that threatens to throw the world into another war, testing all of Aang's powers and ingenuity!

THE PROMISE TPB
Book 1: 978-1-59582-811-8 | $10.99
Book 2: 978-1-59582-875-0 | $10.99
Book 3: 978-1-59582-941-2 | $10.99

THE SEARCH TPB
Book 1: 978-1-61655-054-7 | $10.99
Book 2: 978-1-61655-190-2 | $10.99
Book 3: 978-1-61655-184-1 | $10.99

THE RIFT TPB
Book 1: 978-1-61655-295-4 | $10.99
Book 2: 978-1-61655-296-1 | $10.99
Book 3: 978-1-61655-297-8 | $10.99

SMOKE AND SHADOW TPB
Book 1: 978-1-61655-761-4 | $10.99
Book 2: 978-1-61655-790-4 | $10.99
Book 3: 978-1-61655-838-3 | $10.99

THE PROMISE LIBRARY EDITION HC
978-1-61655-074-5 | $39.99

THE SEARCH LIBRARY EDITION HC
978-1-61655-226-8 | $39.99

THE RIFT LIBRARY EDITION HC
978-1-61655-550-4 | $39.99

PLANTS VS. ZOMBIES

Paul Tobin, Ron Chan

The confusing-yet-brilliant inventor known only as Crazy Dave helps his niece Patrice and young adventurer Nate Timely fend off Zomboss's latest attacks in this series of hilarious tales! Winner of over thirty Game of the Year awards, *Plants vs. Zombies* is now determined to shuffle onto all-ages bookshelves to tickle funny bones and thrill . . . *brains*.

LAWNMAGGEDON
978-1-61655-192-6 | $9.99

TIMEPOCALYPSE
978-1-61655-621-1 | $9.99

BULLY FOR YOU
978-1-61655-889-5 | $9.99

GARDEN WARFARE
978-1-61655-946-5 | $9.99

GROWN SWEET HOME
978-1-61655-971-7 | $9.99